The Spymaster and the Rake

The Spymaster and the Rake

The Andistalkern Sequence
Book One

A S Thomson

First paperback edition 2019

Book and cover design by A S Thomson
Artwork © 2019 A S Thomson

ISBN 978-1-9161431-0-4 (paperback)
ISBN 978-1-9161431-1-1 (ebook)

https://asthomson.com

Table of Contents

PART ONE

The Seventeenth Day of the Eleventh Month of the Thirty-Second Year in the Reign of King Alfred al-Farr (Kingdom Calendar)

"**I**'ve met someone else. Someone special." Jared's voice cracked, turning 'special' into an unintelligible squeak. He coughed, thumped his chest, and repeated his declaration. The muscle below his left eye twitched.

He scowled at his reflection, tilted his head from one side to the other, then ran his hand over the hollow curves of his cheeks, along the firm, hard lines of his chin, and down his long, narrow throat. Several days' worth of stubble scratched his fingers, a rough reminder of his time on the road.

Morgain would approve. 'Fashionably rugged,' she'd called him the first time they'd met. How many years ago had that been? Four? Or was it five?

He frowned and lowered his hand. Dropped his gaze to the sealed courier pouch lying on the bed.

He had no idea what messages it contained. In truth, he didn't care. His clients hired him because they trusted him not to open their correspondence. He accepted to give himself an excuse to visit Morgain.

Not that she would want to see him again after today.

"Watch yourself with that one, my boy. She may have the beauty of a winter rose, but underneath all the glamour, she stinks like a midden heap covered in manure."

He shivered at the recollection of his cousin's oft-given warning, closed the room's tiny window, lifted his shirt from its hook, and slipped it on.

He'd chosen sky-blue silk to match his eyes, gold-embroidered collar and cuffs to complement his deep tan, and mother-of-pearl buttons to catch and reflect the light. A foolish exercise, perhaps, but calling on Morgain without proper preparation would be akin to walking the corridors of the household naked. His clothes were his armour, his jewels his shield. Without them, he'd be leaving himself exposed.

He buttoned his shirt, pulled at the bottom hem to remove the wrinkles, unfastened the top two buttons, puckered his lips, and fastened them again.

Perfect.

He retrieved his jewel box from his travel bag and set it, open, on the dresser.

"I've met someone else. Someone... special. I can't breathe when I'm around her. Can't think of anyone else when we're apart. What we have, it's been good, but what I have with Elise—"

The muscle beneath his eye twitched again.

He scrubbed at his cheeks. Morgain wouldn't be pleased by his proclamation, but couples parted ways all the time. Surely she would understand?

He pawed through his jewel box, picked out a gold, leaf-shaped brooch, held it to his chest, shook his head, and dropped it back in the box. Too much gold. He wanted to emphasise the blond streaks in his hair, not overpower them. Perhaps an earring instead? A simple gold loop to catch the light and draw the eye. He picked out his largest one, pressed it against his ear, swapped it for a smaller one, and nodded.

"Better."

He checked his reflection one last time, paused to straighten a few stray hairs, snatched up the courier pouch, and marched outside.

Gravel crunched beneath the thick soles of his knee-length boots. Wisps of ethereal vapour clouded his breath. The walls of the household and its boundary combined to trap the path in lingering shadow, leaving it as chilled as the bottom of a sunless canyon. He glanced at the ice-blue sky and shivered. Autumn had arrived.

He tightened his grip on the courier pouch and walked faster, heading for the hedge dividing the formal gardens from the lush front lawns. Leaves and tiny twigs brushed his hair as he ducked through the sprouting archway. Warm sunlight washed over his face when he emerged on the other side. He squinted against the sudden brightness and turned onto the flagstone path leading to the household's front door.

A long, skinny shadow stretched across the path, its edges as harsh and uneven as a delimbed tree's. Wind gusted, wood creaked, and the shadow danced.

Jared looked up and stumbled to a halt.

The scuffed soles of a pair of boots dangled overhead. He stepped back and traced the path of the boots' crisscrossing laces up to a pair of uniformed legs, past the buckle of a thick, leather belt, to the flapping lapels of a rumpled jacket. His gaze froze on the grey-blue skin peeking above the neckline of a white tunic for an endless heartbeat before shifting to the body's head.

A young guardsman hung from a roof beam, his elongated neck trapped in a noose, stretched like sap oozing from a shattered branch. Icy sweat crawled down Jared's neck.

Another gust spun the body in a half-circle. Jared stared into the dead man's bulging eyes. His pupils were narrowed to pinpricks, the whites marbled yellow and red. Fear lingered beneath their surface, a dark, rippling shadow captured in the moment of death.

A cough shattered the stillness.

Jared ripped his gaze away from the corpse and sucked in a breath. He blinked several times before the figure in front of him came into focus. Another guardsman; this one alive and staring back.

"What did he do?" Jared raised his hand, not quite pointing at the dead man.

"Fell asleep on duty. Had the misfortune to be caught by Lady Morgain. You Jared?"

"Yes." The sweat crept lower, chilling Jared's back. He eyed the corpse again, the body not yet swollen, the face free of decay. The tip of the dead man's tongue protruded from his grey-white mouth in a fixed expression of eternal mockery. "This happen last night?"

"Aye. The poor bugger woke up just as they tightened the noose around his neck."

The sweat turned hot and clammy, soaking every inch of Jared's skin. He doubled over, gulping in huge mouthfuls of air to keep from vomiting. "Is Lady Morgain—?"

"In her study. She's expecting you."

"Thank you." Jared spat bile and wiped his mouth. He straightened, nodded to the guardsman, and continued on shaky legs.

Another guardsman stood to attention outside the household's towering oak doors; a grey-stubbled, grizzled veteran with puckered lips and a permanent scowl welded to his brow.

Jared lifted the courier pouch, ensuring the seal faced the guard. "Message for Lady Morgain."

"You carrying any weapons?" the man asked, his voice as gruff as his appearance.

"No, sir."

The guard's scowl deepened. He stepped forward a pace. "Arms out. Feet apart."

Jared complied, holding himself motionless. The guard conducted a rough but efficient search, stepped aside, and waved him past.

The household's main doors opened onto a grand entrance hall three storeys tall. Broad, sweeping stairs rose from a marble-tiled floor painted in a dozen liquid colours by the light filtering through the stained-glass windows above.

Jared paused inside the doorway to check his reflection in a highly polished column and frowned. His hair stood up in spikes, burrs clung to his breeches, and a sheen of condensation marred the rows of brass buckles on his boots. He flattened his hair, dried the buckles, brushed off the burrs, and headed for the stairs.

Three more guards waited there, two at the bottom and one at the top. Jared nodded to them as he passed, keeping his gaze low and his pace steady, assessing each man with a hooded glance. If it came to a fight, his height would give him a reach advantage, but he would soon be overcome by their strength—not to mention their daggers, short-swords, and spears.

He reached the first-floor landing and turned left, following the walkway to the front of the entrance hall and the second flight of stairs. The guards on the second floor subjected him to a more thorough search then waved him on. He squeezed between their tense, rock-like bodies and entered Lady Morgain's private quarters. The last door on the left gave access to her study.

He raised his hand to knock and froze.

There's something I need to tell you. I've found someone else. Someone special.

The door blurred, the whirls in the oak melting and reshaping, taking on the form of the dead guardsman's bulging eyes. He hesitated. Half-lowered his arm.

One of the guards snickered.

Jared raised his fist and knocked.

"Come," Morgain called, a sharp edge to her light, lilting voice.

Jared opened the door.

Morgain occupied the chair behind her desk, facing the door. Pale light flooded the room through the skylight, painting white highlights in her thick, black hair, their shifting patterns as mesmerising as sunrays playing across the surface of a lake. She looked up, a faint smile on her lips. The skin around her large, commanding eyes crinkled.

Jared's gaze jumped from the luscious lashes framing her nut-brown eyes, to the stray lock of hair dangling over the bridge of her nose, to the small triangle of sienna skin visible at the neckline of her dress. He curled his lips in appreciation of the ruddy blush rising on her cheeks, looked away when his own blood warmed in response, and coughed. "My lady."

"Jared." She set aside the paper she'd been reading. "Come in."

He approached her, his boots clicking on the tiled floor. A foot from the desk, he dropped to his knees and bowed, buying himself a few seconds to compose his features before he straightened. "Replies from Lords Mattan and Sinshay." He placed the courier pouch on the desk. "Plus letters from Lady Vanra and Godsman Ralmain."

Morgain's eyes appeared to dance as she retrieved the pouch with her left hand and signalled with her right.

Jared started to rise.

Ice-cold metal pricked the back of his neck. A heavy weight pressed into his spine, grinding his flesh like a pestle. Hot breath warmed his cheek as its owner's rough lips brushed his ear. "Don't move."

Jared turned his head towards the speaker, but the blade pressed harder, digging into his skin. He looked back at Morgain. She met his gaze, her expression flat. He opened his mouth to speak, found no words, and closed it again.

The hot breath vanished, the weight lifting from his back. "Put your hands on your head."

Jared obeyed, his eyes still locked on Morgain's, searching for some sign of her intentions.

Her expression never changed.

Hands grabbed his left arm and twisted it behind his back. Metal, rough and cold, snapped around his wrist. A second band locked around his upper forearm. He jerked against its bite.

The blade drove deeper, drawing blood this time.

"Well, this is… new." More hands grabbed his right arm. He locked his muscles, fighting their pull. "I know the messages I carry can be unpleasant, but I've never been arrested for delivering one before." He forced a smile.

Morgain lifted her gaze over Jared's head, propped her elbows on the desk, rested her chin on steepled fingers, and nodded.

More manacles snapped into place, pinning his arms together at elbow and wrist. "Morgain?" His ankles came next, manacled to each other and then chained to his wrists. He shuffled towards the desk, gaining less than an inch before the blade switched from the back of his neck to the front. He froze, barely daring to breathe as its edge shaved his throat. "At least tell me what I'm supposed to have done."

"You are a spy," Morgain said.

Heat prickled Jared's face. He licked lips as dry as scorched scrub. "I would never—"

"Admit it? But you will."

"Morgain, please—"

"Enough." Morgain smacked the desk. "I'm not interested in excuses. The only thing I want to hear from you is the truth."

"The truth? But I'm telling the truth. I haven't—"

"Gag him."

Fingers pried his jaws apart, and a hand shoved a large, iron ball between them. The straps used to secure it cut into the corners of his mouth.

Morgain stood. "I have to leave. Think hard whilst I'm gone. The longer it takes for you to confess, the worse this is going to get."

She picked up the courier pouch and swept past him, her shoes clacking on the floor. The door swooshed open and banged closed. Leather creaked. The unseen guard coughed. Only Jared's ragged breathing disturbed the silence that followed.

❧❧

Sweat soaked Jared's hair and the back of his neck, beading on his forehead and the tip of his nose. He shook his head and flexed his hands. The rough-edged manacles dug into his flesh, rubbing with the voracity of sandpaper on stone. He swallowed a yelp and fresh blood seeped onto his tongue, adding its bitterness to the rusty, metallic taste in his mouth. He swallowed again, and the iron ball scraped his palate.

Prehen Damis, help me. What does she think I've done?

More sweat soaked his armpits and the backs of his knees, seeped down his trousers and squelched between his toes.

His clothes were ruined, as filthy and tattered as a soldier's armour after a day on the battlefield.

Except my battle is just beginning, not nearing its end.

He closed his eyes.

She'd called him a spy.

A spy!

He'd never spied on anyone in his life.

His clients trusted him. He'd thought *she* trusted him.

And she went from sleeping with me to this?

What had happened? Why would she think—?

He'd done nothing. Could think of nothing. *Unless...*

Unless someone accused me to save her own neck.

"*The longer it takes for you to confess, the worse this is going to get.*"

Worse? What could be worse?

Spasms rocked his legs. Pins and needles stabbed his feet and hands. He shifted his weight and ice lanced his spine.

The room grew too hot, the air too thick. He couldn't breathe past the gag in his mouth.

He blinked.

The room swayed.

He closed his eyes.

Felt himself falling.

Heard a distant thump.

A heavy weight smashed into his ribs.

He jerked forwards, cracking his knees on the corner of the desk, and rocked back to stare into the face of a scowling guard.

The guard lifted his foot and kicked him again. "Nobody gave you permission to sleep."

Jared braced his hands against the floor, curled his shoulder, and rolled.

The guard grabbed him by the hair, jolting him to a stop, and hauled him back to his knees. Fire wracked his body, a volcanic explosion sending fresh waves of agony through his hands and feet. He screamed.

"Filthy spy." The guard bent forward and spat in Jared's face.

Jared flinched and would have fallen if not for the guard's hold. He concentrated on breathing, sucking air in through his nose, expelling it through his mouth.

In through his nose.

Out through his mouth.

In. Nose.

Out. Mouth.

In… and out.

His heartbeat steadied. His pulse slowed. He stared at the patterns in the marble-tiled floor.

The splodge next to his knee looked like a maple leaf. The veins to its left resembled a horse's head. Closer to the desk, a monkey stood on its back legs.

The fire in his limbs faded. His mind cleared. And still the question loomed, unanswered.

What am I going to tell Morgain?

He suspected it wouldn't matter; that she'd already accepted his guilt. Even so, he would need to think of something. But for now?

For now, it was enough to breathe.

❧

The rain had started an hour ago. A gentle shower at first, it rapidly built into a driving storm. Raindrops pounded the skylight with the force of chippings thrown by a cartwheel, their reflections dancing across the floor. Jared flinched every time a gust drove the rain harder, imagining the skylight shattering, showering him with glass. He flexed his tongue and swallowed. It did nothing to ease the dry tickle clawing the back of his throat. The pain had passed, at least, replaced by a creeping numbness spreading from his hands and feet into his arms and legs.

A pity he still had no idea what to say to Morgain.

The guard shifted behind him, the creak of leather barely audible over the storm. A huff of air might have been a sigh.

If you're bored, we could always trade places. Jared laughed and almost choked.

A rhythmic tapping sounded on the door, a hollow parody of a soldier's marching cadence. Hinges creaked, admitting a rush of frigid air, and footsteps clacked across the floor.

Something brushed against his shoulder.

He started, his shriek muffled by his gag.

Morgain's laughter filled his ears. "Hush. It's only me."

Jared grunted.

"Does that mean you want to confess?" Morgain placed one hand on his shoulder and used the other to trace the curve of his neck. "Or do I need to give you some extra incentive?"

Something tugged at the straps holding the gag in place, releasing them.

Morgain stepped around him and wiped a fresh trickle of blood from his chin. She tilted her head, her gaze raking his face, and prised the iron ball from between his teeth. "Well?"

"I…" Jared wet his lips and swallowed. "I have… no idea… what you're talking about."

"No?" Morgain cupped his chin with her fingers and wiped his lips with her thumb. "Are you sure?"

"Morgain—"

Morgain looked over his shoulder. "Remove his restraints and help him stand."

Jared had experienced pain before. He'd cried when his cousin spanked him for stealing. Shrieked when he'd dislocated his shoulder falling off a horse. But nothing—*nothing*—came close to the agony that roared through him when the guard loosened his restraints. He screamed—a bellow loud enough to drown out the storm—and screamed again when the guard hauled him upright. Fiery spikes stabbed the soles of his feet. He teetered and toppled sideways, weak as a sapling before a storm.

Morgain caught him by the shoulder. "Fetch a chair."

"Morgain." Jared braced his legs and closed his eyes against a wave of dizziness. "Morgain, can't we talk about this?" He opened his eyes and blinked her into focus. "Surely there's been some misunderstanding? Some mistake?"

"My poor, naïve Jared. Don't you understand the trouble you're in?" She laid an open hand on his chest and leant forward, her eyes narrowed. "Spying is a form of treason, and treason is a capital offence."

Jared's legs buckled. He thunked onto the chair and dropped his head into shaking hands. "So is falling asleep, apparently."

"You saw my guard?" Morgain gnawed on her bottom lip, a twitch that might have been a smile tugging at the corner of her mouth. "That man was responsible for the safety of everyone in this household. I had to make an example of him or risk the rest of the guard growing lax." She crouched in front of him and gathered up his hands. "I don't want to hurt you. I'm doing this to keep you alive. But if you want to live past the end of the week, you need to confess."

"Confess to what? I didn't do anything."

"Very well." Morgain dropped his hands and stood. She stared at him for the length of a heartbeat, her back straight and her expression hard. "You will confess to me, or you will confess to my torturer. You have until tomorrow to decide which it will be. In the meantime, you will remain in my study. Your guard will be armed with a crossbow. If you move from this chair or turn around, you will be shot."

Morgain strode past him, her arm knocking against his shoulder.

Jared shivered at the touch; at the cold indifference of the contact. He lowered his head to his hands and peered at the floor through splayed fingers. She wanted him to confess to keep him *alive*? But confessing would be akin to signing his own death warrant. At least the truth would give him some chance. Some hope.

If he could survive the torture.

He shuddered. How many times had he listened to the older boys' whispered stories as a child? Huddled under his blankets as they regaled each other with tales of the rack, the rat cages, the mock drownings—

I'm dead. Oh, dear gods, I'm dead.

He squeezed his eyes shut and smothered them with the heels of his hands.

❧❦

The rain had ended hours ago, the clouds burnt away by the late afternoon sun. Then the sun, too, had fallen beyond the skylight's edge, to be replaced by an umbrella of stars. Thick glass dimmed and distorted the once brilliant sparks, giving them the appearance of gnarled embers.

Jared sought out the constellation of Prehen Damis and whispered a brief prayer.

'Don't waste your breath.'

He jumped and barely stopped himself from turning. Had the guard just—?

No. Of course not. Then what—?

'The Gods never answer. Prayers are a waste of time.'

"Who—?" Jared bit off the rest of the question and held his breath. There were people outside, laughing and talking. Had he overheard their whispers and misunderstood the words?

He looked away from the skylight and massaged his arms.

It was possible. Weariness had been pulling at his eyes for hours, and there was precious little else for his mind to focus on. Apart from the obvious. But once he'd overcome the initial shock, he'd avoided thinking on *that*. Not that ignoring the issue helped. He needed to find a way out of this trap.

He *had* to.

He sighed and rubbed his eyes.

Why had Morgain told him confessing would save his life? What did she expect him to say? Surely she didn't believe he was guilty. Surely—

Surely nothing. Confess to her or confess to the torturer, those were his only choices now.

But confess to what? Spying? Spying on whom? How?

His stomach cramped, gnawing on nothing. He dropped his head into his hands and groaned. He wanted to get up and pace the room. Shake his arms. Stamp his feet. Do anything—a*nything*—but sit here and wait.

'Then turn around.'

He snapped his head up and peered into the semi-darkness. There was no-one there, and yet—

'Stand up. Turn around.'

I did not *imagine that.*

'One guard. One bolt. If he misses, you walk out of here. If he doesn't…'

…at least my death will be quick. He'd been thinking the same thing not long ago. *Was that all it was, then? Just an echo of my own thoughts? My strained subconscious latching onto stray ideas and echoing them back?*

'You know you want to.'

Yes. Yes, he did. But only part of him. The part that couldn't face any more pain.

And the part that wanted to escape.

"No," he whispered. "No. I'm not ready for death."

The quiet words irritated his sandpaper-dry throat. He ran his tongue across his teeth, but the tiny drop of moisture it produced did little to soothe the pain.

'You could always ask for a drink.'

He shook his head, looked sideways, and squinted at the books lining the nearby shelf. Perhaps if he focused on them for a while. Distracted himself.

The silent whispers continued. The cramps in his stomach intensified. The gnawing turned into the gnashing of rats' teeth slicing through his insides. He leant forward, elbows on knees, and jiggled his legs to gain some relief.

Damn Morgain for all eternity. Now he needed to pee.

18ᵗʰ Day, 11ᵗʰ Month, Thirty-Second Year in the Reign of King Alfred al-Farr

The door behind Morgain's desk flew open and cracked against the adjacent wall with a thunderous crash. Jared snapped upright. His shoulders hit the chair back. His buttocks slid towards the edge of the seat. He swallowed a shriek and planted his feet, halting his slide before he met the floor with his backside.

Morgain swept into the room, a vision of dark beauty in a full-length, black-and-silver dress. Thin slits in the bodice offered tantalising glimpses of her shoulders, whilst slender, silver darts led the eye down the length of her arms to her long-fingered, elegant hands.

His blood stirred as he remembered the touch of those fingers on his shoulders; the press of her hand against his chest; the concern in her eyes when she'd urged him to confess.

Confess?

He blinked, stared at the beaker she carried, and touched his dry lips with his too-thick tongue. "I don't suppose that's for me?"

Morgain glanced at him then traced his gaze to her hand. "This?" She held the beaker towards him. "That depends." She lifted it to her lips and drank. When she lowered it, fresh, clear water glistened on her lips. "Have you come to a decision yet?"

"I..." Jared stared at the bead of water trapped in the corner of her mouth. His stomach clenched. "I've been giving it a lot of thought." He half-stood and froze. "May I?"

"If you must." Morgain set the beaker on her desk and signalled the guard at Jared's back. "But stay away from the doors." She pulled a roll of papers from under her arm and set it down.

Jared heaved himself upright. His legs trembled but held. He staggered to the corner of the desk. "I've been giving it a lot of thought, and…" He pressed his hand against the desktop. *And what?* "And I think we should talk." *Yes. That was it. Talk.*

"About?"

"About?" Jared blinked and took another step. "About us." He swallowed and reached towards her. "About whatever I did to anger you. About—"

"Don't."

He stopped, his fingertips a hair's breadth from her arm, and dropped his hand. "About whatever caused this *misunderstanding.*"

Morgain's stare froze his heart, sending ice crystals through his blood and into his lungs. She smiled and shook her head. "It's too late for talking, Jared. Far too late." She placed a hand on his shoulder and pushed him back to the other side of the desk. "But you can still earn my mercy. Are you sure there's *nothing* you want to confess?"

Her words seemed to take an age to reach him, the sounds distorted and drawn out. It took even longer for those sounds to make sense. There was something about the way she emphasised 'nothing'. Something…

He blinked, and the thought fled. He shook his head.

"I see." Morgain pushed the beaker aside, unrolled the papers, and set them in a neat row along the front of the desk.

Jared squinted at them. The precisely scribed writing swam and twisted before his tired eyes. "What?"

"You want to avoid a fatal appointment with my torturer?" Morgain opened a desk drawer and pulled out an ink pot. "Want to walk out of here alive?" She reached into the drawer again and produced a quill. "All you have to do is sign."

All I have to do is sign? Jared rubbed his eyes. They watered, but he managed to decipher a few words. *"Sold private correspondence… harm the Kingdom… did willingly conspire."* He dug his fingernails into the desktop, bowed his head, and pushed away from the desk.

All I need to do is sign? Confess to treason? Dishonour the up-Arran name?

He pressed his hands to his forehead and staggered across the room. His head swirled and the floor tilted, as unstable as a ship on a heaving sea.

He collapsed against the shelves before he fell.

Confess to treason and escape the torture.

Would that be so bad?

There had been something else. Something he'd thought of during the night. Something he'd meant to say.

If only he could rest. Clear his head.

If I sign those papers...

"No." He looked up at Morgain, his finger raised. "This..." He indicated the room with a swish of his finger. "This is all a trick." He frowned and drew his hand closer. He had rust on his shirt.

Rust? Or blood?

He blinked. The edges of the red-brown stains blurred.

Focus!

"This..." He looked back at Morgain. "...is a trick. A trap. You need me to confess because you have no evidence. No proof."

"No proof?" Morgain turned to the guard. "Is the witness here?"

"He's waiting outside, my lady."

"Send him in."

Jared's heart stammered, each irregular beat sending a fresh rush of blood hammering through his temples. He stared, transfixed, as the guard opened the door.

A grey-haired old man hobbled into the room, hunched over a crooked crutch. He paused inside the doorway and bowed. The stench of week-old fish wafted from his unkempt clothes, a vile miasma that worsened with every twitch and jitter.

Morgain pointed at Jared. "Is this the man you saw?"

The newcomer hobbled closer to Jared and leant forward until their noses touched. "Aye."

"And what was he doing?"

"Meeting one of those foreign chaps, all secret like. They was whispering, and he"—the man jabbed Jared's shoulder with a grubby finger—"gave the foreign folk these papers. Then the foreign chap, he gave this man some gold."

"Did you see what was on the papers?"

The old man shook his head. "Di'n't see no words, but they was all sealed with your seal, m'lady."

"And you'd be willing to say all this in court?"

"Aye, m'lady."

"Thank you. That will be all for now."

The old man bowed again and hobbled from the room.

Morgain turned to Jared. "Well?"

"Well…" What could he say? The man was lying. He'd been framed. But Morgain had made it clear she no longer trusted his word.

Morgain picked up the quill and dipped it in the inkwell. "Sign the confession, Jared."

Just sign. He took a step forward, reached for the quill, and hesitated. "Your witness is half-blind. No judge would accept his word—"

Morgain sighed and tossed the quill on the desk. It bounced and rolled, leaving a narrow trail of ink behind. "I had hoped to avoid this."

"Avoid what?"

"This." She reached into her pocket, pulled something out, and threw it at him. It flashed red and gold as it sped across the room.

He snatched at it and missed. It bounced off his chest and hit the floor with a clatter. He crouched, picked it up, and held it in his shaking palm. A heart-shaped locket rested in his hand. He tilted it sideways, and the small ruby at its centre winked. He flipped it over to trace the inscription with his thumb. "How—?" His voice cracked, his throat too dry for more.

"How did I find out?"

He nodded.

"She—"

"Elise." Jared curled his fingers around the locket and stood. "Her *name* is Elise."

"Her name is irrelevant. Your connection to her is all I care about. Your scullery maid started wearing the locket after your last visit. Discreetly, but not discreetly enough. People noticed. People talked."

"I was going to tell you." He took a step forward. "That's why I came."

"Really? Because you've been here over a day, and you haven't breathed a word."

"Because you accused me of spying!"

"And that stopped you telling the truth?"

"No. I-I was trying to figure out why you were angry."

"Oh? You mean there's more than one reason for me to be upset with you?"

"No! I didn't mean… You did all this because of Elise?"

"I did all of this because you *betrayed* me. And I'm not finished yet. Sign the confession."

Jared tightened his grip on the locket and winced as the point of the heart stabbed his palm. He glanced at the papers and shook his head. "I can see what you're planning, and it's not going to work. Without a confession, you can't touch me. I'm not a commoner. You need proof to move against one of the Blood, and proof is something you don't have. Your witness's testimony is worthless. You can't send me to the torturer on the word of one half-blind old man."

"True. But I can send your scullery maid. Her blood is as common as it comes."

Jared shivered. "You wouldn't."

"Wouldn't I? How long would she last, do you think? How long could you bear to watch her suffer?"

Every word hit with the force of a javelin, spearing his heart. He clutched the locket to his chest, a shield against the dread. "Where is she? What have you done to her?"

"Right now?" Morgain smiled. She actually *smiled.* "I imagine she's at work. As for what I've done. I have done nothing. Yet. If you want it to stay that way, all you have to do is sign."

Jared risked a glance at the guard then charged towards the back door. He only had a few feet to cover.

The guard slammed into him in the same instant as his fingers brushed the handle. An armoured shoulder crashed into his side. Thick arms locked around his waist.

He growled and pushed backwards, clawing at the guard's hands—

—and found himself airborne as the guard heaved him off his feet.

A fist slammed into his midriff, pounding the air from his lungs. He dropped, flailing at nothing, and collapsed in a heap.

Metal scraped against metal, and the sharp edge of the guard's sword pressed against his throat.

He froze.

Morgain laughed. "I see you really do care for her." She retrieved the pen and held it out. "Sign the papers, or your scullery maid dies."

The guard withdrew his blade and stepped back.

Jared struggled to regain his feet. He took the quill and met Morgain's unforgiving gaze. "What's to stop you from killing us both if I do?"

"Nothing but the knowledge that you're more useful to me alive. You'll have to accept my word on that."

Accept her word? He staggered to the front of the desk, pen in hand. *Accept her word, after everything she's done?* He dipped the quill in the ink pot with a shaking hand. Tiny spots of ink spattered the desk when he pulled it out. *Accept her word, or condemn Elise to a long, painful death.* He placed the nib on the nearest sheet of paper and signed.

"Mark them with your thumbprint, too."

He dipped his thumb in the ink and pressed it to each sheet. With the final mark made, he set the quill down and wiped his thumb on his shirtfront. "Are we done?"

"Almost. Hold out your arm."

"What?"

Morgain snapped her fingers.

The guard stepped forward, caught Jared's left arm by the wrist, and stretched it out.

Jared pulled, twisting to break the guard's hold.

The guard tightened his grip and smirked.

Morgain drew the guard's knife and placed it against the crook of Jared's elbow. "You are mine, Jared. Forever. I expect your loyalty, your obedience, and your fidelity. Otherwise..." She slashed the knife down his forearm, exposing muscle and bone.

Jared screamed and cradled his arm to his chest. The room dissolved into a sickening swirl of blacks, blues, and browns, a dizzying maelstrom centred around the throbbing fire in his arm. He stumbled, cracking his hip against the desk. "Why?"

"Why? Because you betrayed me. Do it again, and I'll take your eye." She turned to the guard. "Escort him to one of the guest rooms and let him sleep. Give him food and water, and post a guard. If the cut needs stitching, make him to do it himself. No doctors. I want that wound to scar."

Jared stared at his reflection, his brow creased in an ugly frown. Dirt streaked his face, thick knots matted his hair, and dark bags framed hollow, bloodshot eyes. Twin cuts formed a false smile anchored at the corners of his mouth. He pursed his lips and the wounds cracked open, releasing thick dribbles of blood. He dipped a fresh square of cloth in a bowl of water, dabbed at the left cut, and winced.

'Coward.'

He dropped his hand to the dresser and closed his eyes. He'd done what he'd had to do to keep Elise alive.

'To save yourself.'

If Morgain hadn't threatened her—

'You lasted one day.'

One pathetic day. He sighed and dipped the cloth in the bowl, swirled it, and stared at the bloody trail. *I should have been stronger.*

'*Fought harder.*'
Resisted.
'*Refused.*'
I should have told her about Elise.
'*A long time ago.*'
Why hadn't he said something sooner?

Why had the thought never entered his mind?

He squeezed out the cloth and cleaned the second cut. *Pointless worrying now.* He'd signed the papers; condemned himself as a traitor.

Condemned us both.

He lifted his head. Looked himself in the eye.

'*Coward.*'

He dropped the cloth and turned his back to the mirror. Exhaustion pulled at him, stooping his shoulders and crushing his limbs. Perhaps if he slept, things would make more sense. Perhaps then he'd be able to stop tormenting himself.

He turned back and stared.

Leant closer.

Touched his brow.

Is that a new wrinkle?

'*Does it matter?*'

A day ago, it would have. But now? It gave him something safe to focus on. Something familiar.

He lifted his other hand to investigate and froze, his gaze locked on his bloody palm. He needed to do something about the cut on his arm.

He stepped away from the dresser and plopped down onto the four-poster bed. The oak frame creaked. He tensed, waiting for it to break.

'*And when it does, the ceiling will fall on your head.*'

Given the way things have gone the last couple of days, I wouldn't be surprised. He chuckled, lifted his injured arm, and draped it in his lap. Congealed blood stuck his shirtsleeve to the edges of the cut. He peeled it back, biting his lip to keep from crying out. Fresh blood welled, soaking his arm, but not before he glimpsed exposed muscle and sliced fat.

He doubled over and retched.

'*Coward.*'

He closed his eyes against the self-recrimination, wriggled the rest of the way out of his shirt, bunched it up, and pressed it hard against the cut. Blue sparks filled his vision, dazzling flashes brighter than the sun.

He dropped back onto the mattress, his arm cradled against his chest, and stared at the leafy canopy covering the ornate bed.

This is getting me nowhere. I need a plan. He lifted his head, levered himself onto one elbow, trembled, and collapsed.

He needed to stop the bleeding.

Needed to recuperate.

Needed to escape.

❧

A soft click echoed through the room. Jared opened his eyes and sat up, careful not to jostle his injured arm. He glanced at it. A thin strip of dried blood marred the ragged silk forming his makeshift bandage, but no fresh blood leaked out. He tucked a stray corner of silk into place and smiled. How many people could claim to have wasted fifteen gold octains on a silk shirt to bind a cut?

The door handle turned.

He pulled himself to his feet with the aid of the bedpost, digging his fingers into the carved palm fronds for support, and tensed his legs, preparing to pounce.

The door swung open.

The old man who'd testified against him hobbled inside.

Jared stared, stunned into inaction by the unexpected visitor, only remembering his intentions when the door clicked shut.

The old man leant against the door, tilted his head back to peer at Jared, and grinned. There was a moment of silence as they stared at each other, then the old man straightened and tossed his crutch aside. His stoop vanished. He crossed the room with long, confident strides. "Come. Sit with me," he said, his voice no longer cracked and strained.

Jared edged away from the bed, his gaze darting between the man and the unlocked door. If he was quick, he could make it into the hall before the old man reached the bed, run for the servant's stairs at the end, and—

The old man glanced back at him. "Open it if you like. You won't get far. There are guards on the other side." He took a seat at the table in front of the window.

Jared shuffled forward a few hesitant steps, stopped, and leant his shoulder against the wardrobe. His body trembled, his stymied muscles primed for flight. He crossed his arms to hide his shaking and glowered at the old man, not quite meeting his gaze.

The old man watched him with a mocking, lopsided grin. "Suit yourself." He reached up to slide his fingers under his scraggly, grey hair, winked, and pulled it off. A smattering of short, dark stubble coated his head. He tossed the wig on the table and proceeded to peel layers of oak-coloured clay off his face. Wrinkled brows became smooth, the bulbous nose shrank, and thick, puckered lips narrowed. His skin darkened a few shades and gained a subtle green tinge. Without the disguise, he looked no more than three- or four-years Jared's senior. He bowed his head. "Armon al-Rafael, Spymaster of house Rafael, at your service."

Jared snorted. "Never heard of you."

"That is the idea. I wouldn't be much of a spy if everyone knew me, would I?" He patted the seat beside him. "Come. Sit."

Jared didn't move. He had no desire to share a table with a man who'd helped frame him, nor did he care for the derisive tone underpinning Armon's every word.

Armon shrugged and lounged back in his chair. He stretched his legs out in front of him, placed one elbow on the chair arm, and the other on the table. With a cant of his head, he managed to look down his nose at Jared, despite their relative positions.

Jared waited for him to say more. The moment stretched, the silence scratching at his nerves. He pushed off the wardrobe and moved forward a step. "You're wasting your time. As I told Morgain, I'm no spy."

Armon laughed, a dry, soft chuckle. "Oh, I know that." He sat a little straighter. "Now, please, sit. You're giving me neck ache."

"I don't care about your neck ache." Jared sat. He met Armon's stare for a moment then looked away. There was something dark in the spymaster's eyes; something calculating. He hadn't come for a friendly chat. "Does Morgain know you're here?"

"Of course. You think the guards would let in any random stranger?"

Jared shrugged and turned to stare out the window. Heavy, grey clouds filled the sky, a match for the dreary mood swamping his mind. He'd considered smashing through the lead-paned glass earlier, jumping down and running before the guards noticed he was gone. But even if he'd survived the drop to the gravelled training yard, he doubted he would have gotten far. The guards' barracks loomed at the end of the yard, dominating the space between the household's east and west wings.

'Coward.'

Perhaps. And perhaps he'd made a mistake not charging the guard last night. But jumping from the window now would gain him nothing but an inglorious death. He sighed.

"Are you even listening to me?" Armon asked, a note of irritation in his voice.

Jared turned. Armon's expression hadn't changed, but his fingers now tapped against the table in slow, rhythmic warning.

Jared forced himself to meet his stare. "I'm listening."

"Good. You may not know me, but the guards do. And even when they can't recognise my face, they recognise Morgain's seal." Armon pointed to a small tattoo on the side of his neck; a clover leaf set in a yellow circle, inside a red square.

"You're a slave, then?"

Armon's grin died. "I am a *Rafael*."

"And I've still never heard of you." Jared wanted to slap himself. He'd be safer poking an injured badger with a stick.

Armon's mocking grin returned, the not-quite-smirk sending a chill racing across Jared's skin. "Noble families tend not to boast about their bastards. They like to keep us hidden from the rest of the world."

"Doesn't that make you Armon *bal*-Rafael?" Jared clamped his mouth shut too late.

"Are you always this rude?"

"Is there any reason I shouldn't be?"

Armon's fingers stilled. He pressed his lips together, shifted his feet, and curled his right hand into a fist. A moment of utter stillness followed, a tableau of tense anticipation, his body frozen between one heartbeat and the next.

Then he leapt.

Jared jerked back, his arm raised to block. Fingers caught his wrist and pulled it aside. A fist flew at his face. He flinched and closed his eyes.

Seconds passed.

He cracked one eye open.

Armon towered above him, his arm raised, and his mocking grin back in place. He nodded, uncurled his fist, and patted Jared's cheek.

Jared lunged.

Armon sidestepped, caught his arm, and pulled.

Jared's shoulders outran his feet. His knees hit the floor, sending twin spikes of pain up his legs.

Armon pirouetted, spinning in a half-circle as he twisted Jared's arm up and back. "Stick to wooing girls, dandy boy. You're no match for a real man." He shoved Jared's head towards the floor, released his hold, and returned to his seat.

Jared remained on his knees, head bowed and injured arm pressed to his heaving chest. He watched Armon from the corner of his eye.

Armon sat erect, his muscles tensed, fingers tapping on the chair arm.

Jared balled his fist, pressed it down on the hardwood floor, then released it again. Better to save his strength for a real escape attempt.

He pushed himself to his feet, returned to his seat, and glared out the window. "What do you want from me?" he asked, his voice a bare whisper.

"What do I want from you?" Armon's grin returned. "Why, dear dandy boy, I want to recruit you."

Jared laughed. It was absurd. Completely and utterly absurd.

"I'd hoped you'd appreciate the irony." Armon leant forward, elbows on the table. "You have no idea of the effort I went to, to convince Morgain not to charge you with murder."

"Murder. Treason. The penalty's the same either way. I don't see what difference it would have made."

Armon tutted and shook his head. "You don't? I am disappointed."

"You sound like my old tutor. He was always disappointed with me too."

"I can't imagine why."

Jared scowled.

Armon's grin widened. "Let me explain. I'll try to keep it simple, just for you." He settled back into his chair. "Murders need bodies, evidence, witnesses. You can't pluck them from fresh air. One man with his throat slit. Another with a knife buried in his stomach. But not just any knife. No. It needs to be *your* knife. Perhaps a scrap of cloth from your shirt, ripped off during the struggle. An earring and a bit of ear, clutched in one of the men's hands. And witnesses. Some who saw you in the company of the dead men not long before they died. Others who saw you fleeing the scene, covered in the dead men's blood. That's a lot of effort to go to trap one man.

"Spying, on the other hand? Spying is easy. Talk of foreigners in town. Clandestine meetings witnessed by chance. Rumours on the streets, hinting at hidden goings on. A man who rides from town to town without challenge, answering to no-one, and a member of no guild, serving only himself. All of it pure speculation. But put it all together, add in claims a foreign noble has learnt secrets which could endanger the Kingdom, and *snap*." Armon clapped his hands together. "One little dandy boy snared in a trap."

Jared stared at the darkening sky. He could think of no witty comebacks. No snide replies. He drew in a breath and sighed. "Do you do this to all your potential recruits?"

"No. There really is no need."

"Oh?"

"Most people I approach are happy to work for me. And in the rare instances when they aren't, I find out who they care for and offer them a choice. They can either accept a position on my staff, or their loved one dies."

"And if they still refuse?"

"I kill them, of course. I can't have people running around telling tales on me now, can I?" He said it so easily, as though killing were a thing he did every day.

Jared shuddered. "Then why...?"

"Why go to such efforts with you? I hadn't planned to. But when Morgain found out about my leverage, she wanted revenge. You're lucky I was there to calm her down. She was all for having you whipped to death."

"Am I supposed to be grateful?"

Armon chuckled. "Hardly. I was protecting my own interests. You'd be no use to me dead or covered in scars. Speaking of which, how's your arm?"

Jared stared for a moment then glanced at his arm and shrugged. "It's stopped bleeding."

Armon extended a hand. "Show me."

Jared didn't move. Nothing Armon had said or done made him willing to trust the man. "Morgain said—"

"That you weren't to see a doctor. I'm not a doctor. Now"—Armon's voice dropped to a near-whisper—"show me your arm."

Jared put his wrist in Armon's waiting hand.

Armon unwound the makeshift bandage and probed at the wound, pressing along the sides of the cut, squeezing out fresh squirts of blood. "Can you sew?"

"Well enough to repair my tack."

"That'll do." He released Jared's arm, picked up his wig, and stood. "I'll send for hot water, a needle, and thread. Wash the cut thoroughly then sew it shut. If the puffiness gets any worse, tell the guards. I don't want it getting infected and killing you." He walked to the door, retrieved his crutch, and turned. "In the meantime, I'll have your belongings sent up and arrange a hot bath. Make the most of it. Morgain wants to see you in the morning, and I promised her you would be made presentable. Don't let me down."

19th Day, 11th Month, 32 KAF

Sunlight stroked his cheek, its touch a warm caress against his cool skin. The mattress formed a snug cradle beneath him, whilst the sheets encompassed him in a soft embrace. For a few, brief moments, he knew peace.

Then his arm throbbed.

Jared cursed and rolled from the bed. He stumbled over to the dresser, rubbed his eyes, blinked at himself, and yawned. Morgain would send for him soon. He needed to get ready.

'Or just go naked.'

He laughed. Morgain had certainly enjoyed his nudity before, although...

No.

Too much had changed, and not just with Morgain. Elise deserved better. He would take time to dress and present himself, not for Morgain's sake, but for his own. She had stripped him of his dignity and self-control. He intended to take it back.

The simple ablutions helped, the familiar routine lending an illusion of normality to the situation. He had no time to think as he shaved, dressed, and combed his hair. There would be no jewellery today. No fancy frills or buckles or lace. He wore ankle boots, plain black hose, and a dark red shirt. Simple, smart, and serious. The immaculately groomed face peering out from the mirror did not belong to a broken man.

He tried the door handle, found it locked, and padded across the room to the table where he sank onto one of the chairs. There were too many unanswered questions. Too much he didn't understand. Running blind wouldn't get him anywhere. Neither would antagonising the few people who might help. Galling though the prospect seemed, if he got a chance to earn Armon's trust, he would take it.

The familiar click of the door lock cut across the silence. He looked up but didn't stand.

Armon entered, looking much more the part of the spymaster, his old-man clothes shed in favour of an all-black outfit styled after the uniforms of Morgain's guard. He left the door open and crossed to the foot of the bed, pausing to look Jared over. "You'll do, I suppose." He pulled a small pot from his pocket and tossed it at Jared. "Concealer. For the cuts." He motioned to Jared's mouth.

Jared caught the pot and winced at the jolt to his arm. He peeled off the cloth lid, peered inside, then scooped out a small dollop of the clay-like contents and smeared it on the back of his hand. It blended with his skin as seamlessly as a black cat hidden in deep shadow. "You have a good eye."

Armon crossed his arms over his chest and glared.

"Just trying to be friendly." Jared picked up the pot and nodded to the dresser. "May I?"

Armon backed up until his solid frame filled the doorway. "Go ahead."

Jared crossed to the dresser without sparing him a glance. He set the pot down, scooped out a double-finger-full of concealer, and stole a look at Armon's reflection in the corner of the glass.

Armon had assumed a relaxed pose, but his tense muscles pushed against the fabric of his jacket, and his right hand hovered a hair's breadth above a blackened dagger hilt. He looked up, as if in response to Jared's scrutiny, and flashed him a mocking grin.

The hairs on the back of Jared's neck prickled, but he forced himself to return the grin with a calm smile—a smile he held fixed in place as he applied the concealer to his face. Better to be cursed for eternity than to allow Armon to see how much it stung.

Once his cuts were covered, he rinsed his hands in the wash bowl then slipped the cloth lid onto the pot. He held it out to Armon.

Armon shook his head. "Keep it. I have a feeling you're going to need it."

Jared bit off a retort and set the pot down. "I'm ready."

"This way." Armon entered the hallway.

Jared followed a step behind.

Two guards left their posts at his door and fell into step at his sides.

They walked in silence. Only the clack of studded boots and the creak of leather armour signalled their progress through the east corridors to the top landing of the entrance hall. Armon paused to speak to more guards.

'For someone who claims to be invisible, he appears to be rather well known.'

Jared glanced between all four guards, noted the deference with which they treated Armon, and ran his hands over his hose to dry his sweat-soaked palms. *Well known and well respected.*

'Or well feared.'

Armon finished speaking and moved past the guards into Morgain's private quarters. The guards subjected Jared to a pat down then motioned for him to follow.

Armon stopped outside Morgain's study, spun around, and wrapped his fingers around Jared's throat. "You want to live beyond the next five minutes, you keep your hands to yourself." He shoved Jared back before he could answer and disappeared through the door.

Jared took a step forward and froze. Cold, hollow dread welled inside him at the sight of the familiar doorway, numbing his body and threatening to overwhelm his mind. Ghostly chains closed around his wrists and ankles. Stifling air burned deep in his lungs. The guards shuffled their feet behind him. Then a sharp point jabbed the small of his back. He took a deep breath, willed his hands to stop trembling, and stepped inside.

Morgain occupied the chair behind her desk, just as she had two mornings earlier. Armon had taken up a position to her left, standing with his back to the wall and one elbow resting on a bookshelf. They both watched Jared as he entered—Armon through slitted eyes, and Morgain with an open, intense stare.

Jared stopped a step inside the doorway and crossed his arms, mimicking Armon's earlier pose.

Armon straightened.

Morgain frowned.

Jared rubbed the edge of the bandage encircling his arm. "I want to see Elise."

Morgain's lips twitched. She leant forward and pulled the coverlet off a large tray on her desk. "Sit down." She motioned to the chair in front of her desk.

Jared ceased his rubbing and firmed his stance. "Not until I know she's safe."

Morgain broke off her examination of the tray's contents to meet his stare. "Are you really so eager to lose your eye?"

"No. But I signed the confession to keep Elise safe. I won't cooperate further until I know you've kept your word."

"I see." Morgain plucked the cloche off the nearest plate. The mouth-watering scent of fresh-cooked bacon filled the air. "You will have all the proof you desire soon enough, but first…" She set the cloche to one side. "First, we will eat breakfast like civilised adults."

Jared ground his teeth. His stomach growled. "You promise I'll get to see her as soon as we're finished here?"

"I promise. In fact"—Morgain lifted another cloche to reveal a mound of scrambled eggs—"I will insist. Now *sit*."

Jared sucked on his bottom lip. Trusting Morgain felt worse than trusting a viper, but what choice did he have?

Her glower deepened, growing darker than any thundercloud. His empty stomach cramped. He lowered his arms and approached the chair. From the back, it looked normal, straight-legged and square-framed, with a solid, curved back. But from the side—Jared glanced at Morgain and back—from the side, it looked like something more suited to a dungeon. The back and seat were made from thin slabs of wood drilled full of holes, like a sieve or grate, and—

Jared perched himself on the edge of the seat. He didn't want to think of the and.

Morgain uncovered the final plate to reveal several slices of toast. "Strap yourself in."

So much for not thinking of the and. He glanced at the food on the desk and swallowed. "That really isn't necessary."

"Of course it's not *necessary*, but it's what I *want*." Morgain transferred several rashers of bacon onto his plate, followed by a spoonful of egg. "Now strap yourself in." She added a slice of toast and glanced to the side. "Armon."

Armon pushed away from the wall.

Jared leant forward and strapped his ankles to the legs of the chair.

Morgain waved Armon back. "The one at your waist as well."

'Say no, coward.'

Jared grabbed the restraint's ends and fastened them like a belt.

"And your right arm."

'Why don't you tie a noose around your neck while you're at it? Save everyone a lot of trouble.'

He ducked his head to hide his face. *Where did that thought come from?* He fastened the arm restraints at wrist and elbow and sat back, his face coated with a cloying layer of cold sweat. "Who are you?"

Morgain laughed. "I'm the woman you've been sleeping with for the past five years."

"The woman I slept with would not have done this."

"No?"

"The woman I slept with was kind, compassionate, and gentle."

More laughter. "She also believes in justice and examples."

"You call this justice?"

"No. I call it vengeance."

"Then—"

"Enough!" Morgain picked up a fork and held it towards him. "I had this breakfast specially prepared for us. Let's not spoil it with pointless arguments."

Jared reached for the fork.

Armon edged forward, his fingers clamped around his dagger hilt, and glared at Jared through burning eyes.

Jared held Armon's gaze for a dozen heart-thumping seconds then turned to Morgain. He set the fork down next to his plate. "Do you distrust me so much we need a chaperon now?"

"I suppose it does spoil the intimacy. Armon, don't you have work to do?"

"None more important than keeping you safe."

A frown flickered across Morgain's brow, come and gone like a bolt of lightning. "Then fasten the neck strap, if you must."

"With pleasure." Armon stalked across the room, his hand still stroking his dagger, and disappeared behind Jared's back. A thick, leather strap slipped around his neck a moment later. A soft hiss sounded as the end slid through the buckle. The strap snapped tight. It crushed his throat, not quite blocking his airway, but ensuring every breath became a struggle.

Morgain served herself a spoonful of egg. "Play nice, Armon."

The strap loosened a notch.

She added two rashers of bacon. "Thank you. You may go."

A faint growl tickled Jared's ear. Then the tiles cracked beneath Armon's retreating feet. The door at Jared's back opened with a blast of air and crashed shut.

Morgain frowned after him, blinked, and shook her head. "Tuck in."

Jared picked up his fork and stabbed the egg. His arm trembled.

"Does it hurt?" Morgain reached across the desk and stroked the bandage poking out from his cuff.

He dropped the fork and snatched up a slice of toast. "Why are you doing this? What do you want?"

"What do I want?" Morgain slid her fork into her mouth then slid it out, running the prongs across her lower lip, pulling it down into a pout. She held it there for a moment then lowered her hand. "Can't you figure it out?"

"Armon said he wanted to recruit me."

"Mmhm." Morgain swallowed. "You are very important to his plans."

"And the confession?"

Morgain placed her hand on a beaker of water. "What do you think?"

"Insurance for my good behaviour?"

"Clever boy." She lifted the beaker and drank. "Do you like the chair? I had it made just for you."

"Well, uh, I..."

'You what? Hate it? Despise it? Wish it had never been made? Go ahead and tell her. See what she does.'

"What do you think the holes are for?"

Jared frowned. "The holes?"

"Yes. The holes. What do you think they're for?"

"I have no idea."

"Attachments." Morgain leant forward until her elbows rested on the desk and curled a finger in her hair. "Have you ever wondered what it would feel like to sit on a chair of nails?"

"Nails?" Jared squirmed under the press of a dozen imagined pricks. "I can't say it's something I've ever considered."

"No? I have. If you misbehave, you'll get a chance to find out."

Acid stung the back of his throat. He'd heard that tone before, seen the same look in her eyes. Only the last time he'd seen it, they'd been lying together in her bed.

"I have a job for you."

"A job?"

"Yes, a job. Must you repeat everything I say?"

"I... No. Of course not. What sort of job?"

Morgain dropped her hands to the desk, all her playfulness fled. "One you are eminently suited to. I need you to deliver a message."

✎✐

A steady stream of people moved through the lower service corridors of the al-Rafael household, some shuffling under heavy loads whilst others strode with messages or supplies in hand. Slaves scurried amongst them, their hurried steps and downturned eyes giving them the appearance of scuttling mice.

Jared hugged the sides of the corridors as he wove between them, paying just enough attention to avoid a collision. He clenched and unclenched his fists, running his nails across his palms each time, before shaking his fingers loose.

There has to be a way out of this.

There has to.

He glanced over his shoulder as he neared the corner. The guard still followed. He hadn't let Jared out of his sight since they left Morgain's study. There'd been no way to send a message. No chance to scribble a quick note.

He reached the door to the kitchen garden and pressed himself against the opposite wall. There was no chance of blending into the crowd and disappearing either, not in this gaudy uniform.

He rested his head against the wall and closed his eyes. *Think, Jared. Think.*

He cracked his eyes open and glanced to the side. The guard had taken up a post at the junction. He met Jared's gaze and winked.

Jared squeezed his fingers under his collar and tugged. It did little to ease the itching. The threads of the woollen undershirt and hose scratched like claws every time he moved.

Prehen Damis, help me. Guide me free of this mess.

The guard took a step forward.

Jared tugged at his green-and-yellow striped doublet and pulled up the matching knee-length braies. He caught a glimpse of himself in the door's glass pane and snorted. His appearance would have been laughable if the situation were less strained. The whole outfit was at least a hundred years out-of-date.

The guard took another stride towards him.

He stepped up to the door.

"Please, Morgain, I'll do anything. Anything but this."

He glanced at the guard and sighed. His plea had failed to garner Morgain's sympathy. He doubted it would be any more effectual if he made it to the guard.

He raised his hand to the door and shoved.

"Jared!" His name rang through the enclosed garden, sung by a voice as sweet as a nightingale's. It held so much happiness, so much joy, that it made his blood tingle even as icy tendrils crept towards his heart.

"Elise." Her name slipped from his tongue in a whisper, its taste bittersweet. She moved amongst the runner beans, a basket suspended from one arm and a pod clutched in her upraised hand. Her wild hair had escaped its bonds again, the wayward strands adding a false halo to the gentle, ginger waves. He stared at her as she walked towards him, his gaze travelling from pert, deep-red lips, across freckled cheeks pale as birch bark, to eyes so deep and green they pierced his heart like a barbed arrow, reeled it in, and refused to let go again.

She grinned at him.

He grinned back.

"You look like a marrow." She laughed. A deep, heartfelt laugh, not the high-pitched, nerve-grating, tittering fashionable amongst the Blood.

"A marrow?" Jared looked down at himself and raised his eyebrows. "Not a cucumber?"

She stepped closer and draped her hands around his shoulders. Strong hands, for a strong woman. Independent too. He'd spent more time on the road than he had with her, but she'd never complained.

He placed his hands on her hips. "But marrows are fat."

Elise laughed again and patted his stomach. "*You* are not fat."

"I'm glad you think so." He ran his hands up to her waist, tracing her curves with his thumbs, then slid his arms around her and pulled her in tight. She felt so small pressed up against him. So delicate he feared if he held her any tighter, she'd snap in half.

Her arms slipped under his armpits. Her fingers dug into his back.

He tilted his head down to her shoulder, closed his eyes, and breathed in her scent. Rosewater mingled with polish and freshly turned earth. He breathed deep, sucking every precious drop of her aroma into his lungs.

Please, please, let this moment never end.

He could warn her now, whisper a quick message in her ear, ask her to meet him outside town. They could escape. Get away together before Morgain realised what he'd done.

And if I fail? If we're caught?

If he failed, Elise would be tortured to death. And he'd be forced to watch.

He pulled her even closer.

'Surely your freedom is worth the risk?'

He lifted his head and drew in a breath.

Something thudded into the back of his knee.

He stumbled.

Elise released him and backed away.

A dark, hunched figure darted out from behind him. "Sorry, sir. Very sorry."

Jared grabbed for the fleeing figure, but Elise caught his arm. "Let him be. It's only Jed, the gardener's new apprentice." She leant closer and lowered her voice. "I think the gardener felt sorry for him. He's rather simple."

Jared lowered his arm but kept one eye on the bedraggled man.

Jed scuttled along a grassy side path and stopped next to a lettuce bed. He glanced up, revealing a familiar, dirt-smeared face, and flashed Jared a mocking grin.

"Jared?"

Jared tore his gaze away from Armon and looked at Elise.

Her smile had faded, her laughter-lines given way to a furrowed brow. "What's going on? Why have you been avoiding me?"

"I..." Jared glanced at Armon.

Armon had edged closer; close enough to overhear every word. He met Jared's gaze, drew his dagger, and pressed its blade to his lips.

Iron bands tightened around Jared's ribs like the crushing coils of a python. "I haven't—"

"Three nights you've been back. Three nights, and not a word."

"It's complicated."

Armon shifted the dagger from his lips to the base of his throat, where he tapped it once before pointing it at Elise's back.

"Elise." Jared reached for her hands, but she pulled them away. He held his in mid-air for a moment then tucked them under his arms. "Elise, I..." *Please. I can't do this. I can't.* He looked to the overcast sky and blinked his stinging eyes. "I can't see you anymore."

Elise's mouth moved in silent denial. Her irises appeared to fracture like thin lake ice, black cracks splintering and spreading through the green, each shard mirrored in the depths of his heart. She backed away from him, hugging her chest. "Why?"

"I..." *I can't tell you. If I do, you'll die.*

"No." Her hair cavorted around her shoulders like flames as she shook her head. "You don't get to do this. You don't pledge your undying love to me one visit then break things off without explanation the next. I thought we had something special. I thought..." She bowed her head and muttered something beneath her breath. Her grip tightened on her arms, her knuckles going white. When her gaze returned to his, her eyes were flat, her expression devoid of life. She dropped her arms. "Is there someone else?"

"No!" Jared's denial was too quick—too powerful. He saw the truth register in her eyes.

She stared at him for one stunned moment, snatched a runner bean from her basket, and snapped it in half. The end of the pod dangled from her fingers, the strands as torn and useless as his unvoiced explanation.

"Elise, I... I'm sorry." The hatred twisting her face tore at his heart, ripping deeper than all Morgain's threats. He reached for her again, but she spun away, her basket swinging wide behind her, barely missing his hand.

Armon flipped his dagger over and buried the blade in the dirt.

Elise didn't even glance in his direction as she stormed from the garden.

Jared turned his back on Armon. He would *not* let the black-hearted bastard see him cry.

Gravel crunched behind him. Fingers touched the top of his arm. "At least you didn't try to give her the locket back."

Jared rounded on Armon, his hands curled into fists. "What?"

"Someone stole it from her room. What would she have thought if she'd discovered *you* had it?"

"You bastard."

Armon chuckled and shrugged. "Guilty as charged. Don't you have any more imaginative insults?"

"You're a cowardly, sneaking, thieving, stinking pile of cow dung."

"Better, but still not very good." Armon pressed up against Jared, standing on tiptoe so they stood nose to nose. "You have ten days to deliver Morgain's message. Ten days to get your dandified backside there and back. If you fail, or you're late, I'll assume you've run." He moved his mouth to Jared's ear and dropped his voice to a whisper. "And if you run, your precious scullery maid will die."

Sherna nipped at the grass, snorted, and flicked her head between her forelegs when she encountered a few stubborn shoots. Her simple pleasure brought a brief smile to Jared's lips, but the moment was fleeting, quickly swamped by the dark morass that had threatened to drown him since his meeting with Elise. He walked to the paddock and rested his arms on the fence.

Sherna lifted her head, whickered a greeting, and returned to her meal.

An involuntary twitch tugged at his lips. "At least one thing in my life remains unharmed. Right, girl? Though you'll have to rest here a few more days." He glanced towards the walls of the al-Rafael Household. "Official duty, you see."

The soft tread of feet and hooves squelched in the damp earth behind him. "Your mount, sir."

Jared turned to the stablehand and sighed. The boy led one of the royal courier thoroughbreds. A dark brown gelding of sixteen hands with a lean frame and slender legs. It snorted and shook its head when Jared took the reins, conveying its eagerness to get on the road and stretch its legs. The 'hand stepped aside as Jared leapt into the saddle with practised ease.

"Where to, sir?" the boy asked.

"The al-Arran Household."

"You'll want the north-east road then. It runs straight for about twenty miles, then crosses over the north-south pass. You'll find the next courier station just off the junction. There'll be a warm bed and a fresh horse waiting for you when you get there."

As if I need directions to find my own home. Jared nodded his thanks and kicked the horse into motion.

He held it to a walk whilst they cut across the southern corner of town, giving those on foot time to clear their path. A queue clogged the approach to the outer gate, but the guards took one look at his uniform and waved him through. Once they cleared the string of travellers seeking entry, he nudged the gelding with his knee, steering it off the uneven cobbles onto the more forgiving dirt side-track.

With the track ahead clear of traffic, he relaxed in the saddle and gave the horse its head. It settled into a steady, ground-eating trot, its long, agile legs pounding a rhythmic drumbeat against the dirt. The open, overcast landscape soon turned into a monotonous blur of browns, greens, and greys, as dull and lifeless as the trampled, shredded remnants of his life.

He hunched lower in the saddle and replayed his meeting with Elise over and over, analysing every touch, every gesture, every word.

Searching for something he could have said or done differently, some way he could have lessened her hurt. Wishing he could have held her a few seconds longer, memorising her scent, her warmth, her feel.

The miles disappeared, unnoticed, behind him, insubstantial as a gossamer dream.

The buffeting wind dried his silent tears.

❧❧

Orange light bloomed from the courier station's windows in mockery of the weak sunset, the rich, deep glow promising much needed comfort and warmth. The gelding flared its nostrils and lifted its head. Its pricked ears swivelled forwards as it picked up its pace, trotting with the eagerness of a hunting dog chasing a fresh scent.

Jared leant forward and gave it a solid pat on the neck. A slight tug on the reins turned it onto the gravel road leading up to the station. He dismounted at the gate and led the gelding around the back to the stables.

At his approach, a young woman darted out from the shadows and took hold of the gelding's reins. "Will you be staying tonight?" she asked in a too-cheerful voice. "Or do you require a fresh mount?"

"I'll be staying." Jared handed over the reins and unbuckled his saddlebags. He could have pushed on for a few hours—given his deadline, he probably should—but the cold, fat raindrops spotting the road promised a miserable night to come. The al-Arran Household was only two days' ride away. Even allowing for poor weather, he had plenty of time.

"Very good, sir." The young woman scratched the gelding between the ears. "We'll have a fresh mount saddled and ready for you at first light."

"Thank you." Jared shouldered his saddlebags and pulled a bag of squashed raisins from his trouser pocket. "For the gelding. He's worked hard today." *And I never even asked his name.*

She took the bag with a smile that ruddied her cheeks. "I'll see he gets them in his feed."

"Thank you." *Again.* Jared gave the gelding another pat and headed to the front of the courier station. He stopped when he reached the front yard and stared back down the road. Elise would be elbow deep in hot water by now, scouring the day's dishes before she retired for the night.

Retired to an empty bed and an uncertain future.

Retired alone.

"Forgive me, my love." The wind snatched his whisper and ripped it apart, destroying it as effectively as Morgain had destroyed his life. Even if he did get a chance to explain things to Elise, even if he could make her understand, he doubted she would forgive him now. There had been too much pain—too much hatred—in her eyes for that.

Why have I been such a reluctant coward?

Why didn't I tell Morgain our relationship was over when I had the chance?

An icy raindrop landed on the centre of his head. He shivered and hurried indoors.

An archway to his left opened onto a large common room where warm, bright fires crackled in twin hearths. Only a handful of people occupied the room, sitting alone or in pairs at the long bench tables. Another archway on the right led to the stairs.

Jared approached the counter opposite the door and handed his work papers to the man on the other side. "Do you have any single rooms available?"

The man took the roll of paper, scanned its contents, made a note in his logbook, and handed it back. "The attic room's empty. It'll cost you two pentains."

"Any food?"

"Mead and broth are included. Venison is a pentain extra."

"I'll take the room and the meat." Jared plucked three five-sided silver coins from his money pouch and placed them on the counter.

The man pocketed the coins and replaced them with a key. "Follow the stairs up to the second-floor landing then take a left. Your room's through the door at the end of the hall. Would you like your meal sent up?"

"Please."

The man made another note in his book. "Washing facilities are on the first floor. If you want a private bath, it'll cost another pentain."

"No bath. Thank you." Jared picked up the key and headed upstairs. He located the door the man had mentioned and discovered an unlit flight of stairs behind it. After backtracking to collect a candle, he climbed to the room in the rafters.

It was larger than he'd expected, with a fireplace, clean bed, table, and chair. He dropped his saddlebags on the bed, walked over to the fireplace, and jabbed at the banked coals with the supplied poker. The coals flickered and flared to life. He pulled the chair closer to the fire, straddled the seat, and stared into the flames.

He was in serious trouble—only an idiot would try to claim otherwise—but there had to be *something* he could do to escape.

The last courier station on his route sat ten miles inside the al-Arran border and almost a full day's travel from the household. If he timed it right, he could leave the main road just inside al-Arran lands, cut across country, and earn himself two- or three-days' head start before the station master questioned his absence. Add another two or three days for news to get back to Morgain, and he could put a good hundred miles between himself and the nearest pursuit.

If his life had been the only one at stake, he might have taken the chance. Morgain would release his confession as soon as she learnt of his desertion. He'd be forced into hiding, at least until the initial uproar died down. But he knew how to live off the land. He'd stand a decent chance.

But his life wasn't the only one at stake. If he ran, Elise would die. His freedom wasn't worth her life.

He pressed his knuckles to his eyes, breathed deep, and fought back a fresh bout of tears. Everything he'd done in the last two days had been done to protect her.

Everything.

And yet he feared it wouldn't be enough, that the demands would keep on coming, and Elise's life would continue to be at stake.

He had to get her away.

Had to keep her safe.

He just wished he knew how.

'You should kill Armon.'

The thought came from nowhere, a whisper from the darkest recess of his mind. Three days ago, it would have struck him as abhorrent. *But now?* He had to admit it held some appeal.

If he left at first light, followed the road for a few miles, then circled back, he could be at the al-Rafael Household by nightfall. Once there, he could use his uniform and pouch to trick his way past the guards, convince one of the servants to show him to Armon's room, break in whilst the spymaster slept, and slit his throat.

He stared at his hands and shuddered at the imagined touch of hot, sticky blood.

Faint laughter flitted through his mind. *'Like you could ever kill anyone.'*

There it was again. The same dark whisper. The same sibilant voice.

Is it truly my subconscious?

"Or am I going mad?"

He dropped his arms to the back of the chair and stared into the fire's flame.

22/11/32 KAF

ome.
Its nearness injected some warmth into Jared's frozen bones. After three days in the saddle, the prospect of a good meal, a hot bath, and a night in his own bed lifted the weight from his heart. Relaxation and a good night's sleep might be all he needed to see a way out of this mess.

'Or it might not. It's not too late to run.'

But if I'm going to run, I need to do it now.

Farmland lined both sides of the road, the fields lying fallow after the recent harvest. The Hia Copse loomed ahead, the ring of woods forming the first line of defence for the al-Arran Household. Once he passed under its bows, there would be no turning aside.

He pulled his cloak tighter, hunched his shoulders against the incessant rain, and clicked his tongue, encouraging his mount to keep slogging through the mud. He looked to his right, out across the empty landscape, though he couldn't see far in the dim light.

Nobody else had braved the weather. No witnesses existed to report him if he did leave the road. He would have three days, possibly four, before pursuit started.

He turned his gaze forward and shook his head. Better to kill himself than abandon Elise now.

He reached the edge of the copse. The trees' shadows fell across the road, making it feel more like late evening than midday. At least the thick branches provided some respite from the downpour. He sat a little straighter, wiped water from his eyes, and checked his saddlebags for the hundredth time.

Still secure.

He shifted in his saddle, wet clothes rubbing against wet skin, and patted the side of the horse's shoulder, whispering, "Not far now."

The trees gave way abruptly, the centre of the copse having been cleared when the first al-Arrans settled there generations ago. The land between the edge of the copse and the moat had been kept clear ever since. Anyone foolish enough to attack the household would be forced to cross the barren land under constant fire from catapults and archers atop the walls.

Jared sensed the archers watching and let his cloak fall open to reveal his uniform.

The lowered drawbridge spanned the moat when he reached it, the gate standing open. Two men guarded it, one old and grizzled, the other barely old enough to grow a beard. Jared recognised them both, though he couldn't place their names. He nodded to them as he crossed the drawbridge.

"Welcome back, sir," the young man said. He pressed his fist to his chest in salute.

Jared raised a hand in acknowledgement, dragged up a smile for the young man, and rode through the ten-foot-thick wall into the bailey.

The al-Arran Household was small—much smaller than the al-Rafael's—and their holdings were modest, made up almost entirely of farmland and woods. The main seat of the family reflected that modesty. The bailey housed a small village, with a smithy, tannery, and woollen mill on one side, and a bakers and butchers on the other. A small market square and a tavern provided the only other sources of commerce.

Today, the village appeared deserted. Even the stray dogs had sought shelter from the rain. Jared steered his horse along the cobbled street then cut across the market square to the stables at the foot of the motte. He slipped from the saddle and led the horse inside, blinking in the flickering torchlight.

A boy lay slouched on a hay bale, far enough away from the arched opening to stay dry. He glanced up as Jared entered, gave a polite nod, and went back to chewing on a strand of straw like a mindless, contented cow.

Jared led the horse to the boy, dropped the reins at his feet, untied his saddlebags, and slung them over his shoulder. "She's all yours." He threw a nod toward the horse.

The boy mumbled something unintelligible and carried on chewing at the straw.

Jared dug his fingernails into the leather of the bags. "Now, boy. She's worked hard. The least she deserves is a proper rubdown and a decent meal." He waited for the boy to pick up the mare's reins, then turned towards the rear exit and the motte gate.

The boy muttered something around the straw in his mouth.

Jared thumped his heel to the ground and spun. "What did you say?"

"I said you couriers are all the same. You think you're better 'an the rest of us 'cause you wear the King's uniform."

Jared took a step forward. "I'll be sure to share your opinion with my cousin."

The boy wrinkled his nose. "Your cousin?"

"Lord Ryal al-Arran."

Blood drained from the boy's face, leaving his skin as grey as the walls of the keep.

"Now, see to my horse."

"Y-yes, sir."

Jared struggled to hold his glower as he waited for the boy to scramble off the hay bale and lead the mare to an empty stall. Once satisfied she would be properly cared for, he readjusted his saddlebags and headed for the door.

The guard at the second gate took the time to check him for weapons before letting him through.

Jared stopped on the gate's other side and stared up the steep hill. Rivulets of water raced along the gaps between the cobbles like miniature rivers, frothing and threatening to breach their banks. The rain made the small stones as slick as an ice sheet, and his legs already ached from days in an unfamiliar saddle, on unfamiliar horses, in clothes barely adequate for the job. He sighed and pushed forwards, forcing his tired limbs to move, hauling himself up the last few yards to the top of the motte. Once there, he rapped on the squat, stone keep's iron-bound door.

"Name and business?" a muffled voice asked from behind the thick wood.

"Jared up-Arran with a message for Lord Ryal al-Arran from Lady Morgain al-Rafael."

Keys turned, bolts slid back, and the door opened with the slightest of creaks. "Come in out of the rain, lad. I'll let him know you're here."

"James?" Jared stepped inside. He slid his saddlebags off his shoulder and dropped them to the floor. "What are you doing manning the door?"

"I'm not." Ryal's old adviser smiled and moved aside so the guard could close the door. "I spotted you tramping up the hill and came down to welcome you home."

"Your welcome is most... welcome." Jared laughed at his awkward thanks and shrugged off his cloak.

Behind them, the guard slid the door's deadbolts home.

James waved Jared closer to the wall torch and looked him up and down. "Didn't think I'd ever see you in a uniform, lad."

Jared's smile slipped. "Nor would you have if I'd had a choice."

James's thick white brows drew together in a frown. He leant closer and squinted. "What happened to your face?"

"It's a long story. One I'd prefer not to repeat. Is Ryal—?"

"He's in a meeting with the guild heads. I'll let him know you're here. Why don't you wait up in the main hall? Dry yourself in front of the great fire. I'll have one of the servants bring you a warm meal."

"That would be more welcome than you know. These last few days... I feel like I've been sucked into the Vortex, swirled around until I can't think straight, and spat back out." Jared snatched at his saddlebags with his left hand and almost dropped them again as a line of fire raced up his arm. He feigned a stumble to hide his grimace and switched the bags to his other hand.

James caught him by the shoulder and pulled him up. "Are you—?"

"I'm fine." Jared rocked his shoulder back to fling James off, noticed the concern on the advisor's face, and forced himself to stop. "Sorry. I didn't mean to snap. I'm tired, that's all. I'd hoped to be here yesterday, but with the weather..." He lifted his free hand and shrugged.

"You sure that's all?"

Jared nodded.

James let him go and stepped back. "Go get some rest. We'll be with you as soon as we can."

"I will. Thank you." Jared shifted his bags to his forearm and strode down the corridor to the east tower, where a narrow, spiral stairway wound up to the first floor. The steps glinted in the torchlight, their surfaces worn smooth as river-washed pebbles by the passage of hundreds—if not thousands—of pairs of feet. He reached out and touched the polished stone, just as he did every time he returned home. It gave him a sense of belonging, a connection with those who had gone before.

Thunder cracked, splitting the air overhead.

Jared ducked, shoulders hunched, then glanced behind him. The corridor remained empty. He laughed at himself, shifted his saddlebags to his shoulder, and climbed the stairs.

Vapours from the great fire warmed the air at the top, carried there by a ventilation system that heated the whole of the upper floor. The promise of rest and warmth sped his feet. He quick-marched across the corridor and entered the main hall through the side door.

The fire's blazing flames filled the hall and reflected off the polished, grey stone walls, lighting it as effectively as a dozen torches. Though small by modern standards, he'd yet to discover another household which offered the welcoming warmth created by the hall's high ceiling, great fire pit, and columned central chimney.

He dropped his saddlebags on the nearest table, tossed his cloak over the back of a chair, and approached one of the arches enclosing the great fire.

It crackled in the deep pit. Small sparks flew as a log shifted and split. He edged a little closer. The fire's heat beat against his exposed skin. His woollen shirt and hose started to steam, releasing a stink like damp sheep. He slipped off his gloves and held his wrinkled hands up to the flames.

A dull ache sank into his arm as his warming blood reawakened his half-healed cut. He rolled up his sleeve and stared at the ragged red slash running the length of his forearm. The sight of the ugly, irregular stitches ignited sparks in his teeth. He dropped his arm and hastily rerolled his sleeve.

He was still no closer to a solution—he could see no way to get Elise beyond Morgain's reach. Perhaps Ryal would think of something. A fresh pair of eyes might see something he'd missed.

He sighed and shambled back to the table, all too aware of the relentless passage of time. Every second ground at his patience. Every minute spent idling brought Elise closer to death. The last thing he wanted to do was stand around waiting, yet the best thing he could do for her was regain his strength.

He sank onto the chair, crossed his arms on the table, and rested his head on the makeshift nest.

≈≈≈

"Jared!"

Jared startled and swore. His neck cracked as he lifted his head from the cradle of his arms and wiped a dribble of drool from the corner of his mouth. "Ryal." He pushed himself away from the table in a screech of chair legs on stone. The high-pitched squeal drove through his bones like a drill through granite. He winced and stood. "Sorry. I didn't mean to fall asleep."

"Nonsense. I'm the one who's kept you waiting half the night." Ryal caught Jared as he turned. His giant hands encompassed Jared's forearms, crushing the tender cut.

Jared hid his pain behind a smile and reciprocated his cousin's hold. He studied Ryal as his cousin regarded him with sparkling brown eyes.

Ryal appeared as young and healthy as ever. His broad shoulders and erect posture made him seem a giant, though he lacked Jared's height. His deep brow and crooked nose gave him a fierce countenance, whilst laughter lines and broad, upturned lips added a degree of softness. Only the wrinkles on his forehead and the specks of grey in his brown hair betrayed his true age. He broke off his inspection with a laugh. "It's good to have you back, my boy."

"It's good to be back, sire."

"I hope you'll forgive the poor welcome. I'd meant to come up sooner, but you know how much the guild heads go on. Every one of them has his own opinion, every one of them thinks he's right, and none of them will approve anything until they've all argued their point. It's been a long, tedious day." Ryal released his hold and took a step back. "James said you have a message for me."

Jared followed Ryal's nod to the fire, where James stood warming his hands. James met Jared's glance and walked over to join them.

Jared reached across the table for his saddlebags, flipped one open, and pulled out the courier pouch. "Lady Morgain requested that I not return until you reply."

"I see." Ryal took the pouch and broke the wax seal. "What's going on?" He removed the rolled message and tossed the empty pouch onto the table. "Why are you in official uniform?"

"Well..." Jared glanced between Ryal and James, his throat tightening. He clasped his hands together and rubbed his palm with his thumb. No matter how he looked at it, he couldn't think of way to explain the situation without casting himself in a poor light. He glanced at James again and clenched his hands tighter. "Morgain and I have had a falling out."

"Why does that not surprise me?" Ryal flattened the roll of papers and angled the top sheet to catch the firelight. His eyes narrowed, and he mouthed silent words as he read.

Jared glanced at the floor and back up again. "It's, uh, it's my fault, I suppose. I..."

Ryal's face darkened. He lifted the top sheet, skimmed the second, then handed both to James. His narrowed eyes settled on Jared. "Do you know what this says?" he asked, his words quick and clipped.

"I have no idea."

"Lady Morgain is demanding Kieron's hand in marriage."

Ryal's statement hit Jared like a kick to the stomach. He hugged his wounded arm to his chest. "She is?"

James nodded without taking his eyes off the letter. "She's not being polite about it either."

"Apparently," Ryal said, pulling Jared's attention back to him, "if I refuse, my *cousin* will be declared a traitor."

Oh, Gods.

"Apparently, he signed a confession."

"Ryal—"

"And if my cousin is a traitor, that makes me suspect."

"—I'm—"

"And if I'm suspect, Morgain will take great pleasure in confiscating the al-Arran lands and stripping my family of our titles."

"—sorry."

"You're sorry?" Ryal grabbed the second sheet of paper from James and slammed it into Jared's chest. "Sorry? What good is sorry against *that?*"

Jared took the paper in his shaking hand. He stared at the crumpled confession and shook his head. "I-I never. I didn't think..."

"You didn't think what?" Ryal asked, his voice flat.

"I didn't think she would use it against you."

I didn't think there was anything more she could destroy.

Jared's eyes locked on his signature on the bottom of the paper. The hall's walls closed in on him, the fire's light faded, and phantom thirst clawed at his throat. His shoulders bowed beneath the memories. He pushed them away, lowered the confession, and forced himself to look up—to meet Ryal's gaze.

Ryal's clenched jaw muscles bulged, his left eye twitched, and his larynx bobbed so violently Jared flinched.

James finished reading the letter and handed it back. "She appears to have left you little choice."

"Not so." Ryal's voice hummed with controlled anger. "There's still a choice."

Jared straightened his shoulders. "There is?"

"Of course." Ryal snatched the confession from Jared's hand. "I can take this to a magistrate, declare you a traitor, and order your execution myself."

Where Ryal's previous statement had hit Jared like a kick, this one gutted him with razor-sharp talons. He clapped a hand to his stomach and swallowed vomit. "You can't. You wouldn't."

"I can, and I will."

Jared blinked away sweat. "James?"

James looked away with a shake of his head.

Jared turned back to Ryal, one hand extended in appeal. "Y-you don't mean it. You're trying to scare me."

"I doubt you'll still think that when your neck meets the headsman's block."

Imagined pain sliced through Jared's neck. His legs buckled and folded, dropping him to his knees. "Ryal, please, don't do this. There has to be another option."

"Name it."

"We can appeal to the King. Convince him you had nothing to do with this—"

"Morgain has the law on her side. You think the King would risk civil war to protect a minor lord and a confessed traitor?"

"The confession was forced. She tortured me without provocation."

"Tortured?" Ryal snorted. "Where are the wounds, Jared? Where are the broken bones? The maimed limbs? The missing digits?"

"She was careful. She chained me so tight I couldn't move. Denied me water. Food. Sleep. Then, when she did unchain me, she threatened to have me shot if I so much as *looked* in the wrong direction. She—"

"Do you have proof?"

She would have killed Elise. Jared sagged forwards. "No," he whispered. "No proof."

"James, would you—?"

"Of course." James strode across the hall and exited through the main door. His footsteps echoed from the stone walls before fading down the corridor.

'Like the echoes of a death knell. Your death knell. If you want to live, you need to move. Now.'

The front door would be locked and bolted. The drawbridge raised. The gates closed. But he could get out through the kitchen. Squeeze through the sluice gate. Swim the moat.

"Jared?"

Jared started and tore his gaze from the door.

Ryal stared down at him. "Do I need to call the guard?"

Jared met Ryal's stare and read the warning there. There was more at stake than his life. If he ran, he might survive, but he would condemn himself forever in Ryal's eyes. There would be no chance of forgiveness. No possibility of returning home. "No." Jared placed his hands on his thighs and dug his fingers into his flesh to hide their trembling. "No guards."

"I have one more question, and I want an honest answer." Ryal thumbed the edge of the confession then held it out in front of him. "Is there any truth to this? Did you sell Morgain's correspondence?"

Jared held Ryal's gaze and drew a deep breath. "No. I did not."

Ryal glanced across the room to the far wall. When he looked back, moisture glistened in his eyes. "I love you like my own, my boy, but if it comes down to a choice between you and my son..."

Wood scraped across stone as the main door opened. Soft footsteps announced James's return.

Jared kept his eyes locked on Ryal's. His throat tightened. He nodded. "I understand."

Hands grabbed his arms and pulled them behind his back. Coarse rope bound his wrists. It didn't crush and bite as Morgain's manacles had, but it dragged at him, drawing him down into a lightless mire.

Ryal smiled at him, but his smile held no warmth. He watched as James helped Jared to his feet then turned his back.

James retrieved Jared's cloak and draped it around his shoulders. Then he unhooked an old hessian sack from his belt and pulled it over Jared's head.

Jared bit back a whimper as the drawstring tightened around his neck. He breathed in stale air and the stink of onions.

"Start walking. I'll make sure you don't fall." A hand thudded onto his shoulder.

He stifled another whimper and lifted his foot, but the first step proved impossible.

"The floor's flat. You'll be fine." James tightened his grip.

Jared edged forward, the tip of his boot scraping the floor. His balance shifted. He dropped his foot to the ground.

James gave his shoulder a squeeze.

Jared transferred his weight forward and took another hesitant step. Success bolstered his courage. He picked up his pace, counting his steps. Five. Ten. A turn. Fifteen. Twenty. Twenty-one. Twenty-two.

James pulled him to a stop. "Steps ahead. Take your time going down."

Jared slid his right foot forward until his heel cleared the edge then lowered it, slowly—ever so slowly—until his sole touched solid ground. He released his pent breath in a panicked laugh.

James switched his grip from Jared's shoulder to his wrists.

His standing leg shuddered. His stomach lurched. He pictured himself slipping, falling, tumbling. His bones breaking. Neck snapping. Dead eyes staring.

Stop it!

Crazed laughter cackled inside his head.

"James?"

"I'm right here."

Jared shivered in the cooling air. The stone's chill seeped through the soles of his boots. He descended six steps. Seven. Eight.

"Almost there."

Four more steps brought them to the ground floor.

Another corridor followed. Another flight of winding stairs. He paused at the bottom. "James?"

"What is it, lad?"

"There's something I need you to tell Ryal for me. Something I should have told him myself. If I don't go back… there's a woman. Elise. If I don't go back, if I don't make it to the al-Rafael Household within six days, they'll kill her. Morgain will kill her." He paused to listen, straining to hear anything above the blood thrumming in his ears. "James?"

James patted his shoulder. "I'll do what I can, lad. No promises though, hmm?"

Jared could only nod.

"Come on. It's not much further."

They walked a short way, turned left, then left again, descended a single step, turned right, and stopped. A bolt shot open, the sound like a thunderclap in the silence. James steered Jared forward, pulled off his cloak, untied his arms, and removed the hood. Light pierced Jared's eyes like needle-thin lances. He squinted and blinked.

James had brought him to a tiny square cell.

Jared stretched his arms to his sides. His fingers cleared the walls by inches. His hair brushed the low ceiling. A pile of dirty straw filled one corner, and the stench of raw sewage rose from a small hole in the floor. A bed and a toilet. He backed away from them both. His back thumped against the cold, damp wall. He rolled his head back and slid to the ground, pulled his legs in, and hugged them to his chest.

"Stay strong, lad. Don't give up hope."

The door slammed.

The bolt thundered home.

Darkness swallowed the cell in its jaws.

23/11/32 KAF

Jared could see nothing beyond the tip of his nose; hear nothing but the rhythm of his own breath. If not for the press of stone at his feet and back, he could have believed he floated in limbo. He had no idea how long he'd been sitting there and no way to gauge the passage of time. Only the stiffness in his limbs suggested it had been hours, rather than minutes, since James had locked him in.

He relaxed his arms and let his legs slide forward. Fiery tingles stabbed his feet and hands, stinging with the intensity of a thousand ant bites. He flexed his fingers and toes to soften the pain, then stretched a hand to the right until his fingers bumped into the neighbouring wall. Rough stone scratched at his fingertips as he walked them upwards. He dug his fingers into the crumbing mortar for purchase and levered himself upright. His muscles groaned in protest. He closed his eyes and exhaled.

More finger-walking located the door frame. He felt his way around its perimeter and cursed. The door had been set into a recess, blocking access to its edges from inside the cell.

'You're going to die down here, you know.'

No.

He turned around and pressed the back of his head against the thick wood of the door.

'Yes. You're going to die here, trapped in the dark, forgotten and alone.'

No. Ryal would never abandon me.

'Wouldn't he? It would be much easier for him to deny your existence than order your death.'

A crash echoed in the distance. Faint taps followed. Jared cocked his head. *Are those footsteps?*

Yes. Yes, they are.

He pushed off the door and took two steps forward before his blindness brought him to a halt.

The footsteps stopped outside his cell. He turned in a half-circle and waited for the thud of the bolt. A soft click sounded instead, followed by a nerve-scraping squeal. Light bloomed along the bottom of the door. Then a tray slid through the new opening. He didn't even have time to register its contents before the hinged flap snapped closed.

"Wait!" Jared dropped to his knees and scrambled forward. "Please. Wait." His knee hit the edge of the tray. His hand landed in something cold and congealed. He snatched it out and sucked at his finger. *Porridge? Or gruel?* The mush was so tasteless he couldn't tell. He felt around the tray and found another bowl filled with water, but no spoon.

'It's not much of a last meal.'

It is not my last meal.

He ran his hand along the bottom of the door but found no way to open the flap.

'You heard what he said. He'd rather kill you than permit Kieron's marriage to Morgain.'

He spoke in anger. He'll see things differently once he's had time to calm down.

'Fine. Lie to yourself if you must. You're still going to die.'

The sibilant voice broke off with a snort, leaving Jared's mind as silent as his cell. He picked up the bowl with shaking hands and settled down to a meal of cold, congealed gruel.

"Damn it!" Jared dropped his laces and pounded his fists against his thighs. He lifted his left hand to his mouth and sucked on the finger he'd cut on the cord. The muscles on the back of his neck rippled and twitched as he sensed invisible eyes on his back. He imagined the eyes' owners giggling to themselves as he struggled with his clothes.

'If Morgain could see you now…'

"She'd be laughing her head off. Yes. I know."

He took hold of the laces again.

Something scratched at the floor behind him. Something with sharp little claws. Something that probably had fur and teeth and liked to bite people.

'There's nothing there. You've already checked a dozen times.'

"Yes. I know that too!"

His mind had been working overtime, imagining rabid rats, fatal tumbles down stairs, invisible people watching his every move—

'Strange voices arguing with you inside your own head.'

"Please, gods, don't let me be going mad." He closed his eyes. The darkness remained unchanged, but blocking out its true depth helped calm his overworked heart. He brought his hands together, pulled the laces of his breeches tight, and fumbled with the unseen cords until he'd tied them in a knot. More scratches came from the hole at his feet. He backed up until his shoulders hit the door.

'Do you think you could fit down there?'

"What?"

'Where do you think it goes? Are there tunnels? Sewers? A cave?'

"It'll empty into the moat. All the toilets do."

'It could be your only way out of here.'

"It—no. I'm not squeezing down a chute covered in other people's filth."

'Not even to save your life?'

Jared ground his teeth.

'Not even for Elise?'

He shuffled forward until his toes hovered over the edge of the hole and crouched. His stomach somersaulted at the stench. Slime squished beneath his boots. "No." He straightened and backed up a step. "No. If I run, Ryal will presume I'm guilty. He'll have me hunted down and killed. If I stay..." He turned in a circle. "If I stay, at least I'll have a chance."

'What chance? You saw the way he looked at you. You saw your death in his eyes.'

"No!" Jared clamped his hands to the top of his head. "No. It's not going to end like this. I am *not* going to die down here in this hole. I have been through too much—sacrificed too much—to die knowing... knowing Elise is going to die anyway. That my selfishness... that I..." Jared squeezed down on his skull.

A *crack* thundered through the cell. The door opened on creaking hinges. And then...

And then nothing.

Jared looked up.

James stood in the doorway with a sack in one hand and a rope in the other. Jared started to shake. "Oh Gods..."

"Turn around, lad."

Jared shook his head. He wanted to back away, but his legs refused to move. "No. Please."

"Jared."

Jared turned. The rope went around his wrists. The sack slipped over his head. He bit down on his lip to hold in a scream. *Don't cry.*

"I'm sorry, lad."

Don't cry. Don't cry. Don't cry.

"Ryal's ordered your exile."

Please, gods, I'm not ready to die. Jared blinked. "Did you say *exile?*"

"He's giving you two days to pack and get clear. After that, word will go out that you're to be killed on sight. You won't be allowed to return to al-Arran land."

"How long—?"

"A night and a day."

Five days left. He wasn't going to die. Elise wasn't going to die. He could still make it. He could still save her life.

"Ryal's reply to Morgain's demand is in your room. He doesn't want to see you again. He thinks he might kill you himself if he does."

They were going up the stairs, out of the dungeon, back into the light.

"Sorry about the hood, but Ryal didn't want anyone to know you were in the dungeon."

The sack still stank of onions. It made Jared's stomach churn.

"You've missed the evening meal, but I had some food brought up for you."

More steps. They were on the upper floor.

"If there's anything here you want to keep, you'd best take it with you. I doubt Ryal will be in the mood to send it on anytime soon."

The hood came off, then the rope slipped free. Jared held his hands up to block the light and peered through slitted eyes. They were in the middle of his bedroom. "Thank you."

"Look after yourself, lad."

Jared nodded.

James left.

Jared closed the door. "Gods, I stink."

'I know you do.'

He stripped off the courier uniform, tossed it in a corner, and fell on the waiting food. It was only bread and soup, but after his meal of cold, congealed gruel, it tasted like the best food in the world.

24/11/32 KAF

Jared opened the wardrobe doors and flicked through his clothes. He pulled out his spare riding leathers and winter cloak, skipped past his evening wear, skipped back again, lifted out his best shirt, and tossed it on the bed. His comfiest breeches and a pair of loose tunics followed. Then his spare riding boots, complete with a hole in the sole under the big toe.

What else?

He closed the wardrobe doors and moved on to the chest of drawers. A warm blanket, some nightclothes, and some underwear joined the growing pile. From the top drawer, he took out his mini crossbow and a small dagger. He started to close the drawer again then paused to run a finger along the hilt of his old sword.

The gruff veteran who'd gifted it to him had died years ago, but the texture of the worn, cracked leather brought back memories of his stern visage. The man had been full of tales from his youth; of battles and brawls, duels and street fights. He'd even offered to teach Jared to use a sword. Unfortunately, Jared's enthusiasm had proved greater than his skill, and after a few months of fruitless lessons, the veteran had suggested he try something else.

He lifted the sword from the drawer and leant it against the side of the bed.

Next...

Next, he needed something to put everything in. He returned to the wardrobe and pulled out his old saddlebags and a rucksack. Anything that didn't fit would be left behind. It would have helped if he'd been able to *wear* the riding leathers, but he was still on official duty, which meant he had to dress like an overgrown marrow. At least he didn't stink anymore. He'd taken the time to bathe and wash his uniform before collapsing into bed the night before.

He scanned the room, double-checking for anything he might have missed. His gaze fell on the small desk by the window, and he sighed. He couldn't put it off any longer.

The desk's top drawer opened without a sound. He reached inside and felt along the top until he located the oval depression. A firm press popped the hidden lock, and a panel in the side of the desk swung open. The secret cupboard held a small wooden box and a cloth-wrapped package. He removed the box first and ran his fingers over the soft, smooth wood. The finely carved box appeared seamless on first inspection, but if one slid the short sides back, pulled out the thin panels, and pressed down on the twin mahogany triangles...

The lid flipped open with a snick. He poked at its contents; over fifty gold octains and a handful of uncut gems. A dangerous amount to carry when travelling alone, but Ryal had left him with little choice. He closed the box, set it on the desk, and retrieved the cloth bundle.

The hessian crackled as he removed it, the folds stiffened by age. He let the cloth fall to the desktop and cradled the painting it had protected. He had no memory of the oak-panelled room it depicted, nor the luxurious, padded armchair in which his mother sat. She held him in her lap, a tiny bundle of white swaddling with a dark blob for a face. His father stood behind them, his hands resting protectively on her upper arms. The painting gave the impression of a strong, happy family, but the details were crude. His parents' features were as vague on the canvas as they were in his mind, as indistinct as mountains in the mist.

He closed his eyes and pressed the painting's frame to his forehead. He'd lost them when he was four, when a virulent plague swept through their household. His parents had sent him to Ryal as soon as they realised the danger, but they stayed behind to help. Within weeks of the plague's outbreak, everyone who had lived on up-Arran lands had died, his parents included. The painting and the uncut gems were the only things of theirs he owned. Everything else had been lost when the king declared up-Arran territory off limits to prevent the plague's spread.

He opened his eyes and traced his parents' outlines with his thumb. "I just want to make you proud," he whispered.

'You'll need a miracle to achieve that now.'

He rewrapped the painting, placed it on top of his money box, and picked up Ryal's message pouch.

He'd found it on the desk last night. It hadn't been sealed.

He tapped his fingers against the loose flap, still unsure of his decision, then flipped it open and stared at the two pieces of paper inside. He'd never opened another person's correspondence before.

'And look where it got you. What's left to lose?'

My reputation.

'The reputation of a traitor? I can see why you'd want to protect that.'

He plucked the smaller piece of paper from the pouch and unfolded it before he changed his mind.

"Jared,

"If you have any sense, you'll get as far away from Morgain as you can. Regal will be made ready for you. Head north to Butterfly Cove. Ask for Captain Renault. He'll give you safe passage for a fair price.

"-R"

Jared smiled. Ryal hadn't abandoned him completely, it seemed. As for his advice—he would consider it. First, however…

He picked up the larger piece of paper and unrolled it.

"To Lady Morgain al-Rafael, Third Lady of the al-Rafael Household,

"Thank you for drawing my attention to Jared up-Arran's transgressions. I have exiled him from al-Arran lands on pain of death. The reasons for his exile will remain unannounced for now, but I will be the first to acknowledge his treason should the matter come to light. Please do not send him here again.

"Concerning your proposed marriage to Kieron: I have given the matter a great deal of thought and feel certain conditions must be set before any agreement may be reached. I must insist inheritance of all al-Arran lands and titles remain in the male line. I also propose that, in the interest of fairness, the al-Rafael titles and lands remain in the female line.

"I also feel a substantial dowry will be in order. Kieron is my only heir, and I am unlikely to produce another. As such, I will require sufficient recompense and assurances, in case something should happen to him in the future to prevent him from inheriting his estates.

"I believe the details of any agreement would be best discussed in person. Expect me at your household by the end of the month.

"Yours,

"Ryal al-Arran, Seventeenth Lord of the Al-Arran Household"

Jared let the scroll curl up on itself and dropped it into the pouch. Morgain would not like it, not one bit. A wise person would keep away from her when she received Ryal's reply.

'So what does that make you? An idiot?'

Jared shrugged and returned to his packing. He wrapped the painting and money box in his blanket and was placing the bundle in his rucksack when someone knocked at the door. He pushed the bundle to the bottom and reached for his clothes. "Who is it?"

The door opened in answer, and James stepped inside. "You ready?"

"Almost." Jared folded his riding leathers and placed them on top of his blanket.

"Need a hand?"

Jared glanced up at James and smiled. "Please."

James picked up one of the tunics and folded it.

Jared returned to the desk to collect his spare crossbow bolts.

Once his bags were packed, he strapped his sword and dagger to his belt, slung the rucksack onto his back, and picked up his saddlebags in one hand and the crossbow in the other. He nodded for James to lead the way, followed him across the room, then paused just inside the door.

He turned and swept his gaze around his room, memorising its familiar layout. "When I was out on the road I always thought—always *knew*—I had somewhere safe to come back to. It made all the travelling easier, having that security to fall back on. Now, though—" his voice broke. He looked at James, but the old adviser offered no reassurance. He glanced back at his room one last time and motioned for James to continue.

They moved through the empty corridors in silence. Jared had half-hoped to find Ryal in the main hall, but his cousin wasn't there. The few servants who were about didn't spare them a glance.

James led the way to the east tower, down the stairs, and along the corridor to the front door. "You sure you've got everything?"

"As sure as I can be. Besides..." He hefted his saddlebags. "...I don't think I could carry any more if I tried."

James chuckled and unbolted the door. Jared started forward, but James put out a blocking arm. "Watch your back. Morgain won't hesitate to kill you if she thinks your death will work to her advantage."

"I have no intention of staying around long enough for her to try."

"You have a plan then?"

"The beginnings of one."

James clapped Jared on the back. "Be careful, lad. I don't want you coming back here in a box."

"I will." Jared stepped outside and started down the steep hill. He didn't look back.

❧

A fresh courier horse was saddled and waiting for him when he reached the stables. A small, black-haired boy clutched the gelding's reins in both hands. Every time the horse snorted or side-stepped, the boy flinched and looked around the stables with big, round eyes.

Jared clucked his tongue to calm the gelding, dropped his saddlebags at its side, and transferred the courier pouch and a few other essentials to the courier bags.

The gelding whickered and tossed its head.

The boy shuffled several inches to the side.

Jared caught him by the shoulder. "Don't show you're afraid, boy. You'll only make it more nervous."

"Y-yes, sir," the boy whispered. He didn't sound convinced.

Jared retrieved his saddlebags and took the gelding's reins. He clicked his tongue and gave a sharp tug. The horse started forward.

"Um. Sir?"

Jared stopped and glanced over his shoulder.

The boy stood in the middle of the aisle, open hand extended. He fixed his big, round eyes on Jared's face. "I saddled him and everything, sir. Honest."

Jared didn't believe a word of it. He doubted the boy even knew how. Still, he pulled a coin from his belt pouch and tossed it to him. The youngster had shown some bravery, staying in the stable by himself with a horse three times his size.

"Thank you, sir." The boy caught the coin and clutched it to his chest with the ferocity of a squirrel protecting its nut.

Jared led the gelding outside, into the frigid air, and across the road to the family's private stables. He nodded to the soldier guarding the door and led the gelding inside. A loud whinny punctuated their arrival.

The gelding shied.

Jared tightened his grip on the its reins and stared at the source of the noise.

At almost seventeen hands, Regal was easily the tallest—and broadest—horse in the stables. His huge frame filled most of the aisle. His glossy black coat gleamed in the torchlight, and his hoofs shone. He stared at Jared with dark, clear eyes, pulled at his halter, and pawed the ground.

Jared tied the courier horse's reins to a hitch-ring near the door and went to greet his proud stallion.

Regal bent his head forward and nudged at Jared's hands.

Jared laughed and stroked the top of Regal's nose.

Regal jabbed him in the stomach.

Jared hopped back a pace. "Hey!" He fished a handful of raisins from his pocket and scattered them on the ground. Regal pounced on them, leaving him free to check over the stallion's saddle and tack. He tugged at straps to tighten the buckles, straightened the bridle, and pulled down hard on the saddle. When nothing budged, he holstered his mini-crossbow under the saddle-flap and secured his saddlebags in place.

Regal finished snuffling at the floor and whuffled.

Jared shrugged his rucksack off his back and tied it across the saddle.

Regal snorted and sidestepped. Each stomp of his hoof sent a judder through his body, threatening to dislodge his load.

Jared gave his side a pat. "Easy, boy. Easy. I know it's undignified, but it's only until we reach the al-Rafael courier station. Then it'll be just you and me again." Using the courier horse as a pack mule would have been the better choice, but as long as he was on official duty...

He untied Regal's reins and led him towards the thoroughbred. The big stallion snapped at the gelding's exposed rump. Jared yanked on his reins. "Stop that."

Regal lunged again, and the courier mount shied.

Jared gave another yank and stamped his foot. "No!"

Regal snorted but made no further attacks.

Jared leapt into the gelding's saddle whilst keeping a tight hold on Regal's reins, clicked his tongue, and kicked.

The gelding tossed its head.

Regal stepped forward.

The gelding danced sideways then broke into a trot.

26/11/32 KAF

Thick clouds obscured the stars. More rain fell, heavy and relentless. Regal trudged on, his hoof-steps muffled by the thick grass. Jared leant forward and patted his neck. "Almost there now, boy," he whispered. "Almost there."

The countryside slipped past in a dark blur, with the deep shadow of the distant woods on one side and the less distinct undulations of the shallow hills on the other. Claggy mud sucked at Regal's hoofs, slowing his steps, but the lost time seemed preferential to the risk of being spotted on the road.

The walls of the al-Rafael Household rose out of the darkness ahead, looming like a spider at the centre of its web. The torches lining the parapets sputtered and flared in the wind.

Jared steered Regal towards the dark shadows of the stables and away from the watching eyes of the guards above. Thick, dark lines marked the edge of the paddock, the harsh edges of the rails like gashes corralling the natural curves of the land. He pulled on the reins, bringing Regal to a stop, and slid from the saddle.

The reins slithered like soap-slicked string in his numb fingers as he tied them to the paddock fence. Once the quick release knot was in place, he checked the straps securing his bags and gave Regal another pat. "I'll be as quick as I can, boy. Be quiet for me, and I'll bring you back an apple."

Regal lowered his head between his legs and pressed his ears flat. Chill water ran down his coat in glistening waves.

Jared removed his cloak, draped it across Regal's back to protect him from the worst of the rain, and climbed over the fence. His left boot slipped on the wet wood as he lowered himself over the other side. His right twisted on a patch of mud. He grabbed for the fence, catching the rail before he landed on his backside.

Regal whinnied.

Jared chuckled, pulled himself upright, and padded across the paddock to find the stable doors closed. He placed his hand on one and pushed, but it failed to budge. Not unexpected, given the time and weather. A quick scan of the paddock revealed nothing but Regal's tail swishing through the veil of rain. He dropped to a crouch and crept towards the stable's corner.

A shiver ran down his back, a line of prickles rising behind it. He pulled at the collar of his jacket, sealing off the gap between fabric and skin. The rain drummed against the stable roof and splashed in the puddles forming in the mud. A low creak, like the groan of the rope Morgain had used to hang the young guardsman, sounded in the distance.

He rounded the corner and edged towards the side door, his gaze flicking towards the household walls, imaging the young man still dangling from the eaves, his decaying skin sloshing free in the rain.

Dear gods, what am I doing?

He glanced over his shoulder, searching for Regal's solid form, but the downpour obscured everything now.

'This is a bad idea.'

Yes. But I don't have a better one.

He pulled off a glove, fumbled in his belt pouch, and produced a key.

'I wonder if Morgain ever suspected you'd use it to break in when she gave it to you?'

Jared's fingers trembled. The key scraped against the escutcheon. He lowered it and pressed his forehead to the sodden timber. *No more than I imagined her arresting me in a fit of enraged jealously.*

He wiped the water from his eyes, set one hand next to the lock, and slid the key in with the other. It released with a crack like thunder, and the door swung open on squealing hinges. The ominous creak came again, three times in quick succession, like the dead laughing.

He retrieved the key and slipped through the gap. A mix of straw, horse, and sweat filled his nostrils. Heavy snoring echoed from the hayloft. Soft whuffles sounded in the nearby stalls. He closed the door, and everything vanished.

His pulse beat double-time in his fingertips as he searched along the rough wood of the left-hand wall. *It should be here somewhere...*

His knuckles hit something hard and sharp. Metal squeaked, the lantern's handle shrilling in protest as he knocked it swinging. He snatched at it, snared its base, and pressed his other hand to his aching chest. A flick of his thumb opened the shutter, releasing a whiff of kerosene. Faint light leaked out, casting a narrow, yellow beam across the floor and illuminating the door to the tack room across the hall.

He tiptoed across the gap, wrapped his fingers around the handle, and pushed it open.

Twenty cubbies ringed the small room, each one designed to hold saddle and tack for one of the stalls. His gear had been stored in the fourth compartment. He pulled his saddle free, turned it upside down, and threw in his bridle and two sets of reins—one short and one long.

With his bundle tucked under one arm, he closed the door, unhooked the lantern, and followed the hallway into the aisle running between the four blocks of stalls.

Sherna poked her nose above her stall door and whuffled at his approach.

His heart skipped every time his boots clicked against the stone floor as he tiptoed closer. He hung the lantern on the hook fixed to the post next to her stall and held his hand out for her to examine.

She sniffed it and nibbled his fingers.

"There's an apple in my pocket, girl," he whispered as he reached over to unlatch the door. "Stay quiet for me, and you can have it all."

Her nose dug into his side as soon as he stepped into the stall.

He bit his lip to stop a giggle. Her tongue tickled. "All right. All right." He squeezed his hand into his pocket and pulled out a chunk of apple.

She snaffled it from his fingers and crunched it between her molars.

"Now, hold still whilst I get you sad—" His foot caught on something in the straw. He tripped and crashed against the stall wall.

Sherna whinnied.

The snoring stopped.

"Shit!" Jared dropped the saddle to the floor, shoved it against the stall door, and crouched in the corner.

Floorboards creaked overhead.

Sherna shoved his hip, her tongue questing for his pocket.

The trapdoor to the hayloft groaned.

Lantern light reflected off Sherna's slashing tail. Jared leapt to his feet and slid its cover shut.

Sherna pushed at his pocket.

He stumbled and banged his hip on the door.

She whuffled, her hot breath brushing across his neck.

He placed a hand atop her nose, pulled another slice of apple from his pocket, and tossed it to the far end of the stall.

She chased after it whilst he dropped back down into the shadows.

"What's all the racket then?" a man called from above. Boots thudded on the hayloft ladder.

Jared crouched lower and tucked his head under his arms.

"One of you fall over in your sleep?" The man chuckled. His footsteps echoed along the aisle. Stopped. Moved closer. "You's better not be down here playing tricks!" Pale yellow light washed across the stall.

Sherna snuffled, hunting for the apple in the straw.

"Ain't nice, playing tricks on ol' Art." A shadow fell over Sherna's back. A human shadow.

Jared tucked in tighter and bit his lip.

"What you about?"

The light flared. The shadow grew larger.

Jared curled his toes in his boots and tensed his legs, readying himself to run.

Sherna lifted her head to stare at Art, whinnied, and whipped her tail back and forth.

The man sneezed. "Bloody 'orse. Quit wakin' up ol' Art."

The shadow withdrew, and Sherna returned to her rooting. Footsteps clicked along the aisle. The ladder's rungs creaked. The trapdoor thumped closed.

A dozen seconds passed in silence before several loud crunches announced the successful conclusion to Sherna's hunt.

Jared smothered a laugh and remained crouched in the dark until Art's snoring resumed. "That was too close."

Sherna whinnied.

Jared stood and wiped his clammy hands on his damp shirt before opening the shutter on his lantern. More slices of apple kept Sherna occupied whilst he fitted her saddle and bridle. She nibbled at his ear as he attached the reins then surged forward when he opened her stall door. He led her into the aisle, dropped the end of her reins to the floor, and tiptoed to the front doors.

The central bolt shrieked when he pulled it free. The big double-doors rattled in the wind. Art stopped snoring again. Floorboards creaked overhead. Jared clutched the hilt of his knife and backed into the shadows. A volcanic snort punctuated a lull in the storm, and Art's snores returned to their normal rhythm.

Jared blew out his breath and released his knife.

Two more bolts, one at the top and one at the bottom, freed the right-hand door. He pulled it open. A strong gust carried rain and leaves into the stable.

Sherna tossed her head and backed away.

Jared grabbed her reins. Another piece of apple and a firm slap on the rump convinced her to head outside. He led her across the paddock and tied her reins to the fence.

"I'll be as quick as I can. I promise." He patted her nose.

Regal watched the exchange from the other side of the fence and pawed at the dirt. His large bulk dwarfed Sherna's small, compact frame, but she showed no sign of submission. She'd been around him too long to succumb to his bullying.

Jared gave them both one last slice of apple and jogged inside. He closed the main door as quietly as he could, slid the central bolt home, and pressed his head against the wall.

Part one of the plan was complete.

'And that was the easy part.'

Yes.

'Any sensible person would leave now.'

Yes.

'But you're not sensible.'

So it would seem.

Jared pushed away from the wall and padded down the aisle towards the stable's rear door.

Jared stuck close to the high-cut hedgerows as he crept through the formal gardens. The rain and rising wind played havoc with his senses. Branches cracked like thunder overhead. Loose shutters clattered like hoof-beats. Unseen hinges squealed with the ferocity of a dying scream. Even his own footsteps sounded alien in his overworked mind.

His eyes fared no better, his vision limited to a few feet in any direction. With each step, new details emerged from the gloom. Sculpted trees—beautiful when viewed in daylight—appeared twisted and deformed in the murk, lurking like gargoyles poised to pounce. The eyes of bronze statues followed him, silent witnesses to his trespass. Topiary animals lurked in deep shadows; false wolves, bears, and boars stalking him through the night. He paused to orient himself and wipe rainwater from his eyes.

The household wall loomed to one side, the blank, unlit windows like the teeth of a giant's maw, jaws open and ready to bite. Only the hedgerow bordering the formal garden kept it from its prey.

Something skittered across the path at his back. He swallowed a curse and spun. Shadows wove and danced before him like an army of ghosts herding him to his doom. He held his breath until his lungs burned, but nothing else stirred. His breath escaped in a low sigh. He turned to face the hedge.

The maintenance gate had to be close, but it remained invisible in the dark. He dropped into a crouch and edged along the foot of the hedge, leading the way with an outstretched hand. Wet leaves and small twigs brushed against his fingers. Mud squelched beneath his boots. A few steps later, the leaves and twigs vanished.

He stopped and reached into the gap. His hand thudded against a plank of splintered, weather-worn wood. He felt along its length, located the ring handle, twisted, and pushed. The small gate creaked open. The prickling sensation he'd experienced outside the stables returned. He peered into the gloom behind him, saw nothing, and squeezed his way through the gap.

Overgrown branches clutched at his clothing. A sharp twig scratched a burning line across his cheek. He hissed through his teeth and pushed harder. The hedge released its grip.

He stumbled forward and knocked his shoulder against the household wall. Behind him, the wind caught the gate. It squealed as it started to close. He lunged, catching it before it crashed into its frame, searched the ground for a fist-sized stone, and used it to prop the gate open.

With his escape route secured, he collapsed against the wall and expelled a shuddering breath. *Almost there.*

He glanced at the shuttered window above then looked to his left. If a guard had been posted to watch the side entrance, he'd decided to spend the night inside.

Still in a crouch, he turned right and scrabbled through the leaf-strewn mud, counting each window as he passed. At the eighth, he stopped, raised a hand to the time-worn shutter above his head, and risked a quiet knock.

'You think she'll hear you above the storm?'

Probably not.
He knocked again anyway. Nothing responded in the room beyond.
'Stop dallying and open the shutter.'
What if it's locked?
'It won't be. She never locks it.'
She will after this.
Rain pounded against his head. Cold wind blasted through his drenched clothes. He didn't move.
'Quit sitting there like a marrow and go in.'
I can't.
He knocked again—harder this time—though it was pointless. Even if Elise did hear his knocking, she'd only blame it on the storm. He hooked his fingers around the edge of the shutter and pulled. It didn't move.
Locked.
'Latched. Jimmy the hook.'
Jared stood, unsheathed his belt knife, and slid its blade between the edge of the shutter and the wall. After several seconds of probing, he snagged the latch with the tip of his knife and knocked it loose. The shutter swung open. He caught it, climbed inside, closed it, and reset the latch without a sound.
"Elise?" His soft whisper drifted through the small room, the cave-like darkness deeper than that of the storm raging outside. He side-stepped to the left, towards the black smudge of her bed. "Elise?" His shin hit the bed frame. He hopped back a step and cursed.
Elise's soft, regular breathing stopped.
Jared froze with his foot in mid-air, one hand pressed to his throbbing leg.
Elise muttered something unintelligible and shifted in her bed.
Her breathing resumed, loud and rasping now he'd tuned in to the sound. He knelt beside the bed and searched along the covers until his fingers brushed the mound of her leg. "Elise!" He gave her shoulder a short, sharp shake.
Her body tensed. She turned in his direction. Air stirred as she drew in a breath.
He clamped his hand over her mouth before she could scream. "Shh. It's me. Jared." He relaxed his grip.
She grabbed his arm and shoved. "Jared—"
He locked his hand in place. "Hush. Please. If I'm found here—"
She bit him. Hard.

He bit into his own lip to silence a yelp. Blood trickled onto his tongue. "Elise!"

She stared at him, the whites of her eyes large and vivid in the dark. Her ragged breath blew hot and moist against his palm. "You're smothering me," she said, her voice muffled.

"Sorry." He relaxed his grip. "Give me five minutes to explain. Please."

She nodded.

He removed his hand and settled back onto his heels.

She pushed herself up and pulled her blankets close to her chest. Her eyes never left him.

He stared at her dark outline, his mind blank, licked his lips, swallowed, and coughed. "I'm sorry about last time. My finishing things the way I did. But I had no choice. Lady Morgain, she…"

Elise reached up to the bedside shelf. Metal squealed, and a thin sliver of light appeared, piercing his eyes. She remained masked by shadow. "You slept with her?"

"Yes."

Elise seemed to shrink before him, her head hunching into her shoulders as she pulled her legs to her chest. "Go on," she whispered.

"She found out about us. About you. And she didn't take it well."

"I can understand that." Elise's words were flat. Empty. Cold.

Jared shivered. He only had one chance at this—

'Yes. And you've made a wondrous mess of it so far. Why don't you try talking in full sentences? It might help.'

He dropped his gaze before Elise read the self-loathing in his eyes, ran his hand through his wet hair, took a breath, and tried again. "I came here to break up with her, but when I arrived at her study, she had me arrested before I could say a word. Then she accused me of spying. Told me that if I didn't confess, she would have you tortured in my place. I had to protect you." He paused and glanced up, but Elise's face remained hidden in shadow. He moistened his lips and continued. "I didn't want to end our relationship, but she forced me to. She told me if I didn't, she'd have you killed."

Elise didn't even twitch.

"I would have explained at the time, but her spymaster was watching us. He had a knife."

"Her spymaster?"

"The gardener. Jed. He was behind you when—"

"Jed? The simpleton? A killer?" Elise leant away from him, giving her head a tiny shake.

"Jed isn't his real name. It's Armon bal-Rafael. He works for Morgain."

"Jared—"

"Please, let me explain."

Elise sighed and shifted on the bed, eliciting a creak that drove through his bones like nails ripping through wood. "I'm listening."

Jared sucked on his lip. How to convince her? There had to be something. "He gave me this." He reached beneath his shirt and pulled out the locket that had started all the trouble. "He stole it from your room to prove my infidelity to Morgain."

Elise reached for the locket, hooked the chain with her pinkie, lifted it up an inch, held it for a second, then let it drop again. "Did you give her one too?"

"No. It's you I love, not her."

The beginning, Jared. Start from the beginning.

"Armon wants me to work for him. I don't know why, and I don't know what he wants me to do. All I know is that he stole the locket to prove he knows about us. He told me that if I don't do *exactly* as he says, he's going to kill you. He's using you to control me, and I don't want that. I don't want you getting killed. I want you to be safe. I want..."

Oh, stop dancing around the issue and tell her!

"I want you to come away with me."

"You want me to *what*?"

"I want you to come away with me. Give me a second chance, and I'll never betray you again. I swear. It'll be you and me, somewhere new, where nobody knows us. I'll give up the courier work, stay with you, buy us a house, or a farm, or a... a windmill if that's what you want. We can get married. Have children. And we'll never hear of Morgain or Armon again."

"And this Armon, if he's as dangerous as you say, he'll simply let us go?"

"Well, no. He'll hunt for us, for a while. We'll have to stay hidden. Go somewhere where he won't look. Where we'll be alone. But it won't be forever. And I'll keep you safe, I swear."

"Then what you're saying," Elise said, the chill returned to her voice, her words vibrating with a force so unlike her normal, soft tones, "is I either stay here and hope you don't do anything to get me killed. Or I go with you and spend the rest of my life running from this Armon and Lady

Morgain as well. And the whole time, I'll be wondering if you're being faithful or not. Wondering, every time you leave the house, if there's someone else. Wondering if every woman I see is lying in your bed. Wondering if there is another house, with another warm bed, and another set of children somewhere else."

Jared gritted his teeth, trapping the arguments which threatened to well out in his throat. She would not be swayed by false reassurance. He waited, heart hammering in his chest like a stranded flounder, not daring to breathe.

"No, Jared. Even if you are telling the truth, it doesn't excuse what you've done."

"I know. I know. But..."

"No!"

"Elise—"

"I am not spending the rest of my life as a fugitive."

"I love you, Elise."

"Love me?" Elise snorted. "If you loved me, you would never have slept with Morgain. If you loved me, you'd have respected me as much as I respected you. Love isn't a word to bandy about when it suits you. Love is something you prove every day through your actions and your fidelity. It is a commitment, a promise to another that—" She broke off with a squeak and drew a ragged breath. "A promise to another that they mean more to you than anyone else in the world. No, Jared. You don't love me. The only person you love is yourself."

She stood, pushed past him, and crossed the room to the dressing table. "And the only thing you love more than yourself is your precious coin."

Her words sliced through his chest, burning and freezing in equal measure. "Th-that's not true."

Stone clinked. Light flared. Jared turned to find Elise illuminated by candlelight, her eyes narrowed, her beautiful face twisted in anger.

'You're handling this really well.'

"Lady Morgain's a powerful woman. A *very* powerful woman. You don't say no to someone like her, especially after, well, after..." He stopped. Tried again. "If I had told her it was finished—"

"If you had told her, she would have stopped paying you."

Jared's breath caught in his throat, his insides knotting like unravelled rope. "Paying me?"

"Don't pretend you don't understand. The whole town's talking about it."

"Talking? Talking about what, exactly?"

"About all the women you've got, up and down the country, who are willing to pay you to spend a night in their bed!"

"No…"

Elise started to pace—to the door, to the dresser, back to the door. She spun and glared at him, though she didn't hold his gaze long. "Nobody pays gold octains to get a message delivered," she whispered.

"Elise, I swear, I have never—would never…" Jared got to his feet and took a hesitant step towards her. If he could just hold her for a moment, break through the icy wall she'd erected between them, remind her of the bond they shared. He reached out a shaking hand. "I'm not a whore."

She batted his hand away. "How many other women have you been sleeping with?"

"Elise—"

"How many?"

Jared flinched. "Since I met you? Just Morgain."

"And before that?"

The pain in her voice sawed at his heart. He staggered back until his legs hit the bedframe and dropped to the bed. "Four or five."

"Four or five?"

"It never meant anything. I knew it, and they knew it. Besides, I stopped the moment I met you—"

"And you expect me to take you at your word after you've been caught having an affair?"

The rain continued to pound the wall. The wind rattled the shutter. Jared stared at the light dancing across his hands.

'Brilliant plan, genius.'

He exhaled through his nostrils, uncurled his fists, and lifted his gaze. The candlelight illuminated Elise's face from below, accentuating the deep bags beneath her eyes, the sagging skin, the fresh wrinkles. "I'm sorry, Elise. So very sorry."

"I don't care."

"You don't mean that." He slid off the bed, onto his knees. "If I had met you first." He shuffled forward. "If I had been stronger." He reached up and took her hands. "Come away with me, Elise. Please. Come away, and I'll prove I love you. I'll prove there's no-one else."

Elise tugged her hands free and shook her head. "It's too late. What we had together is gone. Even if I came, I'd never be able to trust you again. You should leave, before someone finds you."

"But..." This wasn't supposed to happen. He couldn't lose her. Not like this. Not now. "Elise."

"Leave, Jared. Please."

'Yes. Leave. Back out the window. Back into the rain.'

The shutter slammed closed behind him, the crack of the impact like a bolt of lightning flashing down his spine. He looked back at the window, tears beading in his eyes. "I'm sorry."

Elise never heard him.

The wind didn't care.

He stood in front of the window, unmoving, unseeing, as he replayed the conversation over and over, wondering what else he could have done, what else he could have said to convince her to go with him, what other arguments he could have used to change her mind.

Why am I so useless at saying what I mean? Why didn't I act when it would have made a difference? Why did I keep on seeing Morgain?

Why, why, why. What use are whys to anyone? Whys won't fix what's broken. Whys won't change the past.

He sighed and looked to the sky. The rain had eased, and the clouds were breaking apart. The moon had started its decent towards the horizon. *Time to go.*

"I'm sorry, Elise," he whispered.

And then he was running, back through the gardens, past the sculpted trees and stone figures that had seemed so daunting not an hour ago, across the yard outside the courier compound, and into the stables beyond. He paused there to lock the door and listen. The old man's snores still rattled the rafters. Horses whuffled and shifted in their stalls. Nothing had changed. No-one knew he was there.

He let himself out through the side door and hastened along the side of the fence. Regal spotted him and snorted a welcome. Sherna's warm whinny followed close behind. He stopped beside the big, black stallion and clapped his neck.

"Going somewhere?"

Jared jumped and started to turn. An arm wrapped around his shoulder. A sharp blade rested against his throat.

Armon pressed the side of his face against Jared's cheek. "Did you enjoy your little meeting with your scullery maid?"

"How did—?"

"I've been watching you since you rode in. You're lucky I'm the one who spotted you. My men have orders to shoot any intruders on sight."

"*Your* men? You mean the guard? I thought—"

"Well, technically, the household guard report to their commanding officer. But they're also under orders to obey Morgain's special adviser. Namely, me. But no. I meant *my* men. My spies. I'm not titled spy*master* for nothing. Now"—Armon jostled Jared's shoulder—"you still haven't answered my question. Are you going somewhere?"

"North. Just north."

"Then you're willing to let your scullery maid die? Or are you calling my bluff and hoping I lied?"

"What makes you think I care?"

"Interesting." Armon straightened, but the knife stayed at Jared's throat. "Nice horses. Both yours, I presume. It would be a pity if anything happened to them."

Jared sighed. "I'm getting sick of your threats."

"Threats?" Armon laughed. "That wasn't a threat. I'm merely concerned they might hurt themselves running around in the dark. They'd be much better off back in the stables where it's safe, don't you think?"

"You don't care what I think."

"True." Armon changed his grip, stepped back a pace, and grabbed the back of Jared's collar in his free hand. "You take the horse's reins, and I'll take yours. We'll take the big one in first." He gave Jared a shove.

Jared feigned a stumble, twisted, and dove to the side. The knife edge scraped his throat. His collar tightened around his neck, cut off his breath for a moment, then ripped. He dropped into a forward roll before Armon could recover, planted his feet when they hit the mud, caught hold of a fence post, and pulled himself upright.

Regal tossed his head and shied back a step.

Jared rested a calming hand of Regal's rump, grabbed his sword hilt with the other, and pulled the blade free. He spun, putting Regal at his back, and held the sword before him in a defensive stance.

Armon stood several feet away, his knife held slack in his right hand and a wide grin on his face. "I've never seen you with a sword before. You sure you know how to use it?"

Jared answered with an experimental lunge.

Armon batted the longer blade aside, ducked beneath Jared's outstretched arm, and spun. His knife raked across Jared's midriff, its tip slicing cloth. Cold air prickled the skin exposed by the cut. A flick of his wrist reversed his grip, and he slammed the knife hilt into Jared's stomach.

Jared grunted and stumbled backwards.

Armon switched hands, rammed the hilt into Jared's armpit, switched hands again, and brought the pommel down atop his shoulder.

Jared's arm went numb. His sword slipped from his lifeless fingers.

Armon jabbed again. The knife hilt cracked into Jared's jaw.

Jared's teeth clacked together. His vision swam. The sky spun, the stars diving towards the horizon. For a moment, he seemed weightless, and then his head smacked into the ground.

A heavy weight crashed onto his stomach, driving the breath from his lungs. He blinked the world back into focus and stared into Armon's still-grinning face.

Armon placed a hand on Jared's shoulder and used it to push himself upright. "Not bad, for a dandy boy, but not very good either. I'm going to let you up now, and you're going to take the horses back to the stables. I don't want you to run, or fight, or argue. Understood?"

Jared nodded. He still couldn't catch his breath.

27/11/32 KAF

Jared stared at himself in the mirror. A nasty, purple-green bruise adorned his chin, dried mud coated the side of his face and matted his lank, too-long hair, and his stubble had grown too long to be fashionable but remained too short for a beard. Rips and stains covered his tunic. He tugged at a loose flap of cotton and found he no longer cared.

He dropped onto a chair, leant forward, placed his elbows on the dresser, lowered his aching forehead to his hands, and glanced sideways at Armon.

The spymaster sat at the small table, gaze fixed on the window, chair tipped back, and one foot pressed against the table's edge. A coin danced back and forth across the knuckles of his right hand. He looked over at Jared and smiled.

Jared looked away.

They were in the guest room Morgain had set aside for his use, where Armon had confined him the night before. He'd collapsed onto the bed as soon as he'd heard the lock turn, only to lie there, tossing and turning, until Armon's return.

Everything had gone wrong after he'd entered Elise's room. *What was I thinking, waking her like that?* She must have been terrified, opening her eyes to find someone leaning over her in the dark. And then he'd pressed his hand down on her mouth, suffocating her. No wonder she'd refused to leave.

And what happened to my explanation? He'd spent hours working out what to say, planning every word, every gesture, every smile, and every frown. And then he took one look at her and forgot everything.

He stared at himself in the mirror then switched his gaze from his reflection to Armon's. "Have you nothing better to do?"

"At this moment in time?" Armon trapped the coin between his knuckles, tossed it up in the air, and caught it. "No. Not really."

"Then the great spymaster is nothing more than a babysitter for Morgain?"

"I'm not watching you for her, I'm watching you for me. I have work for you, and you are going to do it."

Jared straightened and twisted around to look at Armon directly. The man was grinning again; that same insolent, mocking grin. "What work?"

"Work you're eminently suited to." Armon set the coin dancing.

"Such as?"

The coin fell to the table. Chair legs crashed to the floor. His mocking grin vanished, replaced by a hate-filled, tight-lipped glare. "You can't guess? But you're a hero. You ride alone, carrying vital messages, crossing wild country, risking life and limb to deliver them safely. The thought of bandits and wild animals ripping you to shreds is enough to make most women swoon. Then, when you arrive safely, they sigh and clasp their hands to their bosoms and invite you into their beds."

"You sound jealous."

Armon laughed. "Jealous? Hardly. You and I, we both know the truth."

"Which is?"

"That you're a coward." Armon stood. "That you go cross-country because you know most bandits watch the roads." He took a step forward. "That you have fast horses so you can outrun the boars and wolves." Another step. "That you would rather shoot a man with a crossbow than risk a fair fight." He grabbed the arms of Jared's chair and leant forward until their foreheads touched. "You are a coward, and a dandy, and you disgust me." He pulled back and spat. The gobbet splattered between Jared's feet.

Jared stood, forcing Armon back. He took a pace forward, putting them chest-to-chest, and glared down his nose at the smaller man. "I have never attempted to hide what I am, unlike you. You sneak around in the shadows, lurking in corners and spreading lies. You threaten and bully and cajole so you can pretend to be in control."

Armon rose to his tiptoes. "Men like you are all the same. Too rich to learn to do any real work, but too far down the pecking order to earn real respect. You play at being important, strutting around in your fancy clothes with your fancy women and your fancy looks. And when you get caught doing something wrong? Why, you blame it all on someone else."

Jared's reply was drowned out by a loud pounding on the door.

Armon turned his back, ending their conversation. "Enter!"

A guard stepped into the room and bowed his head. "Lady Morgain wishes to see you. She asks that you escort him"—he nodded in Jared's direction—"to her study first. He is to make himself comfortable whilst he awaits her presence."

Armon glanced back at Jared and grinned. "After you."

❧☙

Jared stared at the chair; at its holey seat and thick, confining straps. "Make yourself comfortable," the guard had said. He'd rather damn his soul to an eternity in the vortex than make himself comfortable on *that*.

He walked past the waiting chair, past Morgain's desk, and flopped down into her seat instead. The desk had been cleared except for a pen and inkstand on one corner, and a pile of blotting paper and a small box of fine sand on the other. He put his feet up on the desk and leant back to wait.

Make yourself comfortable, indeed. The last thing Morgain cared about was his comfort, he was sure.

'I wonder what she plans to do with you now.'

I'd rather not think about it.

'Perhaps she'll get out those nails and make you sit on them. All those little spikes digging into your skin, covering your legs in tiny little holes.'

Jared lowered his feet and squirmed. He was *not* going to think about it.

'They'll push in a sliver, forced through your flesh by your own weight. Hundreds of tiny rivulets of blood, running down your legs, dripping onto the floor. Drip. Drip. Drip.'

Jared shot to his feet. "Enough!"

The study door opened, and a guard stuck his head through the gap. "Problem?"

"No. Everything's fine. Thank you." Jared sat.

The door closed.

He frowned down at his shaking hands.

'Maybe she'll cut you again. Give you a matching scar on your other arm.'

He traced the length of his half-healed cut with a finger. The skin looked like it had knitted enough for the stitches to come out, but putting them in had been hard enough.

'Yes. Let's leave the thread in to rot and get infected. Good plan.'

He'd do it now. Get it over with.

'Using what, genius? Armon took your knife.'

He opened the top drawer. It was split into three compartments. The largest held a stack of pristine, plain paper, whilst the smaller ones held two candles, a seal, and a bottle of red ink. He slid the drawer closed and tried the larger one, only to find it locked.

'I wonder what she's hiding in there.'

"Doesn't matter," he whispered. "I don't know how to pick the lock."

'Probably a list of everything she plans to do to you. Starting with those sharp, nasty, rusty nails.'

Jared stood again. He needed a distraction.

'You could always write a letter.'

A letter? Who would I write a letter to? But he knew, of course. He'd known ever since he'd walked into the study and spotted the pen and ink on the desk.

He sat, wiped a smear of dirt off the desk, and took a sheet of paper from the drawer. The bottle popped when he pulled out the stopper. He set it down, dipped the pen in the ink, and wrote.

"Elise,"

He stared at the paper and frowned. *What to write?* He owed her an apology, at least. Some sort of explanation…

"I am so very sorry. What I did last night was wrong. I had no right to break into your room. It was a foolish and desperate thing to do, and I will never forgive myself for scaring you. But I __am__ desperate. Morgain has stolen my life and intends to make me her plaything. Armon seeks to use me in his games, yet he refuses to tell me what I must do and is forever taunting and insulting me. Ryal"

A drop of ink fell from the pen, interrupting his flow. He pressed the blotting paper against it to dry the stain, lifted the it away, and continued.

"Even Ryal has exiled me, leaving me without a place to call home.

"And yes, you are right, it is my own fault for being such a stupid, arrogant fool. I should have given you my fidelity and my time, but I gave you none of the former and very little of the latter. I am amazed, now that I think on it, that you waited for me at all. I will never forgive myself for what I have done to you, and I have no right to ask you to do the same. I can only apologise profusely from the bottom of my heart and pray that one day you will stop hating me."

He stopped and reread his words. They sounded pathetic, even to him.

"Morgain is a very jealous woman, Elise. If you stay, she will target you. Go north, to Ryal, and show him this letter. I am sure he will be able to find you work. I know it will not be easy for you to live in such a remote village, away from all your friends, but at least you will be safe there. Please, Elise, get away from her.

"My love, always,

"Jared"

Jared set the pen aside and sprinkled sand over the paper. He had no way to get the letter to her, and he doubted she would read it if he did, but at least he had tried. He pressed a sheet of blotting paper against the letter to dry the last of the ink, folded it in half, and half again, and slipped it into the inside pocket of his shirt.

'That wasn't very good.'

You write it then.

'I did. I am you and you are me. I can't help it if we're going crazy.'

I'm not going crazy.

'Then stop talking to yourself, fool.'

Jared sighed. He was tired and hungry. He hadn't eaten anything since the evening before—

'Ask the guards for something. I'm sure they'll be happy to play servant for you.'

—and had only managed a couple of hours of sleep.

'Sleep then. Morgain's bed is very soft, and she told you to make yourself comfortable.'

Finally, something they could agree on. Jared smiled.

Thunder shattered the black silence. Jared snapped his eyes open and leapt upright. He scrambled away from the noise, caught his feet in the tangle of sheets, fell off the bed, and landed on the floor in an undignified heap.

His breaths came in big, loud gulps, his veins throbbing in his temples and sweat dripping down his face.

What?

He had been sleeping, oblivious, and then… then there was noise, and panic, and falling.

He untangled his legs from the sheets, searched for the source of the bang, and discovered Morgain watching him from the doorway.

She stepped into the room. "No-one gave you permission to come in here."

True, but... "No-one said I couldn't either."

"You seem to be growing a backbone. I'll have to do something about it."

Jared pushed to his feet, straightened, and met her hard gaze. "And if I like my new backbone?"

Morgain's lips twisted up in a sneer. "I will have the guards break it for you."

"Ah."

Morgain reached the bed, and her face darkened. She brushed a chunk of dried mud off the mattress. "At least you took your boots off first." She picked them up and threw them at him, one at a time.

He managed to catch the first but had to duck the second. When he straightened, he found Morgain staring at him, her eyes promising death. He blinked and looked away.

"Armon tells me you were sneaking around the grounds last night." She flipped open the catch on her clothes chest and lifted the lid. "Says you visited a certain young woman's room."

"I needed to talk to her." He rose on his tiptoes to peer into the chest.

She side-stepped to block his view. "You were told to stay away from her."

"I just—"

"You were told that if I *ever* caught you with another woman again, I would cut out your eye."

Jared's stomach roiled. He retrieved his second boot and edged towards the study door.

"Unfortunately, Armon still needs you, so the cutting will have to wait." She reached into the chest and pulled out a cloth-wrapped bundle. "This will have to do instead." She tossed the bundle at him.

He hopped back, dropped his boots, and caught it. Its weight stung his palms.

Morgain stepped between him and the study door. "Open it."

Jared gnawed a sliver of dry skin off his bottom lip. He pulled back the first flap of cloth with shaking fingers and uncovered the ends of a belt. Only this belt was made of metal sheathed in leather. One of its ends had a row of rectangular slots instead of holes. The other sported a metal loop and a padlock in place of a buckle. He risked a glance at Morgain and swallowed. She watched him with eager eyes, beads of moisture dotting her lips.

He pulled his gaze away and gave the ends of the belt a shake. The cloth wrapping fell free. He stared at the thing in his hands, his mouth working in silent denial.

A triangular, metal plate, slightly curved, hung from the middle of the belt, attached with some sort of hinge. A roll of leather lined its edges and its rounded tip. Two sturdy chains, also padded with leather, dangled from the foreshortened point. But it was the two protrusions which triggered a churning in his gut. The bottom one looked like a miniature colander; spherical, with a sprinkling of holes. The upper one was tubular, with a downward droop. More holes pierced its rounded end.

Acid burnt the back of Jared's throat.

"Put it on," Morgain said.

"No." He held his body rigid, locking his tremors deep inside, and forced himself to return Morgain's stare.

She took a step towards him. "Pardon?"

He squared his shoulders and curled his hands into fists. "I said no."

Morgain's eyes widened for a moment, then her brow furrowed. "Would you prefer I called the guards? I'm sure they would have fun dressing you."

"If you must."

She spun on her heels and headed for the study door.

Jared backed up until he bumped into the wall next to the window. He looked down at the formal gardens twenty feet below, then over to the guard stationed at the side door. If he jumped, the tall hedges might break his fall, but he would be lucky to get more than a dozen feet away before the guard reached him. *Still—*

Morgain opened the door. "Armon!"

Jared glanced at the room's other door. If he could make it over the bed, he might be able to reach it before—

"It's guarded," a new voice observed.

Jared snapped his head around and glared.

Armon grinned at him and banged the study door.

"Boys, boys, no need to be hostile." Morgain took a seat on her clothes chest. "The two of you have a lot more in common than either of you realise."

"I doubt that," Armon said, his voice hard and bitter.

Morgain dismissed his protest with a wave of her hand. "Armon knows his place in my world. He's known it for a long time now. But you." She turned to face Jared. "You have a lot to learn. Let's start with a story about obedience, a skill you clearly lack." She nestled her hands in her lap, straightened her shoulders, and flicked her hair back. "When I was six years old, my parents gave me a present. His name was Armon."

Armon jerked his head around and took a half-step forward. "Morgain—"

Morgain whirled on him. "*Don't* interrupt me!"

He flinched as though he'd been lashed but nodded and backed away.

Morgain stared at him for several seconds then resumed her teacherly pose. "As I was saying, they gave me a gift. Armon, the illegitimate get of my grandsire, fathered on a serving wench after my grandmother's death." She shifted her attention to Armon. "It's a pity nobody thought to put a chastity belt on the old lech. It would have saved us all a lot of trouble."

Armon didn't even blink.

Morgain turned back to Jared. "We couldn't have a bastard Rafael running around like a commoner, of course, so my parents saw to it that his mother went away before her pregnancy became common knowledge. Once Armon was old enough to survive without her, they brought him to me. He was my playmate and my whipping boy. When I misbehaved, he took my punishment in my place. My parents meant for it to teach me compassion and responsibility, but instead I discovered I enjoyed the pain and fear in his screams every time they pulled down his trousers and spanked him."

Jared's muscles trembled. He thumped down on the windowsill before he collapsed. Across the room from him, Armon could have been listening to the latest report on the movement of sewer rats.

"When I realised how much Armon feared being punished," Morgain said, continuing as though she'd never been interrupted, "it made it easy to control him. He resisted at first, just like you, but I taught him better. If he was caught stealing, they slapped his hand and sent him to bed without his supper. If *I* was caught stealing, they spanked him so hard he couldn't sit down for a week. Whenever he refused to obey me, I made sure I was caught. He soon learnt his place. Didn't you, Armon?"

"Yes, Mistress."

Morgain kept her eyes fixed on Jared until he dropped his gaze, then she turned to Armon. "Bark for the cheating fool, Armon."

Armon looked at her, lips twisted, eyes pleading. A heavy silence filled the room. He took a deep breath. And barked.

Morgain smiled. "You see? Armon is a good dog. Now." She stood and stepped around the bed. "Are you going to put your belt on, or will I have to get Armon to do it for you?"

Jared looked over her shoulder at Armon.

Armon stared back at him, the fingers of one hand tapping his sword hilt.

Jared looked away. Why had Morgain shared their story with him now? Did she think it would scare him—?

'If she did, she was right'

—or did she intend to rein in Armon?

'And why would she do that when you're *the one she's trying to discipline?'*

Jared flipped the belt over and traced the edges of a rectangular hole with his thumb. *Armon would have no qualms in doing as she ordered, ripping off my clothes, forcing the belt into place, and pulling it tight.* He shuddered and looked up.

Armon's lips curved into a mocking grin.

Jared switched his gaze to Morgain. "I'll put it on."

She smiled. "I thought you would."

Jared stood, placed the belt on the windowsill, and took hold of his waistband. *I can't believe I'm doing this.*

'You could still say no.'

And let another man dress me? I don't think so.

He lowered his breeches and drawers, stepped clear, and retrieved the belt.

Morgain looked him up and down, assessing him like a slab of meat. "You'll need to be measured for a permanent belt, but that one should be fine for a day or two."

Jared's bowels cramped. His hands trembled as he set the belt around his waist and tucked his genitals into the cages. He winced at the touch of cold metal on his skin and pressed the thin end of the triangle between his legs.

Morgain stepped behind him and caught hold of the dangling chains. They rubbed against the insides of his legs and the backs of his buttocks when she pulled them tight. "Everything tucked up nice and secure?"

Jared forced himself to check, despite Armon's unsettling stare. "Yes."

The belt tightened around his waist, and the padlock clicked as Morgain locked everything in place. "Come back here tomorrow evening and I might let you take it off. *If* you behave." She spun him around to face her and gave the front plate a tug. It didn't budge. "Take the rest of the day off to consider your behaviour. Go into town if you wish. But don't do anything stupid. I'll know if you stray. Won't I, dog?"

"Yes, Mistress," Armon answered, his voice tight.

"Get him out of here."

Jared barely had time to collect his breeches and boots before Armon took hold of his arm and dragged him from the room.

The instant they were alone, Armon grabbed Jared by the shoulders and slammed him against the nearest wall. He wrapped a hand around his throat and squeezed. The tip of his blade pressed into Jared's chest. "If you breathe one word of what happened in there to anyone, I will kill you. Slowly and painfully." His words came out in ragged gasps, and his whole body shook. "I will start by cutting out your tongue. And then I might remove your toes, or your fingers, or maybe both. After that, I might just bite off your balls." He tightened his grip.

Jared fought for breath, his nostrils flaring. Spots danced in front of his eyes, exploding like sap trapped in a burning log. He clawed at Armon's hand. Pushed at his arm.

The blade dug deeper.

Hot blood seeped down his chest.

Armon pulled him forward. Slammed him back again. "I am no-one's fucking dog!" He withdrew his blade and loosened his hold.

Jared sucked in deep gulps of air, his throat burning. "Why don't... you just... kill her?"

Armon cocked his head. "And then what? I'm a bastard, in case you'd forgotten."

"You're still a Rafael. She has no heirs. Nobody knows your origins. You could claim to be a distant relation. Rule in her place."

"And why would I want to do that?"

'Because it's better than barking like a dog?'

"Why wouldn't you?"

Armon sneered and tossed Jared aside. "Enjoy your day of freedom, dandy boy. It's the last one you'll be having for a long time." He kicked the door open and stormed out.

Jared stood in the middle of Morgain's study, half naked, with blood leaking from the hole in his chest and his lungs straining with every breath.

This is a nightmare.

'Wake up then. Get out.'

How? You think I can pinch myself and, poof, it's all over?

'Why not? It's got as much chance of working as anything else you've tried.'

⁂

Armon shoved a pair of guards from his path and stalked down the corridor towards a servant carrying a tray, his eyes locked onto hers, daring her to block his path. She side-stepped too late, her shoulder clipping his arm, and bounced off him into the wall. The empty tray clattered to the ground at her feet. He glared at her, sending her scurrying in the opposite direction, and cursed. The corridor ended at a T-junction. He turned left and knocked on the door.

"Enter!"

He pushed the door open, stepped into Morgain's bedchamber, and slammed the door. A tea set sat on a dresser. He grabbed one of the cups and threw it against the wall.

Morgain looked from Armon to the broken cup and back. "Feel better?"

"A little."

"Good. Do you think it worked?"

He dropped onto the chair across from her and drummed his fingers on its arm. "He's terrified."

"Will he do what we need?"

Armon shrugged. "For now. I suspect he'll still need a reminder or two." He paused his drumming long enough to pluck a teacup chip off his trouser leg and flick it to the floor. "Bark for the cheating fool, Armon? Where did that come from?"

"It seemed appropriate, somehow."

He stilled his hand and smoothed the chair-arm. "If I'd realised what you were planning when you asked me to play along, I might have refused."

"Oh, I doubt it. Not everything I told him was a lie, after all."

Armon dismissed her words with a wave of his hand. "Have I ever told you how beautiful you are?"

"At least twice today."

"Well, it's true."

She rewarded him with a broad smile that brought a glow to her cheeks. "You're incorrigible."

"And you're a tease."

She scowled, but a twitch of her lips spoilt her serious expression. "It will never happen, Armon. You're my uncle."

He started to tap his fingers again. "You don't have to keep reminding me."

"Still jealous of Jared?"

He growled. "I can't believe you slept with him."

"And why would I not? He's handsome, athletic, and very energetic."

Armon stood and paced the room. There was an image he didn't need in his head.

Morgain snagged his arm and pulled him to a stop. "When will you leave?"

"In two days."

"Try to bring him back in one piece. I have a lot planned for him. If you're a good dog, I might even let you watch."

"Woof bloody woof."

Morgain laughed.

❧❧

The Red Pony Inn stood in the centre of the trade district, a stone-faced, tile-roofed structure frequented by merchants, travellers, and one ex-private courier. Jared ducked through the doorway into the well-lit interior and stepped to one side to avoid a collision with a couple on their way out. The soft buzz of a dozen conversations filled the room and mingled with the crackle of the fires to create a calm, welcoming atmosphere. Most of the tables were occupied, but one remained empty near the back, under the stairs, affording some privacy. His boots clicked on the polished wood as he wove his way through the throng of patrons, causing several people to turn and watch as he passed. He ignored them, pulled out a chair, and sat with his back to the room, shifting several times before finding a position where the chains on the belt didn't press into his backside.

"What can I get you, sir?" a pleasant, feminine voice asked.

He glanced up at the waitress and flashed her a half-smile. She was a comely woman. Portly, but not off-puttingly so. He might have flirted with her not so long ago. Now Morgain's threats stayed his tongue. He tossed a gold octain onto the table. "Spiced mead. Your strongest. And keep it coming. There's more if that one runs out."

"Anything to eat?"

He started to shake his head, but the smell of cooking meat wafting from the kitchen made his stomach growl. "What's available?"

"Vegetable broth, rabbit stew, or roast chicken with vegetables."

"I'll have the chicken. Please."

"An excellent choice. I'll be back with it soon." The waitress smiled and left.

Jared traced the grain of the oak table with his finger. Decades of stains marred the polished surface. He dug his nail into a thin crack and picked at a splinter whilst he waited for his meal.

"That's him," a man said, his whispered words carrying over the general buzz.

"Who?" a second man asked.

"You know. What's-his-name. Gerald, or Jarret, or something. Morgain's pet whore."

Jared dug his nail in deeper, twisted his thumb, and gouged out a small lump of wood.

"You sure?"

Chair legs scraped on the floor, and an unsettling prickling spread across his back.

"Yup."

The chair legs scraped again, and the prickling faded. He shrugged to throw off a lingering tingle and pushed the piece of wood back into the hole.

"I heard he fucked some merchant's wife last time he was in the south," the first speaker said. "Got paid ten octains for the privilege. It's why Morgain's got him on a short leash."

Jared's arm trembled. He curled his hand into a fist.

"Hah," a third voice interjected, "I heard he got some poor sot up in al-Ramon pregnant then left her without a penny. She's been forced to beg on the streets to keep the kid fed."

Jared braced his legs and made to stand. Morgain's voice echoed in his head. *I might let you take it off. If you behave.* He hunched his shoulders and punched the underside of the table instead.

"Aye. He's got two in Woodsend as well. Irresponsible fucker."

A plate *thunked* down on the table.

Jared flinched.

The waitress leant in close. "Ignore them, young'un. Men like to gossip is all." The drink thudded down next to the plate and mead slopped over the side of the tankard.

"Thank you." Jared snatched up the tankard, sipped, and winced when the alcohol burnt the back of his throat. He drained its contents and banged it down on the table next to the plate. "More. Please."

"I'll get you a jug."

The men's conversation had moved on to other topics. He tuned out their voices and turned his attention to his meal; chicken covered in pale gravy, roast parsnips, leeks, and turnip. He shoved the leeks to one side, skewered a square of turnip, shoved it in his mouth, and chewed.

"Nobody pays gold octains to get a message delivered."

He stabbed at a chunk of parsnip. It flew off the plate, skittered across the table, and fell to the floor.

Elise was right, it seemed. Everyone was talking about him. And she'd had to listen to the vicious half-truths after he'd split from her and disappeared? He wouldn't blame her if she hated him for the rest of their lives.

The waitress returned with the jug. He refilled his tankard, lifted it, and drank it dry.

Not hard to guess who's behind the rumours either. Armon. Has to be. He's determined to ruin me.

'He's doing an excellent job.'

Why, though?

'Because he hates you. Isn't that reason enough?'

Apparently.

The chicken tasted good. Moist and tender.

Like Elise's lips.

Jared's blood warmed. His penis pressed against the chastity belt. He squirmed, the burn from the belt-chains flaring momentarily before dulling to embers once more, refilled his tankard, and drank.

"What do you think he does that's so special?" the man behind him asked.

"Who?" the second man replied.

"Him. Morgain's whore. He must be damn good, if all them women are willing to pay."

Jared straightened his back and smiled a smile made crooked by numbed lips. Not all the rumours were bad ones, it seemed.

"Maybe he does tricks."

"Huh?

"You know. Tricks. For folks with weird tastes. There's this woman over in Woodsend who'll piss on a man for a quarter octain if he asks."

"Piss on a man?" Jared mouthed.

'Best hope Morgain never hears of it. She might get ideas.'

More mead. Jared stared into the bottom of the empty jug. The edges blurred then snapped into focus. He lifted it above his head and gave it a wave, his arm unsteady.

"Wonder what his trick is then."

"Probably lets them suck his dick."

Jared stood, only his feet weren't listening. They tangled themselves together, tripping him.

The waitress grabbed him by the shoulder and shoved him back in the chair. "Your mead."

Mead. Good. He tried to pour some, but the tankard refused to sit still. He bit his lip, took a tight grip on the tankard, and carefully lined it up with the lip of the jug.

"Hey, handsome. How much for a quickie out the back?"

Jared blinked. A strange woman perched on the edge of his table, staring at him with big, hungry eyes. She had a mole on the side of her face. A big, black, hairy mole.

Where did she come from?

He shrugged.

"You don't know?" The woman leant forward, exposing the tops of her huge breasts. "Come now, don't be shy." She ran her fingers along his thigh in playful little steps.

"I," he said, enunciating each word to ensure she would understand, "am not. A who—"

Her fingers reached his groin and probed at the metal plate. Her eyebrows lifted. "Well now."

"Get your hands off my wife!" Hands grabbed his shoulders, pulled him off the chair, and flung him backwards.

He kicked, scrambled to catch his balance, and landed on his back in the middle of the floor. The ceiling spun in a sickening swirl of colour, only stopping when a shadow moved forward to take its place. He squinted, and the shadow coalesced into a sharp-edged, scowling face. He blinked to bring its swaying eyes into focus. "Wha—"

The face swooped, and hands knotted in his tunic. A yank launched his body upward but left his stomach on the floor.

He stared down at his feet, dangling a whisker above the floorboards, then up at the massive brute whose fists had snared his tunic. "Who?"

The brute arched his back, recoiled his head, and snapped it forward with the speed of a striking adder. Their foreheads collided with a chilling crack.

Jared spun and tumbled, crashed into a table, tripped over a chair leg, and dropped back to the floor. He teetered on his hands and knees for a moment, then lifted a shaking hand to his forehead. It came back bloody.

The inn door opened, admitting a blast of frozen air. He looked up, and his hand fell, limp, to his side.

"Jared?"

"S-sire."

Ryal covered the gap between them in three quick strides, hooked his hands under Jared's arms, and pulled him upright. "What's going on?"

"I... he..." Jared turned to look for the giant and teetered sideways. His stomach cramped in protest, and he lurched forward, blasting Ryal with a rush of breath.

Ryal wrinkled his nose and stepped back. "You're drunk."

Drunk? Me? The skin across his brow stretched, pulling at his latest cut, as he struggled to focus on the buttons of Ryal's coat. "Um. Nope."

Ryal scowled and shoved him towards the bar.

He stumbled, grabbed the edge of the counter, and fixed the floor with an accusatory stare. *When had it gotten all the way down there?*

"Two rooms, please," Ryal said.

Jared looked up, glanced at the innkeeper, then twisted to peer over his shoulder.

The angry brute scowled at him, wrapped a possessive arm around his wife's shoulders, and marched her out the inn.

"Good ridinse."

Ryal slapped the back of Jared's head. "Behave!"

"Room's four and five are free," the innkeeper said. "Up the stairs, end of the corridor, on your right."

Ryal thanked the innkeeper, pulled Jared away from the bar, and dragged him up the stairs.

They entered a generously sized room, with a table large enough for dining, a double bed, dressing table, and a set of drawers. Ryal deposited

Jared in one of the chairs and paced around the table. "What are you doing here?"

"Having a meal and a drink. Trying to think." Jared put his head in his hands. Ryal's pacing made the room lurch and jolt like an out of control spinning top.

Ryal sighed. "That's not what I meant. What are you doing *here,* in al-Rafael territory? You were supposed to go north. You should be on a ship by now, getting as far from Morgain as you can."

"A ship?" *No. That isn't right. I had to come. To see Elise. Couldn't Ryal see—?*

"And what, by the Gods," Ryal stopped pacing and glared down at Jared, "do you think you are doing getting drunk in public?"

Jared tipped his head back, intending to match Ryal's glare, but a halo of torchlight burned his eyes.

"You are an up-Arran. A man of the Blood. It's high time you started behaving like one."

Jared shot to his feet and gave Ryal a shove, knocking him back to serve as a shield against the stabbing light. "Why do you care?"

"Why do I...?" The question started as a shout and faded to a whisper. "How can you...? You're family. As dear to me as a son."

The floor rocked. Jared thumped onto the chair. "That's not... not what you said when you threatened to cut off my head."

"Vortex take my soul, I never meant..." Ryal pulled out a chair and sat. "Jared. My boy. I did what I did for your own protection. Didn't you find my note?"

"I found it."

"Then what are you doing here? Why—?"

"I came back for Elise," Jared whispered, tearing a fresh hole in his soul. "I wanted her to come with me. I got the horses ready and went to her room, but she... she refused. She said she couldn't trust me anymore. That the rumours... So I left. And then—"

"Then you decided to come here and get drunk?"

"No. Yes. I don't know. I needed some time alone. To think. I—"

"You stink. You know that?"

"I—"

"And when was the last time you changed your clothes? They're filthy."

"Mor—"

"It's high time you grew up, Jared. You're not a little boy anymore. You need to start *thinking*."

Jared slumped against the table. A hard lump filled his throat.

"You can't waltz about here, there, and everywhere, doing what you please, when you please, and expect to keep getting away with it."

His eyes stung. His lungs burned.

"Jared?"

Everything he'd been through in the last two weeks hit him at once. The torture. The abuse. The threats. The loss of his love, his home, his life. The strange voice whispering in his mind. It was too much. It was all too much. He sobbed.

"Hey now, lad. No need for that."

Everyone hated him. Everyone had abandoned him. And now…

'Jared up-Arran. Professional whore.'

Huge sobs wracked his body. He pressed the heels of his hands into his eyes and dug his fingernails into his head.

Ryal patted his arm.

Jared batted him off.

Ryal crouched beside him, wrapped an arm around his shoulders, and squeezed. "Shush, my boy, it's not so bad. We can sort this—"

"She hates me, you know," he managed to gasp between sobs.

"Morgain hates everyone. She—"

Jared pushed Ryal away and swiped at his tears. "Not Morgain. Elise."

"I'm sure, once she's had time—"

"No!" Then, more softly, "no."

"Jared—"

"She believes them. All the rumours and lies. She'd rather believe them than me."

'Jared up-Arran. Professional bloody whore.'

"I wrote her a letter." He pulled the crumpled paper from his pocket, touched one corner to the table, held the other between his thumb and forefinger, and twizzled it. "I wanted to explain." He tossed the letter on the table and leant back. "But if she'd rather listen to them."

'Filthy whore. Dirty cheat.'

"If she'd rather…"

Ryal picked up the letter and slipped it inside his jacket. "I'll make sure she gets it."

"You will?" The pressure on his chest eased a notch. He looked up. "Could you take her home with you? Get her away from Morgain?"

"I can't force her—"

"Try. Please. At least promise me you'll try."

"I'll try."

"Thank you."

Jared turned back to the table. He'd run out of words.

Ryal retrieved his chair and turned it so they faced each other. "You should get out of here as well. I can help—"

Jared shook his head. "Morgain's watching me. Always watching. Her and Armon."

"Who's Armon?"

"Her spymaster. He's an evil bastard."

Ryal's face lost some of its colour. "Tomorrow morning, when the gates are busy, I could—"

"No. She'll know. And then she'll condemn you as a traitor as well." Jared crossed his arms on the table and rested his head on them.

The door hinges creaked a few minutes later. Ryal groaned as he stood. His footsteps crossed the room. Then he spoke, his voice low. "I should never have let this happen."

"Don't be so hard on yourself. He brought it on himself."

Jared frowned. That was James, Ryal's adviser, and a man he considered a friend.

"No," Ryal said. "I brought it on him. Morgain's messenger warned me there'd be consequences when I refused her first proposal. I should have ordered him home."

"You think he'd have listened?"

"You think I'd have given him a choice?"

Silence fell over the room. Laughter drifted up from below. Jared's neck itched. He didn't have the energy to scratch it.

"What are you thinking?" Ryal again.

"That it's not too late."

"Not too late for what?"

"To kill him."

"James!"

"Slit his throat whilst he sleeps. He'll never know what happened."

"No."

"It's the merciful thing to do. You forget, I've seen Morgain do this before. She'll play with him for a few months, get bored, and give him to her torturers."

More silence. A shuffle of feet. Then Ryal's voice, closer now. "I promised his mother I would protect him. I won't break my word by killing him now."

"You were all for beheading him a few days ago."

"I was all for giving the boy a good scare. You were the one arguing in favour of the headsman's axe."

"It would have been the right thing to do. For everyone concerned."

"Enough! I will hear no more of this."

Silence followed Ryal's admonishment. Accompanied by what? A look? A nod? A bow? Jared tried to lift his head to see, but his body failed to respond.

"Good." Ryal, just inches away. "Now help me put him to bed."

Two pairs of hands took hold of his arms. He went limp and let them drag him from the chair. They bundled him onto the mattress like an oversized sausage. Ryal tucked him in.

"Then you're going to leave him to suffer?" James asked. He'd already moved away from the bed.

"There's another option, if he's willing." Ryal stared down at Jared for an age, sighed, and turned away.

28/11/32 KAF

Jared probed his latest wound and cringed. It was a small cut—no more than an inch long—but the bruise surrounding it would rival the one on his chin. He sighed and slouched against the chair back, took another mouthful of water from his mug, and swirled it around his mouth in a feeble attempt to wash the furriness from his tongue. His head throbbed, and every little noise or movement sent a fresh lance of pain from his eyes to the top of his spine.

Cursed hangover. Whose stupid idea was it to get drunk anyway?
'Yours, of course.'
Another bad decision in a string of bad decisions.
'Time for that to stop.'
Yes
'Time to take back some control.'
He nodded and winced.

"Pair up!" a man shouted in the courtyard below the window.

Jared pressed his hands to his ears but failed to shut out the noise. Wood cracked against wood as the guards started on their next drill. He groaned. They'd been at it all morning, shouting and stomping, grunting and groaning. *When are they going to shut up?*
'When are you going to learn not to drink so much?'
He stood and padded over to the window.

The guards worked through their routines with wooden swords and shields, sunlight reflecting off polished breastplates and buckles. He squinted against the glare and pulled the shutters closed, shushing them when their hinges creaked.

It helped—a little. He collapsed onto the bed.

"Don't let her see you're broken, lad," Ryal had said when they'd spoken earlier that morning. *"Don't let her win without a fight."*

Jared had snorted at that, but Ryal had silenced him with a wave.

"Not that sort of fight. You never were suited for brawling." Ryal paused to look Jared over. "Clean yourself up and have a shave."

Jared ran his fingers over his smooth chin. He had scrubbed the sweat and grime away and washed his hair. A bath would have been better, but it was a start.

"Present yourself to her as you would have before any of this happened, with your back straight and your head held high."

"With dignity." Jared checked his clothes for the hundredth time. The collar of his white cotton shirt peeked out from beneath a black, short-sleeved tunic. A dragon, picked out in multi-coloured silk thread, adorned his back, and a matching pair of the mythical beasts flowed up the outside of his breeches.

"Show her you're still strong. That you're still a man."

He picked up a plain gold ring and slipped it onto the middle finger of his right hand, next to the dragon-seal band on his ring finger.

"You cannot fight her with your fists. I think you've already learnt that."

His fingers drifted to the bruise on his chin, proof of the truth of Ryal's words. Armon had disarmed and disabled him with three quick, efficient blows delivered with the hilt of a knife, any one of which would have been fatal if the knife had been reversed.

"You must find other ways to resist her, at least until you can escape."

Jared's lips twitched, lifting into a grin, as he remembered what his cousin had said next.

"Find out what she's planning, find me proof of her treachery, and I'll take it to the King."

Jared had burst out laughing, despite his sore head. *"You want me to spy on Morgain? Give credence to her false accusation?"*

"What have you got to lose?"

"Nothing," he answered, both then and now.

He poked at his hair, pushing a few stray strands back into place. He felt more human now he was clean and properly dressed; more like his old self. And yet that old self, the one who had pampered and preened and chased after pretty women, seemed shallow to him now. Shallow and naïve.

'And you're sooo much wiser now, of course.'

No. I'm not. But at least I'm no longer blind.

The door opened without warning, and Armon stepped inside.

Jared stood and turned to face him. "What now?"

Armon laughed. "What now? Is that really any way to greet me?" He closed the door and strode across the room. When he reached Jared, he circled around him, his gaze roving up and down. "Much better. I was beginning to fear this whole exercise had been a waste of my time."

"Meaning?"

"Meaning I need Jared the dandy, not Jared the sulky little boy."

Jared dug his nails into his palms and bit back a retort. *Dignity, remember?*

"Better again. But you need to practice keeping a straight face. You're going to be hearing a lot of insults over the next few months."

"I heard a lot of insults last night."

Armon grinned. "Your reputation does seem to have been ruined somewhat. And so easily, too. I merely mentioned you might have been paid a coin or two for your time between the sheets. Fast forward a few days, and everyone in town had you down as a prize whore with conquests in every village, city, and town. I particularly like the rumour about the al-Rishad bastard you've sired. Apparently, the great lady's husband is searching for you, determined to wreak his revenge on you for cuckolding him."

"I don't know any al-Rishads."

"I know. It's still a delightful story, though." Armon's grin vanished. He stared at Jared through narrowed eyes. "You don't have any children anywhere, do you?"

"No," Jared growled through gritted teeth.

"I thought not, but I needed to be sure." Armon's grin returned. He leant against the door, arms crossed, and waited.

"Are you going to tell me why you're doing all this?"

Armon inspected a fingernail, picked out a bit of dirt, and flicked it away. "Patience, dandy boy. I'll tell you what you need to know, when you need to know it."

"Then why are you here?"

"I came to escort you to lunch. Morgain is hosting Lord al-Arran and his adviser. She wants you to act as their server—"

"Oh, come on."

Armon dropped a hand to the hilt of his knife.

Jared swallowed the rest of his protest. He didn't need more additions to his collection of bruises. Besides, playing Morgain's invisible servant would put him in the perfect position to overhear her plans. Not that she was likely to mention them in front of Ryal, but it would be a start. He held his arms out, hands open and fingers splayed.

Armon smirked. "After lunch, you'll be meeting with Morgain's tailor. You'll be measured for a new wardrobe, amongst other things." Armon tipped his head towards Jared's groin.

Jared buried his hands in his armpits to keep himself from tugging the chastity belt's chains. "It'll be difficult for him to measure anything as long as I'm locked in this thing."

"That shouldn't be a problem. If you conduct yourself in a suitable manner at lunch, Morgain has agreed to remove the belt." Armon pushed away from the door and opened it. "And don't scowl at me like that. I'm not the one who's been sleeping around."

"But you—"

"I what?"

'He's right about you. You do *have a habit of blaming people for your own faults.'*

Jared shook his head. "Nothing."

"Good. Now, come. It wouldn't be wise to keep Morgain waiting."

Jared dodged the corner of a handcart, hopped to avoid a stagnant puddle, and ducked beneath a low hanging sign. "Where are we going?"

"Patience, dandy boy," Armon said, his reply barely audible above the screech of metal wheels and barking of stray dogs. "I would tell you, but given your proclivity for the luxurious, I doubt you'll have heard of the place. No afternoon tea and brandy, you see."

"No afternoon tea and brandy?" Jared vaulted an open sewer and pressed his sleeve to his nose to block the stomach-churning stench. "You think I'm that demanding?"

"Think it?" Armon paused at a junction. "Hardly. I know it." He chuckled and jogged across the road.

Jared glared at Armon's back. He'd had enough of the unfounded insults. They'd grown more tedious than the threats. He wanted nothing more, in that moment, than to pull Armon back, trip him, and drop him face first in the sewer. A little humility might serve to curb his viperous tongue.

He took a deep breath—*dignity, remember?*—and hurried to catch up. "Would it hurt you to show me some respect?"

"Respect?" Armon stopped. "Respect is a commodity you have to earn." He nodded to a nearby side-street. "Down there."

The street he indicated was clean and uncluttered, though nobody moved along its cobbles, and none of the passing crowd spared it a glance. There were no street signs. No stalls or shop windows. No obvious reason to walk its length. He shivered. "Why—?"

"Really? You think I'd drag you all this way to give you a beating?" Armon snorted and shook his head. "Come on." He cut through a crowd of ragged children to reach the side-street, eliciting a cacophony of protests and curses.

Jared wove around the edge of the group and dived into the street moments before an old, two-wheeled cart blocked the opening. He picked up his pace and re-joined Armon as the spymaster stopped and knocked on an unmarked door.

A flap in the door opened with an angry squeal, and a hooded pair of eyes appeared in the gap. After a quick inspection, the flap banged shut, and the door swung open. "Master Malkem," the eyes' owner—a comely, middle-aged woman—said. "Please, come in."

"Thank you." Armon skipped up the step, wiped his feet on the mat, and entered the dimly lit hallway.

"Your usual room?"

"Please."

The woman acknowledged his request with a nod before motioning for Jared to enter. He had time to note the plain brown carpet, red-and-white flowered wallpaper, and gold-framed mirror before the door closed, cutting off the daylight.

Their host squeezed past them and led the way up a narrow flight of stairs to a small, square landing. She opened the door on their right and stepped to the side. "Will you be eating today?"

"Not me," Armon said. "But he will." He nodded in Jared's direction.

"Will you be taking coffee?"

"Three, please. But not until our final companion arrives."

"Very well. I'll be right back with your food." The woman bobbed a bow and trundled down the stairs.

Armon shrugged off his jacket and entered the room.

Jared followed a step behind. The room was modest—big enough for a rectangular table, four chairs, and a miniature sideboard—with a single window overlooking the street at the building's rear. He closed the door. "Master Malkem?"

"One of my aliases." Armon tossed his jacket over the nearest chair and perched on the windowsill. "One you will soon become very familiar with."

"Another half-answer." Jared pulled out the chair across from the window. "Why am I not surprised?" He lowered himself, keeping his lips compressed to contain a sigh. The chains were gone, the chastity belt removed after lunch as Armon had promised, but the bruises left behind ached under the press of his weight.

A knock shook the door, rattling the catch in its frame. Their host let herself in without waiting for a response, thumped a plate onto the table, slid it across to Jared, and left without a word.

Jared frowned at its contents—slices of cold ham, toasted bread, and something green and mushy that might once have been a vegetable— then fetched himself some cutlery from the sideboard. "Now what?"

"Now it's time for you to learn what it is you're going to do for me." Armon switched position, putting his back to the window. "You can eat whilst we talk."

Jared stabbed a slice of ham and ripped off a mouthful. "Very generous of you."

Armon snorted. "I thought so." He lowered his hand, resting his fingertips on the chair arm. "Tell me what Morgain and her guests discussed during lunch."

Jared stuck a finger in the mush and touched it to the end of his tongue; stringy and bitter. He spread it on the toast anyway. "Why?"

"No questions. Just tell me."

"Well..." Jared placed the knife on his plate. *Where to start? With Ryal entering, wincing when he glanced at me then ignoring my presence? Or with Morgain's casual flick of her wrist, sending me scurrying like a slave to pull out her chair?* He huffed and shook his head. "Ryal thanked Morgain for inviting him to lunch, then she said—"

"Summarise, please. I don't need a word-for-word repeat of the conversation. If I want more details, I'll ask for them."

"Right." Jared ate a mouthful of toast. "Ryal explained how he arrived so quickly—"

"How?"

"He came cross-country." *Damnable man should make up his mind.* "Left the pack horses behind with his retainers." *Tell me what they said. Don't tell me what they said.* "The rain held off for most of the journey, so they were able to make good time." *Why am I even answering?*

'*Because you're a coward, that's why.*'

Armon nodded. "What else?"

"They discussed the proposed tax changes." They hadn't even mentioned him first. Ryal hadn't asked about his presence, and Morgain had seemed content to let his standing at her back like a clipped parrot send her message for her.

"What changes?"

"The king wants to tax tanneries and fisheries—"

"Enough. What else?"

"Morgain asked if there had been any problems with the harvest. Ryal said there hadn't."

"And?"

"And that's all."

"You're sure?"

"Yes."

"No-one mentioned the food?"

"No. Yes. James did say—"

"I know what he said. Why didn't you mention it before?"

"You were listening?"

Armon rolled to his feet and circled the table. He stopped at Jared's back. "Why didn't you mention it?"

"It didn't seem important."

Armon rested his hand on the back of Jared's chair and leant over his shoulder. "*My* job is to decide what is or is not important. *Your* job is to listen and report what you hear." He straightened and stepped back a pace. "You did well. For a first try."

"You want me to spy on Morgain?" *Now that would be ironic.*

Armon chuckled. "Hardly. I can do that myself."

"Then what—?"

Another knock cut across their conversation. Armon pushed off the chair hard enough to drive Jared's stomach against the table, strolled to the door, and cracked it open. "Tessa," he said, his voice unusually light. "Please, come in." He opened the door all the way and stepped back. "Our coffee, too. Thank you."

Their host entered first, carrying three mugs. She glanced at Jared's half-empty plate, smiled at him, and set the mugs on the table. A second woman followed her inside, towering over everyone in the room. She paused at Armon's side, dipping her head to whisper in his ear, side-stepped to allow their host to slip out, and turned to Jared.

Jared stared, his breath trapped in his throat.

She glided across the room to the table, loosened the fingers of her gloves with a series of elegant, measured tugs, and slipped them off. A shrug and a dip of her shoulder dislodged her cloak, dropping it into her waiting hand. And all the time her gaze remained on his, locking it in place with invisible chains.

"I wouldn't look at Tessa like that, dandy boy," Armon said. He took Tessa's cloak, folded it, and hung it over the back of an empty chair. "Not if you value your life."

Jared swallowed a mouthful of saliva and looked away. "I wasn't looking at her like anything." *Was I?*

'Yes. But what man wouldn't? All those sleek curves and flexible muscles. Can you imagine what she would be like in—?'

"Jared!" Armon dropped into his chair and dragged it forward, causing its legs to screech across the floorboards.

Jared flinched.

Cackling laughter filled his head. *'I do believe Armon is jealous.'*

Jealous? Jared stole a look at Armon.

Armon wore the same disapproving expression he'd sported on the day Morgain and Jared had shared breakfast. He drummed his fingers on the table, the rhythm fast paced and agitated.

Why? I can understand him being protective of Morgain, but—

'Why?' More cackles. *'I would have thought 'why' was obvious.'*

Tessa pulled out the chair diagonally opposite Jared's. Her thick, black hair fell around her shoulders as she slid into the seat. She looked to Armon, her expression unreadable. "Are you going to tell him, or should I?"

"Allow me." Armon reached across the table for one of the mugs. His arm brushed Tessa's fingers, and they exchanged a look that gave Jared chills. Armon pulled the mug close to his chest. "Jared up-Arran, please allow me to introduce you to Tessa. To most, she is known as Lady Zandra, a relatively wealthy merchant who operates out of the al-Rafael trade district. To a few, she is better known as the al-Rafael assassin. Most of those few are dead."

Jared looked at Tessa again. This time, when their eyes met, her emotionless gaze froze his bones.

She touched the tip of her tongue to her lips and smiled.

Jared looked away. "Why are you telling me this?"

"Why?" Armon reclined in his chair, his mocking grin slipping into place. "Because, dear dandy boy, she is the one who is going to kill you if you decide to misbehave."

His tone, and Tessa's accompanying nod, left Jared in no doubt of the certainty of the threat. He reached for a mug and curled his fingers around it, clinging to it as tightly as he now clung to his newfound confidence. "I presume this means you're finally ready to tell me what it is you expect from me?"

"You presume correctly." Armon lifted his mug to his lips and took a sip. "Can you speak Canri?"

"What?"

"Canri. The language of the Canri people."

"I know what Canri is. But why—?"

"Just answer the question."

"No. I can't."

"Then you'll need to learn." Armon drank more coffee. "Lady Morgain recently secured the right to house a delegation in Canri's foreign district. She intends to use it to establish trade and political ties with the Canri people. We need someone on the inside to ascertain how the Canri people react to our proposals and fix any problems that may arise. That someone is you."

"Me?" A burst of uncontrolled, breathy laughter escaped Jared's lips. "But I don't know anything about politics or trade policies."

"Which is exactly why I chose you. I need someone they'll never suspect. When they check your background, they'll discover you're a minor noble fallen on hard times. You've been exiled from your home for reasons unknown, upset a powerful member of the Blood, and become the subject of vicious rumours concerning your private life. Driven by desperation and the hope of regaining the favour of your one-time lover, Lady Morgain, you have agreed to accept a position as a minor member of the ambassadorial party. A position which, under normal circumstances, you would never have considered. Only three of us will know the truth, and Tessa and I will be saying nothing. So unless you do or say something stupid, you will be completely safe."

"But why choose me? There must be plenty of other people—"

"No. You were the most suitable candidate. You have ties to Morgain but are not in her service. You are of the Blood, which makes you important enough to be subject to general gossip, but you are not so important that you would not lower yourself if you needed to. You have a reputation as a man who goes out of his way to impress women. A man who cares more for his luxuries and fine clothing than he does for politics and trade. And you have this way of looking utterly baffled whenever people start discussing matters more complicated than the weather or the latest fashion. Just like you're doing now."

The skin on Jared's forehead tightened, his frown deepening. "You make me sound very... shallow."

Armon's grin widened. "You are very shallow."

"And what will I be doing in Canri, exactly?"

"To start with, you will simply listen. You will work in the reception area of our embassy, serving our guests with food and drink, and seeing to any other needs they may have. You will listen to their private conversations and report what you hear to me or my representative. You will tell me everything, however insignificant it may seem. If they speak to you directly, you will shrug and show them the confused expression you're so good at. They will soon assume you do not understand them and will thus talk freely around you. But you must be careful not to react to anything they say, no matter how derogatory or suspicious it may be. If you so much as frown, you'll give yourself away."

"And if I refuse to help you?"

Armon looked to Tessa. "You will not leave this room alive."

"You wouldn't kill me in public." Jared took a sip of the bitter coffee. "Besides, if I'm dead, you'll have no-one to play spy."

"I have other plans in place. You are far from indispensable. Your assistance will make my life easier, but I can still achieve my goals without you."

"And if I tell the Canri people your plans?"

"We will show them the confession you signed and convince them you're lying to save yourself. They are even less kind to traitors than we are."

"Then it seems I have little choice."

Armon grinned and drummed a slow rhythm on the arm of his chair. "I'm glad you understand."

1/12/32 KAF

Horses snorted and whinnied. Men conversed in loud voices. Others shouted across the crowd. Grass disappeared under thick mud, trampled beneath boot and hoof. Merchants, diplomats, servants, slaves, and patrolmen milled about amongst supply carts, piles of baggage, and horses.

Jared observed the chaotic preparations from the edge of the field, holding his saddlebags in one hand and Sherna's reins in the other. Most of his possessions were somewhere amongst the mess. Servants had come to his room that morning and packed everything he owned, everything that was left of his life, into two small boxes.

They've taken everything.

'Everything but your soul.'

And my horses. Don't forget my horses.

Sherna chose that moment to nudge his arm. He gave her nose an absent pat as he looked towards his other mount. Regal stood on the far side of the field, carrying the leader of the small company of patrolmen on his back. The patrol leader looked resplendent in his immaculate green and yellow uniform, directing those around him with gestures and shouted commands. People jumped to obey without question, civilians and patrolmen alike. Armon played his role well. Jared had to give him credit for that.

Off to the left, another group had gathered. A tall, slender woman, wrapped in a thick, woollen cloak and sheltered by a wide-brimmed hat, stood next to two men; one short and overweight, the other of average height and solid build. The woman looked up, noticed Jared watching, and winked. *Tessa?* He flashed a smile and looked away.

His gaze fell on a pair of patrolmen; a grey-haired veteran and a youth barely old enough to grow a beard. The veteran pressed his mouth to the youth's ear. The youth nodded and raced across the field, his thick hair bouncing in time with his steps. He stopped when he reached another small group. An older man stood at the group's centre, straight-backed and proud. A second man stood next to him, portable writing slope in hand. Four muscle-bound giants surrounded them, hands on sword-hilts and eyes alert. The youth delivered his message and dashed away.

Jared sighed.

Star Bay lay fifty miles to the east, a distance he would normally cover in one or two days. But given the size of the travelling party, the addition of laden carts, inexperienced riders, and poor weather, they would be lucky to make it in less than a week. Three weeks aboard ship would see them reach Canri, and after that...

After that, I become a spy.

PART TWO

1/12/32 KAF

Armon sat atop Regal and watched the eight patrolmen ride away from him. They kept their mounts in a staggered *W* formation, giving themselves room to manoeuvre whilst still blocking the full width of the road. Anyone travelling in the opposite direction would be forced to stop and yield to the men's questioning.

So far, the precaution had proved unnecessary. Nothing moved on the east-west road. If everything went as anticipated, nothing would. With the full moon due, the road should be as void of life as a chicken-coop raided by a fox. Only the insane and desperate would risk being caught outdoors when Mortis Damis's unblinking eye filled the night sky.

Even so, he had set his patrol out following standard protocol. Eight men rode ahead of the main party to clear the road and watch for ambushers. Eight more followed behind to foil any attack from the rear. The remaining patrolmen rode alongside the caravan to provide protection and a sense of security for the merchants and ambassadors they escorted.

Patrol Leader Malkem was very good at following protocol. He was renowned for it, in fact. Since joining the al-Rafael army at fourteen, he'd worked to establish himself as a competent, though not outstanding, patrolman. His ability to follow orders, memorise protocol, and lead small groups of men earned him promotion by nineteen. His lack of imagination and his tactical ineptitude ensured he would never rise further within the ranks. When the patrol leader became inconvenient, it was easy enough to acquire falsified orders, ride out one gate alone, change out of his uniform, and ride in through another as someone else.

He flexed his fingers, stretching his new gloves. They fit as snuggly as Malkem's persona; a persona he'd worn so often it sometimes felt more real than his own.

Regal snorted and sidestepped.

Armon patted the stallion's neck and turned his attention to the west, where the lead riders of the main caravan were coming into view. He folded his hands atop the pommel, adopted Malkem's upright, rigid posture, and waited.

Ambassador Salem rode at the head of the party, as menacing and alert as an alpha wolf leading its pack. Few lines marred his face, but years spent indoors had robbed his skin of its lustre, turning it a dull, leathery brown.

For over a quarter-of-a-century, he'd led negotiations on behalf of the al-Rafael family, earning himself a formidable reputation in the process. He was known for his ruthlessness around the negotiating table and his ability to ferret out his rivals' secrets to gain leverage over them. He knew how to get under people's skins; to find their weaknesses and exploit them.

Or so people claimed.

Armon had never worked with the ageing ambassador. He intended to use the visit to Canri to discover if Salem's methods justified his status. If he proved even half as astute as his success suggested, it would provide a fun distraction during the endless days of waiting that lay ahead.

And if he doesn't, I'll get the pleasure of plucking one more parasitic weed from Morgain's garden.

Salem's head scribe, Stanin, flanked him on the left, with one of his hulking bodyguards on his other side. His remaining bodyguards rode into view, the rest of his assistants and scribes following in line.

A short gap separated the ambassadorial party from their mercantile counterparts. Alsam Azier, one of the richest—and fattest—merchants in the region, rode at their head. He seemed determined to bore his two riding companions to death. His mouth hadn't stopped working since they'd left the al-Rafael Household, and his free hand wove tirelessly, stabbing and waving in accompaniment to his words, his finger wielded as efficiently as a master swordsman's blade. His barrel-bodied mount staggered with every step, swaying like a rope-bridge in a gale as it struggled to carry his excessive weight.

Behind them—

Armon tightened his grip on the pommel, and his leather gloves creaked.

Behind them, Tessa rode her piebald mare alongside Morgain's latest pet, with her knee so close to his it almost touched. Whatever Jared said as they came into view made her laugh. Some wild tale about the non-existent dangers he'd faced on the road, no doubt. Tessa leant towards him, a smile on her lips.

A smile? For the dandy boy?

Armon supressed a growl, grabbed Regal's reins, yanked them to the right, and gave the stallion a kick in the flanks.

"Is everything well, Patrol Leader?" Salem asked as Armon approached.

Armon dipped his head. "All is well, Ambassador." He turned Regal about and fell in beside the ambassador's bodyguard. When the ambassador said nothing else, he slowed Regal's pace and dropped back until he drew alongside Tessa. "You two seem rather... cosy."

"Just admiring the, uh, view, Patrol Leader," Tessa answered with a nod at Alsam Azier's back.

Armon bit back a laugh. "It is rather remarkable." He let his mocking grin break through Malkem's serious façade for a moment. "But, uh, more dangerous than it looks."

"Isn't everything?" Tessa whispered.

Armon coughed and looked away. "Yes. Well. Uh." He hadn't missed the twinkle in her eye or the suggestive wink that followed.

"You'd best keep moving." Tessa looked into his eyes for a moment then let her gaze slip past him to the surrounding countryside. "We're supposed to be strangers. Remember?"

Armon inclined his head. "We'll talk later." He flashed Jared a warning glare then guided Regal to the side of the road, where he held the stallion steady as the rest of the caravan trundled past.

The delegation arrived at Crossroads Lodge just as the sun touched the horizon, the inviting orange glow in the three-story lodge's windows a welcome sight after a full day on the road. Armon slid down from Regal's saddle and handed the reins to a waiting stablehand. A glance at his sub-patrol leader confirmed the lead patrol had encountered no problems. He rose to his tiptoes to peer over the growing crowd, located the lodge's owner near the front entrance, breathed in, and squeezed his way across the courtyard through the mass of horses and people. He returned the lodge owner's nod of greeting with one of his own. "Is everything set out as we arranged?"

"It is," the man said. "All of the rooms are prepared, and meals will be served within the hour. The rear courtyard has been cleared for your wagons and a temporary pen set up for your slaves. If you have any problems—"

"I will call you." Armon snatched the room keys from the man's extended hand and turned away. Malkem had no time for civilians. "Ambassador Salem! Merchant Azier!"

The two men broke off their quiet conversation and turned unwelcoming glares in his direction.

Like a magpie and a peacock. One elegant and understated, with a covetous eye. The other flamboyant, strutting, and determined to drown out everyone around him.

Armon tapped his fingers against his thigh and smiled at each man in turn. "Your keys, gentlemen. You each have a suite on the second floor." He crossed the small gap between them and held up the keys. "If you require any of your luggage brought to your rooms, please let me know. My men will be happy to carry it up for you."

Azier grabbed his key. "I have my own servants, thank you, Patrol Leader."

Armon dipped his head. "My apologies, sir. I didn't mean to imply—"

"Then don't." Azier tipped his head back to stare down his nose at Armon, snorted, and shuffled away.

Armon turned his attention to the ambassador. "My men will be guarding the front and rear entrances. If your guards would—"

"Do not presume to command my bodyguards, Patrol Leader. Do so again, and I will see you stripped of your rank and cleaning out privies for the rest of your very short career."

Armon bowed his head and squeezed the remaining keys in his fist, the hard metal serving as a poor substitute for Salem's neck. "Of course, Ambassador. It was not my intention—"

"Do you have anything else to tell me, or do you intend to waste my time with your babbling?"

Armon gulped an exaggerated swallow and lifted his head, not quite meeting Salem's eyes. "Uh, yes, Ambassador. I mean, I'm sorry, Ambassador. I..." He paused, as though taking time to clear his head, and added, "Food will be served within the hour. You may eat in the common room or in your suite. I am requesting everyone be in their room by ten. We rise at dawn and depart an hour after."

"Thank you." Salem plucked the key from Armon's fingers and dismissed him with a wave.

Armon turned his back, allowed himself a small smirk, and searched the crowded courtyard for his next target. He found her near the stables, engaged in conversation with one of the lodge's servants, coughed to get her attention, and bowed when she turned. "Your key, my lady."

"Thank you, Patrol Leader." Tessa took a moment to dismiss the servant then reached for the key.

He pulled it out of her reach. "Your room's on the third floor. End of the hallway. Overlooking the stables."

"What time?"

"Midnight." He placed the key in her outstretched palm.

She nodded, picked up her saddlebags, and headed for the lodge. Armon permitted himself a moment to admire her swaying backside, tucking the memory of it away with all the others, using it to fill the hollow in his heart.

He scanned the faces of the remaining merchants and ambassadorial staff. Most of them would be sleeping two or three to a room. Tessa, as the only senior female, would have hers to herself—a situation that suited them both.

He headed for the stable next. The thin windows along its long walls let in little of the failing sunlight, and only a couple of the overhead lanterns had been lit to compensate. It took him several seconds to pick out Jared in the shadows halfway along the aisle, giving Sherna a brush down. He sauntered up to the former courier, sidestepping once to avoid a stable boy. "Predictable as ever, I see."

Jared stopped his brushing and rested his arms on Sherna's back. His lips curled up in what might have been an attempt at a friendly smile. "I wanted to settle Sherna myself. She's growing restless. She needs a proper run, not this constant plodding."

"Of course." Armon managed not to laugh at the obvious ploy. "And when I let you take her for a canter, you'll disappear over the horizon, never to be seen again."

"And leave Regal behind? I'd—"

"—give up a chance at freedom for the sake of a horse?" Armon's cheek muscle twitched. "I don't think so."

"Then send one of your men with me. He can—"

"No." Armon's cheek twitched again, but he felt no amusement this time. "If you're that worried about your cursed horse, ask one of the stable boys to take her out. Otherwise, she stays here."

Jared sighed but said nothing more.

Armon handed him one of the keys. "Third floor. Second door on the right. You're sharing with a man called Stanin. Be polite. He's Salem's head scribe."

"Arm—"

Armon covered Jared's mouth with his hand, shushing him. "It's Malkem. Patrol leader Malkem. Don't forget again." He lowered his hand. "Be in your room by ten. I'll be checking on everyone."

Jared looked towards the stable doors and stared with glazed eyes for a handful of seconds before turning back. He juggled the key in his hand, then slipped it into his breeches pocket. "I'll be there."

Armon nodded. "Good choice."

Jared pulled off his socks, tucked them into his boots, folded his breeches up to his knees, and stepped into the river. The shock of the icy water sent a shiver through his body. He kept walking, wading into the middle of the Gormglais, not stopping until the water reached the tops of his calves. Then he turned to look upstream, tracing the path of the river to the north.

The Gormglais began its journey somewhere in the Monadh Geal as a modest brook trickling through the rocky heights. As it flowed south, it merged with other streams and rivers, growing wider and faster until it became a gushing torrent pounding its way through the Am Monadh Liath. Over the centuries, it had carved a path through the harsh landscape, eroding its rocky banks and carrying the stone south. When it reached the softer grasslands, it grew wide and shallow, the flow of water slowing until it lost the power to carry its load.

At this point, where the Gormglais passed through the Bogha-froise valley, the chips of rock, smoothed into pebbles by the constant motion of the water, fell to the riverbed to form a natural ford.

Jared stood in the centre of the ford, the waters of the Gormglais washing around him like drifts of silk as they flowed south to the sea. He'd always wanted to see the spot where the Gormglais originated. He'd planned to take Elise with him but never found the courage to ask her to come. And now?

Now it was too late.

He took a deep breath, willing himself to relax, and lifted his head, seeking to catch a glimpse of the hills and mountains to the north. A mass of broken black clouds obscured the view, blocking out everything except the grass, the river, and a few dark smears on the horizon. One of those smears was the edge of the Darkwood Forest, the source of the timbers used in the Crossroad Lodge's construction. The other, smaller, smears were farm buildings, tiny blots on an otherwise undisturbed landscape.

Standing there, with nothing but the wind in his face and the gurgling of the river for company, he felt whole. It was for moments like these that he had become a courier; moments when he could simply stand and admire the beauty of the world. Seeing nature's strength—scenery that had taken hundreds, if not thousands, of years to form—put everything into perspective.

Armon had stolen his life, destroyed his reputation, and denied him his freedom. But Armon was only human. With time and patience, he would wear him down. He would probe and prod, just as the river wore at the rock, until he discovered Armon's weaknesses. Then he would exploit them, turn them to his advantage, and use them to escape.

'Poke, prod, exploit, and escape? All that in five days?' A snort sounded in Jared's head.

Jared sighed and returned to the lodge as the first raindrops fell.

His inner calm shattered when he entered, destroyed by a wave of heat and noise. The tables, normally set in small groups, had been arranged to form two longer tables running almost the full length of the common room. Ambassador Salem sat at the head of one, quietly observing its other occupants, whilst Alsam Azier sat at the head of the other, gesturing wildly as he relayed yet another tale of his amazing adventures from his youth. Tessa sat about halfway down the merchant's table, nodding and smiling at Azier as she sipped her soup.

Jared considered taking his place at the ambassadorial table—one seat remained empty at its foot, next to one of Salem's servants—but the thought of exchanging pleasantries with a group of people who'd spent an entire day staring down at him drove him away. He sought out one of the lodge's waiters and requested his meal—pea soup followed by fish and root vegetables—be brought up to his room. Salem's gaze bore into him the entire time, tracking him across the room to the stairs.

His saddlebags sat slumped on the floor outside his room door, dropped there by the servant who'd insisted on taking them up. He unlocked the door, retrieved his saddlebags, and stepped inside.

"Wonderful. Just... wonderful." The room held one bed, pushed up against the left-hand wall, and a small dresser with a single cupboard jammed into the far-right corner beneath the small window. A straw-filled mattress, covered with an old, raggedy blanket, had been dragged into the room and crammed between the bed, the dresser, and the door. After seeing the arrangements at the tables downstairs, he had no doubts over which bed was his.

He dropped his saddlebags on top of the straw mattress, tucked his boots against the wall behind the door, and sighed.

'What did you expect? A full suite with a four-poster bed and feather pillows?'

No. But a better mattress would have been nice.

He wriggled out of his riding jacket and wrinkled his nose. A quick search located a jug of clean water and a bowl inside the dresser. He poured some water into the bowl, chipped a corner off the small bar of soap, and scrubbed his face and hands.

Beyond the window, the water of the Gormglais, now pockmarked by the falling rain, glowed a deep orange as it reflected the last rays of the setting sun. Directly above the river, bridging the sky from horizon to horizon, the valley's famous rainbow glowed.

A sudden rap at the door made him jump. He coughed, clearing his throat, and looked over his shoulder. "Yes?"

"Room service."

"Leave it outside the door, please."

He washed his hands a second time and dried them on the legs of his breeches before he collected his food. The crookery on the tray rattled as he picked it up and glanced about the room. With a shrug, he settled for a seat on the bed, placed the tray on his lap, and picked up a spoon. "Well. This is cosy."

"Do you always talk to yourself?"

He flinched, sending soup slopping over the sides of the bowl, and snapped his head towards the door.

Armon stood in the doorway, right shoulder leaning against the door frame, right ankle crossed over his left.

Jared suppressed a glare. "What do you want?"

"Just making sure you're indoors. My men saw you walking towards the river a while ago."

"I needed to clear my head."

"As long as that was all."

"You think I'm stupid enough to try running away on foot?"

"Apparently not." Armon uncrossed his ankles and pushed himself away from the door frame. "I'll be checking again at ten. Make sure you're still here."

"I don't have anywhere else to go."

And that was it. Armon left. No mocking grin. No half-hidden insults. No angry glares. Just a few simple comments, delivered with unnerving calm.

Jared shuddered and went back to his soup.

Jared studied his left boot, running his fingers over the leather to ensure he hadn't missed a spot. Satisfied, he set it to one side, retrieved the right one, and propped it between his knees. He dipped the cloth into the polish and breathed. The scent of beeswax settled over him like a cooling summer breeze. He slipped his left hand into the boot and began to rub in the polish with his right.

It was dark outside now. The clouds hung heavy in the sky, hunkered down like brooding ravens, threatening to shed more rain. The candle on the dresser barely gave off enough light to work in, but it held back night's creeping shadows and the memories threatening to rise with them. The burble of the river filled the little room, drowned out by an occasional burst of laughter or shout from below. It almost felt like a normal night on the road.

Almost.

He studied his right boot, checked the sole with his thumb, and set it beside the left. A quick twist secured the lid on the polish tin before he wrapped it in the cloth and pushed the bundle back into his saddlebags.

He picked up his jacket next and stuck a finger through the small hole in the sleeve. The thought of sewing it in the poor light was enough to give him a headache. He tossed it in the corner and stripped for bed.

The door opened just as he added his breeches to the clothes pile. He turned, making no attempt to cover himself, and painted a grin on his face. "Yes?"

"Jared, I presume?" the intruder, an older, silver-haired man, asked.

"Yes. And you are?"

"Stanin." Stanin closed the door.

Jared crossed his arms over his chest and studied the newcomer. Stanin stood almost a foot shorter than him, looked scrawny beneath his baggy tunic, and suffered from slouched shoulders. A pair of round, wire-framed spectacles sat in the middle of an equally round face, and patches of his skin seemed permanently ink-stained. "Let me guess. You're a scribe."

"How observant of you." Stanin lifted the square case he carried and turned sideways.

Jared shuffled back half a step to give him room to squeeze past. When Stanin said nothing else, he shrugged and turned his attention to the wash jug on the dresser.

"This is for you," Stanin said, just as Jared splashed cold water onto his chest.

Jared glanced over his shoulder.

Stanin held four copper rounds in his palm.

Jared snorted and went back to washing. "I don't need your charity."

"It's not charity, it's your pay. One month, in advance."

The soap slipped from Jared's grip and plopped into the water. He turned. "One *month*? I can make more than that in one *day*."

"Not whilst you work for the Lady al-Rafael."

"But... a round a week? That's less than a common labourer makes!"

"True." Stanin lowered his hand until the coins clinked together in his curled fingers. "But once you take off taxes, stabling and feed for two horses, room and board for yourself, and the repayment of the loan she gave you, this is all that's left."

"Loan? What loan?"

"One moment." Stanin pulled a ledger from his case and flicked through the pages. "Ah. Here we are. Monies are owed for one portable wardrobe, fifteen outfits, four pairs of shoes, four pairs of boots, and a, uh, chastity belt."

Jared sank onto the mattress, mouth working but unable to form words.

"I've also been instructed to inform you that you're not to accept any other forms of employment whilst engaged by the Lady al-Rafael, unless Ambassador Salem, Armon, or I order otherwise."

Jared took the offered coins, the rounds clinking together in his shaking hand. "I'm supposed to survive on four copper rounds a month?"

"Plenty of people survive on less."

"And Armon. You know Armon?"

"Yes."

"You work for him?"

"Yes."

"Willingly?"

"Yes."

Jared sighed. Just what he didn't need, another pair of eyes watching him.

"Armon requested I teach you Canri. Can you read?"

"Yes." *What sort of daft question is that?*

"Good." Stanin produced a small, worn book from his case and tossed it on the straw mattress. "You will read and memorise one page a day. I will test you each night, both on the page you have been studying and the previous pages. I suggest you start now. You have a lot to learn and very little time in which to learn it."

Jared opened his mouth to ask more, but Stanin had already turned his back. He picked up the book, flipped to the first page, and skim-read the first paragraph. It listed the letters of the Canri alphabet along with each letter's pronunciation.

Well, this looks like fun. Not.

He sighed, shuffled closer to the candle, and read through the paragraph again, sounding out each letter in turn.

Armon threaded his way across the common room, first stepping over the mounds of sleeping servants, and then picking his way between the resting patrolmen. He pushed open the front door, slipped outside, and saluted the two men on duty there. "Melf. Winton. Anything to report?"

"No, sir," Melf replied.

"Very good. Carry on." He turned towards the stables.

The crunch of his boots alerted the men stationed outside the stable door to his approach. They lowered their pikes and pointed them towards him. "Who goes there?"

"Patrol Leader Malkem."

The patrolmen pulled their pikes to their sides and saluted, fists to chests. "All quiet, sir."

Armon returned the salute. "Very good. Keep alert." He turned again, strolled down the path between the stables and the lodge, stopped halfway along, and glanced at the sky. Something small and light brushed his shoulder. He bit back a yelp and spun, his hand on his sword hilt.

Tessa stood to the side of the path, one hand pressed to her mouth to suppress her laughter.

Armon relaxed his grip. "Must you sneak up on me like that?"

Tessa pressed a finger to his lips. "Got to keep you on your toes," she whispered.

He caught her finger in both hands and kissed it. "How are things going?"

"Much as you expected. Salem is keeping himself to himself. He seems determined to ignore anyone who isn't a member of his staff. I tried to speak to him, but he brushed me off."

"And Alsam Azier?"

"Ah, the great merchant Azier, hero of a thousand tales, or so he would have people believe. The man never stops talking, and the only thing he seems capable of talking about is himself."

Armon smiled and stepped closer, resting his hands on Tessa's shoulders. "And the mission?"

"Oh, he intends to conquer Canri for us. He has brought dried herbs and candied fruits, tools and rare metals. Luxuries he believes the Canri lack."

"And the trade agreements?"

"He intends to establish exclusive trading rights, both to import and export goods to and from Canri. All in Morgain's name, of course."

"Of course."

"He's also brought several slaves with him."

"Really? I hadn't noticed." He winked.

Tessa laughed. "He intends to trade them, too."

"To the Canri?"

"He heard they make slaves of their conquests, and he wishes to set up an exchange."

"Does he now?"

"He's brought four beautiful, utterly docile females, two boys, and one educated male."

"Beautiful and docile?" Armon slipped his hands from Tessa's shoulders to her waist. "Sounds like my kind of woman."

Tessa swatted his cheek, the sound of flesh striking flesh startling in the quiet night.

"Oww."

"Serves you right."

Armon grinned. He peered into her eyes, his heart beating thrice for every passing second, and reached up to cup the back of her head. The silken strands of her hair tangled around his fingers. Motes of lavender and sandalwood scented the air. He inhaled, drawing her fragrance deep inside, tipped his head, and kissed her.

Her arms enveloped him, her chest pressing against his. Tiny explosions ignited on his skin, lit by her fingers walking the length of his back, lingering to explore the curves at its base. Then she grasped his buttocks and squeezed.

A sonorous, primal groan rose from the bottom of his lungs.

She broke off the kiss to stare into his eyes.

"Tess?"

"Mmmm?"

"What were you and Jared talking about today?"

She stiffened and took a step back. "What do you think we were talking about?"

"I have no idea. It's just…" He caught a strand of her hair and twisted it between his fingers. "You were laughing and—"

"And you hate seeing me happy unless I'm with you?"

"No. Of course not."

"Don't you trust me?"

"Of course I trust you!"

"Then why ask?"

"Because I don't trust him."

Tessa snorted. "It was your idea for me to come."

"I know." Armon let go of her hair and looked away. "I'm sorry. But I know what he's like. He's—"

"He's nothing. You're the man I love." She tapped him on the nose.

Armon lifted his eyes, smiling again. "I know. I'm sorry."

"I have to go. Your men will come looking for you if you're not back soon."

Armon sighed and stepped away. "Let me know if anything happens."

"I will."

"I love you, too."

"I know." Tessa reached up and grabbed the rope dangling a few inches above their heads. She pulled herself up, hand over hand, until she could press her feet against the lodge wall, then climbed to her room, slipped through the window, and pulled the rope in behind her.

6/12/32 KAF

Five days on and nothing had changed. Armon and Tessa continued to watch him, and on the odd occasion when neither of them were around, Stanin took their place, his beady little eyes locked on Jared's back. He'd considered making a run for it anyway. He'd wait for Armon to ride ahead, perhaps around a bend or over a hill, drop back to the rear of the caravan, and then turn off the road.

'And risk getting a crossbow bolt in your back.'

Possibly, if Tessa's reactions are quick enough.

'Or just get caught and dragged back in disgrace.'

Much more likely. Sherna was the faster horse, but Regal had the stamina to outrun her going cross-country, even if she had a head start. Better to wait for a more realistic opportunity.

'Of which there have been exactly none.'

Jared sighed and glanced around. The countryside they travelled through had changed, growing more cultivated as they drew closer to the east coast. It started with a few scattered farms, their fields filled with flocks of sheep or herds of cattle. Livestock gave way to arable crops as the soil grew richer, until the land on either side of the road formed a patchwork of small fields, most lying fallow after the harvest, although a few still held masses of towering green or yellow stalks. And now those fields gave way to orchards, the perfectly spaced trees providing dappled shade to anyone on the road. They would arrive in Star Bay before sunset, where they would board the waiting ship.

'And there'll be plenty of chances to get away then. You could wait until nightfall and slip overboard. A short swim to shore, and you'll be free. A wonderful plan. Unless you drown first, of course.'

Jared checked a growl and dropped his gaze to the Canri language book he held. Lists of verbs filled the pages, broken down by type and form. He mouthed each foreign word as he read it.

'He's gone. And fatty's distracting the assassin. This is your chance. Run. Now. Before it's too late.'

Jared looked up.

Tessa glanced over her shoulder at the same time, smiled, and turned back to Azier.

She'll kill me.

'Better than being tortured by Morgain when you get back.'

Jared bit back a retort and returned his attention to the book.

Perhaps escape was the wrong option. After all, what was there to gain? Freedom? Of a sort. But he doubted Morgain would give him up without recourse. She would send someone after him, and he would spend the rest of his life running from her; running, with no-one beside him, and nowhere to call home. Ryal would keep to his word and refuse to lift his exile. Unless he somehow escaped, returned to the al-Rafael Household, broke into Morgain's study, and stole the information his cousin had asked for.

Laughter echoed inside his head. *'Like that will ever happen.'*

Perhaps his original instincts had been correct, perhaps he should try to make friends with Armon or, if not friends, allies. Morgain treated Armon more like a slave than an uncle. They could have something in common there.

If I can get Armon on my side, perhaps I can persuade him to help. Or trick him into revealing Morgain's plans. Would I stand a better chance than if I fled? Possibly. Would I live longer? Buy myself time to come up with a better plan? Definitely.

'Then it's decided. You'll choose the coward's path.'

Not a coward's path. A prudent one. He would sneak away when they reached Star Bar, find a way to send a message to Ryal, then re-join the ship before—

"Reading something good?"

Jared almost dropped the book. Tessa had slowed her mount to ride beside him. He looked at her and shook his head.

"May I see?"

"Of course." He moved the book towards her.

"Thank you." She reached out to take it. Her shoulder brushed against his. Their fingers touched.

Pain erupted in the back of his head. The book tumbled to the ground. A hand grabbed Sherna's reins and wrenched them from his grip.

"You were told to keep your hands to yourself!" Armon nudged Regal closer, pinning Sherna between the stallion and Tessa's mare.

Jared blinked but couldn't focus through his watering eyes.

"What is going on, Patrol Leader?" Salem shouted, his voice coming from somewhere up ahead.

"Following Lady Morgain's orders, sir." Armon turned to Jared and lowered his voice. "Hold out your hands."

Jared started to turn his head. The spot where Armon had hit him flared, sending aftershocks radiating through his skull. He dabbed at the knot and checked his fingers. No blood. "What?"

"Hold out your hands."

He looked around, careful to keep his head movements slow. Everyone had stopped to watch. Most of them frowned, their lips compressed or downturned, but a few leant forwards in their saddles, lips parted or eyes glistening.

'Like jackals eager for their supper to expire.'

Then they'll be going hungry this time. Jared turned to meet Armon's gaze and extended his hands.

Armon bound his wrists together with Sherna's reins then used the remaining length of leather to secure them to her pommel. "You were told to stay away from other women."

"I wasn't—"

Armon slapped the back of his head.

His vision blurred. He swayed in his saddle. Something pressed against his right palm. He curled his fingers around its hard edge. When his vision cleared, he discovered he held Stanin's book clutched in his hand. He lifted his head.

Ambassador Salem twisted in his saddle to look back at them. "Are you quite finished, Patrol Leader?"

Armon kneed Regal away from Sherna. "I'm finished, Ambassador."

"Then might I suggest we keep moving? I do not wish to be late."

"Of course, Ambassador."

The caravan resumed its monotonous trudge.

Sherna snorted and settled into a steady walk.

Jared rubbed at his aching skull. He risked a glance at Tessa.

She stared past him, her eyes fixed on Armon's back, and her eyebrows drawn together, her glare wolf-like in its intensity.

❧

Armon led the caravan off the road a little before noon and brought them to a stop on an untamed strip of land running between two orchards. He nudged Regal to the side of the strip and waited for Azier and Salem to join him. "We'll rest here for half an hour," he said when he judged them close enough to hear. "If anyone wants to eat or stretch their legs, they'll need to do it now. We won't stop again before we reach Star Bay."

Salem reined up first. "Thank you, Patrol Leader."

"Sir." Armon dipped his head. He ignored the look of haughty disdain on Salem's face, guided Regal towards the patrol's picket, slid from the saddle, and tied Regal's reins to one of the hitching posts his men had driven into the ground. Behind him, a cacophony of shouts, grunts, and horse whinnies broke out as the caravan prepared a hasty camp. He gave Regal a solid pat on the shoulder and shifted position to watch the chaos, putting his back to the approaching rider.

"I don't suppose you're going to let me down?" Jared asked.

Armon made a show of stretching his arms, back, and shoulders before he turned to answer. He flashed his mocking grin at Jared. "You don't suppose right."

Jared sat straight-backed in his saddle, his gaze fixed on a distant point. His chest swelled, shoulders rising and falling. He dropped his gaze to meet Armon's. "Don't you think you're overreacting? All I did was show her a book. It's not like you're married to her."

Heat exploded in Armon's veins, as volatile and violent as an erratic volcano. He turned before it transferred to his face. "I don't care if you showed her a spot on the end of your finger, I will not have you—"

"Patrol Leader Malkem!" Tessa's shout cut across the noisy camp. Those closest to her moved apart, clearing a path between them.

He clung to a polite smile, though he couldn't resist stealing a glance at her stockinged legs, visible through the slits in her riding skirt. When she reached him, he inclined his head. "How may I help you, my lady…?"

"Zandra. May I have word? In private."

"Of course." He bowed and spread one arm, using it to indicate the orchard to his right. "This way?"

Tessa nodded.

He led the way, weaving a path through the trunks of the apple trees. Once the hubbub from the caravan had faded to a low murmur, he stopped and turned to face her. "Te—"

Her glare turned his words to vapour, evaporating them like water tossed on hot stones. She took a pace forward and seemed to gain an inch in height. "What do you think you're playing at?"

"I'm *playing* at being Malkem."

"Malkem?" Tessa barked a laugh. "Since when did Malkem care about anything outside his own patrol?"

"Since Lady Morgain—"

"No." Tessa shoved him against a tree trunk. "You will *not* use her as an excuse."

"I wasn't—"

"Have you forgotten what happened the last time you let your emotions get in the way of your work?"

"I'm not—"

"Oh, but you are." She shoved him again. "You're going to ruin everything."

"You think I would jeopardise—?"

"I don't have to think it. I'm watching it happen."

"Tessa, please." Armon lowered his voice in a vain attempt to calm her ire. "I have to—"

Her punch hit the tree before he could duck, leaving it shuddering from the impact.

He stared at the splintered bark for a heartbeat then lifted his gaze to meet hers. "Why?"

"You once called Lord al-Ayire a useless, lazy, power-crazed idiot. Remember?"

"What has that got to do with anything?"

"You were as blind and stubborn then as you are now."

"Because I told the truth?"

"Because you let your emotions overrule your common sense."

He sucked on the inside of his mouth. "I did not—"

"He gave you plenty of chances to apologise. The first time you refused, he had you arrested."

"I really don't see—"

"The second time you refused, he had you locked up at the top of his watchtower."

Armon's eyes lost focused. Three days he'd spent there, hands and feet bound, with no food and very little water. Dark, jagged rocks had waited for him below, ready to shatter his body if he happened to fall. He shivered.

"And when he had you brought down, you *still* refused to apologise." Tessa plucked a speck of bark off his cheek and flicked it to the ground. "He had to dangle you over a cliff on the end of a thief-catcher's pole to get you to come to your senses."

Armon saw it then, the U-shaped hook wrapped around his neck, his feet dangling over empty air, hands clutching futilely at the pole. A sudden crack. A sickening lurch. Large splinters of wood where the pole had cracked. A garbled apology. Al-Ayire ordering him pulled back in.

"Why bring this up now?"

"Why? Because you're losing your self-control. I shouldn't have to explain—"

The snap of a twig drew them both up short. Armon pushed away from the tree trunk and smoothed down his jacket.

Tessa backed up several paces.

A whip-like crack came from the same direction as the snap. Whoever approached cursed, the words crude but cultured. A monochromatic figure tramped through the trees with all the nimbleness of a beached seal.

Ambassador Salem.

Several leaves adorned a snarl in his hair, his breeches had rucked around his knees, and mud spattered his normally immaculate boots.

He reached the area where Armon and Tessa waited and assessed the situation with a single sweep of his impassive gaze. "Is everything well, Lady Zandra?"

"Yes, thank you, Ambassador." The smile she shared with him wouldn't have looked out of place on a blood-drenched warrior. "I was just telling the patrol leader I'm more than capable of looking after myself, and I don't need him to play guardian to my virtue."

Salem's gaze flicked between them, his nose wrinkled in disgust. "I see."

Armon bowed his head to Tessa. "If that is all, my lady?"

"That is all," she said, her voice as cold as the northern wind.

Armon had only taken two steps when Salem called him back. He stopped and looked over his shoulder. "Yes, Ambassador?"

"If, in future, you have a problem with a member of my staff, I would appreciate it if you spoke to me about it first."

"Of course, Ambassador. My apologies if my actions offended you."

Salem dismissed him with a wave.

❧

They reached Star Bay as the last ripples of a weak sunset faded from the sky. The moon was yet to rise, and thick clouds blocked out the stars. Freshly lit streetlamps added their warmth to the glow of firelight flooding from dozens of windows to keep the town alive.

The caravan kept to the main road, led by Armon and half his men as they forced their way through the thinning crowd towards the harbour on the far side of the bay. Jared held Sherna's reins in one hand and rubbed his chaffed wrist with the other. He'd spent most of the afternoon with his wrists tied to the pommel. Armon had refused to release him until Salem ordered him to during an unplanned rest break. The black look Armon threw his way afterwards told him the matter wasn't over.

A light tug on Sherna's reins slowed her imperceptibly. A nudge of his knee guided her closer to the edge of the road. The caravan had spread out as it travelled through the town, and a bend in the road separated those at the front from the rest. Neither Armon nor Stanin were in sight, which, with luck, meant neither man could see him either. Tessa remained visible, separated from him by a dozen horses and riders. She rode straight-backed, head unmoving, as she conversed with her riding companion. Nothing in her body language or posture suggested she'd noticed his measured retreat. He tightened his grip on Sherna's reins, clicked his tongue, and turned her down a quiet side street.

"Well, that was easier than I'd expected." He leant forward and gave Sherna's neck a pat. She danced beneath him, the clicks of her hoofs mirroring his erratic pulse. He patted her again, straightened, and glanced over his shoulder. Nobody followed them; nobody even looked around to see where he'd gone. "Good."

At the next junction, he turned Sherna again, placing them on a street paralleling the main road but travelling west, towards Star Bay's courier station. A fair number of people still traversed the street, most of them on foot. He pulled Sherna to a stop and slid from the saddle. Sweat prickled his scalp, and his back tingled. He spun on his heels, searching the crowd. No-one. He chuckled and rubbed Sherna's rump. "Come on, girl."

He led her through the streets, sometimes sticking to the busy roads, sometimes cutting down empty side streets to check for signs of pursuit. His route took him across the closed market square, through a twisting series of alleyways, and back to the square a few minutes later. If anyone followed, he failed to spot them. Even so, the itch between his shoulder-blades persisted. He returned to the main road, the tail end of the caravan at his back, and joined the flow of traffic heading out of town.

Several inns lined the road; large, well-maintained establishments with firelight leaking around the edges of solid shutters and bright porch lights creating pools of safety against the encroaching night. The prospect of a table near a warm fire, hot food, and a soft bed tugged at him with the persistence of a fisherman reeling in his line, but he walked on until he reached a narrower street a hundred yards from the town gates.

More inns—and likely brothels—intermingled with tea houses and black-windowed shops. He chose one a fair distance back from the main road. Though smaller than the other inns he'd passed—only two stories, rather than three—the noise coming from inside suggested it provided a better service than the peeling paint on its sign and the wonky shutters implied.

A second sign on the side of the building pointed to stables at the back. He opened the side gate and led Sherna down a narrow alley to a small, dirt yard.

The stable block held no more than four or five stalls, but it appeared clean, and the boy at the entrance looked tidy and alert. He stepped forward at Jared's approach. "Stabling's a pentain a night. Hay's two rounds. Oats are three."

"How much for an hour?"

"An hour?" The boy pursed his lips and sucked. "I'm not s'posed to but—" He glanced towards the inn's back door. "Seeing's as we've two stalls empty, I'll do it for a pair of rounds."

Jared handed him three. "Is there a privy I could use?"

"Down the passage on the left."

"Thank you." He handed over Sherna's reins and strolled in the direction the boy indicated.

'Really? You're doing this before you send the message?'

I'm desperate.

And now he'd thought of it, the pressure built tenfold. He hurried his steps and darted through the dimly illuminated opening. Three paces in, he stopped, pressed his back to the wall, and looked back into the yard.

Sherna's tail lashed out as she disappeared through the stable doors, but nothing else moved in the small, enclosed space.

He crossed his legs and waited, alert for signs of pursuit, uncomfortably aware of the thump-thump of his own heartbeat and the rush of his breath through his nose and mouth. Still nothing but the flicker of shadows across the inn's back windows, accompanied by a burst of shouts and laughter from within. He counted his heartbeats, continuing to a hundred to allow for its rapid pace, before he turned in search of the privy.

A sputtering torch lit the passage, so low on fuel it gave off more smoke than light. The 'privy' turned out to be little more than an open trough lined with straw, with plank dividers fitted to the wall to separate it into stalls. He hurried to the last stall in the row, unlaced his breeches, leant back to check the passage remained empty, and slid his cod piece free. The release of pressure on his bladder was instant. He closed his eyes and sighed.

A rush of air stirred his hair. Cloth scuffed the wall at his back. The sensations had barely registered when a cold point touched the underside of his penis.

The stream of urine cut off. He cracked one eye open, stared at the long, narrow blade set against his genitals, and stilled his breath. "Uh..." He turned his head slowly—ever so slowly—and stared into Tessa's eyes.

Her lips curled up in a voracious smile. "Going somewhere?"

"Well..." He raised his right hand, palm open, elbow pointing backwards, measuring the distance between them. He considered twisting away and knocking her arm clear, then winced as he imagined the likely outcome.

Tessa chuckled. "How far did you think you could run?"

"Wasn't running. Just needed to..." He motioned to the trough.

"I'd be more inclined to believe you if you hadn't put so much effort into sneaking away." Tessa twisted her wrist, and the edge of the blade shaved his skin. "Where were you going?"

"To the courier station. To send a message. To Elise." The last came out as a squeak, provoked by a poke of the stiletto.

"That I can believe." Tessa withdrew her blade. "Finish your business then join me in the yard. Ride back with me without causing any problems, and I won't mention this... incident... to Armon."

"I... thank you." Had he detected a touch of sympathy behind her words?

'Pity, more likely. Amusement. Mockery. Rid—'
Shut up.
Shut up?

Why am I arguing with myself?
He finished his business, covered himself, and returned to the yard.

᪥

They re-joined the caravan as the last of the wagons turned into the harbour. Jared guided Sherna past the slow-moving vehicle, his eyes tracing the path of wagons and horses ahead of him, following its course to the largest of Star Bay's piers. "Is that our ship?"

"Yes." Tessa brought her piebald mare level with Sherna. "Impressive, isn't she?"

Jared nodded. The four-master had to be over a hundred and fifty feet long and at least a third as tall. Three full decks rose above the waterline, the second housing a double bank of oars, with the split-level forecastle, upper, and lower poop decks above that. The ship's name, *The Hunter*, was emblazoned across the bow, each letter standing as tall as a man.

"*The Hunter* is Morgain's flagship," Tessa said a few seconds later. "And the second largest ship in the Kingdom's fleet. She could hold a party twice our size and still feel spacious compared to most ships I've travelled on. Your cabin's in the lower forecastle. Sherna's stall's in the stable underneath."

"You hear that, girl? Your very own stall." Jared patted Sherna's shoulder.

Sherna whinnied and tossed her head.

Tessa laughed. "Come on. Let's catch up with Azier before Armon notices our absence." She flicked her reins, and her mare stepped up to a canter.

Jared held Sherna to a walk and glanced over his shoulder. He could still run; bring Sherna alongside one of the wagons, use its side to hide her turn, and pray she could put enough distance between himself and the caravan before anyone noticed they'd gone.

And spend the rest of my life in exile? I don't think so.

᪥

Armon was exhausted. After twelve hours in the saddle and three more spent overseeing the loading of the ship, he wanted nothing more than to collapse into bed and sleep. He let himself into his cabin and took a breath. The air smelt of sandalwood and lavender. "Tessa?"

A hard, sharp point jabbed the front of his shoulder. He glanced down at the long, needle-like stiletto poking him and smiled. "Does this mean I'm forgiven?"

Tessa leant forward, her breath hot against his ear. "No." She ran her knife across his body to the base of his neck. "You haven't earned my forgiveness." The knife slipped under his top button. "Yet." A flick of her wrist sent the button spinning across the tiny cabin.

He reached behind him. Stroked her thigh. "I've been thinking about what you said."

"Oh?" Another button went flying.

He paused, his fingertips soaking up her warmth through her clothes. "You were right. I've been letting my emotions get in the way." A third button popped free. "I promise not to let it happen again."

Tessa snorted. "Words are cheap." A flick of her stiletto removed the final button and his jacket flapped open. She sliced through his shirt, slid her free hand into the slit, and rubbed his chest.

He tensed, his muscles hardening beneath her touch, his lungs tightening. "What, exactly, do you want me to do?"

"That's easy." She yanked his shirt off his shoulders, trapping his arms behind his back and exposing his torso. "Give him a carrot." The tip of her stiletto traced a path down his bare flesh, leaving behind a thin, bloody scratch.

He shivered. "Give him a what?"

"A carrot." She spun him round to face her. The confines of the small cabin forced his body tight against hers. "You know. Donkey. Cart. Stick. Carrot." She kissed him.

Armon returned the kiss and groaned in frustration. He wanted his hands free to touch her; to pull her clothes off her body and run his fingers over her skin.

She broke off the kiss. "If you keep pushing him the way you have, he's going to snap." Her leg slid between his. She rubbed it against his groin. "You can't risk him turning on you."

Another groan, this one longer and deeper. *Damn this teasing. Why won't she let me touch her?*

She lowered her leg. "I shouldn't have to tell you this, love. You know better."

"I know. I'm sorry."

She let him go.

He wriggled out of his shirt and reached for her.

Her fingers locked onto his wrist, stopping his hand an inch from her face. "Not now."

His skin tingled beneath her fingers. "Why not?"

"People will hear."

Armon stepped back. His heel caught on the side of the bed, and he fell backwards onto the mattress. "Cursed ships."

Tessa grinned. "A carrot. Don't forget." She placed her hands on his shoulders and shared one final, passionate kiss. "I'll see you on deck tomorrow."

Armon nodded. He watched her slip through the porthole and imagined her climbing along the hull, her fingers seeking out cracks in the planks, her hobnailed boots digging little holes into the wood. She would find the porthole to her own cabin, wriggle her way inside, and close the window behind her. No-one would ever know she'd left.

He touched his tongue to his lips, sampling her salty-sweet taste. His flesh pressed against the fabric cage of his breeches.

He growled and punched the wall.

7/12/32 KAF

Jared yawned and rested his arms on the ship's rail. Sleep had eluded him. The creaking of the ship's timbers and the constant lapping of the sea had merged with his dreams; dark dreams filled with shadow and terror. The weight of them still haunted him, though he recalled no details. He'd tossed and turned all night, occasionally rising to pace his cabin before throwing himself back atop his bunk. And then he'd opened his eyes to find the first streaks of daylight lighting his cabin. The sun was rising. He'd chosen to rise with it.

The ship had already set sail when he emerged on deck. The growing light revealed nothing but sea in all directions. The crew scampered around like rats, checking ropes, scrubbing decks, and climbing about the rigging.

A portion of the upper poop had been kept clear for the passengers. He stood there now, leaning against the rail, watching the churning wake tumbling and crashing behind the ship like soil beneath the plough.

'Constantly moving. Constantly reacting. Never in control.'

Just like me.

'Yes. Just like me.'

Jared sighed.

"You look like a man with the weight of the world on his shoulders." The speaker's soft voice triggered a shiver, accompanied by the memory of a blade scraping the underside of his genitals.

He stepped back and sideways, putting a safe gap between himself and Tessa. "I find the troubles of Jared up-Arran weight enough."

"Are your troubles really so bad?"

Do you really expect me to answer? He turned away, hoping she would get the hint and leave him in peace. When the silence grew heavy, he swivelled back. "How many people have you killed?"

Tessa laughed. "How many women have you slept with?"

Jared forced himself to look into her eyes—eyes sparkling with amusement. "I don't keep count."

Her smile thinned. "Neither do I."

"But still, you must remember—"

"Oh, I remember some of them. The murderers. The rapists. The traitors." She winked at him.

"I am not—"

More laughter. She stepped forward, closing the gap between them. "I know you're not. But neither am I the thoughtless killer you assume."

"I never said—"

"No. You didn't. But you were thinking it." She paused, as though inviting him to contradict her. Several seconds passed in silence, then she bent her head closer and whispered in a voice dripping honey, "Not everyone I kill is a criminal. Some people just... get in the way."

"Get in the way? How?"

All signs of amusement fled her face. "Keep asking personal questions and you'll find out."

Jared dug his fingernails into the rail to mask his shaking. After their encounter yesterday, he knew she could end his life whenever she chose. But why threaten him now? She'd approached him, not the other way around.

'And you threw her offer to talk back in her face.'

I never.

He had. Of all the foolish things. How did he ever expect to find information for Ryal if he went around alienating everyone? She'd done him a favour yesterday, keeping knowledge of his excursion from Armon. Why, he didn't know, but that was no reason to aggravate the only person in the delegation who'd shown him a shred of kindness. He watched the ship's wake flow past for a time then looked back at her. "Please, my lady, accept my apologies. It wasn't my intention to pry."

'Liar.'

Tessa held his gaze until sweat beaded on his forehead, then her mouth lifted in a warm smile. "Apology accepted." She let her words hover in the air for a second then leant in so close her breath heated his face. "This time."

Someone coughed.

Jared started.

Tessa pushed away from the rail and turned to face the newcomer, her movements smooth and her expression bland. "Patrol Leader." She inclined her head to Armon. "Jared and I have concluded our discussion. I hope you won't consider me rude if I leave you two gentlemen to it?"

"Not at all." Armon bowed. His eyes followed Tessa as she crossed the deck.

'And now for the repercussions. What do you think he'll do this time? Beat you?'

I have no idea.

Jared reclined against the rail, crossed his ankles, and blotted out the taunting whisper. He'd done nothing wrong. Not that that counted for much when it came to dealing with Armon.

Armon turned, fists clenched at his sides, facial muscles taut. He looked into Jared's eyes then glanced away. "I came to apologise."

Jared swallowed, choked on a mouthful of saliva, coughed, and thumped his chest. "You came to what?"

"To apologise." Armon uncurled the fingers of one hand and tapped them against his thigh.

Jared waited, expecting mockery or laughter.

"For yesterday," Armon added. He puckered his lips and swallowed. "I overreacted when I saw you with Tessa. I'm sorry." He shifted his gaze to stare out to sea and rested one arm on the rail. "There's a small cargo hold underneath the stable. The ship's captain left it empty so my men can train during the voyage. Meet me down there in an hour."

Jared bowed his head, clasped his hands, and touched his fingers to his forehead. Could he? Dare he? Dare he refuse? He lowered his hands, lifted his head, and nodded.

"Good. I'll see you then."

Jared crossed his arms and stared at Armon's receding back. There had been no smile hidden behind his eyes as he spoke, no hint of his mocking grin. He had spoken quickly, his words hard and clipped, but the apology had sounded genuine.

He didn't like it. Not one bit.

≈✥≈

Armon paced the length of the cargo hold, getting a sense of its size. Despite being roughly half the width of the forecastle deck, the shelves running the length of the partition and the sloping hull gave the space a claustrophobic feel. He stood in the middle of the floor and stretched out his arms. His fingers cleared the walls by several inches on both sides. It would do.

"A carrot," he muttered as he stripped off his jacket and tossed it onto one of the shelves. "Need to give him a carrot."

He stretched his arms out again and traced a series of circles in the air, warming his muscles.

"He doesn't deserve a damned carrot."

He slid his left foot in front of his right and stretched.

"He can't even accept a damned apology."

But Tessa had been right. Every man had a breaking point, and Jared was dangerously close to his.

The steps leading down from the stables creaked. Armon took a deep breath and tamped down the heat racing through him, snuffing it like a candle flame. He curled his lips into their customary grin and spun around.

Jared stepped onto the deck.

Armon ran his gaze down Jared's body. He was fit, he'd grant him that, but it was a fitness gained from hours spent in the saddle. His muscles were built for strength and stamina, not quick, coordinated bursts. It would take weeks to retrain his body. Still, he'd worked with worse. "Take your shirt off."

Jared stiffened. "Excuse me?"

"I said, 'take your shirt off'. Unless you want it covered in sweat and grime? I don't care if it gets ruined."

"Why would it—?"

"You need to learn to fight."

Jared opened his mouth, closed it again, frowned, and shook his head.

"I'm offering to teach you. It's an offer I won't repeat."

"You're…" Jared glanced behind him then ran his gaze around the room. "But…"

"If something goes wrong, you need to be able to defend yourself." Armon took a step forward.

"Why?"

"Why?" Armon chuckled. "You really need to ask?"

"No. I mean, why you? Why now?"

"Because." Armon took another step forward and stood on his tiptoes, bringing his eyes level with Jared's. "I cannot afford for this mission to fail. I don't have time to teach you properly, but you can at least learn to defend yourself so you don't end up getting killed." He dropped back to his feet and spun away. "Either take off your shirt and accept what I'm offering or leave." He waited, his back to Jared. Long seconds stretched by in silence.

The deck creaked and rolled.

Jared stumbled and cursed.

Armon laughed and turned to face him. "Well?"

Jared took off his shirt.

"Good choice." Armon moved to stand underneath one of the lanterns and waved Jared closer. "Let's start with something simple. Punch me in the face."

Jared clenched his fist, drew back his arm, and swung.

Armon raised his hand to block the attack, ducked beneath Jared's arm, and pivoted on his heel to finish with his back to Jared and his elbow pressed against his stomach. He pushed Jared back with his arm and stepped clear. "Think you can do that?"

"Uh…"

Armon read the confusion on Jared's face and swallowed a curse. "I'll do it more slowly. Bring your arm up, as though you're going to punch me."

Jared did as instructed.

"Use your left hand to block the attack. Like this." Armon pressed his hand against the inside of Jared's outstretched wrist. "Or you can catch the attacker's wrist"—he continued to demonstrate as he spoke—"and pull him towards you. Next, step inside the attacker's reach, pivot on your heel, and jab your elbow into his stomach. Hit him hard enough and you'll wind him, giving you time to retaliate or run." He released Jared's wrist and turned to face him. "Ready to try?"

"Yes."

Armon aimed a weak punch at Jared's chin.

Jared grabbed Armon's wrist and pulled, turning and ducking so the blow passed over his shoulder.

An elbow slammed into Armon's gut, driving the breath from his lungs. Then fingers tangled in his hair and pulled, ramming him forward. His forehead cracked against the edge of a shelf. Pain exploded in his skull and blood flooded his eye. He staggered backwards, one hand clutched to his face. Two Jareds waited for him, standing in front of two swaying sets of shelves. He blinked.

Jared lunged.

Armon sidestepped and grabbed Jared's wrist as he passed. A vicious tug forced him to his knees, his arm twisted behind his back. Armon switched his grip to his right hand and wiped blood from his eyes with his left. "Do that again... and I'll break... your arm." He grabbed Jared's hand and bent it backwards, eliciting a muffled scream. "Understood?"

"Understood," Jared replied through gritted teeth.

"Good." Armon released Jared's wrist and shoved him to the deck. "Now get up and try again." He put his full strength behind his next punch.

Jared's block deflected the blow, but not enough to stop it from clipping the bottom of his chin, knocking him off balance.

Armon grabbed a fistful of his undershirt to keep him from falling and grinned. "A fair attempt, but your block needs to be faster and stronger. Try again." He gave Jared a second to settle himself then attacked.

He pushed Jared hard, making him repeat the counter over and over, criticising and advising in equal measure. On the few occasions when Jared succeeded, he kept his praise to a minimum, offering no more than a nod or a simple 'well done', then he stepped up his own efforts, adding more speed or strength, altering the angle of his punch.

Jared showed minimal improvement during his first lesson, but he worked hard and refused to give up. Armon smiled in silent approval. He'd anticipated complaints, objections, and excuses, but dandy boy was proving himself tougher than expected.

The small hold grew hot and stuffy as they worked. Sweat soaked Jared's undershirt, his muscles ached, and his breath came in laboured gasps.

Armon bounced on his toes across from him, clenching and unclenching first one fist then the other as he rocked his shoulders. He chuckled, his face flushed but not dripping. His right forearm bulged, his foot shifting forward—

Jared jerked his forearm up but failed to block the incoming blow. Armon's fist caught him square on the chin, sending him crashing into the shelves. Blood sloshed between his ears with the ferocity of a river in flood. He slid to the floor.

"Enough." Armon pulled Jared to his feet. "Get some rest. I want you back here this evening for another lesson."

"Yes, *sir*." Jared slapped his fist to his chest in mock salute.

Armon shook his head, retrieved his jacket, and slipped it on. "I hope you've been working on your language lessons. I'll be testing you later."

Jared managed a nod, picked up his shirt, draped it over his shoulder, and climbed the stairs to the stables. The familiar scents of horse and hay filled his nostrils. He'd need to come back later and clean out Sherna's stall, but first he wanted a good soak, a long drink, and a change of clothes. He followed Armon up to the main deck, squinting against the strong sunlight, and bumped into his back.

Armon took half a step sideways, giving Jared a partial view of the obstruction.

Ambassador Salem stood at the top of the stairs, his arms crossed and his back straighter than *The Hunter's* masts. He scowled, his irises burning like dark flames beneath his thick brows. "My cabin, gentlemen. Now." He pivoted on his heels and led them up the stairs to the senior staff's cabins. One of his bodyguards stood watch outside his door. The man bowed his head to the ambassador and pushed it open.

Salem entered first, took a seat on the room's only chair, and glared across the small table at Armon and Jared. "I've had a report that the two of you have been fighting."

Jared glanced at Armon.

Armon lifted his shoulders in a minute shrug.

Jared pulled his shirt off his shoulder and clutched it before him in both hands. "Ambassador Salem, sir, Armon and I weren't fighting, we were—"

Salem cut him off with a slash of his hand. "*Don't* try and deny it. One of my servants stumbled across your scuffle. What he witnessed, *Patrol Leader*, was your good self holding Jared in an arm lock and threatening to break his arm."

Armon bowed his head and shuffled his feet. He looked up, glanced at Jared, and swallowed. "I can explain, sir."

"Please do."

"Well, sir, I—"

"It was my fault, sir," Jared said. He kept his eyes fixed on the handful of grey strands criss-crossing Salem's lined brow, though he sensed Armon's hot stare locked on his side. He had spoken on impulse, hoping to earn a smidgen of Armon's trust. A pity he hadn't thought of an excuse first. "We were discussing my... indiscretion... with Lady Zandra, and I..." He paused and glanced away. What could justify the scene Salem's servant witnessed? "I insulted the patrol leader, sir. I insinuated his anger towards me may have been triggered by impotence, sir."

"I see." The ambassador leant back in his chair, pressed the tips of his fingers together, and tapped his chin. The whites of his manicured fingernails glistened. "Still, that is no excuse for fighting aboard ship." He turned his stare on Armon. "If you have no discipline, your men will follow suit. Consider this a second warning, Patrol Leader. There will not be a third. Dismissed!"

"Sir." Armon saluted, clicked his heels together, and left.

Salem dropped his hands to the table and fixed his gaze on Jared. "It's about time we met, young man. If you're to be a member of my staff, it's only fair I lay down some ground rules." He stood and stepped around the table. "Lady Morgain gave me some very clear instructions about you. She told me you've got yourself into some bother and were sent along to make amends. Is that correct?"

Ah, shi—"Yes, sir."

"Then I think it best I set some ground rules. First, you will avoid being alone with any woman whilst aboard this ship."

Jared twined his fingers in his shirt. "Sir."

"You will also dress yourself more appropriately for polite company. You will wear an undershirt, shirt or tunic, and coat at all times. I will not have you wandering around in your shirt sleeves when there are ladies present."

The shirt bit deeper into Jared's fingers with Salem's every word. He bowed his head, his cheek muscle twitching. "Yes, sir."

"You have met Stanin, I believe."

"Yes, sir."

"He will be instructing you on the duties you will be expected to perform whilst working at the embassy. Your lessons will begin this afternoon." Salem retrieved a wooden box from behind a curtain and placed it on the table. "Lady Morgain gave me this. She informed me that, should I find you engaged in inappropriate behaviour, I am to use it to discipline you. The duration of its use will be determined by the extent of the offense. Why don't you take a look?"

Jared licked his lips and swallowed. He didn't need to look to know what lay inside, but he lifted the lid anyway. Lantern light whorled across the dull metal of the chastity belt. He squirmed. "I-I understand, sir."

"I hope so." Salem slammed the lid shut. "Because I won't give you a second warning. Now leave. I have work to do."

"Sir." Jared bowed and backed out the cabin.

❧❦

Armon stalked across the main deck, headed for the upper poop. His hands were clutched into fists, his nails digging furrows into his palms. He growled when one of the ship's crew got too close, sending the man running. Several people glanced in his direction when he climbed the stairs to the upper deck, but one glimpse of his face was enough to make them look away again. Anyone foolish enough not to take the hint earned themselves a glower. And then someone shouted, "Patrol Leader!"

He swept his eyes over the deck, seeking the source of the shout.

Tessa waved to him from the port railing.

He waved back, some of his anger fading, and strolled over to her. "Lady Zandra." He bowed.

"My dear man," Tessa said, her voice pitched to carry, "what happened to your head?"

"I lost my balance and cracked it on a shelf. It's not as bad it looks." He flinched when she probed the cut with a finger.

She tsked and shook her head. "This needs to be cleaned before it becomes infected. Come to my cabin, and I'll dress it for you."

"Thank you for your concern, my lady, but I have duties—"

"Nonsense!" Tessa wrapped his arm in hers and pulled him towards the stairs. "It will only take a moment."

"As you wish." Public protests completed, Armon allowed Tessa to lead him to her cabin.

"What really happened?" she asked.

"I offered Jared a carrot." Armon dropped onto the narrow bunk. "He repaid me by snatching the whole damned bunch."

"Armon—"

"I offered to teach him self-defence. Went easy on him on his first attempt. He thanked me by giving me this." He waved a hand at the cut on his head then dropped both hands to his lap. "Guess he's got more fight left in him than I gave him credit for." He laughed and slouched against the cabin wall. His head throbbed.

"And Ambassador Salem?"

"Lectured us for fighting aboard ship. Wanted to know what started it." He sat up straight and stretched. Half his body ached, his muscles objecting to the abuse they'd suffered now he'd relaxed. "I was about to spin some nonsense about teaching Jared some discipline when Jared interrupted. He told Salem he called me impotent."

Tessa laughed.

Armon caught hold of her hands and pulled himself upright. "You think it's funny?" he asked in a deep throated growl. He tried to glare at her, but his body betrayed him. His lips twitched as he struggled to suppress his grin. "You think it might be true?" He pressed his forehead to hers; ran his hands over the curves of her hips.

"No." She pulled him closer; draped her arms over his shoulders. "I know you too well to believe that." She kissed the tip of his nose. "It was a good excuse, though. Quick thinking on his part."

"Indeed." Armon straightened and pushed Tessa away, his ardour dampened by her praise. "Why though? Why not use the incident to widen the rift between Malkem and Salem?"

"Perhaps he fears Salem more than he fears you. Or perhaps—" Tessa pulled a kerchief from her pocket and dabbed at the cut on his forehead. "Perhaps he simply realised his life would be a lot easier if he worked with you instead of fighting you all the time."

Armon caught her wrist, holding her hand away from his skin. "What have you said to him?"

"Me? Nothing."

Her soft smile made him doubt the truth of her claim, but he didn't push her. He trusted her, even though knowing she and Jared had been talking made him want to smash everything in sight. "So you suggest that I what? Let his interruption slide?"

"Thank him for it."

Armon pulled Tessa's hand down, his grip tight enough to turn her skin white. "Excuse me?"

"Thank him. Praise his quick thinking. He'll be a lot more useful if he can see the benefit of working with you instead of fighting you all the time."

"I suppose." He released his hold then kissed her wrist where he'd crushed her flesh. He hadn't hurt her, not truly. She'd break his arm if he tried.

Tessa extracted her hand, shook out her kerchief, and folded it so a clean section was on the outside. "What else is bothering you?"

"I need to find somewhere else to train Jared. I can't risk Salem seeing me with him again. Not whilst we're aboard ship."

"I'll find somewhere for you."

"Thank you."

"Is that everything?"

Armon nodded.

"Good. Now enough with the jealousy. I'm not interested in Jared, and I never will be."

"I'm sorry."

"You should be." Tessa leant over and kissed his lips. "Now let me finish cleaning your cut before people start wondering why we've been alone so long."

27/12/32 KAF (One)

Jared groaned and rolled onto his side. He had bruises layered atop bruises, and every inch of him ached. Armon had trained him for three weeks solid, with every session more intense than the last. And when he wasn't with Armon, he'd been shut away with Stanin, learning everything he could about Canri.

Alongside the language lessons, there'd been lectures on protocol and manners, overviews of the Canri hierarchy, and instructions on the differences between Canri culture and their own. He could still hear Stanin droning on, even though their last lesson had ended hours ago.

"Always bow your head when someone enters the reception room. Only your head, mind. You may be serving as a junior official, but you're still of the Blood. Meet their eyes, but do not stare at them. When you're serving food or drink, look over their shoulder, not directly at their faces. If they say something shocking or surprising, do not react. If they realise you understand what is being said, your cover will be ruined."

Jared slid his legs over the side of the bed and sat up.

"Not that you'll understand much to start with. We've barely scratched the surface of their language. That will change once we're in Canri. Nothing speeds up learning a new language better than being surrounded by its native speakers. In two or three months, when the real negotiations begin, you should be reasonably fluent."

"Two or three months?"

"These are very sensitive negotiations. There is much to be gained here if everything goes well. Both parties will take their time getting to know each other before they risk anything. It is not unusual for these things to take several years."

Jared stood and stretched, pushing Stanin's words from his mind. He didn't want to think about it anymore. What he wanted was a hot, soothing bath.

That's assuming Canri has baths.

He shrugged. He would find out soon enough. For now, however, he'd make do with a bucket of cold water and a cloth.

A laundry would be nice, too.

He glanced at the clothes he'd laid out the night before and sighed. Saltwater had made the fabric of his undershirt coarse, myriad creases gave his shirt the appearance of a dish rag, and his tunic had a hole in it where it had snagged on a nail. Thankfully, his jacket would hide most of the damage, but still, it didn't give the best first impression. It'd be a relief when he regained access to the rest of his clothes.

The ship had arrived in Canri sometime during the night. Not that he'd seen anything of the city yet. As soon as the lookout had called sight of land, the captain had ordered the passengers to return to their cabins to give the crew room to work. An hour or so later, a deckhand had knocked on his cabin door and informed him someone would ring the ship's bell when it was safe for him to come back on deck. He had accepted the news with a nod. What other choice did he have?

He finished dressing, stuffed his scattered belongings into his saddlebags, and sat on his bunk to wait.

Jared's first sight of Canri was not a memorable one. *The Hunter* had docked in a small, semi-circular cove surrounded by sandstone cliffs. Half-a-dozen ropes secured her to a pair of jetties barely two-thirds her length. A single building—a small wooden hut—sat at the far end of the shingle beach. Only one man came to greet them, and when Jared came on deck, he was already talking to Ambassador Salem and Alsam Azier. Jared tried to get a look at him, but the mass of people and horses crowding the deck acted like a living screen, obstructing his view. He adjusted his saddlebags on his shoulder, scanned the crowd, spotted Stanin in the middle of the chaos, and walked over to him. "Is there anything I can do?"

Stanin scowled, ran his finger down the list he held, tapped it, and nodded. "Collect your horse from the stables and get in line."

"There's a line?"

Stanin pointed at the ramp leading onto the jetty.

"Thank you."

Jared worked his way across the deck to the stables. Sherna stood in her stall, saddled and swishing her tail in irritation. She greeted him with a whinny and lipped his hand.

He gave her nose an affectionate rub. "Sorry, girl. No apples today."

She snorted.

He unhooked her reins and led her outside. A young sailor stationed at the stable entrance pointed him towards the growing queue of horses and riders winding across the deck like a chain of ants.

Jared nodded his thanks and guided Sherna to the back of the line.

She sidestepped and tossed her head.

He patted her neck and whispered to her as they waited. Ahead of them, those at the front of the line snaked forward. He tightened his grip on the reins and readjusted his saddlebags once more.

The delegation marched off *The Hunter* in single file, stepping down the ramp to the jetty, across the beach, past the hut, and onto a narrow, rocky path. It led inland, winding up the side of the cliff at a steep angle, forcing the party to slow, to pick each step with care to avoid catching a foot or hoof on the rubble-strewn rock.

Three-quarters of the way up, the path levelled, the cliff giving way to a gently sloping hillside. Rock and rubble turned to short, scraggly grass and sun-baked earth. Up ahead, the Canri guide and the leaders of the delegation waited for the rest of the group to catch up.

Jared led Sherna towards them, crested the top of the hill, and stared.

The land fell away before him, the sudden drop revealing the outer walls of Canri not far from its base. They formed a horseshoe, with the rounded end facing the hill, and the two arms curving forwards before plunging into a vast lake. At their narrowest point, their ends had to be at least a mile apart.

Someone broke from the tail-end of the procession to join him. "Impressive, isn't it?" Armon asked.

Jared nodded, his gaze fixed on the city below. Whilst the sheer scale of Canri's walls had stilled him to silence, the layout of the city within left him breathless. There wasn't a single narrow, winding street or tall, cramped building in sight. Long, straight roads spread across the city like veins in a leaf, each one wide enough for two wagons to pass each other with ease. Hundreds of narrower streets sprouted from those veins, criss-crossing the city in gentle curves. And though they lacked the breadth of the main thoroughfares, a horse and cart could pass through with room to spare.

More striking still were the colours; reds and oranges, greens, purples, and blues. Every road and street cut a vivid slash through the city. Large, open squares punctuated the streets, adding their own bright splash to the mix. Walls, streets, and squares worked together to form an irregular pattern, its meaning tickling the back of his mind but remaining out of reach.

"It's a message to their gods," Armon said. "A reflection of their faith. No mere mortal can understand it, especially not foreigners like ourselves."

"Not even the people who designed it?"

"But of course. But its designers were not mere mortals, they were Vortai. Men hand-picked by their gods to serve as messengers to the people."

"Like godsmen?"

"In a way. But Vortai are held in much higher esteem. When a Vortai speaks, the entire world listens."

"The entire world? I doubt most of the world even knows they exist."

Armon chuckled. "I'll leave the philosophical discussion to those more suited to the task. I'm just an ignorant patrolman, after all. Now come, before we're left behind."

Jared tore his gaze away from the city. Beside him, Sherna grazed at the short, scraggly grass. Ahead, the majority of the delegation had already started on the long descent. He clucked his tongue, gave Sherna's reins a gentle tug, and led her forward, falling into line behind Armon.

The descent proved easier than the ascent, with the path less steep, and the compacted earth surer underfoot. Even so, he didn't look up again until they reached the hill's foot.

Tilting his head back, he felt like a mouse in the wall's shadow. Four grown men could have stood one atop the other and still failed to reach its top. And the absence of a single crack or seam would make it impossible to climb. It appeared to have been carved out of a single length of solid rock, then smoothed and polished by a thousand hands until it glistened like fine-cut white opal under the rising sun.

His toe caught in a divot. He stumbled, his face warming when Armon chuckled. The imperfections in the stone became evident as they neared the wall. Veins of blue and black mottled its surface, but even they didn't reveal a single seam. Nor was it completely flat. Its top curved outward to form a concave overhang, suspended from which—

Prehen Damis preserve me...

—suspended from which were several cages, each one occupied by a man.

'Two men, one woman, and a child.'

The party stopped within spitting distance of the wall, granting Jared his first glimpse of their guide. He stood an inch taller than Salem's biggest guard, though he lacked the other's girth. Long, light brown hair framed an angular, forest-green face, heavy brows, narrow eyes, and thin, bloodless lips. A loose-fitting tunic and trousers, decorated with a colourful, abstract pattern similar to the one created by Canri's streets, shrouded his lean frame.

"Green skin?" Jared whispered, dipping his head to mask his words from everyone but Armon. "I'd heard the stories, but I thought people meant their skin was tinted like yours, not, well, actually *green* green."

Armon snorted and shook his head, his smile threatening to break into a grin. The last of the travellers drew up behind them, and their guide began to speak, his deep voice pitched to carry to the whole group.

"He welcomes us to the mighty city of Canri," Armon whispered, "the heart of the great Canri Empire. He hopes we will find a warm welcome within her walls. Accommodation has been prepared for us within the foreign district, and a feast will be held in our honour tonight. He invites all of us to attend."

The guide stopped speaking, and Salem responded in Canri.

Armon paused to listen, then smiled. "The ambassador thanks our guide for the warm welcome and hopes our two nations may become good friends. He also asks about the people in the cages above."

Jared looked up at the cages. Misery lined the occupants' slack faces, their dull gazes staring straight ahead. Only the child seemed interested in their arrival as he pressed his forehead against the bars to peer down at them.

Armon continued his translation. "Those in the cages are criminals the magistra has chosen to serve as examples. The two men were caught brawling in public after drinking during the daylight hours. The boy is a thief. The woman..." Armon turned to look Jared in the eye. "The woman practised prostitution without a licence. I suspect she's been placed there as a warning for you."

Jared swallowed and looked away, a heavy weight settling in the pit of his stomach. "What will happen to them?"

Armon shrugged. "He didn't say."

The welcome over, the guide lowered his voice and spoke directly to Salem. The ambassador half-turned, pointed to Jared, and waved him forward. "Our hosts wish to speak with you before you enter the city. Stanin will take your horse and make sure she is looked after. I will come with you, to translate."

"Sir." Jared let Stanin take Sherna's reins.

The guide said something in rapid Canri, noted Jared's confusion, and added, "Follow. Please." He led them the short distance to the base of the wall and through a small gateway. It led to a stone-lined tunnel with a curved roof. Narrow slits and dark holes lined the walls and ceiling.

The back of Jared's neck prickled. He glanced up and down the length of the tunnel but saw no-one besides Salem and their guide.

The guide stopped halfway along the tunnel and knocked on a door partially hidden in shadow. He waited for a reply, pushed the door open, and waved Jared and Salem through.

A second man waited inside. He shared the guide's angular face and narrow eyes, but his lips were fuller and his hair darker. He stood in front of a small table—the only piece of furniture in the sombre room—with his hands clasped in front of him and his face set in an expression Jared couldn't read. He wore a strange, padded tunic made up of hundreds of tiny coloured squares, each fitted together to form a pattern as complex and confusing as a chameleon's scales. The tunic reached his knees and was belted around his waist. Simple, leather-soled sandals covered his feet.

He stepped forward and said something in Canri. Jared thought he caught the words for "welcome" and "thank you".

Salem's reply proved easier to follow. "Hur kan jag hjälpa dig?"—*"How may I help you?"*

The man spoke again, his rapid speech almost musical in the way it rose and fell.

Salem held up a hand to stop him. "Kan du prata långsammare tack?"—*"Can you speak more slowly please?"*

The man nodded. "Förstås. Tyvärr."—*"Of course. Sorry."* He continued, slowing enough for each word to be distinguished from the others, though most remained indecipherable.

Salem watched him, nodding each time he paused to show he understood. When the man finished, Salem turned to Jared. "Our Canri friends have been checking into our backgrounds. Your presence in our party is causing some concern. You have a rather... unwholesome... reputation. It has also been claimed that you work as a prostitute—"

"That's prepost—"

"Don't interrupt." Salem paused, said something to their host, waited for his reply, then nodded. "They are not accustomed to men selling their flesh for money, but they are willing to admit you to the city if you agree to certain conditions."

Salem's words snapped around Jared like an iron-barred trap. The room suddenly felt too small, the walls too close, the air thick and stale. He edged towards the door. "What conditions?"

"That you register yourself as a prostitute, that any work you do be recorded in a log, and that you pay all appropriate taxes on the first day of each month."

Damn you, Armon. He reached for the door handle.

Salem side-stepped to block his path. "This is not optional. Either you register, or you do not enter."

Jared lowered his gaze to meet Salem's uncompromising stare. "Tell him I'm not a prostitute. Tell him I'm a courier. That the rumours are lies." He glanced at the Canri official, smiled in response to the man's bemused expression, and turned back. "Well?"

"I will not."

"You have to."

"This is not a matter for protest." Salem bit the ends off every word. "We have just arrived. Cooperating now will help our future negotiations."

"I will not—"

"Then you will return to Lady Morgain."

Jared curled his toes, digging them into the soles of his boots. Return to Morgain in disgrace? Enjoy a seat in his 'special chair' as a reward? Put himself through all of that without uncovering a jot of information to give to Ryal for his trouble? He'd be better off jumping from the nearest cliff. "Fine." He dropped his hand and stepped back. "Tell him I'll do it."

"I thought you would." Salem turned back to the waiting man and spoke to him in Canri.

The man pointed to a sheet of paper on the table then waved at Jared.

Salem motioned towards the table. "You need to sign the registration paper. It explains that you may only work in the licenced brothels, that ten per cent of your earnings must be paid to your place of work, and that a further twenty per cent is to be paid in tax. All work is to be recorded in the logbook provided, and you must wear the earring supplied whenever you are seeking a client."

"This is ridiculous." Jared accepted the pen their host held up and signed next to the 'X' at the bottom of the paper. The man nodded and said something else. Jared looked over his shoulder at Salem. "Now what?"

"There is a fee to pay. Two quarts in gold."

"Tell me you're joking."

"Just pay him."

Jared scowled, pulled out his money pouch, picked out two octains, and handed them over.

The man bit on one of the coins, examined its edge, and nodded. He then retrieved a set of weighing scales from beneath the table, dropped two small weights in one dish, and the octains in the other. They failed to balance. The man held up a single finger and said, "Ett."

Jared shook his head.

"Ett!" the man repeated. He picked up one of the octains and waved it.

Jared handed over a third octain and watched as the man added it to the scales. They tipped, the dish holding the octains dropping like a skewered pigeon to thunk against the base. The man retrieved the coins and tucked them into his tunic, picked up a red candle, dribbled a small pool of wax onto the paper Jared had signed, and pressed a circular seal into the puddle. He handed the paper to Jared, speaking to Salem as he did.

Jared waited for Salem to translate.

"Do not lose your license. It will cost another two quarts to replace. If a guard thinks you're engaged in improper behaviour, he may request to see it. If you don't have it on you, you will be fined a gold quart and ordered to report to a magistra. If you fail to report, or report without your licence, you may be jailed… or worse."

'Such a warm welcome. Aren't you glad you came?'

Jared resisted the urge to laugh.

The man reached into his tunic and produced a small, leather-bound book and an earring. He handed them to Jared.

"Thank you." *Prehen Damis take your soul.*

Salem plucked the book from Jared's hand and added his own thanks to Jared's.

Jared glared at him. "I don't need a pimp."

"And I don't need to be one. I'm keeping the book to ensure you don't do anything stupid." Salem looked away from Jared, cutting off further protest, and addressed their host in Canri.

The man nodded several times and pointed to the door.

"It's time to go," Salem said. He motioned for Jared to precede him. "Our guide is waiting outside, and I do not wish to be late."

Their guide led them along the tunnel at a pace just shy of a run, not slowing when they emerged onto a major thoroughfare. The street ran arrow-straight, passing high sandstone walls set with a series of ornate, black, iron gates. Fine gravel coated the road; small white stones with clear flecks sparkling in the sunlight. There were no separate walkways, no gutters or open sewers, no ruts from wagon wheels or carriages. There was, in fact, not a single piece of litter or spot of dirt for the entire length of the street.

Jared would have stopped to confirm his impressions, but at the fifth set of gates, their guide led them off the road and into a large open courtyard. He marched across the courtyard, past a long, narrow building on their left, to a single storey mansion at the rear of the compound.

Stanin met them in front of the massive double doors, nodded to Salem, and thanked the guide.

The guide dipped his head, said something Jared didn't hear, and left.

"Settled in already?" Salem asked.

"Hardly." Stanin gestured for them to step inside. "Malkem and his men are taking the horses and slaves to the stables. I've sent most of the servants back to unload the cargo. Rooms have been assigned..." Stanin switched his gaze to Jared. "Speaking of which." He snapped his fingers, and one of the delegation's servants came running. "Show envoy up-Arran to his room."

The servant nodded and gestured for Jared to follow.

He set a brisk pace, the drum of his footsteps drowning out the rest of Stanin's report. They walked to the end of the corridor and turned left into a second as broad and high-ceilinged as the first. Plain, pale-wood doors lined the right-hand wall, whilst alcoves housing smooth-lined marble pedestals topped with potted plants injected some colour on the other side. Off-white light emanated from a dozen translucent globes suspended from the ceiling like trapped, miniature moons. Jared stopped to examine one but failed to discern the source of the strange light. No flames flickered within the globes, and no pipes or tubing ran along the ceiling to supply them with oil.

The servant's footsteps fell silent. Jared abandoned his inspection and raced to catch up.

The servant waited for him outside a room two-thirds of the way up the corridor, one of a handful whose doors stood open. He extended his hand towards it. "Your room, sir."

"Thank you." Jared slipped the servant a coin and stepped inside.

The room appeared reasonable enough, with rough, pale-yellow stone walls, ceiling, and floor. Though unfurnished, it had space to fit a wardrobe and a small dresser or desk alongside the bed.

The bed?

He frowned at the raised stone platform running the length of the room. A bolster pillow sat at its far end, with an old brown blanket heaped nearby. He dropped his saddlebags beside it and sighed.

The room had one window, small and rectangular, cut into the stone above head height. He rose to his tiptoes, craned his neck, and managed to see outside. A strip of pale blue sky sat atop a wider band of bland, white wall.

There was no glass in the window or shutters on the wall, just a thin strip of wood set into the underside of the opening, about two inches back from the edge. He compressed his lips for a moment, reached up, and gave it an experimental tug. A wooden panel slid down, blocking out the light. At least he'd be able to shut out the elements if he needed to. He pushed the panel back up, dropped to his heels, and surveyed the room again.

It wasn't the best room he'd ever stayed in. Probably not the worst.

He picked up the blanket and rubbed it between his fingers. Thin, threadbare, but clean. He dropped it and perched on the edge of the bed, as lost as a moth caught in the middle of a butterfly swarm. He'd spent most of his life travelling; visiting new towns, meeting new people. But there'd always been a sense of familiarity before; a shared language, shared beliefs, shared laws. Accents varied, and styles changed, but at its heart every town felt the same. But Canri?

Canri felt like a mantis disguised as a flower to lure in its prey.

His first view of the city, with its wealth of colour and order, had spoken to his soul. There'd been a message there, hidden just out of reach. But it wasn't meant for him, it was meant for gods; gods he'd never heard of and didn't understand. It had drawn him in like honey, and then the bee had stung.

He reached into his pocket and pulled out the licence he'd signed. He could pick out a few words—'the', 'and', and 'agree'—but he'd have to trust Salem had told him the truth about the rest. He tucked the paper away and pulled out the earring. Even it seemed alien to him. It didn't have a post or hook, but a curved clasp shaped to fit the top of the ear. The setting looked like silver, with six arching claws clutching small, pink stones. He ran his finger across their surfaces. The facets were smooth; the edges sharp. He lifted the earring to his ear and clipped it in place.

'If Elise could see you now…'

He removed the earring and put it away.

He'd never heard of a town registering prostitutes before. Or seen people locked in cages suspended from a city wall. *And for what? Fighting, thieving, and whoring? It isn't right.*

'It was a message. A warning to behave.'

They could have just said—

'Would you be thinking about it now if they had?'

There's more to it than that. The streets are too clean. Too quiet.

'Streets can't be clean now?'

"Of course they can. But there's always some rubbish. Some dirt. Pure white stones without a single mark on them? It's not natural." He closed his mouth, suddenly aware he'd spoken out loud, dropped his head into his hands, and rubbed his hair.

A soft knock sounded on the door.

He looked up.

Stanin watched him from the doorway, eyes narrowed.

'Keep this up, and you'll have everyone convinced you're mad.'

Keep this up, and I might believe they're right. He summoned his most innocent smile. "Yes?"

"I'm assigning furniture to rooms. Do you have any specific requests?"

"Uh…" *Furniture. Right.* "I need a dresser. And a mirror. A big one, if possible."

Stanin lifted the book he'd held at his side and made a note in it. "Dresser and mirror. Anything else?"

"A large bed with a feather mattress and silk sheets?"

Stanin chuckled and shook his head. "I'll put you down for extra bedding. You look like a man who'll appreciate an extra-large pile of straw." He placed his pencil in the spine of the book and snapped it closed. "The patrol leader wants to see you. He's waiting in the baths. Follow this corridor to the end, go left at the corner, and take the first door on your right. Big wooden one. You can't miss it."

So Canri did have baths. Something positive at last. "Anything else I should know?"

"Take your clothes off before you go. It's considered rude to arrive fully dressed." Stanin pulled something from behind his back and threw it at Jared's head.

Jared jerked his arm up and caught it just before it hit his face. A towel. He lowered it.

Stanin was gone.

৶৩

Jared pushed the door to the baths open with one hand whilst holding his towel in place with the other. Heat and steam washed over him, coating his skin in a thin layer of moisture. He stepped inside and closed the door, buying himself a moment to take in his surroundings.

Blue-grey marble covered the floor and walls of a bathing room twice the size of any he'd seen back home. Benches lined all four walls, with small cubbyholes underneath for storing towels. Two sunken baths dominated the room, each one large enough for ten men or more. The steam came from the left-hand one, rising from the water's surface.

Armon lounged in the hot bath, his legs stretched out in front of him and his head resting against its rim. He cracked one eye open and smiled. "Coming in?"

"I'm not sure it would be appropriate."

"Oh, come now." Armon opened his other eye and cocked his head. "You can't be a prude. You've probably slept with more women than most men have met."

"You're not a woman."

"True. I'm also not trying to sleep with you. Get in, before I get a crick in my neck."

Jared pulled his towel free from his waist, tucked it into the nearest cubbyhole, and lowered himself into the bath. The heat seeped deep into his skin, relaxing muscles and soothing aches with the efficiency of a masseuse. He sank until the water tickled the underside of his chin and let out an appreciative sigh.

"Feels good, doesn't it?"

Jared nodded. He closed his eyes and let the warm water carry away his pain. Let himself forget, imagining, for a moment, that the last two months had never happened.

Then Armon spoke. "What did the Canri want with you?"

Jared huffed out a breath. "Apparently, the rumours you spread arrived here before us. They insisted I register as a prostitute before they let me through the gate."

Armon raised an eyebrow. "So soon? I'd expected them to take a week or two to get here." His eyes went out of focus, and he gazed into the distance for a moment, blinked, and shook his head. "They gave you a licence?"

"Sold me a licence. Yes."

"You could have some fun with it."

Jared stared, open mouthed. "What?"

"Don't pretend you haven't thought about it. You get to have sex *and* get paid for it."

"I am not—"

"A whore? So you keep saying. But you're wrong." Armon leant forward, his gaze intent. "All those women you've slept with... did none of them give you gifts? Buy you clothes or jewellery? Promise you more if you came back?"

Jared swallowed and clenched his fists. "It wasn't like that."

"No?"

"I cared for them."

"You cared for what they could give you."

Jared's denial was halfway out his mouth before Armon finished speaking. He clamped his teeth together and looked away; looked inwards, examining the words he'd suppressed. *The truth, Jared. A little truth won't hurt.* "I cared for the pleasure we shared. The conversation. The company."

"And the gifts?"

Jared looked up, studying the reflection of himself mirrored in Armon's eyes, reading the selfishness others must see in him. The vanity.

The faithlessness. It didn't make for a pleasant sight. "And the gifts," he agreed.

"But you refuse to have sex for money?"

"I will not betray Elise."

Armon's laughter filled the room. "It's a little late for that."

"Perhaps. Or perhaps I can still make amends."

"Why bother? It's obvious you don't love her."

"Don't love her? You think—" Jared thumped the surface of the water, sending droplets flying everywhere. "How dare you? You have no idea how I feel. None!"

Armon sat back, his cruel, mocking grin blossoming on his lips. "Then why are you so angry?"

'It's a good question, Jared.'

Piss off.

"I don't have to listen to this." Jared tucked his feet beneath him and stood.

"Oh, sit down. What are you going to do? Go back to your room and mope?"

He hesitated, one foot on the floor, the other still in the bath. "It beats listening to your drivel."

Armon chuckled. "Why do you never speak of her? A month of travelling, and this is the first time her name has passed your lips."

Jared dropped his foot back into the bath and sat. "You were going to kill her."

"You were going to let me."

Silence. Jared stared at Armon, searching his face for some clue, some hint as to where he was going. Armon's mocking grin gave him nothing. *Only one way to find out, then.* "I was bluffing."

"Perhaps." Armon stretched his hands above his head and rolled his shoulders. "But we both know where you were headed that morning." He stretched his arms to the sides, gave them a shake, and lowered them to rest along the edges of the bath. "And it wasn't Elise's bed."

Jared continued to stare.

"The morning of your arrest," Armon clarified.

Jared clenched his teeth so tight his jaw spasmed. "I had to—"

"No. You did not have to, you chose to. Why didn't you go to Elise the moment you got back? Why wait until after you'd seen Morgain?"

"I had messages—"

"That could have waited or been delivered by another's hand. You had time during the night to visit Elise if you'd really wanted to."

So why? He had no answer, or none he could justify, not even to himself. He'd told himself he needed to end his relationship with Morgain, that he wanted it over before he committed himself to Elise, but... had he? Truly?

"Who did you dress up for that morning?" Armon asked, firing his words at Jared like a hunter shooting a sling. "Who did you seek to impress with your silks and jewels? Who...?" He paused, saying nothing more until Jared looked at him. "Who did you dream of during those long, lonely nights on the road? Whose face did you see when you slept with one of your conquests?" Another pause, this one longer. Jared opened his mouth, but Armon spoke over him. "I notice the necklace you commissioned had no name engraved on it. Did you not know how to spell 'Elise'? Or did you have it made for someone else?"

Jared shook his head.

"Speak her name. Tell me who you love."

"Elise." It came out as a whisper; a word barely formed.

Armon's grin lost its mocking tilt; faded to a sympathetic smile. "Try 'Morgain', Jared. Morgain al-Rafael."

No. Jared drew breath to say the word but couldn't force it past his lips. He had not... did not...

"She loved you too, you know."

"No." The word came out as a croak, the 'o' sticking in his throat.

"That's why she hates you so much." Armon's smile vanished. "That's why your behaviour here is completely irrelevant."

"Meaning?"

"Meaning, even if you're perfectly chaste and don't even glance at another woman whilst we're in Canri, all you'll be doing is buying a little time. Morgain wants revenge. She wants to hurt you like you've hurt her. Once we go back, she'll watch you like a hawk. Smile at a woman the wrong way, and she'll punish you. Thank a female servant for bringing you food, and she'll punish you. Fail to thank the same servant, and she'll double the punishment. Every moment you're alive pains her. Every breath you take is a reminder of your betrayal. Once you're back at her side, you won't be able to piss without asking for permission."

Jared pulled his knees up to his chest and wrapped his arms around his legs. "Why tell me this now?"

"Because I owe you. I thought you were a naïve, self-centred wastrel, and I was wrong. That's not to say you're not a shallow, thoughtless fool, but there's more to you than I assumed. You've proved stronger and more resilient than I expected, and for that you've earned a degree of my respect. Consider this my payment."

"By threatening me?"

"By telling you the truth. And by making a promise. Flirt, or kiss, or sleep with as many women as you like whilst you're here. I won't report it to Morgain. My word on it."

Jared dug his fingernails into his arms to keep from shaking and reran Armon's words through his mind.

Why offer me this now? What does he stand to gain by giving up his hard-won control? Is he trying to bribe me? Buy my cooperation? My trust?

No. If he'd wanted that, he'd have done it from the start. He wasn't the sort of man to give something unless he gained at least as much in return. *Give self-defence lessons and gain a man who can look after himself. Give a degree of freedom and… what?* He replayed the conversation and thought he understood. "Your promise is meaningless."

Armon frowned. "You doubt my word?"

"No. But you don't need to report anything. Salem will do it for you."

Armon recoiled, and his finger drummed the marble, once.

"You didn't know?" Jared forced himself to release his arms and relax. "Salem spoke to me on *The Hunter*. Told me Morgain had asked him to watch me. She gave him permission to do whatever he felt necessary to keep me under control. He took the logbook, too. I couldn't use my licence if I wanted to."

"That… complicates things." Armon resumed his tapping, and his gaze turned inwards, his lips pursing in thought. The speed of his tapping increased, going from the regular tip-tap of a weary peddler to the drumbeat of a galloping charger. He slammed his hand down, the slap of flesh on marble echoing in the sudden silence. "Ask me for something else."

"What?"

"I rescind my promise. Ask me for something else." He held up a hand before Jared could respond. "Think carefully. I'll only consider your first request, and if I think it will endanger the mission, I'll refuse it."

Jared opened his mouth, hesitated, and closed it again. He took a deep breath, closed his eyes, and plunged his head beneath the surface.

'Ask him for a bigger room.'

Jared shook his head, pushing the stray thought away. He needed to be sensible about this.

'A pay rise?'

No. This isn't the time to be frivolous.

'Then make him promise not to harm Elise.'

Jared let out some breath, sending a stream of bubbles up to the surface. It was tempting, but he had no reason to trust Armon to keep his word.

'Then why ask for anything?'

Because there's no reason not to trust his word.

He tucked his legs beneath him and rose to a crouch. He knew what he wanted to ask for, he just didn't know if he should.

'Coward.'

He straightened, opened his eyes, and shook his head, spraying droplets of water everywhere. Armon still lounged in the opposite corner, waiting for his response. He blinked several times, clearing the remaining water from his eyes. "Your hair's changed colour."

Armon shrugged. "It's wet."

"It's shorter, too."

Armon chuckled and rewarded the observation with a mocking grin. "Shorter? Last time you saw my real hair, I had stubble."

"You've been wearing a wig?"

Armon nodded. "Malkem's not known for his stubble. Now make your request. I doubt we'll have this place to ourselves much longer."

"Help me escape."

Armon sputtered, his burst of laughter cut-off half formed. "Excuse me?"

"Once the mission is complete, and you have whatever it is you came here for, help me to escape."

"You're serious?"

"You said it yourself. It doesn't matter what I do here, Morgain is going to do whatever she pleases to me when we return. Why should I cooperate with you at all if that's all I have to look forward to?"

"Because."

"Because what? You'll kill me? What makes you think I care?"

Armon's eyes narrowed. "Don't pretend you're ready to die. And don't think for one second I cannot hurt you. I know more ways than you can think of to force you to obey, and not one of them will leave a mark."

"So I obey now and look forward to being tortured later? Not much of an incentive, is it?"

Armon's fingers began to tap. "You have no idea what you're asking me to do."

"I thought it was simple myself. I spy on the Canri for you. You let me go free."

"I'll consider it."

"And I'll—"

"Enough! You're in no position to bargain. You may think you can refuse to obey me, but you are very, very wrong." Armon stood and took several steps forward. "I have said I will consider your request. Now let it go, or I'll kick you in the balls so hard you'll be pissing blood for a week."

Jared glanced down, swallowed, and looked away.

Armon climbed out of the bath and padded over to one of the benches.

"Are you at least going to tell me what I'm supposed to be listening for?"

Armon reached into a cubbyhole, pulled out a bar of soap, and brought it back to the bath. "No."

"And if I miss something important because you refuse to tell me?"

Armon wet the soap and began to wash. "You're much more likely to miss something if I do tell you than if I don't. I need you to report everything, not just the things you think might be important."

"Then tell me what your mission is. Don't I at least deserve to know that?"

Armon threw the soap at Jared. "No."

Jared snatched at the soap, dropped it, snatched at it again, and snared it before it hit the water. "I could watch Salem for you."

Armon walked between the two baths. "Stanin is already watching him."

"Stanin didn't know Salem had been ordered to watch me. Or he knew and didn't consider the information important enough to pass on."

Armon pressed a small metal disc into the floor with his toe, and something in the wall clunked. Water cascaded from a series of tiny holes in the ceiling, washing over him like a miniature waterfall. "If you're caught, I won't protect you."

"I wouldn't expect you to."

Armon released the disc, slipped into the second bath, and shivered. "Then we have a deal."

❧

Jared returned to his assigned room to find it furnished. His clothes chest sat in the far corner with his saddlebags dumped on top. A dresser—an old, dark wood affair with battered sides and a stained top—had been set against the wall opposite the bed. A mirror sat on top of it, its glass marred by several scratches, and the silver backing showing signs of wear. Nothing fancy, but it would serve.

'Not what you're used to though, is it?'

He pushed the room door closed, pulled off his towel, and tossed it on the bed. A glance to the side revealed his reflection in the mirror. He sighed. The man glancing back at him had bags under his eyes, frown lines across his brow, and a month's worth of scraggly beard covering half his face like moss clinging to age-cracked bark. The beard would be easy to fix, the rest, not so much.

One thing at a time.

He opened the clothes chest, retrieved his jewel box, placed it on the dresser, and opened it. His fingers trembled, his mouth growing dry. Elise's locket lay in the top of the box, the inset ruby winking at him.

"You don't love her," Armon's voice echoed inside his mind.

He picked up the locket. It felt more like a boulder in his palm, a tiny vessel filled with all the hurt and heartache he'd caused. He flipped it over and rubbed the back with his thumb. It felt cold and lifeless, the inscription rough against his skin.

"Did you not know how to spell 'Elise'?"

Pain stabbed his fingers then shot up his arm. Hot, sticky blood ran down his hand. He stared at his clenched fist, seeing nothing.

"Try 'Morgain', Jared. Morgain al-Rafael."

He shook his head. "You're wrong."

'Then why spend fifteen gold octains on a shirt you chose to impress her?'

He blinked. *When did I close my hand?*

He forced his fingers to uncurl, wincing when he discovered the four bloody, nail-shaped cuts in his palm. He wiped the locket clean and placed it to one side. Armon had been trying to confuse him. *Why?* He couldn't say. But it wasn't going to work. Yes, he had gone to Morgain first, but it was Elise he loved.

'Do you? Really?'

He sighed and closed his eyes, squelching each thought as it threatened to rise, blotting out Armon's accusations and his own doubts.

What he felt for Morgain and Elise were two different things. He'd enjoyed his time with Morgain, enjoyed the company and intimacy. But when he'd met Elise, he'd discovered something deeper and more fulfilling. With Morgain, conversation was like a starter, an appetite wetter eaten before the main meal. But with Elise, a few exchanged words, a look, or a touch could be an entire meal by itself. They didn't need sex to be intimate, didn't need to speak to understand how the other felt. Yes, he'd loved his time with Morgain, but he loved Elise far more.

He opened his eyes, picked his razor out of his jewel box, turned to the mirror—

—and swayed as the blood drained from his face. The razor slipped from slack fingers and hit the dresser with a bang. He took a step backwards, caught his heel, tripped, and fell. For a moment, he sat where he'd landed, his mind blank. Then he laughed.

"Fool." He clambered back to his feet. "It was just a trick of the light." He forced himself to look in the mirror again. His own reflection looked out at him. "See. Just me."

But for a split second, it hadn't been. He'd looked in the mirror and seen someone else. The face had been the same—same beard, same hair, same skin—but the eyes had been wild, almost crazy; the lips pale and thin. And the man had been grinning a cruel, malicious grin.

"Just the light," Jared repeated, reassuring himself. Even so, long minutes passed before his hands stopped shaking enough to allow him to shave.

Armon strode through the embassy's barracks, nodded to Winton and Melf—the two members of the patrol he'd assigned to unload the patrolmen's belongings—and pushed open the door to his private chamber. A creak from within brought him to full alert. He tucked his right hand behind his back, slipped inside, and let the door close behind him. His hand was halfway to the sword he'd propped up beside the door before he recognised his uninvited guest. Tessa reclined on the bed, nibbling at a grape. He glanced from the bed to the half-sized window and shook his head. "What if I'd been someone else?"

"Then you'd have entered and found the room empty. I recognised your footsteps."

"My footsteps?" Armon chuckled and kicked off his sandals. "You…" He shoved the door to ensure it was latched, crossed the room in three quick strides, and sat on the bed. "I've missed you."

"Missed me?" Tessa turned onto her side, propped herself up on an elbow, and ran her hand down his side. "You've spoken to me every day."

"No." He leant into her touch, shivering at the tingles it raised in his skin. "I've spoken to Lady Zandra every day. It's not the same."

"Ah. So it's my body you've missed?"

"Hardly." He turned towards her, lifted his knee onto the bed, and draped his arm across her waist. The soft mattress gave under their weight, pushing them together. "I've missed your witty conversation, your wonderful charm, and"—he reached for the bowl resting on the pillows—"your grapes."

Tessa laughed and slapped his hand away. "Dirty beggar."

"I don't beg."

"No?"

"No."

"Never?"

"Never."

"A pity. I like a man who knows how to beg."

"I can imagine." Armon shifted his voice into a higher pitch. "Please, miss. Please don't kill me. I di'n't mean to beat the boy so bad. Honest, miss. I di'n't mean t' kill 'im. I beg—"

Tessa silenced him with a breath-stealing kiss.

"Mrmm," he mumbled against her lips.

She pulled away. "Pardon?"

"More."

"Not until you tell me where you've been."

"Isn't it obvious?" Armon hooked a thumb under the towel at his waist and wiggled it.

"For over an hour?"

"I was talking to Jared." He pulled his arms back and stared at his hands.

Tessa set the bowl of grapes on the floor and wriggled backwards to sit on the pillows. She tucked a finger under his chin and pushed his head up. "What happened?"

"Morgain's been keeping things from me." He snagged her finger and pulled it down. "She's got Salem watching Jared to make sure he behaves." He trapped her finger in his hand and stroked it with his thumb. "I can't help thinking she doesn't trust me." A sudden itch jabbed his wrist. He snatched his hand back and scratched.

Tessa curled her fingers around his, stopping him. "It sounds like a reasonable precaution. You can't watch Jared every minute of the day, and Morgain had to tell Salem something to get him to agree to bring Jared along."

"I suppose." Armon shrugged then looked away. "She still should have told me..." The itch intensified, crawling under his skin from his wrist to his elbow.

Tessa leant sideways, her head tilted to one side.

He turned away to avoid her gaze.

She poked him in the sternum. "What else?"

He squeezed her fingers, took a deep breath, and lifted his head. "Jared asked me to help him escape."

"And...?"

"And I said I'd think about it." He watched her—studied her eyes, her expression—for signs of disapproval, but saw only patience and understanding. A laugh tickled the back of his throat, unwelcome and uninvited. He swallowed it down. "I don't even know why I said it. I would never betray Morgain."

"Guilt, perhaps?"

Armon snorted.

"Jealousy, then."

He rocked back and dropped her hand. "What?"

"You can't stand the thought of him, or anyone else, being with her. You're more protective of her than most daughters' fathers. If you help him escape, you'll never have to see them together again."

He started to shake his head, but the truth resonated too strongly for denial. He stood, turned his back, and tucked his hands into his elbows to keep from scratching. "Tess..."

"I forgive you." Her reply was a whisper, barely audible over his own heavy breath.

He jerked around, noted her soft smile, the slight droop in her brow, and his chest tightened, crushing the air from his lungs. "You do?"

Her smile widened, the lines in her brow smoothing, though a tightness still pulled at the corners of her eyes. "I do."

He dropped onto the bed and wrapped her tight in his arms. "I don't deserve you." He kissed her on her forehead, her cheek, her neck. "I never deserved you." He kissed the underside of her jaw, her chin, her soft, moist lips.

She ran one hand through his hair, the other down his back.

He rocked forward and abandoned himself to her love.

❧

Jared sat cross-legged on his bed, back pressed to the wall and brow furrowed in concentration. The Canri language book lay open on his lap. Bright afternoon sunlight flooded through the small window above his head, lighting the room with the vibrancy of a radiant stream. It hadn't taken him long to appreciate the purpose of his little window. Anything bigger and he'd suffocate in the heavy heat, cooked like a fish stranded on the beach by the sea's retreat.

His clothes for the evening's feast lay neatly folded at his side. A few pieces of jewellery—a pair of diamond stud earrings and a simple signet ring—waited for him atop his dresser. A month's worth of beard covered the bottom of the waste bin, alongside several clumps of overlong hair.

He'd missed his old routines; the simple acts of washing and grooming, picking out an outfit and the jewellery to match. By the time he'd finished, he'd relaxed enough to focus on his studies, but every so often his concentration would shatter, his eyes would slip towards the mirror, and he'd catch himself listening, waiting for the whispering voice to speak.

27/12/32 KAF (Two)

Jared skittered sideways to take advantage of the fading daylight. The tiny writing blurred on the page. He closed his eyes and massaged his eyelids. A knock rattled the room door. He looked up. "Yes?"

The door cracked open, and a young servant popped her head through the gap. "We leave for the feast in thirty minutes. Everyone attending is to gather in the courtyard."

"Thank you." Jared closed the Canri language book with a soft whump and slipped it inside the folds of his blanket.

The servant bobbed her head and left, pulling the door closed behind her.

Jared stood, his stiff muscles screeching in silent protest. He stretched, working his way through a series of exercises Armon had taught him, and started to dress. He didn't rush, despite the urgency in the servant's voice. It wouldn't do for him to make a poor first impression.

"Run and find me a hairbrush, boy. Quickly!" The unfamiliar, booming shout came from somewhere to the right, loud enough to be heard above the hubbub rising in the hallway.

Jared shook his head, gave his sleeves a quick tug, and frowned. *Cufflinks.* He'd forgotten to take out his cufflinks. He hunted through his jewel box until he found a pair of onyx and diamond links and fitted them in place.

"That's a *clothes* brush, boy. I said a *hair*brush. Blasted fool."

Jared chuckled and slipped his jacket on. He checked himself in the mirror and made several adjustments, straightening his collar and brushing a few wrinkles out of his shirt sleeves. The jacket was, perhaps, a little too revealing, with sleeves that ended just above the elbow and breast panels that left a two-inch gap at the front. But this was the first chance he'd had to wear it, and he had no intention of letting it go to waste.

'Very dashing.'

Jared froze, hands halfway to his ear. His eyes snapped to the mirror, but he found nothing unusual there.

'What did you expect to see? A monster?'

You tell me.

Nothing.

Jared scowled and finished putting in his earrings, cursing himself for a fool. He had enough problems to deal with without starting an argument with himself. He was *not* going crazy, he was tired, that was all.

'You and me both.'

You aren't real.

He checked himself one last time, straightened a few stray hairs, and headed outside.

Most of the embassy staff had already gathered in the courtyard when he arrived. Tessa waited off to his left, speaking quietly with several other merchants. Armon stood at the gates, looking stiff and uncomfortable in his dress uniform. Several of his men waited beside him, some scanning the courtyard and others facing the road, all of them alert and armed with short swords and knives.

"Jared!"

Jared flinched, then glanced about, his gaze flitting from face to vaguely familiar face as he searched for the source of the shout. Two younger men stepped apart, and Stanin pushed his way through the gap. "Salem wants you with him tonight. This way."

With a nod, he fell into step behind Stanin and followed him to where Salem waited with his advisers. The ambassador examined Jared and sniffed, his thick brows knotting. "Couldn't you find something more appropriate to wear?"

Jared slipped his hands behind his back, curling his hands into fists. "I'm fully dressed, sir. Breeches, undershirt, shirt, and jacket, as you instructed."

"That... thing"—he motioned at Jared's jacket—"barely qualifies. At least remove those earrings. They make you look like a, well, like a—"

"Like a whore, sir?"

"Precisely."

"They were my mother's, sir. Are you implying—?"

"Of course not. But you are a man. It's about time you started acting like one."

"How—"

'No!'

Jared almost choked. *What?*

'What was it Salem said? "This is not a matter for protest." You will achieve nothing. Let it go.'

Jared uncurled his fingers and shut his mouth.

Salem's brows angled down, their ends joining to form a beak-like point above his nose. "'How' what?"

"Um…" Jared wet his lips. "How much longer must we wait?"

"We will leave when Azier deigns to join us. Until then, stay out of the way and keep quiet." The tails of Salem's long coat flared as he turned his back, the silver embroidery flashing orange as it reflected the dying sun.

"Sir." Jared dipped his head and stepped away. He squeezed between a small gaggle of whispering, giggling servants and two older, frowning merchants to reach a relatively quiet corner of the courtyard. *This morning you called me a coward. Now you tell me not to defend myself?*

'Standing up to Armon was a calculated risk. Arguing with the ambassador will gain you nothing. It is good that you… we… have found a backbone, but we must use it wisely.'

We? What do you mean 'we'? What happened to 'I am you and you are me'?

'I am. You are. We are together.'

"Jared?"

Jared's heart thudded against his ribs and sweat tickled his palms. He bit down on his tongue. Took a breath. "Lady Zandra."

"Jared, look at me."

He turned, his head bowed. His gaze fixed on the appliqué work running the length of her skirt's hem, then he lifted his head, following the loose lines of her dress past her waist to the spiral-work choker resting against her neck. He paused, swallowed, and tilted his head to meet her piercing gaze.

Her eyes narrowed, stealing away her smile. "Are you well? You look pale."

"I'm fine." *Why is she looking at me like that? Like she's trying to see inside my head?*

"You sure?"

He nodded, not trusting himself to speak. He was certain Tessa meant to ask more, but Azier's booming laughter filled the courtyard, cutting her off.

"Time to go," Salem said as he walked past.

Jared fell into step behind him, all too aware of Tessa's gaze following him as he crossed the courtyard.

❧❦

The Canri guide met them at the embassy gates. Ambassador Salem offered the man a polite greeting then narrowed his lips and gestured in Azier's direction. Armon stood off to the side, speaking to the other patrolmen. He glanced up at Jared's arrival, met his gaze for a split-second, then turned his head to survey the courtyard. Jared stopped beside Stanin and nodded.

Stanin stared straight through him.

Azier arrived a few seconds later. The guide spoke to him briefly, said something to Salem, then led them onto the main road and to the left, away from the city gate. The patrolmen flanked the group, the thud of their boots mingling with the whispered conversations of those who followed. Nobody else moved on the road.

They passed more embassies as they travelled, each one closed off behind a set of black iron gates, their courtyards shrouded in shadows. Jared counted them as they walked. They'd reached the seventh before he noted the flicker of distant flames; the eleventh before he heard the hum of human voices. By the thirteenth, he'd picked out five separate fires within a mass of shadowy figures. By the fifteenth, he could separate individuals from those shadows. Individuals whose colourful clothes made them look like wildflowers in an untended meadow.

Bright, multi-coloured shirts clashed with trousers so baggy they looked like skirts. Patchwork tunics, like the one worn by the official who'd greeted Jared inside the city gates, overhung cuff-less, knee-length trousers. Fuller, looser outfits featured slits granting glimpses of naked arms, backs, and legs. One man stood before the fire bare-chested, glints of flame reflecting in his oiled skin.

And Salem complained when he caught me in my undershirt?

The street opened onto a large square just past the seventeenth gate, revealing a further five fires that had been hidden by the walls. The people closest to the road turned to watch the delegation's approach.

The guide led them straight to the fire at the centre of the square. Three men waited there, separate from the crowd.

The guide stopped several paces away and bowed.

The man on the left of the waiting trio raised a hand. "Steg framåt, Davin."

Their guide—Davin?—straightened and stepped forward. "Du ära mig, Magistra."

"You honour me?" Jared asked in a whisper.

Stanin nodded.

Salem and Azier joined Davin at a signal from the magistra. The six men conversed quietly in Canri, the magistra doing most of the talking, although his dark robes and lack of height made him the least imposing of the three. The man in the centre interrupted with an occasional gesture or word. Each time he did, the magistra dipped his head respectfully before continuing. The third man never spoke. Even so, he was the one who captured Jared's attention.

The decoration on his robes echoed the view of Canri from the hillside, with straight lines intercepting gentle curves to form a criss-crossing grid, each segment filled by a distinct colour. Tattoos carried the design onto the man's face; solid blocks of colour separated by thick, ropy lines formed from...

Are those scars?

'Yes'

Jared's breath caught in his throat. *Why would anyone—?*

The group before the fire broke apart. The scarred man stepped onto a small platform and raised his hands. Ripples of silence spread across the square. The scarred man spoke, voice raised to carry over the crackle of the fires. "We, the people of Canri, extend our greetings to you, our honoured visitors." His accent gave his words a musical lilt, though his voice was rough, worn by age or other pleasures. "Tonight, we will feast, both to celebrate your safe arrival, and to honour agreements yet to come." He paused for breath, then repeated his speech in Canri. The crowd cheered. The man lowered his hands, stepped down, and addressed the delegation "It is our tradition to hold a series of games during these celebrations. They are designed to test a man's skill, strength, and stamina. We would consider it a great honour if your people were to participate."

"We would be honoured to accept." Salem turned around. He made a show of inspecting each of his advisers before his gaze settled on Jared. "You will represent the embassy."

"Me?" The word came out as a squeak. "Surely one of your guar—?"

"My bodyguards are not here. And even if they were, it is not their job to play games. You will represent us. This is not an issue for debate."

Jared lowered his gaze. "Sir."

"Ruskin will represent the merchants," Azier said, pointing to a tall, brawny man.

Armon coughed to catch Salem's attention.

"Yes, Patrol Leader?"

"I would like to volunteer to represent the patrol, sir."

"Very well." Salem turned back to their hosts. "These three men"—he pointed to each in turn—"will stand for us."

The scarred man clasped his hands to his chest and bowed his head. "May the gods grant you much luck." He straightened. "Arvid will show you to an area where you may prepare." He gestured to his right, where a fourth man hid in the shadows like a wildcat awaiting its chance to pounce.

Arvid stepped forward and bowed. "Please to come."

Armon and Ruskin returned the bow and moved forward. Jared hesitated a moment before doing the same.

Arvid led them through the crowd to a fenced off section of the square, opened a small gate, and led them inside. "Armour," he said, pointing to several neat piles laid out atop a crude wooden bench. "You wear."

Armon picked up a rectangle of padded leather and turned it over in his hands. "Thank you, Arvid."

"Welcome." Arvid bowed and left.

Armon looked at his companions. "Do either of you need help putting this on?"

"I can manage." Ruskin selected a set of armour and carried it to a second bench.

"Jared?"

Jared stepped closer and frowned. The straps dangling from the pad looked simple enough, but he had no idea if it fitted to a leg or a forearm or— "Please." *What sort of games required their participants to wear armour?*

'Violent ones, perhaps?'

Armon spread the armour from one of the piles across the bench. "Take your jacket off. This looks like it'll be a tight fit even without the added padding. Your jewellery too, unless you want to risk it getting ripped off in whatever fun's to come." He selected the pad he'd first held up and strapped it over Jared's shin. "How much did Stanin tell you about the men who greeted us?"

"Nothing." Jared shrugged off his jacket, frowning at it a moment before folding it and placing it on the bench. So much for his choice of outfit. He'd probably look like a swollen bread roll by the time Armon finished. He removed his jewellery and slipped it into his jacket pocket. "I gathered the one in the dark robes is a magistra—"

"Magistra Justus. He enforces civil law within the foreign district. Every criminal, no matter how petty their crime, must stand before him for judgement. He has the power to order imprisonment, torture, or death for any crime." Armon strapped the second shin-guard in place. "The one with the scars"—he picked up a larger section of armour and strapped it to Jared's thigh—"is Vortai Yngve."

"Vortai? Like the ones who built the city?"

"Yes. So they claim. He acts as a conduit between the Canri and their gods, interprets the gods' messages, and helps prepare the Canri for their lives in the next world."

"The next world? Not their rebirth?"

"That's what I said." Armon strapped on the second thigh guard. The edges of the straps dug into Jared's skin. He glanced up at Jared's hiss and loosened it a notch. "Vortai Yngve is also responsible for enforcing spiritual law. He doesn't have the same power as the magistra, but he can have you exiled if he thinks you're trying to corrupt the souls of his people."

"Corrupt them how?"

"By telling them of our gods. Beyond that?" Armon shrugged. "The Canri do not share their beliefs with outsiders."

"And the third man?"

"Furste Hjalmar. He is the Canri equivalent of a prince of the Blood, although it is more complex than that." Armon lifted one of the larger segments of armour, held it to Jared's chest, and motioned for him to hold it in place. "He'll need to approve any agreements between our people but otherwise is unimportant. I doubt you'll see him again after tonight." He picked up a second segment of armour, walked behind Jared, and held it against his back. "Can you see the fires through the gaps in the fence?"

Jared shuffled around until his back was to the bench. "A couple."

"There's a man at the nearest fire. Average height, for a Canri, but built like a wall, with hair so pale it's almost white. You see him?"

"Yes."

"That's Verner Olsson. One of the richest traders in Canri, and the most influential willing to deal with outsiders. It's vital we win his support. If he refuses to deal with us, most of the others will follow. That cannot be allowed to happen." Armon fastened the chest armour's shoulder straps and spun Jared around to face him. "If he comes to the embassy, give him your full attention. Pamper him, even if it means ignoring our other guests." He knocked Jared's arm aside and fastened the first of the side buckles.

Jared watched him for a moment then went to work on the buckles on the other side. "Is there anyone else I should know about?"

"Yes, but they can wait." He picked up another pad and fitted it to Jared's upper arm. "For tonight, I want you to focus on making a good impression. Do your best in the games and try to pick up some of the Canri language." He moved on to the next piece of armour. "Once we've finished with your armour, you can help me with mine. I want to be ready before Arvid returns."

❧❧

The last of the sunlight had vanished below the horizon by the time Arvid returned to lead them towards the opposite side of the square. Strange snorts, grunts, and squeals carried over the whispers of the gathered crowd. Jared glanced at Armon, eyebrows raised in silent query. Armon shrugged and grinned. Ahead of them, the crowd parted to reveal a dozen boar-like creatures penned within a small enclosure.

Jared stopped. "What?"

"Wild hog," Arvid said. He waved them forward.

Jared stepped up to the waist-high fence. He'd once watched a wild boar as it rooted through wet leaves and detritus on the edge of an old forest. He'd thought it large and vicious at the time, but in comparison to these hogs, it seemed tame. They were taller, broader, and more muscular, their tusks sharper and longer, their mottled skin thicker, and the line of bristling black hair running the length of their spines more pronounced. Their short front legs kept them in a perpetual crouch with their heads low to the ground. One flick of those powerful neck muscles and—

Arvid slapped a hand down on Jared's back. "You catch. We cook and eat." He thumped Armon's shoulder and squeezed Ruskin's arm. "Quickest to catch be winner."

"Uh…" Jared peeled his fingers from the railing and stepped back.

Arvid grinned at him. "Come. All come." He led them towards a knot of men at the far end of the pen.

The four men broke off their conversation at Arvid's approach and stepped back to form a half-circle. Firelight flashed off oiled, green skin. Each man stood naked beneath his padded armour like a barnacle-dotted whale. If those hogs' tusks ripped into their exposed flesh…

Jared glanced at the hogs and shuddered.

Arvid stopped in front of the men and waved Armon, Ruskin, and Jared forward to complete the circle. "Straws. Each to pick. Shortest go first." He held out his hand, his fist curled around a clutch of straws, and nodded to Ruskin. "You draw."

Ruskin plucked a straw from Arvid's grasp with a steady hand and held it up. It was about three inches long.

Arvid turned to one of the Canri. "Du nästa."

The man picked out a straw, held it up, and laughed. It was less than two inches long.

"You," Arvid said, holding his hand towards Armon.

Armon plucked a straw from the centre. Longer than the Canri's, shorter than Ruskin's.

"Du nästa."

The next Canri chose. A four-inch straw.

"You."

Jared stared at the cluster of straws Arvid thrust in front of him. Only four left. He chose the tallest and held it up. Just over two inches, putting him second.

The last two Canri made their selections. They would go third and last.

Arvid tossed the remaining straw aside. "Make line. Short straw first." He repeated his instructions in Canri.

Jared shuffled back and sideways, taking his place in the hastily formed line. Arvid led them around the pen to an adjoining corral. The hum of the crowd rose in volume. Those nearest the competitors jostled, pointed, shouted, and laughed. Dozens of coins changed hands.

Armon leant past the shoulder of the man in front of him. "Observe and learn," he said, his voice pitched low to carry.

The Canri who'd drawn the short straw vaulted the fence into the corral and settled into a half-crouch opposite the small run joining the corral to the pen. An older man lifted the gate between the run and the pen. The wild hogs stampeded towards it, grunting and snorting as they fought to escape. A heavy, muscular hog battered its way through. The pig herder dropped the gate, trapping it in the run.

The Canri in the corral rose onto the balls of his feet and nodded.

The pig herder opened the second gate.

The hog charged, the clatter of its hooves drowning out the cries of the crowd. Its powerful legs tossed great wads of mud skyward. It dipped its head, tusks angled to gore, opened its powerful jaws, and roared.

The Canri dropped a shoulder, feigned a rush to his right, then dove to his left a second before the hog tore through his intended path.

An ear-piercing squeal silenced the crowd. The hog dug its hoofs into the dirt and skidded across the mud. It slammed into the corral fence headfirst, snorted, and shook its head.

Already recovered from his dive, the man circled the stunned hog, approaching its rump.

It sniffed and raised its head, sniffed again and started to turn.

The man leapt.

The crowd roared.

The hog bucked.

Hoofs cracked against leather as the man twisted clear.

Jared pressed a hand to his stomach and winced. "He's insane." He looked to the second pen, where the remaining hogs stomped and snorted. "*I'm* insane."

The crowd gasped.

Jared snapped his head around.

The hog's tusks missed the man's thighs by a whisker as he vaulted over its head, twisted in mid-air, and dropped. He hit the hog's back with a resounding slap, wrapped his arms around its middle, and dug his heels into the ground.

The hog danced beneath him, grunting and kicking as it sought escape. Thick, corded muscles rose along the sides of his neck and across his shoulders as he struggled to keep his grip. He flailed out with one leg, hooked the hog's back foot, and threw his weight to his left.

The hooked leg buckled, sending the hog scrambling sideways, hooves scrabbling for purchase, before it collapsed on its side.

The pig herder raised a red flag.

The crowd cheered.

Jared wiped sweat from his brow.

Armon nudged his arm. "You'll be fine. Just try not to let it pin you on its tusks."

"I think I'd already worked that part out, but... thank you."

Armon chuckled. "Stay out of its way. Let it tire itself out. Move in when it's worn down. It may have the weapons and the brawn, but you have the brain. Use it."

"And if I refuse?"

"You'll shame us in the eyes of the Canri, shame our people by association, and put us at a disadvantage during the negotiations. You'll also risk having a certain confession appear on Ambassador Salem's desk."

Jared turned his back to the pen. "I should have asked you to burn the blasted thing."

"You think there's any chance I'd have said yes?"

"About as much chance as us becoming best friends."

Armon laughed, but at least this time he was laughing with Jared, not because of him. "You never know." He stepped closer and lowered his voice. "Carry on like this and it might just happen."

Jared blinked, caught himself staring slack-jawed, and snapped his mouth shut. He struggled to find a response, but Armon had already turned away, shaking his head and chuckling.

'Good try. But he has a lot more experience playing with words than you do.'

You think you could do better?

'There's only one way to find out.'

Get the fuck out of my head.

Laughter echoed inside his skull, a disconcerting imitation of Armon's dry, mocking chuckle.

"Yared?"

Jared blinked the green blur into focus. Arvid. Frowning. He glanced around. Several other Canri stared at him, their expressions ranging from confused to disapproving. He swallowed and turned back to Arvid. "It's Jared. With a J."

"Yes. Yared. You turn now."

"Right. Of course." Jared followed Arvid to the corral. Had he been talking out loud again? In public? Surely he would have noticed—

'They saw nothing. Relax. Focus on the pig.'

The pig. What did he know about pigs anyway? He'd helped round up Big Ness when he was a boy—she'd been strong, stubborn, and intractable—but a fat old sow was nothing like an angry, tusked hog.

He climbed into the corral and dropped into a half-crouch opposite the run's entry gate, his leg muscles tensed, ready to leap clear as soon as his chosen hog charged. The crowds' gazes burned his skin, their collective breaths held in anticipation. *But anticipation of what? Seeing a foreigner master one of their hogs? Or seeing that same foreigner mauled?*

'Concentrate.'

Right. Pigs. He—

—leapt, twisted, and dove to his left. The hog crashed through the space where he'd stood. A chill breeze buffeted his skin and clothes. He sucked air into a chest too tight to hold breath, scrambled to his feet, and stared at the hog standing less than a yard away. He hadn't even noticed the gate opening.

'I told you to concentrate.'

How—?

'Down. Now.'

Jared dropped, hitting the dirt an instant after the hog charged.

Its leap took it over his head, clearing his back and legs. Its front hooves hit the ground with a crack. Its rear hooves followed, one hitting the dirt, the other catching the back of his calf.

He groaned, scuttled clear on hands and knees, and pulled himself upright with the aid of the corral fence.

'You see what we can do when we work together?'

The shouts of the crowd washed over him, waves of noise rising and falling in time with the thrum of his pulse. He took a step forward and shifted his weight to his injured leg. It trembled and held.

The hog watched him from the other side of the corral.

So like Regal…

Jared let his gaze slide, focusing on a point to the hog's left. He sank into a crouch, drew his arms into his sides, and dipped his head, making himself as small and nonthreatening as possible.

The hog's sides bellowed. It lowered its head, snuffled, and snorted at the dirt.

Jared let himself breathe.

The hog charged.

Jared rolled to the right, twisting clear of its path, snatched at its haunches, and snagged its calf.

It kicked and bucked, dislodging his fingers before he secured his hold.

'Any other bright ideas?'

Could he do what the Canri had? Leap over the hog's front, snare it around the middle, and—

'Gore yourself on its tusks. Scream as it tears open your flesh and rips out your intestines. Writhe on the ground whilst it—'

Shit!

Jared rolled.

The hog's hooves cracked against the ground less than an inch from his shoulder.

He tucked his knees and rolled again, used his momentum to regain his feet, and staggered sideways until he reached the fence.

The hog stumbled to a halt, snorted, and shook its head. Foam bubbled from its nostrils with every breath.

What was it Armon said? Let it wear itself out? Move in when it's worn down?

'Yes.'

Sounds like a good plan. A pity it isn't the only one struggling.

The back of Jared's calf throbbed, the pain focused on a hoof-shaped area the size of an apple. Aches he'd thought banished by his earlier bath weighed down his muscles. The hot evening air burned his lungs. Each dive and roll required more effort than the last; demanded more time for him to recover. He'd slowed as the hog slowed. One mistimed jump and—

The hog let out a long, high-pitched squeal and charged.

Jared dropped and rolled. The hog's tusk caught his shoulder, its point snagging the edge of his armour, spinning him around. He lashed out, grabbing the first thing that came to hand. A leg. He clung to it with every ounce of strength he had left, twisted to get his feet under him, grabbed the leg with his other hand, and pulled.

The hog squealed; a shrill cry more piercing than a child's.

Jared ground his teeth against its pain and hauled himself closer. He inched his hands up to its flank, momentarily released his hold, and wrapped an arm around its hindquarters. Another pull brought it hard against his legs. He collapsed onto its back and used his weight to hold it in place.

The hog stilled.

The roar of the crowd crashed in around him. A ring of strangers surrounded the corral, their faces half hidden in shadows, and their voices blending together to form a low, mumbling hum. He drew in a deep breath, looked up, and froze.

She stood less than five feet away, her body pressed against the corral fence. Her eyes locked onto his, holding him, pulling him in. The crowd faded. The pig ceased to exist. Nothing mattered but those eyes; those beautiful, black eyes.

The hog squealed and bucked.

Jared barely got his foot off the ground before its hoof slammed into his shin. The impact broke his grip. He flew backwards, spinning to land face down in the dirt.

Hands grabbed his shoulders and rolled him onto his back. "Can you stand?"

He stared at Armon in stunned incomprehension.

Armon cursed and dragged Jared to the corral fence. They passed a group of Canri youths surrounding the hog like a pack of wolves. Jared stared at them. "Where...?

Armon propped Jared's back against a fence post. "Can you stand?"

Jared turned. Blinked. "Did you see where she went?"

"What? Who?"

"The woman with black eyes. She was right there." He pointed to an empty spot in the crowd.

Flesh cracked against flesh. Armon shook his hand.

Jared touched a hand to his burning cheek and winced. "What...?"

"Get. Up."

"But—"

Armon grabbed Jared by his chest armour and dragged him to his feet. "Did you hit your head?"

"I don't think so." Jared spotted the group of youths leading the hog from the corral and frowned. "Where did they come from?"

"They climbed over the fence when you were red flagged. The hog saw them coming and panicked." Armon let Jared go. "You're sure you didn't hit your head?"

Jared nodded. "I was looking right at her." He put his full weight on his injured leg. Iced lightning lanced down his shin, into his foot. He bit his lip to stop a scream. "Oww."

"What did she look like?"

"Her eyes. She had black eyes."

"And?"

"And… uh…" Jared shrugged.

"Smitten by a pair of eyes." Armon laughed. "Come on. I'll get the patrol medic to check your leg whilst you're waiting."

"Waiting? Waiting for what?"

"For the next game, of course."

❧❦

Arvid insisted Jared return to the preparation area to receive treatment and ordered a Canri boy to guide him there. The patrol's medic, a young man Armon introduced as Mevin, supported Jared as they followed.

"You know, when I first saw you," Jared said as he hobbled clear of the crowd ringing the hog pen, "I thought you were the patrol's messenger boy, not its medic."

"Most do, sir." Mevin laughed, the warm, inclusive chuckle mirrored in his bright eyes and open smile. "But I started younger than most. Been training since I was eleven." He blew a thick lock of hair from his eye and tightened his hold on Jared's arm. "I'll set you right, sir. No fears there."

Jared nodded, though Mevin's reassurances did little to ease the tightness in his chest. He studied the youth's soft face for a few moments longer before switching his attention to the people they passed.

It had only been a few minutes since the end of his bout with the hog. The woman with the black eyes couldn't have gone far. But the light from the fires made looking for her near impossible, casting the features of those who turned to watch them pass in shadow. He searched anyway, drawn by an inexplicable tug—

His toes caught on something hard. He stumbled, grabbed Mevin's jacket, and almost pulled the medic down after him. "Sorry."

Mevin laughed. "No harm done." He dipped his shoulder under Jared's right arm, wrapped his own arm around Jared's waist, and helped him hop the last few yards to the preparation area.

The Canri boy opened the gate. Mevin led Jared inside and deposited him on the nearest bench. Jared leant his head against the fence and closed his eyes. Black eyes stared at him from the shadows of his mind.

"Could you lift your foot up onto the bench for me please, sir?" Mevin asked.

"Sir?" Jared cracked an eye open and smiled.

"You're one of the Blood, aren't you, sir?"

"I'm also here in disgrace. Jared's fine." He lifted his foot onto the bench and flinched when his heel came to rest against the wood.

Mevin removed the armour from Jared's lower leg and tossed it aside. Jared's boot followed the armour to the ground, the torn remains of his stocking joining it a moment later.

Jared glanced at his bruised shin and cursed.

Mevin placed his hands on either side of Jared's leg. "This will hurt, su—uh—Jared." He pressed on Jared's shin with his thumbs.

Pain shot through Jared's leg, double lines of fire racing down to his toes and up to his groin. He gritted his teeth and arched his back, refusing to cry out.

Mevin shifted his grip and pressed again.

Sweat soaked Jared's undershirt.

Mevin released his hold. "It's not broken."

"It's not?"

"No. Just bruised, as far as I can tell." Mevin settled back into a crouch. "There's a chance it might be fractured, but you'd probably be in more pain if it were. Either way, it's going to hurt like the soulless for a while."

"How long's a while?"

Mevin shrugged. "A few days. A week. Maybe a month. Longer, if the bruising's deep."

"And after that?"

Another shrug. "It'll heal. Eventually."

"That's not very reassuring."

"You're young. You're healthy. You'll be fine." Mevin probed the area around the injury, gradually working his way backwards. Cold fingertips pressed the spot the hog had stomped. Jared flinched. Mevin frowned, lifted Jared's foot by the heel, and winced. "That's a nasty bruise." He lowered Jared's foot back to the bench. "Stay here and rest. I'll see if I can get some ice to put on it."

Jared let out a shaky breath and nodded. He couldn't believe he'd been distracted so easily. He hadn't even seen her properly. He didn't know what she looked like, what she was wearing, what colour hair she had. He didn't even know if she *had* hair. And yet, when he closed his eyes, she was there, watching him, demanding his attention. He wanted—no, *needed*—to see her again.

'And here I thought you loved Elise.'

I do.

'You don't sound very sure.'

I am. I do. I just—

'—want to talk? Why do I not believe you?'

Why would I care?

'Because I'm part of you. I feel everything you feel. Think everything you think. I know the truth. Stop lying to yourself.'

Vortex take you.

The gate creaked.

Jared looked up.

Mevin entered the enclosure, a small bucket in hand. He nodded to Jared. "They didn't have ice, but they promised this would work as well." He set the bucket on the bench next to Jared's foot, reached inside, and pulled out a sopping rag. "It might sting a little." He draped the rag over Jared's leg.

"Nyah!" Jared yanked his leg away. "That's cold!"

"It's meant to be." Mevin pulled Jared's leg back, looking far too pleased with himself. "It'll numb your leg and keep down the swelling. Now sit still and let me work." He pulled out another rag and wrapped it around Jared's shin.

Jared sagged against the fence and chewed on his lip to keep from whimpering as the liquid on the rags chilled his leg.

'Wimp.'

The gate's hinges squeaked. Armon strode through the opening and walked up to the bench. "How bad is it?"

"Bone's bruised, sir," Mevin said. "So's the back of his calf."

"Can he continue?"

"I would advise against it, sir."

Armon shifted his gaze to Jared and lifted an eyebrow, questioning.

Jared sat up straighter. "I'll be fine."

"You will not." Mevin tugged on the rag, drawing a wince. "You need to rest. Your leg's weak. If it gets hit again, it could break."

"I can't—" Jared gasped as Mevin placed a fresh rag just below his knee. "I can't afford to let the Canri think I'm weak."

"It is not weakness to—"

"Enough, Mevin." Armon thunked onto the bench at Jared's side. "He's made his decision."

Is that approval in Armon's eyes?

'Aww, man love. How sweet.'

Shut up.

'When did you start caring what he thinks?'

I said. Shut. Up.

'I'll shut up when I decide.' Alien laughter filled Jared's mind.

Ruskin strolled through the half-open gate. He stopped in front of the bench, stared down at Jared's rag-wrapped leg, then lifted his gaze a little higher. "It's a miracle. A whore with balls."

Jared leapt to his feet, regardless of his injured leg, and grabbed a fistful of Ruskin's shirt. "Care to repeat that?"

Ruskin held his arms out to his sides. "Just telling the truth."

"The truth?" Jared tightened his grip and hopped closer. "What do you know about the truth?"

"I know they issued you a licence to play whore."

"You—" Jared tensed his arm and shoved. Ruskin didn't budge. "You have no idea—"

Armon stood, caught hold of Jared's belt, and pulled him back. "Sit down."

"But he—"

Another pull. "Sit!" Armon spun on Ruskin. "As for you, why don't you keep your opinions to yourself? You want to pick on him, you do it in your own time, not mine."

"Whatever you say, Patrol Leader." Ruskin gave Armon a mock salute then sauntered over to the bench he'd used earlier.

Armon wiped at his forehead. A thin stream of blood trickled down from his hairline.

"Eh, sir." Mevin pulled a clean rag from the bucket and stood. "I should take a look at that for you."

Armon touched his fingers to the cut and frowned at the spots of blood. "It's nothing, Mevin."

"Head wounds are never nothing, sir. I must insist—"

"You have no right—"

"Actually, sir, when it comes to field wounds, I do."

"Cursed know-it-all boy." Armon thudded onto the bench beside Jared. "Do your worst."

"Sir." Mevin knelt in front of Armon and dabbed at his forehead.

Jared sagged back against the fence and stared across the enclosure at Ruskin. "What's his problem, anyway?"

Armon glanced sideways at him. "You're serious?"

"It's not like I've done anything to him. What business is it of his what I do for a living?"

Armon's chuckle turned to a squeak when Mevin pressed the rag to his cut. "Not done anything to him? That's typical Blood thinking, that is."

"Meaning?"

"Think about it for a minute, Jared up-Arran. I'm sure you can figure it out for yourself if you try hard enough."

Mevin retrieved a pouch from inside his jacket, rolled it open, and pulled a needle from one side and a thread from the other.

Armon scowled and fixed his gaze on Jared. "Well?"

Mevin poked the end of the thread through the eye of the needle and tied it in place.

Jared lifted his leg back onto the bench. "You're right. I probably could work it out if I tried. But why should I waste the effort? I'm sure you'll tell me anyway, Malkem-of-no-family-that-matters."

Mevin touched the tip of the needle to Armon's cut.

Armon slammed his fist into the bench.

Jared flinched.

"Damn it, Mevin! You could have warned me."

Mevin grinned and pushed the needle through Armon's skin.

'Well. That was unexpected.'

Tell me about it.

Armon may have addressed his admonition to Mevin, but his glare had been directed straight at Jared. For all his mocking of Jared's heritage, he couldn't take a dig at his own.

"It's simple," Armon continued, his voice calm again. "Ruskin, and those like Ruskin, have spent their lives working their fingers bloody to get an opportunity like this. They've learnt their trade the hard way, risked everything in a bid to get noticed by those who matter, and then you—" Armon pushed Mevin's arm aside. "You come along, sleep with the wrong woman, and get punished—*punished,* not rewarded—by being given a place in this delegation. It makes a mockery of their success."

"But—"

"No buts. Try looking at things from someone else's perspective for once in your pathetic life. When they look at you, all they see is a spoilt brat who's had his hands slapped and is playing at being a commoner to set things right. You'll pretend to be a servant for a few weeks, earn forgiveness, and fuck off again."

And only Armon and I know otherwise. "Damn..."

Mevin knotted the thread and snapped off the excess. "All finished, sir."

"Thank you." Armon pressed his lips together, his gaze on Mevin as he collected his things and left. "You want to make friends out here? Try showing a little humility. Next time Ruskin makes a comment like that, play along. No-one cares for a man who's too proud to laugh at himself."

"But it's a lie."

"It's a cover story. Your life will get a lot easier if you accept it."

Jared opened his mouth to answer then hesitated. By his standards, Armon's entire life was a lie. He swallowed his words and nodded. "I guess it wouldn't hurt to try."

"Finally. Finally, he understands." Armon leant his head against the fence and closed his eyes. "And, Jared..."

"Yes?"

"Never, ever, cast aspersions on my bloodline again."

27/12/32 KAF (Three)

Mevin had returned and was in the process of unwrapping the rags from Jared's leg when Arvid entered the preparation area. He watched Jared squeeze his foot back into his boot and strap on his discarded armour then waved all three competitors over. "Next, we race horse. Do relay. One of you need ride twice. Choose who."

Jared raised his hand. "I'll do it."

"Says the man hopping on one leg." Ruskin lifted his shoulders and growled. "What gives you the right—?"

Jared turned on the merchant. "Have you ever ridden a horse at speed?"

"Well, no…"

"Patrol Leader?"

"I have. During drills."

"And in action?"

Armon shook his head.

A smile tugged at the corner of Jared's lips. He'd seen Armon handling Regal, he knew the truth. "Then, as the most experienced horseman here, I should ride twice."

"And your leg?" Ruskin asked, leaning forward.

Jared glanced at his leg and shifted, putting his full weight on it. "It won't be a problem." He fixed his gaze on Armon.

Armon dipped his head. Ruskin frowned but grunted his agreement.

"Good, good," Arvid said. "Come. Pick horse." All three men stepped forward, but Arvid held up a hand. "Just you." He pointed at Jared.

"But I need a translator."

Arvid held his hands out wide and shrugged. "No understand."

Jared turned to Armon. "Could you…?"

"With pleasure." Armon addressed Arvid in Canri, his words coming out smoothly, if not as quickly as a native speaker's.

Arvid shook his head, his accompanying reply short and clipped. He turned to Jared. "No need talk. You point, I understand. Come. Follow." He led Jared out of the preparation area and away from the square, along one of the curving side streets to a small yard where two horses had been tied to a makeshift hitching post. "Pick."

Jared limped into the yard, careful to stay in the horses' line of sight. He held his hands out, palms up, and let them have a good sniff. "They're a handsome pair." He glanced back at Arvid, who nodded and grinned, though whether in agreement or to humour him he couldn't tell. "I have a small horse too. Sherna. Though these two would look like yearlings next to her."

The horse on the left was copper coloured; the one on the right closer to bronze. He pulled back the copper's lips and examined its teeth. "Young still. Only two or three." He repeated the inspection with the bronze. "This one's older. Six or seven." He stepped around the bronze, ran his hands along its body, and noted Arvid watching, his head bobbing.

"He's strong. Compact. A stallion." Jared circled back the way he'd come and examined the copper. "This one's a gelding. He's leaner. Slightly smaller. Probably easier to control. Slower too, I suspect." He stepped back, re-joining Arvid.

"Which?" Arvid asked.

"If it was just me? The stallion. Armon can probably handle him too. But Ruskin? I saw him riding on our journey here. He's competent in the saddle, bu—"

"Saddle?" Arvid smirked. "Saddle for boys, but you want saddle..." He shrugged.

Jared pursed his lips and strolled forward to stroke the horses' necks. The stallion snorted and pawed the ground. Even saddled, an expert hand would be required to ride him safely. Armon had shown skill with Regal, but Ruskin—

'Ruskin is irrelevant. He's treated you like dirt all evening. Why should you consider his needs now?'

He has good reason to dislike me. I'm the one who's come along and trampled on his toes. Besides, this is about more than Ruskin.

'Yes. It's about proving yourself in front of the Canri. They already look down on you for being a whore. Do you really want them seeing you as a

child as well? Do you think Armon would appreciate the label being attached to his precious delegation?'

No, but... Jared glanced towards the square then down at his injured leg. *What if Ruskin gets hurt?*

'Then it's no less than he deserves.'

Jared lifted his head to meet Arvid's steady gaze. "We'll take the gelding." He patted the copper's neck. "No saddle. Ruskin will have to make do."

When they returned to the square, the Canri had created a racecourse around its perimeter, the boundaries defined by the crowd lining its length. Arvid led Jared to the start line, where Salem and Azier waited alongside the three leaders of the Canri foreign district. They stood at the inner boundary of the course, talking quietly amongst themselves. Ruskin, Armon, and the four Canri competitors were already in place.

"Listen good," Arvid said, waving everyone closer. "You race withershins, yes? See stone at corner?" Everyone looked at the large boulder in the middle of the bend and nodded. "Good. Touch boulder, lap good. No touch, no count. Yes?" Another round of nods. Arvid poked Jared's chest. "You first." Ruskin's chest. "Second." Armon. "Third." Jared again. "Last. Understand?" More nodding. Arvid turned to the Canri and repeated his instructions.

Ruskin turned to Jared and Armon. "Sounds simple enough."

Jared grunted. He'd intended to give Ruskin a few pointers, but if he thought it was simple, well, then the voice in his head was right, he didn't deserve any help.

The clatter of hoofs echoed over the hubbub of the crowd like an avalanche cutting through a storm. A young boy came into view a second later, leading the two horses towards them.

Jared accepted the reins of the copper and let the horse sniff his hand. He checked its teeth and flanks to confirm the Canri hadn't switched horses, led it to the start line, and vaulted onto its back. Fire flared through his lower leg. He gritted his teeth, trapping a hiss.

The first Canri rider guided the bronze to the copper's side and gave Jared a nod.

Jared nodded back and turned his gaze forward. He closed his eyes for a moment and took a breath as he tried to shut out the watching crowd, the rising chatter, the horse and rider at his side. It was a straight dash to the first corner, hard turn left, another straight—

A young man darted from the crowd in front of them, the end of a rope clutched in his hands. Several people on the other side of the course caught its end as he neared and helped him pull it taut.

Arvid stepped between the horses and placed his arms on their shoulders. "Ready?" he asked.

"Ready," Jared replied.

Arvid looked up at the Canri rider. "Redo?"

"Ja."

"Tre… Två… Ett…" He dropped his hands. "Go!"

The rope fell. The crowd roared. Jared slammed his heels into the copper's side and flinched.

It leapt forward, going from trot, to canter, to gallop in a dozen strides. Jared leant forward, clinging to its mane with both hands. The crowd vanished, hundreds of people blending into a single, multi-coloured blur. The cobbles ran together in a stream of grey and white. Wind buffeted his face, cooling his skin and tugging his hair.

He laughed.

Gods, but I've missed this.

The bronze reached the bend first, leading by over a length.

Jared nudged the copper wide, rounding the boulder on the outside. He released its mane with his left hand and leant into the curve, letting his fingers trail along the top of the boulder.

The copper planted its lead leg against the pull of Jared's weight. Its back hoofs skidded, throwing its rump sideways. Its left shoulder tipped towards the ground.

A jolt spasmed through Jared's body. He jerked himself back and up, clinging to the copper's mane, trying to pull the gelding up with him. His knee brushed the cobbles.

Then his weight shifted enough for the copper to straighten its buckled leg. It scrambled to regain its footing, tossed its head, and leapt forward again.

The bronze had gained another length.

"Come on, boy. Come on." Jared reached back with his free hand and slapped the copper's rump. It lengthened its stride, its neck muscles straining with the effort, but the bronze continued to pull away.

They'd dropped a third length by the end of the straight.

They made the next turn without a hitch—the copper leaning away from the boulder in anticipation of Jared's shifting weight—and pulled out of the bend two-and-a-half lengths behind.

"That's my boy!"

The bronze's rider risked a glance over his shoulder, yelled something in Canri, and slapped his mount's side. The bronze pulled away.

"Oh no you don't. Push on, boy," Jared shouted into the streaming wind. "Push on."

The copper doubled its effort, its muscles straining as it fought to close the gap.

Jared's blood sang in his ears. His buttocks and thighs burned. His bruised leg throbbed in time with the copper's strides. He leant into the next corner, brushed his hand across the top of the boulder, and slipped.

"Shit." He clamped his thighs to stop his slide, grabbed the copper's mane with his dangling hand, and hauled himself upright. The copper skipped sideways several steps before recovering.

Jared settled back into place, cursing his own stupidity. They were down four lengths. "Sorry, boy."

The bronze reached the final corner. Its rider shuffled back.

"What the...?"

The copper charged into the bend.

Jared leant over to slap the final boulder, looked up, and gaped.

The bronze's rider crouched on its back, reins held loosely in his left hand. As they approached the finish line, he tossed the reins towards his waiting teammate and jumped, pushing off to the right. His teammate caught the bronze's reins in his right hand, wrapped his left arm around its neck, and swung himself onto the bronze's back. The bronze never broke its stride.

"I am not... doing that." Jared spotted Ruskin waiting on the line and held the copper's reins out to his left, planting his other hand between his legs at the same time. He pushed down on his mount's back, taking most of his weight on his arm. Three feet before the line, he tossed the reins to Ruskin and launched himself backwards, pushing with his hands and knees to clear the copper's back. His feet hit the cobbles. His right leg buckled, ditching him on his backside.

Ruskin snatched at the reins and dragged the copper to a halt.

Jared slapped the ground. "What is he doing? This is a race, not a jolly in the countryside."

"He's a merchant. He's doing his best." Armon offered Jared his hand.

Jared accepted and pulled himself upright. His eyes never left the little copper and its newest rider. "I just hope he remembers to hold onto its mane."

The copper dived into the first corner. Ruskin leant sideways to slap the boulder—

—and his backside shifted to the side. His arm smashed into the boulder. His legs flew free of the copper's back. He flipped in mid-air, rolled down the boulder, and hit the cobbles with a sickening crunch.

Ice chilled Jared's heart. He took a single pace forward, lifted his hand to the back of his head, and stared.

Armon ran.

I should have used a saddle.

'You wanted him to get hurt.'

No. Not hurt. Just... humiliated.

'He's alive, isn't he?'

But...

Jared's breath rattled in his lungs. He'd caused this. He'd refused the saddle. Had avoided giving Ruskin advice when it might have helped.

Armon drew level with Ruskin, Mevin following a few paces behind. Ignoring the fallen merchant, Armon sprinted past him to the copper's side, snatched up its reins, jumped on its back, and spurred it forward.

Mevin dropped to his knees beside Ruskin and rolled him onto his back.

Ruskin twisted and moaned. His right arm was shattered, his bone sticking through flesh. Blood from the sickening break soaked his chest.

Jared swallowed acid. *I never meant—*

'He volunteered. No-one forced him to get on the horse.'

I should have warned him—

'He got what he deserved.'

Mevin helped Ruskin to sit.

What am I turning into?

'A man?' Mocking laughter filled Jared's head.

More members of the patrol arrived at Mevin's side. Together, they helped Ruskin to his feet and walked him off the course.

Behind Jared, the crowd roared. Hoofs pounded on cobbles. The next Canri in the relay stepped up to the line.

Hands grabbed Jared's arms and pulled him clear seconds before the bronze would have mowed him down. He stared at it, mouth working soundlessly and body shaking.

"Anyone would think you'd never seen a broken arm before," a woman said in his ear.

He turned his head. "What?"

"Snap out of it, Jared. The patrol leader's almost here."

He stared up at the woman. Tall. Muscular. Dark hair. "Tessa?"

Tessa slapped him.

The blow re-hitched his mind. "Sorry. Lady Zandra."

"Better." Tessa nudged him towards the start line. "Armon's almost back. You'll have to take the next lap."

"The next lap? But Armon's supposed to ride next. I—" He glanced to the side, noticed Arvid's frantic waving, and stepped forward.

He heard Armon before he saw him, the roar of the crowd and the hammering of hoofs accompanying his approach. He stepped up to the start line as the copper flew around the bend, Armon already halfway clear of its back. He met Jared's gaze, tossed the reins in his direction, and jumped.

Jared caught the copper's reins with one hand, the front of its neck with the other, and rolled himself onto the copper's back. He dangled for a second, his foot skimming scant inches from the ground, locked his fingers in the copper's mane, and pulled himself into place. The move wasn't as smooth as the Canri riders', but the copper only slowed for a few strides. Then they were at full gallop, heading for the corner where Ruskin had fallen at body-shattering speed.

He released the copper's mane with his right hand, tightened his grip with his left, shifted his weight, and stretched. His fingers brushed the top of the boulder and came back bloody.

"Ugh." He wiped the sticky mess onto his leg.

He didn't catch sight of the bronze until he rounded the third bend, and then the glimpse was fleeting; a flash of rump and tail disappearing around the final bend. "We can catch him, boy. We can do this."

Jared leant sideways to slap the final boulder, set his hands on the copper's shoulders as he straightened, drew his legs up to his sides, and pushed. For a heart-stopping moment, he wobbled, then he managed to slide his feet into place. He crouched on the copper's back, struggling to keep his balance, and held out the reins. Armon stood less than five feet away.

Jared threw the reins and jumped, aiming for the crowd. Hands reached for him, catching his arms and legs, cushioning his fall. His feet touched the ground a few seconds later. Strength drained from his legs like water trickling through the cracks in a parched pond. Only the press of the people around him kept him upright.

Dear gods, did I really do that?

The Voice laughed.

❧

Jared waited on the edge of the crowd, his eyes fixed on the last corner of the racecourse, his heart slowing as he recovered his breath. Flickering reds and oranges from the fires washed over the cobbles and the expectant crowd. The succulent aromas of roasting meat and exotic spices merged with smoke, strange perfumes, and the cloying odour of human sweat. It was a mixture of smells found in cities the world over, but it was ever so slightly wrong.

Sight, sound, and scent came together in a dizzying mix that left him wanting to vomit. He looked up to clear his head, and his stomach flipped. Thousands of stars filled the cloudless sky, impossibly bright, impossibly distant, impossibly different. The moon, a half-crescent hovering above the city walls, looked half the size it had in the Kingdom. He'd expected it, of course, but standing there, surrounded by so many not-quite-familiar things, reality hit home. He was alone.

'*Almost alone.*'

Oh?

'*You've got me.*'

Ah, yes. An imaginary voice inside my head. You'll forgive me if I don't find that very comforting.

A growing roar dragged his attention back to the race. He looked down as the bronze rounded the final bend. Frothy sweat soaked its coat, and its nostrils flared with every breath. It ran with its head down, ears drooped, hooves low. Its rider stretched along the length of its neck, coaxing out the last of its strength with a shout and a slap. They crossed the finish line accompanied by deafening cheers.

Armon came into view seconds later. He pulled the copper up beside the bronze, dismounted, and tossed the reins to a waiting boy. The Canri racers surrounded him, their overlapping words an unintelligible gabble as they slapped his back. He took a moment to respond then stalked up to Jared. "Care to tell me what all that was about?"

"All what?"

"Climbing onto the horse's back and jumping into the crowd. You're not much use to me if you break your neck."

"It felt like the right thing to do."

"It felt like the right thing to do?" Armon shook his head. "Sometimes—"

The crowd cheered, drowning out the rest of his words. Jared turned to find Vortai Yngve standing in the middle of the racecourse, holding the winning captain's hand aloft. The Vortai dipped his head towards the two foreigners, and the crowd cheered again.

"At least someone appreciated it," Jared muttered.

"Sirs, sirs," Arvid called, hurrying forward. "Come, please. You must prepare."

Armon scratched at the inside of his wrist. "Any news on Ruskin?" he asked, his eyes on Jared.

"Broke arm." Arvid said. "Hurt... there." Arvid pointed at his midsection.

"His ribs?"

"Yes. Ribs. Hurt. No broke."

"Did he lose much blood?"

"Huh?"

Armon repeated the question in Canri.

The flow of words that followed left Jared baffled. "Well?" he asked when the exchange ended.

"Ruskin's arm is broken in two places, and he's bruised his ribs." Armon glanced at his wrist, scowled, and clenched his fist. "He's lost a lot of blood, but it's not fatal. Their healers are tending to him now. We're on our own for the final game."

"Any idea what it is?"

"A test of strength and prowess. Arvid wouldn't tell me more."

Their stop at the preparation area didn't reveal anything either. The fenced off section hadn't changed since they left. Armon flopped onto one of the benches, glanced at Jared's injured leg, and ordered him to apply a fresh set of icy rags.

Arvid arrived just as Jared pulled on his boot. The young Canri man waved them forward.

"Try not to do anything stupid this time," Armon said, pitching his voice so it wouldn't carry. "You might not believe this, but I'm not eager to watch you die."

Arvid didn't give Jared time to reply. He turned and hurried through the gate, barking his requisite, "follow."

27/12/32 KAF (Four)

Arvid led them across the square to a roped-off section near the central fire, stopped, and pointed to Armon. "You wait." He marched away, glancing over his shoulder to wave for Jared to follow. His path took them around the central fire to a second roped-off area. The youngest of the Canri competitors waited within, bouncing on his heels and waving to the gathered crowd. Arvid signalled for Jared to join him.

Jared stepped over the knee-high rope. The young Canri glanced over, flicked his hand in Jared's direction, and barked a few quick words at Arvid, his tone disapproving. Arvid's response was swift and sharp, but the young man shook his head, gestured at Jared, and stamped his foot.

Arvid silenced him with a slash of his hand.

A third Canri stepped into the square, an older man with weather-worn skin and greying hair. Naked to the waist, he carried a pair of dark wood batons in each hand. His arrival stilled the waiting crowd.

Arvid bowed to the newcomer, and the young competitor quickly followed. A frantic, partially concealed wave from Arvid convinced Jared to do the same.

The older man strolled into the middle of the square and extended his arms, offering one pair of batons to Jared and the other pair to the young man. Jared accepted the batons, and the older man began to speak.

Arvid shuffled closer to Jared. "Referee," he whispered, pointing to the older man. "You fight. Use batonger. Three touch win. No bite. No kick. No hit here." He tapped Jared between the legs. "Understand?"

"Yes."

"Stay in ring, safe. Leave ring, lose. Yes?"

"Yes."

"Good, good." Arvid nodded to the referee and left.

Jared stared at the batons clutched in his hands. The horse race had been perfect for him, but this? This could be a disaster. How many hours had he lost failing to learn the art of the sword? Hours during which he'd spent most of his time sprawled in the dirt. His lessons with Armon might prove more useful. The batons were closer in length to a dagger than a sword. He'd just have to remember to hit rather than grab, stab rather than elbow.

The referee raised his hands, and a hush fell over the crowd. He pointed to Jared with one hand, the young Canri man with the other, waved for them to approach, and pointed to the ground on either side of him.

Jared walked to the spot indicated, sucking in his stomach to quell the worms squirming there, and settled into a ready stance.

The young Canri man relaxed into a crouch, batons held loosely in his hands. His pale blue gaze locked on Jared's. He smirked.

Jared looked him up and down, and the tips of his batons sagged towards the dirt. Blue Eyes was built for fighting, with his slender, wiry body lacking any trace of fat. He set his batons twirling with a smug flick of his wrists.

Jared tightened his own grip, his palms sweating.

"Tre... Två... Ett..." The referee stepped back, dropping his hands. "Kämpa!"

Blue Eyes stepped forward, right arm swinging.

Jared blocked the first blow, ducked under the second, and jabbed at Blue Eyes' ribs.

A swift, almost casual, back hop took Blue Eyes clear. He bounced on the balls of his feet and spread his arms, exposing his chest.

Jared growled and shook his head. Going toe to toe would be a mistake. He needed to hold back, block, and counter. Fool Blue Eyes into underestimating him, break through his defences, and score a hit.

'I'll enjoy watching you try.'

Blue Eyes extended his hands toward the crowd and lifted his shoulders in an exaggerated shrug. The performance drew a mix of cheers and laughter. He dropped his arms, brought his batons up in front of him, and gave them a twirl.

Jared returned to his ready stance, keeping his muscles loose as he studied his opponent, watching for a tell-tale twitch or tensing of muscles, leading glance or head tilt.

Blue Eyes rocked, shifting his weight from his front foot to his back, and leapt, arms sweeping low and wide.

Jared drove his batons down in an inverted V, flinching when wood cracked against wood, wincing at the sting in his palms. The pressure against his batons ceased. He twisted, ducking to avoid an inrushing blur. Air blasted the side of his face. He raised one arm for balance—

—and Blue Eyes's batons slammed into his, one after another, forcing his arm wide. He stumbled, shifting one arm to protect his face and dropping the other to cover his stomach.

Blue Eyes stepped back and laughed. He pointed his batons at Jared then tapped them against his chest.

Jared resumed the ready stance and waited.

A snarl twisted Blue Eyes's lips. His gaze dropped to Jared's waist. His left arm darted forward, baton extended to stab.

Jared held his ground. The glance had been too obvious, the attack lacking in power. He forced himself to meet Blue Eyes's gaze and smile when the attack fell short.

Blue Eyes stepped right and tried again.

Jared shifted his weight back, his arms tensed and shaking. If he had misread Blue Eyes's intent—

Blue Eyes's baton missed by inches. He scowled and stepped forward, right arm swinging in a repeat of his initial attack.

Jared blocked, ducked, and lunged. A solid impact confirmed a hit on Blue Eyes's flank.

Cold wood tapped the inside of his elbow. A blunt point jabbed his stomach. The blows had barely registered when Blue Eyes crouched and slammed the side of his baton against his bruised leg.

Jared screamed and dropped his batons, clutching his right leg in both hands and hopping on his left. Hands clamped onto his shoulders and shoved. He hopped back a step, stumbled, and fell.

Blue Eyes held his hands above his head.

The crowd cheered.

Tears leaked from Jared's eyes. He hugged his leg to his stomach, pressed his forehead against his knee, and growled. Heat burned his cheeks. He didn't look up; didn't want to see the expressions on the onlookers' faces.

"Can you stand?" someone asked.

Jared swallowed and rubbed at his eyes.

"Jared? Can you stand?"

Jared peered at the speaker through blurred eyes. *Mevin?* He shrugged. "Not sure."

Mevin reached for Jared's leg. "May I?"

Jared dropped his arms and nodded.

Mevin eased Jared's boot from his foot and unbuckled the armour covering his shin. Jared kept his gaze focused on a spot over Mevin's shoulder. The crowd was already breaking up, people drifting away in pairs and small groups.

"Malkem won his bout," Mevin said as he probed Jared's leg. "He'll be fighting that young show-boat next. He'll show him what's for if he tries that nonsense again."

"You know how to make a man feel good about himself, you know that?"

"Fah. There's no shame on your part, sir. The Canri are fighters. They train for it from birth. You're an amateur. You made a good show of yourself. You didn't react to that lad's taunting, and you played to your strengths. The Canri'll respect you for that."

"You seem to know a lot about them."

"They're just people, sir. Same as all of us."

৵৶৶

"You're a lucky man, you know that?" Mevin asked.

Jared snorted. "You call getting beat up lucky?"

"No. But I call not getting your leg broken lucky. That young show-off missed."

"It doesn't feel like he missed." Jared rested his head against the fence and watched Mevin through slitted eyes. The young medic smiled as he worked. In fact, he'd been smiling every time Jared had spoken to him. He hadn't judged him either, or made snide, suggestive comments; hadn't threatened him or sought to use him. He'd simply spoken to him like a, well, like a friend.

Mevin lifted a dripping rag from the bucket and pressed it against Jared's shin, chuckling when he flinched. "You were favouring your leg when you fought. It wasn't obvious, but he spotted it. He tried to hit the same spot the hog kicked. Caught you too high. Now you've got two bruises instead of one. There's a lesson to be learnt there."

"Yes." Jared sank back against the fence, relaxing under Mevin's expert touch. "Don't fight with an injury."

"Well, that goes without saying." Mevin grinned, reminding Jared of Ryal's son. Kieron would often flash him that same 'don't be stupid' look when he thought Jared had done or said something foolish. Mevin retrieved another rag. "I did warn you not to."

Jared chuckled. Kieron would have said that as well.

"But no, that's not the lesson I meant." Mevin laid the second rag over Jared's leg. "I meant you shouldn't let people see your weakness. They'll take advantage of it if they do. That one applies to everything in life, not just fighting. It's like when you twitch every time someone calls you a whore. They see it affects you, so they use it to hurt you. But you know what I don't get? I don't get why it bothers you. I mean, you're a good-looking man, and you must be good at your work. Everyone knows you're plenty rich, even though you've no lands and no other income, so you must be doing something right. I'm guessing you're pretty good between the sheets too, or none of those women would want you back. If I were you, I'd be bragging about it every chance I got."

Jared sighed. This wasn't a conversation he wanted to get into, but there was something innocent about Mevin's enthusiasm; something heartfelt about his advice. And it'd been too long since he'd simply talked to someone without worrying about the consequences. His answer slipped out before he had time to think about it and change his mind. "I don't doubt you would. But you don't have one of the most powerful women in the Kingdom monitoring everything you do and say."

"You mean Lady Morgain? But she's harmless."

"You think so?"

"It's common knowledge." Mevin finished applying the last of the rags and sat back. "Since coming into power, she's lowered taxes, started giving hand-outs to the poor, and set up hostels for the homeless. There's even talk of her giving thieves and cutpurses a second chance. Making them slaves instead of cutting off their hands."

"How noble of her." Jared couldn't keep a touch of bitterness from his voice.

"Are you really scared of her?"

Jared nodded. "She gave me a gift before she sent me here. Want to see it?"

"Sure."

Jared pulled at the straps holding the armour on his arm. It took him a few seconds to unfasten the buckles and pull the bracer free. He twisted his arm sideways and pointed at the ragged scar.

Mevin caught hold of Jared's arm and ran a finger along it. "Lady Morgain ordered this?"

"Worse. She did it herself. And she promised me another one through my eye if I so much as looked at another woman the wrong way."

Mevin whistled. "She got someone watching you?"

Jared hesitated, not sure how far to trust the young medic. But the ambassador's antagonism towards him was hardly a secret, and Armon had spoken openly in front of Mevin. Surely he wouldn't have if Mevin couldn't be trusted? "Ambassador Salem," Jared said. "Maybe others."

"Makes a bit more sense now, I suppose. Still, there's nobody else around. Care to give me some tips?"

"Tips?"

"Yes, tips. You know. For when you're... with someone."

"You need tips?"

"I don't *need* them, but, well, it'd be nice to, uh, do something special." Mevin suddenly found the discarded bandage very interesting.

Jared put a hand to his mouth, masking his smile. "Have you ever been with a woman before?"

"Of course!"

Jared averted his gaze, coughing to cover a laugh, not wanting Mevin to realise his earnest declaration had given away his lie. Or worse, assume he was being laughed at or mocked. "It's easy, really. You just need to figure out what she likes."

"Just figure out... How am I supposed to do that?"

"Spend time with her. Watch what she does. Listen to what she says. Experiment." Jared managed to bring his twitching lips under control long enough to look Mevin in the eye. "Most important of all, don't make it all about sex. If she thinks that's all you want from her, she'll run a mile."

"Have you...? I mean, did you...?"

"Yes. That's why I'm in this mess. Take my advice, don't make the same mistake."

"Right... Uh..."

"You finished with my leg?"

"Yes."

"Could you help me get this armour off?"

"Sure. Of course."

"And fetch my jacket for me? I'd get it myself but—"

"I'd break your leg myself if you did. You need to rest. I'll help you to one of the tables first. That way you can elevate your foot and—"

"No."

"No?"

"I want to watch the remaining fights."

"You really shouldn't."

"Don't you want to see if the patrol leader wins?"

"Well... yes."

"Me too."

"All right then. But you have to promise to keep the weight off your leg."

"I promise."

"And promise you'll rest it all day tomorrow. And the next day."

"You'll have to take that up with Salem. I doubt he'll be inclined to listen to me."

"I... Right. I'll be as quick as I can."

By the time Jared and Mevin reached the second ring, Armon had already fought and defeated Blue Eyes. The young man hovered on the fringe of the crowd, sporting an unhappy scowl and a fresh black eye, giving him the appearance of a petulant puppy. Armon stood in a corner of the ring, speaking with Arvid. A second Canri man waited opposite them.

"That's their ring champion, Andreas," Mevin said, with a nod towards Armon's opponent.

Jared released his hold on Mevin and leant on the crowd-barrier, suppressing a wince. "How—?"

"I overheard Salem and Azier talking about him. Apparently, he's undefeated for over twenty matches now."

"Impressive."

"Yup." Mevin released Jared's arm. "Will you be all right on your own? I want to ask Arvid about Ruskin."

"I'll be fine. Thank you." Jared adjusted his grip on the barrier then looked towards the ring.

Unlike Blue Eyes, Andreas held himself still and silent, his gaze fixed on a point somewhere above Armon's head. He wore no armour, just a leather loincloth and hard-soled sandals with straps crisscrossing up his legs to his knees; an outfit that left his well-muscled physique on full show. He held his batons in a firm but relaxed grip.

The crowd on the far side of the ring parted, making room for the referee to stroll through the gap. He stepped into the centre of the ring and motioned for the combatants to approach.

Andreas strolled forward with an easy grace and dipped his head to Armon. Armon returned the gesture then bowed his head to the referee. The referee raised his hands and commenced the countdown.

"Your patrol leader's a fair fighter," a man said at Jared's shoulder.

Jared turned just as the referee called, "kämpa." Batons cracked against batons, and the crowd cheered. The cacophony saved him from needing to make an immediate response. He stared at the speaker, Armon's earlier words echoing inside his head. *Average height...... Built like a wall... Hair so pale it's almost white..."* Verner Olsson. A man Armon had identified as vital to the success of the delegation.

"He dealt with young Oskar well." He nodded at Blue Eyes. "It's a pity you missed it."

"A pity. Yes." Jared curled his lips in a lopsided smile, a softer mirror of the mocking grin Armon often wore. "Patrol Leader Malkem is a far better fighter than I."

Armon side-stepped, blocking Jared's view of Blue Eyes. He and Andreas circled each other, testing one another's skills with thrusts and feints—attacks both men easily deflected.

Jared half-turned, shifted his weight to his good leg, and bowed his head. "Jared up-Arran at your service. It's an honour to meet you, sir."

"An honour?"

"Malkem, the patrol leader, mentioned you." Jared motioned towards Armon.

Armon stepped forward, right arm swinging in high, left sweeping low. Cheers and applause accompanied Andreas's block as he twisted sideways and out of range. Armon spun past the block and flicked his right arm down and back, aiming for Andreas's hip.

Andreas brought his baton across his body, pushing Armon's baton wide, and launched a quick counter. An adept backwards roll took Armon clear of Andreas's double jab.

"Well played." Verner added his applause to the crowd's. "So"—he fixed his gaze on Jared—"what did he have to say of me? Good things, I hope."

"He said your word carries much weight."

"In certain circles, this is true." Verner smiled and rested his forearms on the barrier next to Jared. "But this is not a time for such talk. Tonight is a night for having fun and making friends. You intrigue me. I would know more of you."

"Me?" Jared rubbed at his palm with his thumb. *Why target me? Even if the mention of friendship is genuine, his befriending me won't gain him any advantage in the negotiations.*

'*Unless he sees you as a weak link. Someone to pry information from without your realising what you're giving away.*'

Jared swallowed a sigh. "There's not much to know."

Armon and Andreas clashed again.

Andreas appeared to have the edge, with his blocks coming a fraction sooner than Armon's; his attacks knocking Armon back a fraction further.

Armon, on the other hand?

Armon showed neither the speed nor the finesse he'd exhibited aboard *The Hunter.*

Why is he holding back?

"Come now." Verner half-turned. "Everyone has a story to tell. Is it true you make coin from selling your body?"

"I—" Jared bit off the automatic denial and glanced at Armon. One wrong word, and he'd lose the little trust he'd managed to earn. "I think rumours and gossip have greatly exaggerated my situation."

Andreas launched a fresh attack, leading with his left baton, following up with a series of jabs to prevent Armon from countering. He clipped Armon's forearm and spun away an instant before Armon launched his own thrust. The referee raised a hand, acknowledging the touch.

"I would very much like to know what leads a man, especially one of high birth, to such a thing," Verner said once the cheers died down. "Did you have ambitions to follow such a path as a child?"

"As a...? No!" Jared shivered. *What sort of person even thinks that?* He shifted his feet, wincing at the stab of protest in his leg as he edged sideways. "I, uh—"

Armon feinted to his left then tried a low thrust to his right, only for it to be blocked. His second thrust came in just above his first, sliding over Andreas's baton like a snake, but a flick of Andreas's wrist sent it wide.

The two men broke apart.

Andreas dipped his head in approval.

Jared straightened, grasping the barrier with both hands. "I had many dreams as a child, but not that one."

Verner grunted. "Tell me of your dreams."

Jared hopped to the side, putting a few more inches between them. "Do you always ask strangers such personal questions?"

"What?" Verner jerked his head around, the full weight of his gaze hitting Jared with the force of one of Andreas's thrusts. "Have I offended you?"

"No. No. It's just... It's customary for people to get to know each other before asking such things."

"Ah. But this is not a customary situation. You have come here, to my home, seeking my goods and my favour. I would get to know the men with whom I must negotiate. If I were the one visiting your home, I would expect you to do the same." Verner returned his attention to the fight. "Now, tell me, what did you dream of when you were a boy?"

Jared stared at him, at a loss for a reply.

"Come now. Whatever it is you say, I will not hold it against you. I know you are not a diplomat. It is why I sought you out."

A flurry of movement drew Jared's gaze back to the ring as Andreas stepped back, planted his back foot at an angle, and dropped into a forward roll that brought him inside Armon's guard.

Armon scrambled back, swinging both his batons down in a desperate block. He diverted one of Andreas's jabs, but the second caught him on his thigh. Off-balance and unprepared, he jerked his own baton backwards, slapping Andreas's outstretched arm. The referee raised both hands—one hit apiece.

Jared took a deep breath and looked down at his hands. "I dreamt of many things as a boy." He looked up, across the ring, over the heads of the crowd. "I dreamt of becoming a farmer, raising and herding sheep. I dreamt of becoming a soldier, defending the weak. I dreamt of becoming a ruler with my own lands." A faint smile tugged at Jared's lips. "I dreamt of marrying. Having children. Settling down."

"Your parents approved of these dreams?"

"My parents are dead."

"Ah. That explains much." Verner glanced at Jared. "You lacked guidance as a child."

"My cousin—"

"A cousin is not a parent, no matter how hard he or she may try. Your friends were all older—a shepherd, a soldier, and a ruler—the latter your cousin, at a guess. Correct?"

"Yes."

"And there were others. Other friends and other dreams?"

"Well... yes."

Verner nodded and smiled to himself. "But the dream you followed, that one was all your own?"

"I always wanted to travel. To see the world."

"And the prostitution? It was an accident?"

"Yes."

The two fighters clashed again, their batons coming together with such speed the crack of their collisions merged into one continuous ring. Sweat dripped from Armon's brow, and his muscles showed more strain with every blow, his veins pushing against his skin like thirsty roots desperate to break through the soil.

Andreas targeted Armon's right baton, buffeting it with blow after blow, forcing it wider with every hit.

Armon's arm trembled under the barrage. His shoulder dipped.

Andreas swept his baton wide, blocking the disguised counter. Then he drew his right hand back past his shoulder and launched it forward, putting all his power into the swing. The blow sent Armon's baton flying. He ducked as Armon's second baton came in again, stepped inside his reach, and tapped his nose.

Armon spread his hands wide, accepting defeat.

"It has been a pleasure to speak with you," Verner said, his words almost lost in the eruption of cheers. "But your friend looks like he would have words with you. I look forward to speaking again another time."

"My friend?" Jared looked round, but Verner had gone. When he turned back, he spotted Armon heading towards him. "I would hardly call him my friend."

"Talking to yourself again?" Armon asked when he reached Jared's side.

"No, I was just..." Jared shook his head "It doesn't matter."

Armon turned to stand with his back to the barrier and surveyed the dispersing crowd. "What did Verner want?"

"He'd heard the rumours about my being a prostitute. Wanted to know how it came about." Jared shifted his grip and pushed away from the barrier. "You lost on purpose."

"Excuse me?"

"You're better than that. You were holding back."

"I was exhausted."

"I've spent the last three weeks training with you. I know you're better."

"Then try using your brain for a change. The reason for my restraint's obvious if you would take a moment to think on it."

Jared matched Armon's stare. He opened his mouth, closed it, and ran his hand through his hair. "You didn't want to offend the Canri by defeating their champion?"

"Oh, for..." Armon stepped closer and lowered his voice. "Do you honestly think Malkem would still be a lowly patrol leader if he was anything other than average? Average thinker, average leader, average fighter. Andreas would have defeated me regardless. He was being polite." Armon straightened and stepped back. "Now, if you'll excuse me, I need to eat."

Well. That could have gone better.

'Indeed.'

A finger tapped Jared's shoulder. He turned, glanced at the newcomer, and dipped his head. "Lady Zandra."

"Jared." Tessa returned Jared's bow with a smile. "There's a chair free at my table if you'd care to join me."

Jared started to shake his head. "I—"

"Salem is aware of the seating arrangements."

"Then I would be honoured. Thank you."

"And don't mind the patrol leader. He growls more when he's hungry."

27/12/32 KAF (Five)

The crowd split apart, individuals breaking away in ones and twos to locate their seats, leaving Jared with an unobstructed view of the square. The hog pens and fighting rings had been cleared, and the central fire reduced to a low blaze. The nine fires ringing the square had been banked, and trestle tables and benches now surrounded each one. Tessa supported Jared's weight as he hobbled to the fire on the far right of the square, guiding him to a bench on the outer edge, facing towards the centre.

He took a seat to Mevin's right. Tessa slipped onto the bench beside him. Ruskin, his arm bound in a sling, sat on Mevin's left. Several other patrolmen and an equal number of Canri filled the remaining benches. Jared nodded to those he recognised: Oskar and Andreas.

Andreas nodded back.

Oskar scowled.

Jared dropped his gaze to the fire.

A dozen squared posts enclosed the banked blaze, supporting a large grill resting an inch above the glowing coals. Roasting meats covered the criss-crossed iron, juices dripping to hiss and spit upon contact with the fire's heat.

Jared swallowed before he drooled.

"Smells good, doesn't it?" Mevin asked.

"Very."

A butchered wild hog lay on the grill, its head in the centre, surrounded by leg joints, ribs, chops, and gammon. Several smaller animals—chickens, fish, and what appeared to be oversized rabbits—had also been prepared and laid out to cook. Cabbages and onions nestled with other, less familiar vegetables, including a dozen six-inch long cylinders covered in small yellow nodules.

"I'm having the ribs," Mevin said, looking at his fellow diners as if daring them to argue.

"Ribs are for children," Ruskin scoffed. "All bone and scraps of meat. You'd be better off with a chop or two. Or a big slice of gammon."

"Nonsense. The flavour's all in the ribs. And the sauce they use—"

"Sauce. Pah!"

Jared's gaze drifted as he half-listened to the continuing debate, lifting over the guests across from him to take in the rest of the square. The three Canri leaders, Furste Hjalmar, Magistra Justus, and Vortai Yngve, were seated around the neighbouring fire. Their Kingdom counterparts, Ambassador Salem and Alsam Azier, sat across from them. A third man occupied the bench on their far side. "Is that Patrol Leader Malkem?" Jared asked.

"Yes. He's there to represent the patrol," Tessa said, leaning close and keeping her voice low. "I imagine Salem won't be too pleased with the arrangement."

"Is he ever happy about anything?"

"Probably not."

A shadow detached itself from between Justus and Yngve, circled the table, and mounted the small stage near the central fire. The fire's flames painted the shadow's face in a mask of oranges and reds, revealing his identity to everyone gathered in the square. Arvid turned in a slow circle, his hands raised for attention. The crowd quieted as everyone present turned to watch. He lowered his hands and began to speak. "Tack, ärade gäster..."

"Thank you, honoured guests," Tessa said. "Your representatives have performed well and provided good competition. You honour us by partaking in our games."

Arvid paused for breath, and Tessa added, "I'm afraid it's not an exact translation. My Canri is not the best."

Arvid resumed his speech, and Tessa continued, "All players successfully caught their hog, but it was Pol Artursson who proved most efficient." Arvid pointed towards the man who had drawn the short straw earlier that night. Pol stood and waved, earning a loud cheer.

Arvid waited a few moments before raising his hands for silence. "In the horse relay, our people took victory." Another cheer. "And finally, in the baton contest, Patrol Leader Malkem fought valiantly, making it to the final round. But it was our champion, Andreas Kristofson, who proved the strongest." This produced the loudest cheer of the night.

Several minutes passed before the crowd quieted again. "It is our hope that these games help bond our people with our honoured guests. And that these games, and this feast, provide a solid base for future negotiations. And now, please, eat."

"About bloody time," Ruskin grumbled.

Mevin took Ruskin's plate and started piling on food.

Jared picked up his, meaning to do the same, but Tessa pulled it off him. "Sit still and rest your leg. I'll get it."

"At least I'm not the only invalid here," Ruskin said, loud enough for everyone seated at their table to hear.

"True," Jared said. "But I've got a beautiful young woman to look after me. You, on the other hand…" He grinned and nodded at Mevin.

"Hey!" Mevin set Ruskin's loaded plate on the table with a thunk. "I'm not that ugly."

"No, lad," Ruskin said. "But you're not much good for extra convalescent services, if you get my meaning."

Mevin turned on Jared. "What have you been saying?"

"Not a word, I swear."

"But… he… oh. Oh!" Mevin busied himself filling his own plate, his blush darkening his face by a half-dozen shades.

Ruskin guffawed and slapped Mevin on the back. "Don't worry, lad. I won't be asking you for that. Although I imagine our friend here might have someone on his mind." Ruskin looked from Jared to Tessa and back, his suggestive wink so exaggerated everyone laughed.

"No." Jared noticed the smile slip from Ruskin's face and rushed to explain. "I mean, I barely know Lady Zandra. For all I know, she's secretly married and has ten children hidden at home. I wouldn't—"

Tessa placed two full plates on the table and picked up her cup. "That's not what I've heard."

"No. Really. I would never cuckold someone. I do have some standards."

That drew a burst of laughter from Ruskin. "What about this al-Rishad that's supposed to be hunting for you?"

"Never heard of him." Jared picked up a chop and ripped off a chunk with his teeth. It dissolved on his tongue. He took another bite, taking time to savour the meat.

"Never heard of…?" Mevin looked at Jared as though he were crazy. "Prince Akran al-Rishad, the King's cousin, and the ruler of Inchlass. How can you not have heard of him?"

"Not everyone's obsessed with the Blood like you," Ruskin said around a mouthful of pork.

"But Jared *is* Blood."

"Minor Blood." Jared finished the chop and picked up one of the strange yellow cylinders. He'd noticed several of the Canri biting the nodules off theirs and did the same. Hot juice filled his mouth and ran down his chin. "No title. No lands." He took another bite, enjoying the vegetable's sweet taste.

"But still... You're *Blood.*"

"Stop changing the subject. We were discussing his integrity." Ruskin leant past Mevin to look Jared in the eye. "You're honestly telling me you've never had sex with a married woman?"

"Never. Nor will I."

"Son of a... Not even if they offered to pay double?"

"No."

"Not even by accident?" Mevin asked.

"No." Jared lowered his hands. "Well... There was one time. But I didn't actually sleep with her."

"What happened?"

"I—" Jared hesitated, glanced at Tessa, then at the hilt of the knife she kept tucked in her belt. "Perhaps another time."

Tessa laughed. "Don't stop on my account. I'm a woman of the world, not a shy, retiring noble's daughter."

"Uh—"

'What's wrong? Afraid your audience will listen to your sordid little tale and disapprove?'

No. I doubt their opinion of me could get much lower. And it's hardly sordid.

'Perhaps. Perhaps not. But why hesitate? Why not use the reputation Armon built for you to your advantage for a change?'

My advantage? I don't see what advantage I'll gain by boasting of my lack of judgement. I've already confessed my ignorance—

'And you've only just realised?' Cackling laughter bounced around Jared's skull. *'Don't you want to be accepted, to bask in Mevin's wide-eyed worship and laugh with Ruskin instead of being laughed at again?'*

Well... Jared blinked and looked around, expecting everyone to be staring, waiting for him to respond, but none of them had moved more than a fraction, his silent conversation having taken less time than was needed to draw a breath. He recalled Tessa's prompting and shrugged.

"If you insist." He tossed the odd yellow vegetable onto his plate and wiped its juice from his mouth. "It happened when I was seventeen—"

"How old are you now?" Mevin asked.

Ruskin jabbed Mevin with his elbow. "Don't interrupt."

"Sorry."

Jared sipped his wine to hide his grin, placed his glass on the table, and started again. "As I was saying, I was seventeen, and my cousin had asked me to deliver a message to one of his outlying villages. I'd carried a few messages for him before, but it was the first time he'd trusted me to go by myself."

"So this courier thing wasn't just a cover?" Ruskin asked.

"No." Jared took another sip. "The village was two days ride away, so I stopped at a small farm for the night. A woman greeted me at the farmhouse. A tall, elegant, confident, curvaceous woman. A beauty to my inexperienced eyes. Looking back, though…" He chuckled and shook his head. "She invited me to eat in the kitchen with the rest of the farmhands, served me herself, sat next to me, spent the whole evening talking to me and dropping hints.

"Then, after the farmhands left, she invited me upstairs. Young and naïve as I was, I never thought to question her. She took me to her room and suggested I strip off whilst she got into bed. So there I was, naked as a newborn, standing in the middle of her room, trying my best to look at her face and not her large breasts, when the front door slammed, and a man called her name.

"She turned as pale as bleached mahogany, leapt from the bed, and rushed me to the bedroom window, shoving my courier bag into my hands. I climbed out onto a small roof, but before I could ask for my clothes, she slammed the shutters in my face—"

"Now *that* is a sight I would have paid to see," Ruskin said.

Jared tried the ribs whilst he waited for Ruskin to stop laughing. The sauce was hot and sticky, with a sweet, smoky taste. He took another bite and chewed it slowly.

"Well," Mevin asked, looking tense as a coiled spring about to launch, "what did you do next?"

"I listened to them fu—" Jared glanced around the table, caught sight of Tessa's raised brow, and coughed. "I mean, I listened to them have sex." He bit his lip, trying not to laugh at the shock on Mevin's face.

"You did what?"

"Think about it. This man comes home late and finds his wife sprawled out on his bed without a stitch on. What would you expect them to do?"

"You could have left."

Jared shook his head. "Their bedroom was in the attic. I was stuck on a tiny tiled roof two floors above the ground, and all my clothes were still in her room. If I'd survived the drop to the ground without breaking my legs, there was still the minor problem of the stable hand sleeping in the hayloft. Can you imagine how he'd have reacted if he'd found me trying to retrieve my spare clothes from my saddlebags? I had no choice but to wait—"

"Whilst they—"

"Yes."

"And then?"

"I waited some more, until I heard snoring. Then I risked tapping on the shutter."

"Was she awake?"

"No. But the shutter opened at my touch. I crept inside, terrified her husband would wake and find me. Gods only know what he'd have thought if he'd found me sneaking about his house in the nude. Thankfully, he slept on.

"I found my clothes bundled under their bed and was in the middle of pulling them out when the snoring stopped. I dived under the bed, scraping the skin off my back in my hurry, but he just snorted and rolled over before going back to sleep. I crawled back out and got dressed, putting my tunic on backwards in my hurry. I was in the middle of adjusting it when I realised the woman was wide awake and watching me.

"She flashed me a mischievous smile, winked, and pointed back at the window. 'Guest room. On the right,' she whispered, before cuddling up to her husband and going back to sleep. I lay awake all night, imagining all sorts of horrors that might have been inflicted on me had I been discovered. I couldn't get out of there fast enough in the morning. I've avoided that farm ever since."

"To the follies of youth," Ruskin said, raising his glass. Several of the patrolmen joined him.

Jared raised his own glass, and Ruskin nodded. Having earned that small token of respect, he turned his attention to his food, happy to let others take over the conversation.

He tried the chicken breast and found it stuffed with cheese and mushrooms. The cabbage had been soaked in red wine, and the onions were caramelised, making them a perfect accompaniment to the gammon. He sampled it all, determined to try everything, although the sheer quantity of food left him overwhelmed.

"Have some of the hare," Tessa suggested. "The big rabbit," she added when he frowned at her.

He took a sip of water to cleanse his pallet and followed her advice. The meat fell off the bone and seemed to melt inside his mouth. "Mmm…" he smiled and nodded.

"You certainly seem to be enjoying it," Tessa said.

"The Canri know how to cook. And all these sauces and spices they use… they're wonderful." He picked up the half-eaten yellow vegetable and showed it to her. "What do they call this?"

"Sockermajs. We'd call it sweetcorn."

"It's well named." He looked at his plate—at the mound of half-eaten pieces of food on it—and his cheeks burned. "I don't normally eat like this. I seem to have worked up an appetite."

"I'm not surprised." Tessa picked at her own meal. "How's your leg?"

"There's no permanent damage. Mevin assures me it'll heal by itself."

"That's good. Any other problems I should know about?"

The question buzzed in Jared's ears, but its meaning went over his head. He stared at the head table and the woman sitting there, statuesque as a queen. She'd had her back to him since the meal began but had turned at a shout from across the square, granting him a glimpse of her face. Even at a distance, in the mix of firelight and starlight, he recognised her eyes; her captivating, black eyes. He ran his gaze over her arched back and her thick, black hair nestled in its curve. "Who is she?"

Tessa caught the whisper and followed his gaze. "No-one I've been introduced to. She must be important though, to merit a seat at the head table."

Jared continued to watch her, hoping for another look at her face, but she didn't turn around again.

❧

Jared's leg throbbed in time with the pulse thrumming in his aching head. His muscles had stiffened in the cool night air, and his stomach felt as heavy and full as an overripe pumpkin. He closed his stinging eyes, wanting to rest them for just a moment—

"Hey." Mevin elbowed him in the ribs. "No sleeping."

"I wasn't—"

"Were too."

Jared straightened his back and rubbed his eyes. "It's been a long day."

"A long day? It's just past midnight—"

"Did you get any sleep this afternoon?" Tessa asked.

Jared blinked at her. "Was I supposed to?"

"Mevin, help Jared back to his room, please."

"But we haven't had the—"

"Please, Mevin. It'll only take ten minutes."

The scowl which had accompanied Mevin's protest smoothed away. He bowed his head. "If it pleases you, my lady."

"It does. Thank you." Tessa smiled.

Mevin blushed.

'What? No protest?'

Should there be?

'They're packing you off to bed like a child whilst they stay up and enjoy the party.'

I'm tired.

'So go stick your head in a water trough and come back. Why miss all the fun?'

I just want to—

Tessa caught Jared's chin and pulled him around to face her. She stared into his eyes, searching.

Jared squirmed under her intense gaze. "Lady Zandra?"

"Are you feeling well?"

"I'm tired. I ache. I ate too much. Apart from that, I'm fine."

"You sure? It's just that, for a moment there, you looked… different." She let him go.

"Different?" Jared glanced down at his hands then forced himself to meet her eyes, even as he recalled the not-quite-right reflection he'd glimpsed in the mirror earlier. "Different how?"

"I'm not sure, just… different." She shrugged and laughed. "It was probably a trick of the light. Forgive me."

"There's nothing to forgive, my lady." Jared lifted Tessa's hand in his and touched it to his lips. "It's been a pleasure to spend the night in your company."

"The pleasure was mine." Tessa pulled her hand back. "Goodnight, Jared."

"Goodnight, my lady." Jared stood and straddled the bench. He glanced towards the head table, but the black-eyed woman was gone. She must have slipped off whilst he was distracted. He scanned the square, but only a few people moved about, and she didn't appear to be amongst them. He turned back, and his eyes locked with Armon's.

Armon held his gaze for a breathless second, scowled, and looked away.

Mevin appeared at Jared's side, ducked beneath his arm, and supported his weight whilst he lifted his other leg over the bench.

"So," Mevin asked once they were clear of the square, "you really don't wish to get to know Lady Zandra better?"

Jared shook his head. "After my... difficulties... with Lady Morgain, I want to stay clear of women for a while." He paused, glanced up and down the street to make sure they were alone, then chewed on his lip for a moment before adding, "I've discovered a lot of things about myself these last few weeks. Things I'm not particularly proud of."

"What sort of things?"

Jared almost told Mevin to mind his own business, but he'd been the one to bring the topic up. He couldn't fault him for being curious. Besides, it felt good to have someone to talk to; someone who hadn't pre-judged him and found him wanting.

It isn't as though I have anyone else I can trust—

'Trust? Yes. Trust the immature young man you've known for a handful of hours. An excellent choice.'

And what would you suggest? That I trust Armon instead? Or perhaps you'd rather I talk to Tessa?

'Tessa would be the better choice. At least you'd get to have some fun before you die.'

I doubt Tessa's idea of fun is compatible with mine. Besides, if I don't confide in someone soon, I'm going to explode. He cleared his throat. "Lots of things. I'm not very good at defending myself, for one."

"Most people aren't. That's why they employ bodyguards and soldiers."

"My unwillingness, or inability, to commit."

"To Lady Morgain, you mean?"

Jared made a non-committal grunt. "My ignorance of politics."

"Politics are boring."

"Maybe, but even you know more about them than me. And you, if you'll forgive me saying so, are still a boy."

Mevin shrugged. "I wouldn't have a clue if it weren't for the patrol leader. He makes a point of telling us what's what. Says we can't do our job properly otherwise."

"He's a wise man." Jared almost tripped, startled by his own words, but they were true. Armon always seemed a step ahead of those around him. He read people better than most people could read books, kept up with the latest news and gossip, and knew precisely how to manipulate a situation to his best advantage. As for himself, he hadn't found a jot of information for Ryal, and he'd been gone a month.

They completed their journey in silence. The patrolmen on duty at the embassy greeted Mevin with nods and salutes and waved them inside.

Mevin helped Jared across the courtyard, through the embassy door, and along the corridors to his room. "Do you need help getting changed?"

Jared shook his head. "I can manage. Thank you."

"Just doing my job." Mevin looked around the room, plucked Jared's saddlebags from atop his clothes chest, and moved them to the foot of the bed. "Rest your leg on there while you sleep. The elevation will help stop any swelling."

"Thank you." Jared waited for Mevin to leave then pushed the door closed. He pulled off his clothes, tossed them in a corner, and flopped onto the bed, too tired to complain about the hard, unforgiving stone base. Once he was asleep, however, images of angry hogs, bucking horses, and broken bones haunted his dreams. And hovering above it all, watching everything, were those eyes; those haunting, beautiful, black eyes.

28/12/32 KAF (One)

Armon crossed to the left-hand side of the corridor, pushed on the first door to ensure it was latched, then crossed back to check the opposite alcove. His feet still moved to the rhythm of the drums that had roared the beat for the feast's final dance, and his heart still pounded from the exertion. He peered behind the pedestal, confirmed the shadowed area was empty, and returned to the corridor.

Exhaustion pulled his eyelids closed, and his head bobbed on his neck as he walked. He blinked, and Tessa's smiling face swirled before his eyes. Firelight painted highlights in her hair and glistened on her sweat-soaked skin as she whirled and swayed in time with the thundering drums. A soft hum rose from his chest as he checked the next door. He crossed the corridor, the hum deepening to a growl. He saw Ruskin, nodding and laughing. Mevin, eyes wide with boyish delight. Jared—

Armon slammed his fist into the wall.

Jared hadn't been there.

He stood, fist planted and head bowed, and sucked in a breath to steady himself. He'd known when they left the Kingdom that this would happen. He'd known when he agreed to Tessa's coming the part she would play. He needed to take control of himself.

He took another breath, straightened, and checked the alcove. Empty, of course. He scratched the back of his hand.

The chances of finding anything out of place were slim—his men knew their job—but the occasional random check would ensure their continued vigilance. And it gave him a means to work off some of the energy buzzing through him like lightning trapped in the clouds before a storm. He checked the next door and scratched his other hand.

Footsteps echoed off the walls.

He dropped his hand to his sword hilt and shifted into a fighting stance.

The footsteps grew louder. A shadow crossed the end of the corridor.

He flexed his fingers to keep them from cramping, rocked his weight forward, then laughed when he recognised the grey-haired form of his sub-patrol leader. "Pavel." He saluted, fist to heart.

Pavel snapped to attention, his heels cracking against the floor tiles, and mirrored the salute. "Surprise inspection, sir?"

"Aye." Armon tucked his hand behind his back and rubbed it against his belt. "Any problems to report?"

"No, sir."

"Very good. Carry on."

"Sir." Pavel acknowledged the order with a short, sharp nod and resumed his patrol.

Armon watched him for a moment before returning to his own inspection.

He turned into the next corridor and passed the doors to the baths on his left, the doors to the dining and kitchen facilities on his right. A quick check confirmed all were locked securely for the night.

The final turn took him into the servants' section, with more doors and more decorative alcoves. He repeated his routine, pushing on the doors, crossing to the other side, and inspecting the alcoves.

Door.

Alcove.

Door.

Al—

He froze. Faint light flickered underneath the opposite door. He switched his weight to the balls of his feet, drew his sword with a slow, silent motion, and tiptoed to the wall. A pause, one ear pressed to the door. Nothing stirred on the other side of the thick boards. He turned to put his right side to the door, double-checked his grip on his sword hilt, and slammed his left hand down on the handle.

The door flew open and cracked against the side wall. He ducked in behind it, using its movement to mask his own, holding his sword across his body to block any attack.

Jared stared at him from the bed, open-mouthed, with one hand holding a book in his lap and the other pressed flat against the wall. His right leg lay propped up on his saddlebags. His left was half-bent, his weight on his foot. His body was twisted sideways, as though he were about to rise.

Armon stared for a moment longer, then straightened and sheathed his sword. "You're awake early," he said, struggling to keep his voice light.

Jared lowered his hand and settled his weight back onto his backside. "I woke about an hour ago and couldn't get back to sleep, so I thought I'd read." He lifted his book, as if to prove his explanation, then let it drop into his lap. "You could have knocked," he said, a touch of irritation colouring his words.

"And risked giving an intruder time to attack or escape?" Armon shook his head. "The safety of the embassy outweighs your privacy and comfort." He took a step towards the door and hesitated. "How's your leg?"

"Not too bad."

"Think you can walk on it?"

"Maybe. Why?"

"There's something I'd like you to see."

The look Jared threw him could have melted iron, but he closed his book without protest, set it aside, and extended his hand.

Armon grabbed it and pulled, helping Jared to his feet. "I need to finish my patrol first. Go on ahead. I'll meet you in the courtyard. It should only take a few minutes."

Armon watched Jared stroll down the corridor and nodded to himself. A smattering of pride had squared Jared's shoulders and straightened his back, and despite his newly earned limp, he'd regained his graceful stride. This was the man Armon had been looking for; the man he was going to need. He checked the remaining doors and alcoves then hurried outside.

҂

A few small clouds drifted across the pre-dawn sky—a sky turning purple on the horizon. Jared waited in the middle of the embassy courtyard, head tilted back and arms crossed over his chest. He dropped his gaze when he heard the embassy door open and acknowledged Armon's arrival with a dip of his head. "What did you want to show me?"

"Patience, dandy boy. You'll see soon enough." Armon marched past without slowing, saluted the men guarding the embassy gates, and squeezed through the narrow gap they created for him. Jared followed on his heels, limping as he struggled to keep pace.

Silence enclosed them, made more powerful by the contrast to the raucous shouts and cheers that had dominated just a few hours before. Jared softened his step to minimise the crunch of his footfalls, aware of Armon having done the same a moment before. Nobody else moved on the road or stirred behind the other embassies' high walls. No lights bloomed in the wall sconces or glowed in the few visible windows. No fires illuminated the vast market square.

A high-pitched caw cut the air. Jared shuddered, glanced over his shoulder, turned back, and ploughed into Armon's back. "What—?"

At that moment, the sun broke over the horizon. Where its light touched the square, the stone glowed. Hundreds of miniature rays rose from the ground, each one reaching skyward, fighting to return to the sun. They stretched, growing taut as bowstrings and translucent as insect wings, froze for the length of a heartbeat, then exploded, each one like a tiny, yellow-sparked firework.

The front line of light rolled forward, rising, stretching, and collapsing like a giant wave, its march as inexorable as the coming of the sun. Jared took an involuntary step backwards, but Armon held his ground. The light washed over him without visible harm.

"What...?" Jared repeated, bracing himself against the wave's unavoidable touch. Where the light passed, the city gleamed. The thin layer of dirt covering the square had vanished, revealing a complex mosaic made up of thousands of glistening tiles. He walked forward half-a-dozen paces, dropped to a crouch, ran a finger over the them, and stared at its unsullied tip. "Impossible," he whispered.

"It's part of the Vortai's message," Armon said as he stepped up beside him. "What we witnessed is a minute part of the power protecting Canri."

"But we raced on cobbles. Fought on dirt." Jared stood. "The fires. They should have left some scorch marks."

"The cobbles and dirt were temporary. Slave crews cleared most of it when the celebrations finished. You saw what happened to the rest."

Saw it? Yes. Believed it? Jared shook his head. He crossed to the centre of the square, dropped to his knees, and ran a fingernail along the gap between the tiles. His probing uncovered nothing but fine-grained sand. "Magic?" he asked when he returned.

"Of a sort. But not the magic you hear about in stories. The Canri can't wish something into being or whisper a few words and produce fireballs to throw at their enemies. This magic takes longer. Goes deeper. The entire city is one giant spell."

"A spell of cleanliness?"

"A spell of strength and renewal. For the city and its people. Every pure blooded Canri who touches the pattern benefits. That's why they covered the square last night. To give us a fair chance during the games."

"How do you know all this?"

"It's my job to know." For a moment, it looked like Armon would say more, but then he looked away, shook his head, and signalled for Jared to follow.

෧෫

Armon shrugged his shoulders, left then right, to ease the itch at the juncture of his shoulder blades. How did Jared do it? How did the fool dandy boy manage to get under his skin even when they were getting on? One second they'd been discussing the Canri magic, the next Jared had smiled that fool smile of his and—

Armon growled deep in his chest and clenched his fists to keep from clawing furrows in his skin. *Together. We need to work together.*

The reminder didn't help. He pictured Jared in the great hall, smiling in admiration at Morgain. Jared, lounging on *The Hunter*'s rail, talking to Tessa. Jared, at the feast, hands waving as he told some tale, oblivious to the appreciative stares and giggles of the chestnut-haired woman and her companion on the next table over.

"It looks like a stormy sea," Jared said, his voice carrying across the empty square.

Armon paused at the entrance to a side-street and looked back. "What does?"

"The mosaic. All the dark blues and greens and greys swirling about. And the splashes of colour could be sails, a convoy scattered by the wind."

Armon expelled his agitation with a breath and crossed his arms over his chest. "I've always thought it looks like a forest late at night, filled with nocturnal flowers and prowling animals. The reds and yellows remind me of flames. Human invaders carrying torches, or campers, perhaps." He met Jared's contemplative gaze, cast one more glance over the abstract pattern, shrugged, and moved on.

The street he led them along curved away from the square. Three-storey buildings, built from a variety of brightly coloured stone bricks, towered over them on both sides. Heavy doors and thick shutters kept passers-by out, though here and there the shutters had been thrown open, only to reveal empty, dark rooms within.

"Does nobody live here?" Jared asked.

"Not many foreigners can afford these houses." Armon slowed his pace a fraction. "Most of them live in poorer parts of the district."

"Then why—?"

"To maintain the pattern. And to house visitors, when they get them."

"It feels like a ghost town."

Armon checked a nod. He wasn't too enamoured of the uninhabited shells himself. "Ever seen a ghost?" he asked, spurred on by an irresistible need to say *something*.

"No."

"I have." He turned left along another, identical street and slowed his pace. "When I was ten or eleven. I'd been sent to the kitchens to collect Morgain's breakfast. On my way there, I saw a woman out the corner of my eye. She wore a heavy, dark green dress. Velvet, I think, with lace trim around the neckline and wrists. And her hair—black, or very dark brown—was coiled atop her head like a giant hive. She reminded me of one of the women in the household's portraits, but when I looked at her directly, she vanished."

"Sounds scary."

"Not really." The street ended at a tall, reinforced oak gate. Armon rapped his knuckles against the gatepost, drumming out the patrol's signal. "I was more scared of Morgain's reaction if I let her food get cold." He shook his head at himself and knocked again.

The gate opened a few seconds later, just wide enough for the patrolman on duty to peer out. He took one look at Armon, snapped a salute, and stepped aside. Armon motioned for Jared to enter the paddock first.

It was a fair size, walled in on all sides, with a triple-aisled stable block toward the back. "Sherna's in the central aisle. Second last stall on the right," Armon said as he followed Jared across the sun-dried grass. "I put Regal in one of the outer stalls so he won't upset the rest of the horses."

A small, plank door set into the larger, arched one gave access to the central stable. Armon ducked instinctively as he entered then waited whilst Jared headed for Sherna's stall. Sunlight streamed past him through the open door, but the rest of the stable languished in shadow, with the shutters on the skylights closed against the fading night. As Jared moved further up the aisle, he disappeared into the shadows, swallowed like a toad hiding in detritus.

Armon rubbed at the back of his neck to ease the building pressure; the inexplicable urge to speak. "Regal's a good mount," he called. "Knows how to follow orders and doesn't spook. I don't suppose you'd consider selling him?"

A soft whisper emanated from the far end of the stable, a low whinny, a thud, and a laugh. A few more seconds passed in silence, then, "I'd starve before I let him go."

"Fair enough." He didn't even know what he wanted to talk about. No. That wasn't true. He knew *what* he wanted to talk about, but he didn't know why. And why now? There'd been plenty of opportunities for him to mention it during their voyage on *The Hunter*. Or he could have said something in the baths yesterday afternoon, or anytime they were together during the feast. But it had made no sense to mention it then, and it made even less to do so now. He was tired, that was all. Tired and not thinking properly. He would go back to the embassy and sleep on it. Consider the matter again when he woke. Perhaps then he'd be able to think clearly. Perhaps sleep would rid him of this incessant *itch*. "I saw you with Tessa last night." *So much for that plan.*

"I didn't have a choice."

"I know. I wasn't complaining. I..."

Jared's silhouette broadened. "You what?"

"I need her. She's the most precious thing in my life. When I see her with other men, it terrifies me." Armon paused, trying to restore order to his thoughts, but they refused to still, swarming about inside his head like midges. He ran his hands through his hair, grabbed a handful, and pulled. "When I saw you kiss her hand, it was like being stabbed in the heart. But I know—I *know*—you were only playing your part, and I still hate you for it." He turned and pressed his forehead against the stable wall. "I don't know what I'd do if I lost her. She's the only one who understands."

"Understands what?"

"Me. She's the only one... the only one who really knows me."

"What about Morgain? Stanin? Your men? From what I've seen, they'd follow you anywhere, even if it meant their deaths."

"No. No, no, no. It's not the same. They see Malkem. Or they see an employer. Or they see the spymaster. But me?" He touched a hand to his chest. "Me?" He laughed and shook his head. "You have no idea what it's like. Always pretending to be someone you're not, always acting out a part. Tessa is the one—the *only* one—who has ever seen the truth." He pushed himself away from the wall and turned to face Jared's silhouette. "Every day, I think I'll lose her. Every day, I see a thousand reasons for her to walk away. And then I see her with you, and every part of me burns with anger because I know... I *know*... you could tear her away from me."

"I have no intention—"

"Neither does Tessa. But that doesn't stop me thinking... doesn't stop... doesn't change..." He tipped back his head. Took a deep breath. "I've spent my life being invisible, a thing of shame to be hidden away. I can't go back to that. I can't."

"Why are you telling me this?"

"Why?" Armon shook his head and half-turned, bit down on his lip, and turned back.

"Why?" he asked again, as though by doing so he could stem the flow of words.

"Why?" he whispered, aiming the question at himself this time.

Why did I go and open my big, stupid mouth?

"Because she's my wife, that's why!" He stalked from the stable before Jared could reply.

Sherna lipped Jared's trouser leg, coating it in slobber. He reached into the nearby bag of almonds, his gaze fixed on the stable door. *His wife?*

'So he claims. You should follow.'

Yes, but... his wife? He took a step forward.

Sherna butted his chest with her nose. He staggered back, frowned at her, and opened his hand. Puffs of hot breath warmed his skin as she snaffled the almonds.

'You're wasting time.'

I know! He gave Sherna's neck a solid pat and limped down the aisle. By the time he reached the exit, Armon had already left the paddock.

The patrolman on guard scowled at Jared but didn't challenge him as he hurried past. Jared glanced at the sky as he hobbled along the path. Light from the rising sun caught the edges of the thin spread of clouds, turning them various shades of pink and orange. Several large birds had taken flight to the east, their high-pitched calls piercing the morning quiet like children screeching during prayer.

He reached the gate, pulled it open, and stepped into the street outside.

Armon hadn't gotten far. He traipsed along the road, his steps unsteady, his course meandering from one side of the street to the other.

"Wait!" Jared ran after him, wincing as each step sent pain stabbing up his leg.

Armon didn't slow, either failing to hear Jared's shout, or choosing to ignore him.

"Wait," Jared said again. He drew level with Armon and fell into step beside him. "You can't say something like that then walk away."

"Can't I?"

"No. I mean. Your *wife*?" He placed his hand on Armon's shoulder to pull him back.

Armon had one hand around Jared's wrist before he realised he'd moved. The other latched onto his collar. With a deft twist, he set them both spinning and slammed Jared against the nearest wall. "Keep your hands to yourself," he said, his face an inch from Jared's. The whiff of alcohol accompanied every word.

"How much have you had to drink?"

"How much...?" Armon stepped back, loosening his grip. "No more than anyone else. I'm not drunk, if that's what you're implying."

"You sure?"

Armon let Jared go, helped him to get his balance, and straightened his jacket. "I've had a couple of glasses of wine. Some mead. No. It's this city. It makes my skin itch."

"I know it's a little strange here, but—"

"No. I mean it literally makes my skin itch, under the surface, just out of reach. Can't you feel it?"

"No."

"It's driving me crazy." Armon waved his hand about his head and started walking. "About earlier..."

"I'm sorry."

Armon stopped and stared at Jared like he was crazy. "What?"

"You and Tessa. If I'd known you were married, I never would have... It's not a line I'd cross."

"Not a line...?" Armon looked up and down the street, as though to check they were still alone, then turned back to Jared, one eyebrow raised. "I reveal my most private, best kept secret, and you…?" He shook his head. "You are not that stupid."

"No, I'm not. But who would I tell? Ambassador Salem?" Jared paused just long enough for Armon's expression to darken towards a scowl, then let out a soft chuckle. "To what gain? He dislikes me as much as you do. At least with you, I know what I'm getting." *And as long as you think I might tell him…* Jared smiled.

Armon responded to the smile with his familiar mocking grin. "Very well. If that's how you want to play it, consider your apology accepted." He resumed his slow walk.

Jared fell into step beside him. "You can't say you didn't deserve it though."

Armon grunted.

Jared glanced at him but couldn't tell if he were amused or irritated. "You did destroy my relationship," he said after a few more paces. "I'd been planning to propose."

"And the day you announced your engagement, Morgain would have had you both killed."

Jared stopped, staring at Armon's back. Why had he never considered what might have happened without Armon's interference? He'd just assumed… "You cannot tell me you did this for my benefit."

"Of course not." Armon paused until Jared drew level with him. "But your naivety astounds me sometimes. You're like a child playing at being a grown up. You think the world is full of roses, but you never see the thorns."

"You think I'm that stupid?"

"Not stupid. Innocent. Sheltered." Armon lifted his hands, stared at them for a moment, scowled, and stuffed them under his arms. "Tell me something. When you travel through towns and cities, do you ever consider the beggars in the streets?"

"It's impossible not to see—"

"I said consider, not see. Do you ever think about their circumstances? Ever wonder how they ended up so destitute they're forced to beg to stay alive?"

"I… No."

"Ever wondered what drives a woman to work as a serving wench or sell her body as a whore?"

"Not really."

"What about the street urchins? Did you ever wonder why they resort to thievery and crime, rather than getting a paying job?"

"All right, all right, I get it. I'm an ignorant, self-centred bastard. You don't need to keep going on."

Armon chuckled. "I'm the only bastard here. But no, you don't get it. Everyone thinks of themselves first. It's perfectly natural. Most people spend their entire lives in ignorance, happy to overlook anything that doesn't affect them. But some of us… some of us are forced to see the ugly truth." They reached the square where the feast had been held the night before. He walked forward a few steps before turning to face Jared. "When we see that truth, we have three choices. We can ignore it, we can become a part of it, or we can try to put it right."

"And you're trying to put it right?" Jared asked, queued by the emphasis Armon put on his final words.

"Yes."

Jared had to bite his tongue to silence a laugh. "How can you say that after everything you've done?"

"Walk with me. I'll try to explain." Armon started on a path cutting across the corner of the square, his route taking him towards a wide thoroughfare opposite the embassy road.

Jared planted his feet and crossed his arms. "Tell me something first."

Armon stopped, turned, and motioned for Jared to continue.

"Do you enjoy watching people suffer?"

"In what way?"

"Do you enjoy destroying their lives? Stealing their futures? Ending their dreams?"

"Not particularly."

"Yet you seemed to take immense pleasure in it when you did it to me."

"That was personal, and I was wrong. I've already apologised for misjudging you." Armon turned to go.

"What about torture?" Jared asked, raising his voice a fraction. "Do you enjoy that?"

Armon closed the gap between them in a dozen short, snappy strides. He lifted his hands, fingers curling towards, but not quite grasping, Jared's jacket. "Torture is a necessary evil but certainly not something I would ever enjoy."

"And yet you serve a woman who revels in torture and humiliation."

Something flashed across Armon's face. Doubt, or guilt, or both? Whatever it was, it vanished as quickly as it had appeared, replaced by his mocking grin. Only this time, the grin seemed forced, a mask slammed into place to hide the truth. "As I said, a necessary evil."

"One you hate?"

Armon spun away, heading for the thoroughfare once more, not bothering to check if Jared followed or not.

'Well that hit a nerve.'

Jared hurried after Armon, glancing to the side every few strides to take in his surroundings. Two-storey buildings, in a variety of shades of pastel stones, lined both sides of the street, each one separated from its neighbour by a narrow alley. Signs hung above each door—the first painted with a needle and thread, the second with an old boot, the third a saddle and bridle. Several had stalls set up under their large windows.

"You can't pretend it doesn't happen," Jared called.

Armon looked over his shoulder, glanced down at Jared's injured leg, and slowed his pace. "I'm not."

"No. You're running away instead."

Armon's fists clenched, and his chest expanded, his brow compressing as he appeared to ready a retort. But then he came to an abrupt halt and released a long sigh. "Not here. Not now. There are too many ears listening."

"But we're alone." Even as Jared said it, he realised it wasn't true. Most of the shops had their shutters thrown back, and some of the doors stood open, the shop owners working inside. Others had come out onto the street to set up their stalls. Still, he doubted any of them would understand a word he said.

"Not here." Armon scratched at the back of his hand, digging his nails in so hard they drew blood. "I can't stand this."

"Was it like this last time you were here?"

"What?"

"The itching."

Armon nodded. "There's a herbalist. Her shop's not far from here." He started walking again, his pace slow, his gaze searching. "She sold me a tea..."

Jared followed close behind, keeping silent.

Whatever was bothering Armon, it seemed to be growing worse. He scratched incessantly now, clawing at his hands as if he sought to tear off his own skin. He stopped without warning and clenched his fists, forcing his trembling arms down to his sides. "Wait here," he said, before disappearing inside one of the buildings.

Jared looked at its sign. It depicted a bunch of herbs tied with a piece of string. He sighed and turned his attention to the other shops, intending to browse whilst he waited, but most of the shopkeepers were still setting up their stalls—pulling off the covers, folding down tabletops, or bringing out boxes of goods, ready to unload. He didn't want to head inside in case he missed Armon coming out, so he walked over to the corner of the herbalist's shop to wait.

As he watched the shopkeepers work, he became aware of subtle differences between the men and women here and those he had met last night. There were variations in the shades of their skin. Some of them were darker, some paler, but none of them shared the Canri's forest-green tone. Their faces seemed less angular, less uniform in design. One woman had red hair, and there, one stall along from her, was an old man so short he must be considered a dwarf amongst the Canri. Jared studied them as he waited, wondering why none of them had been present at the feast.

'Isn't it obvious?'

Foreigners...

'Yes.'

Several of the shopkeepers glanced at him as they worked, but if they felt anything more than mild curiosity, it didn't show. One of them even pointed towards her shop, waving him forward. He refused with a firm shake of his head.

Several minutes passed before Armon emerged from the herbalist's. "See anything you like?"

Jared shook his head. "There's not much to see."

"The feast has thrown off their schedule. Market Street would normally be thronged with people by now. You'll have plenty of time to browse later. Come on." Armon set off, heading deeper into the city.

Jared followed a step behind.

Armon walked more easily now, the tension gone from his frame. He reached up to scratch his neck, caught himself doing it, and laughed. Then he glanced back at Jared and motioned for him to catch up. "What have you been saying to Mevin?"

"Stop changing the subject."

"I'm not... I need... We will discuss *that* later. My word on it."

"What makes you think I've been saying anything to Mevin?"

"After you left the feast, once everyone had finished eating, there was music and dancing. Strange, hypnotic dancing. Our groups split up. My men and I watched from the side. Mevin didn't stop talking about you the entire night. He told the tale of your leap from the back of the horse at least a dozen times, and he wasn't even there to see it. You must have said something to make such an impression on the lad."

"I just gave him a little advice."

"About?"

"Women."

"Ah. That would explain it." Armon rubbed at his arm, his hand trembling. "There's this young lass back home. He's got his heart set on her, but he's never found the courage to ask her out."

"How old is he?"

"Mevin? Seventeen. Maybe eighteen. He doesn't know his exact birthdate."

"Isn't he a little young to be a medic?"

"He's still training, but he knows enough to patch up a man and keep him alive until a real healer can take over. I've often thought about recruiting him."

"And here I was thinking you liked him."

Armon snapped his head around, his eyes darkening under a heavy scowl. "Excuse me?"

"What would you use to blackmail him?"

"Nothing. Mevin's Morgain's man to the core. He'd jump at the chance. No. It's his immaturity that holds me back. And his incessant talking. He doesn't know when to shut up. In a year or two though, if things work out..." Armon halted. They'd reached the crossroads at the end of Market Street. "He grew up on the streets. He knows what it's like. When I explain what we're trying to do..."

Jared followed Armon across the road, their path still taking them along the main thoroughfare. Armon said nothing more for several minutes, seeming content to walk in silence.

A dozen questions flitted through Jared's mind, but they were all questions he had asked before. Why had Armon felt the need to force him to serve? Why did he not give him the benefit of asking first? And what, exactly, did he and Morgain have planned? He almost asked his questions out loud, but he worried that, if he pushed too hard, Armon would clam up again. So he waited, let Armon walk, let the tea take full effect. And then he realised there was one question he could ask. One that had been bothering him all night. "Who is she?"

Armon stopped, looked around, then turned to Jared, his brows furrowed in a puzzled frown. "Which 'she'?"

"The one who was sitting at your table last night."

Armon smiled and started walking again. "Any particular one, or should I describe them all for you?"

"She had black eyes. Dark hair. She was seated to your right, with her back to me."

"Ah. Let me think." Armon lifted a hand, tapped one finger against his lips in an exaggerated gesture of thoughtfulness, and grinned. "I think I know which one you mean."

"And?"

"She is not a woman you want to mess with."

"She's married?"

"Not married, no, but she is one of the most powerful women in Canri. When she was younger, she fought in her father's war band. Worked her way through the ranks until she earned her command. She more than tripled her family's holdings before her father died and she became head of her family. Now her son leads her war band in her stead."

"Her son? But you said—"

"Her husband died three years ago. She's a widow."

"I see." It had been a foolish dream anyway. A fantasy built around a glimpse of her dark, commanding eyes.

Armon's grin softened. "Take my advice, dandy boy. Stay away from her."

"At least tell me her name."

"Karolina. Karolina Andersdotter."

A second street cut across the thoroughfare, its far side butted against a wall that looked to be the twin of the one enclosing the city. The thoroughfare they followed narrowed, the high city walls turning inwards to enclose the street on both sides. Armon led them into the walls' shadows.

Chill air filled the alley, prickling Jared's skin with the echo of winter's touch. The high walls and wide overhangs gave it a claustrophobic feel, despite there being room for four men to walk abreast. Arrow slits lined both walls, two or three feet overhead. Smaller slits filled the spaces in between, positioned at waist height. Wide arches spanned the gap between the two walls at regular intervals, their bottoms studded with dark holes.

It would have made a perfect rat run, were it not for the side gates.

At over twelve feet high and six or seven men wide, the foot thick, latticework iron barriers dominated the walls below the third arch. But they stood open and unguarded, allowing anyone to wander through.

Jared looked inside, and the world *shifted*.

Dozens of invaders charged along the alley, crushed together by the high walls. Arrows rained down from above and spears stabbed at their waists. Hot oil and acids poured from the arches onto their heads. Screams of agony and fear turned to yells of desperate hope when they reached the gates. They rushed inside—

—and the gates slammed shut. Terror and panic took hold. The invaders raced towards the sheer walls enclosing the yard, fingers and weapons digging at impenetrable stone as they searched for a way out. A single, deafening blast of a horn drowned out their shouts. Defenders emerged from their hiding places atop the walls to attack, their arrows and spears flooding the courtyard, slaughtering those inside.

Jared staggered back, one hand over his mouth and the other pressed to his stomach. "What the...?"

"A warning from the city," Armon said. "All foreigners see it the first time they pass through."

"Was it—?"

"Real? I don't think so. As far as I know, Canri has never been attacked." Armon started walking again, waving for Jared to follow.

They passed three more sets of gates before they emerged from the alleyway. The walls parted from each other, turning outward before curling in again, forming a curved 'Y'. They enclosed a small gravel beach which sloped down to meet the shore of the giant lake. Several large boulders had been pulled onto the beach to form a ragged barrier. Armon sat down on one them and indicated for Jared to do the same.

Jared chose the boulder nearest the water's edge and gazed out at the lake. Pale blue water lapped the shore, turning darker and greener as the bed of the lake dropped away. Sunlight reflected off its surface in dazzling sparkles, mirrors of the light explosions that had rolled across the market square at dawn. Shrill cries pierced the air, the gulls' calls competing with the gentle crash of the waves as they circled a dozen distant sails.

"Fishing boats," Armon said. "There are harbours on either side of us, cut off from the foreign district by the walls. Not many people come here. It'll be a good place for us to train once everyone's settled."

Jared nodded, only half-hearing. He could feel the waves pulling at him, washing away the images of terror and death that had assailed him in the courtyard. It felt peaceful here. Safe.

"It's also a good place to talk."

Jared pulled his gaze away from the lake and studied Armon instead. His eyes were bloodshot and sunken, his lips drawn and pale, and the green tones in his skin had turned a muddy grey.

"Do I look that bad?" Armon asked.

"You look like a worn-out old dish rag."

"I'd still beat you bloody in a fight."

"I don't doubt it."

Armon managed a smile. "Ask me your question then."

"You. Morgain. Torture."

"Right." Armon pulled out a knife and started to pare his nails. "It's... complicated."

❦

"What you have to understand," Armon said, "is that Morgain and I grew up together."

"So she said," Jared muttered.

Heat flashed through Armon's blood. He started to stand, caught himself halfway to his feet, and expelled his breath in an exaggerated sigh. "Don't interrupt. Please. This is hard enough without..." He waved a hand at Jared's mouth.

"Sorry." Jared's lips contorted, his left cheek twitching, as he struggled to form what he likely intended to be a placating smile. His gaze slipped sideways to the lake. "Please. Go on."

Armon lowered himself back onto the boulder. He held his knife in both hands and rubbed the hilt with his thumb as he spoke. "Morgain and I grew up together. The al-Rafaels claimed me when I was four. I don't remember anything about my mother. My father... He spoke to me twice. The first time, he made his claim on me official. The second time, he told me to shut my stupid little mouth and stay out of his sight." He paused, noted Jared's frown, and shook his head. "I didn't tell you to get sympathy. I never knew the callous bastard. For all I know, he did me a favour, taking me away from my mother.

"But Morgain? Morgain was always there. And yes, sometimes she could be an evil bitch. Sometimes, when the mood took her, she'd deliberately misbehave to get me punished. But then there were the other times. The times when we did things together. When we found ways to sneak past our nanny and escape into town. The times when she would play at being Queen and I..." *...I would be her gallant, loving consort.* Armon laughed and shook his head. "It doesn't matter what I did. What matters is we grew close. Formed a connection. A connection I feel inside of me, deep down, in my bones." He patted his chest over his heart.

Jared raised his eyebrows, his lips parting, before he clamped his mouth shut.

"Oh, don't look at me like that. You're hardly in a position to judge." He lowered his hand. "I always knew she enjoyed hurting people. I knew, but I still lied to myself, telling myself I'd imagined it. It worked, too, until the day I saw her order a page boy beaten. She looked... aroused. Seeing her like that, it disgusted me, but something inside me twisted. The connection we shared..."

Armon shifted his grip and let his knife dangle, point down, with the pommel trapped between his palms. "I don't know how to describe it, except to say it felt right." He wrapped his fingers around the knife hilt, drew his arm back, and threw it as hard as he could. It flew above the water, spinning pommel over tip, and seemed to hang in the air for a second before plummeting earthward to disappear beneath the waves. "It sickens me just thinking about it, but I can't help myself. When Morgain and I are together, it is wrong. So very, very wrong."

"Then don't go back."

"It's not that easy. I'm the bastard son of one of the Blood. The king's law would make me a slave. Morgain saved me from that. I owe her everything."

"Even your soul?"

Armon glanced over at Jared, a faint warmth washing through him, bringing tingles to a cold spot deep inside, but he dismissed the question with a shake of his head. "I don't know if I could resist her pull. I don't even know if I want to."

"But—"

"No. Hear me out. I told you earlier I wanted to put things right. That I would explain how." Armon bent forward and picked up a small, thin stone. Its weight felt good. Solid. Dependable. "The evils we do, they are small. Individual. But the good we do, it affects everyone."

"Like changing the law so thieves are enslaved rather than maimed?"

Armon sucked on his lips, fighting the tug of a smile. "Mevin's been talking to you?"

"Yes."

"That's one of the changes," he said.

"And you think a lifetime of slavery is the better choice?"

"Don't you?" Armon leant forward, pulled by the need to hear Jared's answer.

"I..." Jared locked gazes with Armon for a moment, swallowed, and looked away. "Didn't you say you owed Morgain everything for saving you from the same fate?"

"But I'm not a thief. My only crime was being born." Armon stared at the stone he held; at the scratches on the back of his hands. "Don't you see? The loss of a hand is a death sentence to most people. At least in slavery they have a chance. They can earn redemption if nothing else. But the ones who work hard enough can earn their freedom. Buy themselves a second chance."

"And when they end up back on the streets because no-one will give them work?"

"That won't happen. Morgain's setting up hostels. We'll find them employment."

"I guess it could work."

Armon looked up, read the doubt in Jared's eyes, and understood. He'd doubted too, when Morgain first told him her plans, but given time to consider her words, he'd come around. "There will always be real criminals, of course," Armon added, not wanting Jared to think he was blind to the downsides. "The ones who don't want to do honest work. But if they refuse all the help they're offered, well, then they'll be getting what they deserve."

"Does Tessa know about this?"

"Tessa knows everything. She understands." Armon stood, strode to the edge of the lake, and stared down into its depth. "Do you know how we met?" He held up a hand before Jared could answer. "No. Of course not. How could you? It was a stupid question." He kicked at a pebble, sending it skittering across the beach. "Morgain sent me to spy on one of her rivals. An old lord with some... unhealthy... habits. The lord discovered my presence and hired Tessa to kill me. I was young. Arrogant. I took her to my bed. She drew a knife on me. Pressed it against my throat." Warmth returned to Armon's limbs alongside the memory.

The pressure inside him eased, the urge to confess fading. He allowed himself a small smile. His first real smile that morning. "At that moment, she looked into my eyes—into my soul—and forgave me."

"Yet you doubt her loyalty?"

"I don't doubt her loyalty. Never that. It's my own worth I question. My own heart I doubt. One day, I'll overstep the boundaries. One day, I'll go too far. And when that day comes, I know she'll kill me. Of that, I have no doubt."

⁂

They remained in frozen silence as the sun crept into the sky, Armon at the edge of the lake, staring into its depths, and Jared perched atop a boulder, staring at Armon's back. He didn't know what to do next; didn't want to say the wrong thing. What had Armon hoped to gain? He'd been in control, arranging everything to happen as he needed. His sudden confession made no sense.

'Perhaps he hopes you'll kill him.'

No. If he wanted that, he wouldn't have warned me not to fight. Does he really strike you as someone who's keen to die?

'He wants your sympathy, then. Your understanding.'

Armon? I don't think so. A man like him needs nobody's pity.

'Which means...'

What?

'He's lying.'

Why? Why lie about something like that? Why confess to being a monster if he's not?

'To make you afraid of him again. To keep you under control.'

No. He doesn't need lies to do that. This is something else. Something deeper.

'Such as?'

I don't know.

Jared uncrossed his legs and pushed to his feet. Pebbles scraped and shifted beneath his boots. He took several steps forward, until he stood at the spymaster's side. "Armon?"

Armon flinched and jerked his head around. Tears glistened in his eyes. "Yes?"

"What happens now?"

"We carry on as before. And, if I'm lucky, you forget every word I just said."

"I don't think I can."

Armon nodded. "I didn't think you would." He glanced at the stone he clutched in his hand, shrugged, and sent it skipping across the lake. "Don't think I'll go any easier on you because of our little chat."

"I wouldn't expect you to."

"Good." Armon turned his back to the lake. "We should get back."

"And then?"

"And then I sleep. You too. Salem will expect you to start work this afternoon."

"And you just want me to watch and listen to the Canri?"

"Yes."

"You do realise I can barely understand a word they say?"

"It's better that way for now. Be a good boy, do as Salem says, and avoid rousing his suspicion. That's enough to start. You'll pick the language up soon enough, now you're surrounded by it."

"And you?"

"I'll watch, listen, make friends, wait for reports. When it's time to do more, I will."

"I'd have expected a spymaster's life to be more interesting."

"Trust me, it is. But without the proper foundations"—Armon pressed his hands together in front of him then yanked them apart—"everything falls down."

Armon left Jared at the gates to the embassy and headed for the barracks. The patrolman on the duty saluted as he passed. He returned the gesture with an effort, his limbs heavy as granite. A boy with a toothpick could have attacked him at that moment and he would have struggled to defend himself. He'd just reached up to open the barracks door when it swung away from him. He locked his legs to keep from stumbling, stared at the young man on the other side of the door for a second, blinked, and smiled. "Mevin."

"Sir?"

"See that I'm not disturbed before noon."

"Yes, sir." Mevin slammed his fist to his chest, likely bruising himself in his enthusiasm.

Armon returned Mevin's quick salute and squeezed past.

Inside, the barracks were blessedly dark, the only light coming from a handful of low-lit lanterns mounted around the walls. He stalked past the men's bunks, noting who slept, who rested, and who sat together chatting. Only eight of his men remained in the barracks. A third of the patrol would always be on duty, whilst the second third would be available for errands or escort work, and the final third would be at rest. He nodded to those who were awake enough to notice him, crossed to the far side of the barracks, and entered his private room.

The door clicked shut behind him, the soft sound acting as a signal to stop. The last of his strength leaked from his body like water draining from a broken bucket. He sagged against the door and rubbed grit from dry eyes. They watered, the salt stinging his corneas until tears leaked out. He squeezed them shut, pinched the bridge of his nose, and waited for the pain to pass.

"You've been gone a long time," a woman said.

He didn't even have the energy to flinch, not that he was in any danger. He cracked one eye open, searched the gloom, and smiled when he located Tessa reclining on the bed, watching him. He lowered his hand. "Jared and I have been talking."

Tessa slid her legs off the side of the bed and sat up. "Is that man-talk for 'beating seven bells out of each other'?"

"No. It's man talk for 'we were talking.'" He pushed away from the door and started across the room.

Tessa rose from the bed, swung her hips in a seductive strut, and met him at its centre. "What did you talk about?"

"Things."

She placed her hands on his shoulders and rested her forehead against his. "What sort of things?"

"Canri magic. Mevin. Me." He rested his own hands on her shoulders, intertwining his arms with hers. "Us."

Her fingers dug into his flesh. She pulled her head back. "Us?"

Armon closed his eyes, took a deep breath, and told her everything.

She stroked his shoulders, enticing a fresh flow of hot blood in his weary limbs, bent forward, and touched her lips to the top of his head. "I'm proud of you."

"You are?"

"Very."

"But it could ruin everything. He could turn against us, go to Salem, and—"

Tessa silenced him with a finger to his lips. "Hush. You did the right thing."

"Really?"

"Yes. Jared's driven by his emotions. He'll respect your honesty."

"And if he doesn't?"

"There's nothing he can do. Salem's unlikely to believe the word of a disgraced noble over your own. Besides." She kissed his forehead. "You could both do." His nose. "With a friend." His lips.

He sank into the kiss, relishing the press of her lips against his, wrapped his arms around her waist, and pulled her close. "You know," he mumbled when he broke off to draw breath, "if I weren't so tired, I'd be extremely happy right now."

Tessa flashed him a toothy smile, her eyes sparkling with mischief. "Perhaps I can do something about that." She lowered her arms. Kissed his chin.

"Hey. Hey!" Armon swatted her hands away from his sides, dancing backwards. "That tickles!"

Tessa grinned and lunged for him.

He batted her attack aside, twisting sideways as he did. "Please, Tess. I need to sleep."

"Mmhmm." She caught his wrist as he dodged past and stepped behind him, tugging on his arm, forcing it tight against his back. "The bed's that way." She pushed with enough force to send a jolt of pain up his arm, triggering a shiver, dispelling his weariness further.

He shuffled forward, keeping his steps small to avoid putting extra pressure on his shoulder. "I do like it when you play rough."

"I know." Her lips brushed his neck. His skin tingled at their touch. "And if you play along, I might even reward your good behaviour."

28/12/32 KAF (Two)

Jared fastened his belt, reached for his undershirt, and flinched when a knock rattled his bedchamber door. He opened it to find a young man—one of the servants who'd travelled with Ambassador Salem's party—standing outside, food tray in hand. Jared accepted the tray and nodded his thanks.

"Ambassador Salem requests that you attend the reception at two hours after noon," the young man said.

"Uh—"

"Big double doors opposite the main entrance."

"Thank you."

"He also bids me to remind you that you are to come fully clothed." The young man raised a thick eyebrow, slid his gaze down Jared's naked torso, and smirked at the undershirt dangling from his fingers.

"Fully clothed." Jared curled his fingers, not quite crushing his shirt in a fist. "Anything else?"

"Yes. If you must wear jewellery, you are to keep it simple and discreet."

"I see. And?"

"That was all."

Jared turned back into his room and kicked the door closed with his heel. "If you must wear jewellery, keep it simple and discreet," he mimicked, voice pitched high. "Who made Salem my bloody mother?"

Laughter echoed inside his head.

"I'm glad you agree."

He ate his meal—some sort of meat stew—and finished dressing. Putting his boots on proved a challenge. His injured leg had swollen whilst he slept. There was barely enough strap on the buckles to allow him to fasten them. He glanced out the window, trying to gauge the time, but the restricted view made the task impossible. It had to be at least an hour past noon, but not close to two—he hadn't taken *that* long to dress.

He checked his appearance once more, turned to leave, hesitated, and turned back to the mirror.

Show yourself, then.

Nothing happened.

If you're going to keep arguing with me, the least you can do is let me see you.

'What fun would that be? You're expecting it.'

So it was you I saw?

'In a manner of speaking. I am you, after all. A braver, stronger, more intelligent you.'

A sneaky, conniving, cruder me would be more accurate.

'But you don't deny I'm you? Ha! A victory.'

Well?

'What?'

Let me see you.

'No.'

Coward.

'What does that make you?'

Confused.

'Try crazy. Only crazy people argue with made up bits of themselves.'

Cowardly, crazy, and confused. Not a promising combination.

'But we are more than the sum of our parts.'

Jared's reflection flashed and, for a split-second, he saw it again—the wild eyes, pale lips, and malicious grin. But it wasn't just his reflection that changed—he felt it in his face too. For that split-second, his muscles were beyond his control, stretching and contracting with a will of their own.

The Voice cackled. *'I am the stronger. I am the better. I will take control.'*

Jared grabbed the wash bowl and vomited.

Sweat beaded on Jared's brow. He dabbed at it with a handkerchief, praying the turmoil roiling within wasn't reflected without. It wasn't just the heat causing him to sweat, although it certainly didn't help. It was the second glimpse of the Voice in the mirror. The reflection of the man he could become.

What's happening to me?

There was no answer. The Voice had been infuriatingly silent since revealing itself. That's if it existed at all. *What if there is no Voice? What if I imagined everything?*

What if I'm insane?

The patrolmen guarding the heavy oak doors leading to the reception signalled for him to stop. They gave him a quick pat down then waved him through.

Did I imagine the whole thing? Everyone talks to themselves, after all. Everyone debates matters inside their own heads.

What if, stressed as he was, he'd simply taken things a step further and convinced himself something was there when it wasn't? It was perfectly possible. The spasm he'd felt in his face could have been a simple twitch, the changes in his reflection nothing more than his subconscious showing him what he desired to see.

I'd be more inclined to believe that if it hadn't happened twice.

He stepped through the double doors, forcing the matter from his mind. There would be time to consider it later, when he was alone.

"Jared." Stanin glanced to his right, at a short, balding man seated behind a large desk, stepped forward, and extended his hand. "Come inside."

It seemed an odd thing to say to someone already five paces into the room, but Jared took his offered hand and shook it anyway.

"Are you well?" the balding man asked, squinting up at Jared. "You look pale."

"I'm fine. I'm not used to this heat. And my leg's still sore from the games. It's nothing. Really."

"Good." Stanin pursed his lips and frowned. "If you're done chatting, you have work to do"

"Sorry." Jared dipped his head to the balding man and turned to Stanin. "Where should I start?"

"You'll spend most of your time either in here or in the main hall." Stanin nodded at a set of double doors at the back of the room, past a dozen small tables. "The ambassador's private office is to your right." He motioned to a door behind a second large desk. "Azier's is on your left. Speak to his secretary if you have a message for him."

Jared glanced at the balding man and nodded.

Stanin motioned for Jared to turn around and pointed towards a sideboard next to the entry doors. "You'll be stationed there. Drinks are kept in the right-hand cupboard. Glasses and trays in the left. There are plates in the central section, and snacks will also be provided. As well as serving our guests with food and drink, you will be expected to act as a waiter when meals are taken in the hall. The embassy opens its doors at sunrise until noon and again from four in the afternoon until midnight. You will be in attendance at all times."

Jared looked around the reception again and nodded his understanding. "Do I get any days off?"

"Unless the ambassador says otherwise, no. Go through to his office. He's expecting you."

Jared approached the door and knocked on the dark wood.

Salem's answering, "Come," drowned out the knock's echoes.

Jared dropped his hand to the door handle, twisted it before he lost his courage, and opened the door.

The office could have housed his bedchamber five times over and still had room to spare. The few pieces of furniture present appeared lost within its walls, with the desk, chairs, and storage chests taking up less than a third of the floor. Ambassador Salem sat behind the desk, the surface of which was littered with papers. He glanced up, looked Jared over from toe to head, and returned his attention to his work. "Come in. Don't sit down."

Jared stepped into the room, padded across the empty space between the door and the desk, and waited, his hands clasped behind his back to hide his fidgeting.

"Are you ready for a hard day's work?" Salem reached for a sheet of paper and added it to the pile in front of him.

"I believe so, sir."

"You understand your duties?"

"Make our guests feel welcome and see to their needs."

"Good. Has Stanin shown you the hall yet?"

"No, sir."

"Ask him to do so."

Jared waited, expecting more.

Salem laid aside the paper he'd been reading and glanced up, brow furrowed. "Still here?"

Jared backed out the way he'd come, groping blindly behind him like a mole searching for its hole. He snagged the handle on the third attempt, opened the door, and slid out the gap. Salem's eyes never left him.

"Any problems?" Stanin asked.

Jared jumped and strangled a yelp before he embarrassed himself. He turned to Stanin, who'd taken a seat at his desk during Jared's absence. "Does he look at everyone like that?"

"Like what?"

"Like a father who's just caught his child doing something very, very bad?"

"Ah. No. That's a look he reserves for incompetent servants and men he particularly dislikes."

"Right. Well. He, uh, wants you to show me the hall."

"Go on through." Stanin nodded towards the door. "It isn't locked."

Jared hurried across the reception to the door Stanin indicated, yanked it open, and darted inside. Once it closed, he collapsed against it and stared at the floor. With each breath he took, his panic eased, the churning inside subsiding, until he recovered the strength to lift his head.

Marble columns marched down both sides of the hall, wrapped in trailing ivy and pockmarked with patches of yellow-green lichen. One column had cracked down the centre. A second had lost its top. Golden hills spotted with trees stretched beyond the columns, rolling towards the horizon where they reached up to meet a cloudless sky.

"Impossible." Jared approached the nearest column, reached out to touch it, and breathed an "oh," of surprise. Up close, the illusion became obvious, the hills unveiled as nothing but painted stone.

At least ten feet above his head, perched atop the fake columns, stretched a ceiling he couldn't have imagined in his strangest dreams. It looked like a skyscape grown from gems, with clouds of amethyst, ruby, and amber floating in a sky of turquoises, topazes, and sapphires. Stacks of wafer-thin gems, layered one atop another, combined to make a translucent display of incredible depth. A cluster of giant sunstones nestled in the false sky's centre, each cut to gather and reflect the sun's radiance like exposed seams of gold.

The golden light painted a pattern of bright lines and puddled shadows on the circular table in the centre of the room. A table he could have lain on spreadeagled with room to spare. He tapped its top, searching for joins, but it appeared to be carved from a single piece of wood, a giant horizontal slice of an ancient tree. Hundreds of pale-brown growth rings radiated from its centre, interspersed with contrasting circles of ash-blond wood, some as thin as a sheet of paper and others thicker than his thumb.

Two dozen chairs circled it, each one's seat a miniature copy of the table it complimented. He perched on the edge of one and watched the sunlight play across the ceiling, feeling his body growing lighter by the moment, losing himself in its mesmerising dance.

A throbbing in his injured leg pulled him back into himself, each beat shearing away another layer of illusion like a sculptor chipping at stone. He rubbed it until the throbbing stopped, stood, and turned towards the door. Swirls of orange and red around the frame drew his gaze upwards. His breath lodged in his throat.

A creature out of legend stared down at him, its visage engulfing the entire front wall. For the most part, its features lay in shadow, but its vibrant eyes gave it the illusion of life. Long and narrow, they slanted downward towards its nose. Black, ovoid slits sliced vertically across irises the colour of flames. Fire filled the background, highlighting the edges of the beast's face, liming its scales in oranges and reds. Its great maw stretched wide, its giant teeth poised to chomp down on anyone who walked through the door.

Jared cringed.

'It's just a painting, stupid.'

He whirled, eyes straining as he searched the room. A v-shaped shadow swept across the floor, heading straight for him. He backpedalled, stumbled over the leg of the chair, and banged into the wall before realising the Voice had returned. *Your timing is—*

'Perfect. And the shadow was just a bird. If you keep jumping at nothing, you really will go mad.'

Madness might prove to be a blessing given the mess I'm in. Jared scrambled from the great hall, sweat prickling his neck as he ducked to avoid the monster's teeth.

Azier's secretary looked up from where he hunkered over his desk and grinned. "Impressive, isn't it?"

Jared nodded and coughed to clear his throat. "Are the jewels in the ceiling real?"

"As far as I know." The secretary stood his quill in its stand. "The question you have to ask yourself is, 'why?'" He waved his hands as he spoke, punctuating his words with slashes and waves. "Why go to all that effort to decorate a meeting hall? Who are they trying to impress? Certainly not their own people. They built this city and every building inside it. So if it's not the Canri they're trying to intimidate, it must be us. The room is a reminder of the Canri's strength. It shows us their wealth, reminds us of the lands they have conquered, and stands as a testimony to their artistry."

"Consider me suitably intimidated."

Stanin coughed. "I doubt the Canri were thinking about the likes of you when they designed this embassy." He tipped his head towards the sideboard. "Our guests will be here soon. Prepare the drinks. Pour a mix for now, but keep the liquor and liqueurs back until after the evening meal. Once the snacks arrive, lay out a selection at each table. Keep track of what everyone chooses, and don't let anyone's glass go dry. That should be enough to keep you occupied."

Jared pulled off his boots, tossed them into the corner of his bedchamber, and sank onto his bed. His coat landed on top of his boots, his tunic joining it a few seconds later. He wiggled out of his breeches, tossed them on the heap, and did the same with his hose. Stripped down to his underwear, he lay back on the bed, closed his eyes, and sighed. A gentle breeze drifted in through the window, cooling his exposed skin and drying his sweat.

Someone knocked at the door.

"Come in," he called, cracking one eye open.

Armon slipped through the door and nudged it closed. "You'll catch a chill if you fall asleep like that."

"I needed to cool down." Jared forced himself to sit back up, wincing when he caught sight of his injured leg. It looked even worse than it had at lunch time, swollen to almost twice its normal size and covered in purple and green bruises like a rotting marrow. "Pass my saddlebags over, would you?"

Armon glanced around the small room. "Where...?"

"In the corner." Jared pointed.

Armon looked at the pile of dirty clothes and frowned. "Are you always this messy?"

"Only when I feel like I'm cooking alive." Jared took the saddlebags from Armon and used them to prop up his leg. "Any idea how we get our laundry done around here? Should I take it to the baths with me or—"

"Leave it outside your door. The slaves will pick it up in the morning and bring it back in the afternoon." Armon glanced around the room, started toward the clothes chest, stopped, and perched on the edge of the dresser instead. "Busy day?"

"Busier than I expected."

"Lots of visitors?"

Jared nodded. "Most of them just made appointments and left again."

"Tell me about the ones who stayed."

"Marta Aasen arrived first—"

"Describe her."

"Five-foot-eight-ish, chestnut hair cut short, brown eyes, oval face."

"What was she wearing?"

"Ankle length dress, belted at the waist, made from the colourful, patterned cloth the Canri seem to favour."

"Anything else notable?"

Jared shook his head.

"That's a little... general."

"I can't help it if they all look alike."

Armon snorted. "I suppose if you're not used to Canri features... What did she have to drink?"

"Red wine. No food."

"Was she alone?"

"No. She had two companions. A second woman, Aina something, and a servant." Jared grabbed a blanket and wrapped it around himself to keep the chill wind off his bare skin.

Armon poured some water, offered Jared a glass, then resumed the interrogation, pummelling Jared with questions for almost an hour, dragging out every detail he could. By the time he finished, Jared's mind was spinning. He drank the last of his water and stifled a yawn.

"This will get easier with practice." Armon pushed himself away from the dresser. "What time are you due back?"

"A little before dawn."

"Then I'll leave you to sleep. Try to pick out more details next time. Look for unique jewellery or unusual features. Anything to help me identify individuals in a crowd."

"As you will, Patrol Leader, sir."

Armon snorted and left.

❧

'When did you get so friendly with that monster?'

Jared rolled over, groaned, and opened his eyes. *What?*

'Have you forgotten what he did to you? To us?'

Who?

'Armon bal-Rafael. Who do you think?'

Jared tumbled out of bed, scrabbled to his feet, hobbled to the window, and sighed. The moon still hovered high in the sky. He'd been asleep less than an hour. *He's not all bad.*

'Yes. You're right. Because being tied up so tight you can't move, without access to food or water, is such fun, isn't it?'

Morgain did that, not Armon.

The Voice grunted. *'He's the one who found out. He's the one who reported us. He knew what she'd do to us, and yet he did nothing.'*

Jared climbed back into bed and pulled his blanket over himself. He shoved the Voice into the darkest recess of his mind and imagined walling it in. His thoughts became blessedly silent, but when he drifted back to sleep, his dreams turned to nightmares. He sat, immobilised, on a hard, wooden chair, surrounded by darkness. Hunger gnawed at his stomach. Thirst filled his mouth with dust. And behind him were the watchers, waiting for him to move.

Waiting to kill.

8/13/32 KAF (One)

Jared headed straight for his room when his morning shift finished, eager to remove his boots and rest his leg. The bruising had faded from bluish-purple to a sickly yellow-green in the days since the games, but it still ached after hours spent on his feet, serving food and wine to the Canri visitors whilst dodging the attention of Marta's assistant, Aina.

She'd started flirting with him the day after their arrival, growing less subtle and more persistent with each visit. He'd done everything he could think of to put her off, from an open-handed shrug accompanied by an, "I don't understand," to turning his back on her mid-flow to serve Marta instead. Short of telling her he wasn't interested—something he'd been warned not to do to avoid upsetting a potential trade partner—he had no other recourse but to smile, serve her as swiftly as possible, and move on.

He let himself into his room, pushed the door closed, stepped back, and pressed his head against the bare wood. His leg throbbed, his bone feeling as weak as splintered kindling. He wiped his sweaty hands on his breeches, drew in several long, slow breaths, and became aware of a faint pressure on his side; the incorporeal touch of another's stare. A glance to his right confirmed his suspicions. Armon stood in the corner behind the door, arms crossed over his chest, and—for the first time since they'd left the Rafael Household—out of uniform.

"People are going to start asking awkward questions if you keep sneaking in here like this," Jared said as he pushed away from the door.

"They'd have to see me first." Armon pulled a hand free from the crook of his elbow, uncurled his fingers to reveal a small brown pot, and offered it to Jared. "A salve. For your leg. From Mevin."

Jared took the pot. "Thank him for me."

Armon nodded. "The ambassador gave you the afternoon off?"

"How did you—?"

"Our ship came in. The *Elfin*. Somebody should be here any—"

A heavy knock shook the door.

"—minute." Armon edged into the corner behind the door and signalled for Jared to open it.

Jared did so and scrambled out of the way as two men entered, hefting a large wardrobe between them. He grabbed his clothes chest and slid it out of the corner, freeing up a space. The men struggled over to the far wall, grunting with effort, and half-placed, half-dropped, their burden into place. One of them gave it a shove, pushing it against the wall, and then they both filed past him without a word. Jared stared at the wardrobe. "What...?"

"Jared up-Arran?" a soft voice asked.

Jared whirled, hands curling into fists.

A small, skinny man stood on the threshold, fingers latched onto the door frame and body leaning forward so his head was inside the room.

Jared stared at him. There was something familiar about his narrow face, pointed chin, and well-groomed goatee. Where...? Morgain's tailor? Yes. Though he looked paler than he'd been at their last meeting, and his brown hair had grown scraggly and unkempt. Jared relaxed his hands. "Yes?"

"I've come to deliver the clothes the Lady al-Rafael commissioned for you." The tailor released his hold on the door frame, darted into the room, and paused to brush down his dishevelled clothes. "Please excuse my appearance. I'm afraid sea voyages don't agree with me."

"I daresay I was even more of a sight when I first arrived." Jared grinned.

The little man laughed and appeared to relax. "Sanworth far-Fay, at your service." He held out his hand.

"A pleasure to meet you, Master far-Fay." Jared shook his hand, finding he liked his slightly awkward manner and infectious smile. He seemed more amenable without Morgain breathing over his shoulder.

Brief handshake complete, Sanworth squeezed past Jared and flung open the wardrobe doors to reveal a rail bursting with clothes. "We have dress coats, short coats, and waist coats. Shirts, tunics, and under-shirts. Full-length breeches, knee-length breeches, and braies." He closed the doors again, knelt in front of the wardrobe, and pulled open the large drawer on the bottom left. "A full set of underclothes. Vests, hosen, loincloths, and codpieces." He shut the left-hand drawer and opened the one on the right. "Boots. Four pairs." He closed the drawer and opened the one above it. "Shoes. Four pairs." That drawer closed and the matching one on the left opened. Sanworth glanced at the wooden box within and hurriedly closed it again. He pulled open the last drawer, a thin thing the width of the wardrobe. "Jewellery for all occasions. Silver and gold." He closed the drawer and stood. "I hope you find it to your satisfaction."

Jared looked from Sanworth to the wardrobe and back. "Did I see Monadailshire embroidery on one of the shirts?"

"You did. There's also Aaral lace and South Islands cotton."

"South Islands cotton?" Jared took a half-step forward, sensed Armon's brooding presence behind the door, and lifted a hand to rub his neck. "I'm sure it's all of the highest quality, Master far-Fay. Thank you."

Sanworth's smile broadened. "Of course, I must insist you try it all on. Everything should fit, but it may be a few minor adjustments are needed."

"Now?"

"The sooner we start, the longer I'll have to make the adjustments." Sanworth threw open the wardrobe doors again and started pulling out clothes. A knee-length dress coat in sky blue with silver trim was joined by an off-white shirt with ruffles at the cuffs and collar. He added knee-length breeches two shades darker than the coat, pulled out a pair of shiny black boots with silver buckles, and finished with a small pile of underclothes.

Jared fought off a frown. He could feel himself overheating just thinking about wearing so many layers. "Uh, perhaps later, Master far-Fay. You have just arrived, after all, and—"

"No. No. My work must come before my own comfort. I insist—"

"He said no," Armon said, loud enough to make Sanworth jump.

Sanworth turned towards Armon, his eyes going wide. His smile faded. He lowered his head. "Master Raf—"

Armon crossed the room in two brisk strides and covered Sanworth's mouth with his hand. "No-one knows me by that name here, Unworthy. You should know better than to say it out loud, hmm?"

Sanworth nodded, and Armon lowered his hand. "I'm sorry, uh…"

"Malkem. Patrol Leader Malkem."

"Yes… well… forgive me. You startled me. I didn't mean—"

"I forgive you, Unworthy. Just don't do it again." Armon's words were smoother than churned butter, but his eyes were hard, and his mouth drawn down in disapproval. He lifted his hand, and for a moment, Jared feared he would hit the other man, but then he reached forward and patted Sanworth's cheek. "Did Morgain have any messages for me?"

Sanworth shook his head. "She didn't even mention you would be here."

Anger flashed across Armon's face, so intense Sanworth stumbled back a step. "And Salem? Did she send a message for him?"

"I can't—"

Armon grabbed Sanworth by the collar and hoisted him up onto his tiptoes. "Don't give me reason to mistrust you."

"You want me to betray Lady Morgain?"

Armon cursed and shoved Sanworth so hard he tripped over the clothes chest and smacked into the back wall. "What did she send him?"

"A-a package." Sanworth scrambled to his feet.

"Give it to me."

"But—"

"Give it to me!"

Sanworth pulled a leather wrapped bundle from his coat pocket and extended it in a shaking hand.

Armon snatched the bundle from Sanworth's fingers and slipped it inside his tunic. "I suggest you go and bathe. Tidy yourself up. Put on some fresh clothes. Have some lunch. Jared will be ready for you four hours past noon. Then you and he can play dress up to your heart's content."

"A b-bath would be nice." Sanworth tugged on his sleeves as he squeezed his way between Armon and Jared before scurrying for the door.

"And, Unworthy..."

"Yes?"

"Say nothing to Salem about this. I have reason to suspect his loyalty. If I find out you've warned him..."

Sanworth gulped. "I won't breathe a word."

Jared watched Sanworth leave. He regained his composure remarkably quickly, straightening as he opened the door and striding from the room with a swagger suggesting nothing amiss had happened.

Armon slammed the door closed on Sanworth's heels. He paced up and down the small room, fists clenching and unclenching in time with his ragged breathing.

Jared's stomach cramped, squeezing down on a small sliver of ice. "Why do you call him that?"

Armon stopped pacing. "Unworthy? To remind him what will happen to his reputation if he steps out of line."

"Did you have to be so hard on him? Surely—"

"He's a vile snake. He makes a fortune tailoring clothes for the rich and important, but he still delights in selling rumours and lies."

"And you are better than him how, exactly?"

Armon spun on Jared, a snarl on his lips. "How dare you?" He took a step forward, arms half-raised and fists clenched. "How dare you compare me to him?"

Jared's drop to a defensive crouch was automatic, a response drilled into him by hours of training aboard *The Hunter*. He lifted his own hands before him—with muscles loose and shoulders relaxed—poised to deflect any attack.

For a count of ten, the tableau held, then Armon lowered his fists, tilted his head back, and laughed.

For a startled second, Jared could do nothing but stare, then he half-rose, hands still raised. "Now what?"

Armon shook his head. "You wouldn't understand."

"Try me."

A swipe of a hand dismissed the request. Armon reached past Jared and picked up the ruffled shirt Sanworth had selected. "Don't you like it?"

"Shirts like that went out of fashion fifty years ago." Jared straightened, backed up a step, and lowered his guard. "I doubt my grandfather would have worn that monstrosity when he was my age."

"But it's made from the finest silk, measured, cut, and stitched by a master tailor. I'd have thought you'd jump at the chance to wear it..., dandy boy."

Fire warmed Jared's blood. He took a half-step forward before registering the amusement in Armon's eyes. The twitch at the corner of his lips. The teasing delivery of his words. He pulled up short. "Surely I was never that bad."

"You still are. I'm relying on it."

"But... I'll melt in those."

"You will look a perfect idiot." Armon hung the shirt back up. "Come on. We've both been penned up here too long. Why don't you join me for lunch?"

"I should be studying…"

Armon dismissed the protest with a shake of his head. "You can study as well outside, and the fresh air will do you good. You'll turn into a ghost if you don't get some sun soon."

"But my leg—"

"Can rest as well in a food tent as it can here. Meet me at the gates in ten minutes. That should give you time to slab a generous dose of salve on and change into something more comfortable."

Jared leant back in his chair, tipping it onto its back legs, and sipped at his drink. The iced fruit juice cooled and refreshed as it slid down his throat. A soft breeze drifted through the slits in the tenting behind him, the air stirred by giant fans worked by a dozen slaves.

Armon sat at Jared's left, his eyes fixed on the open front of the pavilion, his gaze distant. His glass sat on the low, slatted table, its contents untouched. He'd said very little since they'd met at the embassy's front gate.

They hadn't travelled far, just to the market square where the Canri held the feast, but even that short walk had been enough to bring beads of sweat to Jared's brow. Armon had led them into the closest pavilion— one of over a dozen ringing the square—and picked a table near the back, where the roof offered shade from the noonday sun. Then he'd turned his attention to the busy market filling the square, only looking away once to answer the boy who came to take their order. Now he sat biting at his lower lip, staring at nothing.

"What's wrong?" Jared asked.

Armon started, glanced at Jared, and flashed a smile that faded as quickly as it appeared. "See the blue and white pavilion on the right, about a third of the way up the square?"

Jared turned his head to the side and ran his gaze along the line of pavilions. "Yes."

"There's another stall, three up from it and across the gangway. Small and nondescript. Plain canopy. Black cloth covering the table."

It took Jared three attempts to locate the stall, tucked as it was between two much larger ones. "Got it."

"Look at the man talking to the stall holder. Short. Slouched. Silver hair. Ash-brown skin. I think it's—"

"Stanin?"

Armon nodded. "He's been there since we arrived. I wish I could get close enough to hear what they're saying, but I'd stand out like a mourner at a festival in this crowd."

"Perhaps he's haggling for a better price."

"For over ten minutes?" Armon snorted. "Besides, this isn't the first time he's been seen here. Mevin mentioned bumping into him in the market a couple of days after we arrived, and this is the third time I've spotted him here during the afternoon break. He goes to the same stall every time. Talks to the same man. But he never mentions these meetings when I debrief him."

"Is that why you're suspicious of Salem?"

Armon's brow crinkled. "What?"

"You told Sanworth—"

"That I had reason to suspect Salem's loyalty. I remember. But it has nothing to do with this."

"But what if it does? What if Stanin is acting as a go-between?"

"He would tell me. Unless—"

"Unless whatever they're doing goes against Morgain's orders, and Stanin wants it to succeed."

Armon stopped watching Stanin and picked up his glass. "Now you're starting to think like one of the Blood. I'll ask Tessa to watch him. See what she can find out." He took a long drink.

The serving boy returned to their table carrying two odd bowls formed from a series of interlocking yellow-green hexagons with brown spikes at their centres. The boy set the bowls down, said something Jared didn't understand, and hurried away. Jared peered into the bowl and frowned.

"Hollowed out pineapple," Armon said. "It's a fruit."

"And this?" Jared picked up a pale-yellow disc. It squashed between his fingers and plopped back into the bowl.

"Banana."

Jared shrugged. The name meant nothing. He poked at the chunks inside the pineapple, spotted a grape, and fished it out with his spoon.

Armon picked up his pineapple and laughed. "It's just fruit. It's not going to bite you." He dug into his own salad with relish.

⤳⤲

After they finished their meal, Armon led the way into the bustling market, pushing and weaving through the mass of shoppers. Jared followed close on his heels, not wanting to get lost in the chaos. One minute he was squeezing past a woman bent double by age, and the next he had to jump clear as a large hound careened through the crowd. A rosewood-skinned giant glared down at him as he recovered his balance, his red-tinted skin a shocking contrast to the powder-blue lustre of the woman clinging to his arm. He ripped his gaze away, lest he be accused of staring, and increased his pace to catch Armon.

A flash of light drew his eye. A young woman draped in a white, knee-length tunic darted through the throng, her arms stretched before her as she attempted to catch an escapee chicken before it was crushed underfoot. The chicken veered to its right, darting between a pair of bearded men, each wearing a billowing shirt resembling a giant, exotic flower, then zigged back to its left, its new route putting it in Jared's path.

Jared hopped back to avoid the chasing woman and cracked his hip against the corner of a stall. The stall's owner chose that moment to call to the crowd, his deep-throated bellow booming with the ferocity of a signal drum.

Clapping a hand over his ringing ear, Jared edged around the stall and hobbled clear. He'd closed the gap to Armon to a couple of feet when a high-pitched shriek sliced through the buzz of the crowd. His heart beating double, he whirled towards the sound, only to spin away again when he saw the brightly feathered birds squawking in the cages in the neighbouring stall.

His spin carried him into the side of a hefty woman in a flowing, brown robe. He bounced off her and jolted a young boy whose head barely reached his waist. The lad went sprawling. The woman barked what might have been an apology or an insult and scurried away.

Jared offered the boy his hand.

The boy shouted at him, scrambled to his feet, and dashed into the crowd.

Jared dropped his hand to his belt, feeling for his money pouch. A chill shivered down his spine when he found nothing, but then he shifted his foot. The hard edges of the coins he'd hidden in his boot pushed against his heel. He glanced around, fearing he'd lost track of Armon, only to spot him standing a few feet away, chuckling.

Armon waited for Jared to catch up then pushed forward, aiming for the far end of the market.

"There are no Canri," Jared said, when the crowd thinned enough for him not to need to shout.

"Pardon?" Armon asked, glancing at him without breaking stride.

"All these people, all this diversity, and yet I've not seen one Canri."

"This is the foreign district. Why would there be?"

They entered another aisle, and the noise level rose, though it wasn't loud enough to obscure the oinks and snorts coming from a nearby stall, where a dozen piglets rooted around in mud and straw.

Jared wrinkled his nose and frowned. A market like this should have reeked of human sweat, rotting produce, and animal waste, especially on such a hot afternoon. But he could barely smell the unwelcome odour of hundreds of bodies, hidden beneath the scents of flowers and odd, yet pleasant, perfumes. He glanced at the pigs again, just as a thin stream of light twinkled in the straw. The Canri magic destroying the pigs' manure.

A few feet further on, Armon stopped at a stall filled with pottery and picked out a large, terracotta bowl. He handed it to Jared without a word and turned back. Two large, corked bottles and a palm-sized bowl joined the first. Armon studied the stall for a moment longer then waved the vendor over and pointed to his selection.

Jared stood at Armon's side, laden with the chosen goods, sweat running down his forehead and dripping into his eyes. He leant closer and heard Armon say the Canri words for "plain" and "crude".

Armon finished speaking and held out his hand, palm up, to reveal half-a-dozen copper rounds.

The vendor shook his head, hands gesticulating wildly, but he spoke too rapidly to understand. He then pulled over a set of scales and set three small weights in one side. "Tre quartains."

Armon dropped his handful of coins into the scales.

The vendor removed first one weight, then a second, before the scales balanced. He shook his head and dropped both weights back in the pan. "Tre quartains."

Armon pulled another six rounds from a slit in his belt and added them to the pile. He picked up one of the weights and set it aside. "Två quartains."

The vendor picked up one of the coins, spun it over in his hand, banged it on the table, and shook his head. "Två quartains och fyra." He tossed the coin back into the pan and crossed his arms.

Armon added two more coins. "Och två?"

The vendor shook his head, keeping his arms crossed.

"Två quartains och fyra." Armon handed over the last two rounds. He did not sound happy.

The vendor flashed a wide smile, scooped up the coins, and turned to his next customer.

"Bad price?" Jared asked when they started walking again.

Armon shook his head. "Reasonable. But he only knocked two rounds off his starting price. He didn't trust our currency. If it's the same throughout Canri, the trade negotiations will be difficult." He stopped at a second stall, this one selling bolts of cloth, purchased a length of fine netting, and added it to the bowl Jared carried.

"What—?"

"You'll see." Armon glanced at him and grinned.

They'd almost reached the edge of the market when the aromas of roasting meat and baking bread rose above the other smells. Jared breathed in, inhaling the scents of freshly cooked chicken and pork. His mouth watered, and his stomach growled, demanding a more filling meal than the earlier fruit salad.

Armon approached a stall selling a selection of meat-filled pastries and picked out six. After a quick exchange of words, the stall holder wrapped the pastries in brown paper and then took the bottles Armon had purchased earlier and filled them from a barrel of water. Armon tucked the pastries into the bowl beside the bottles, glanced at Jared, and laughed. "Later."

With the shopping finished, Armon led the way to the walled-in gravel beach at the far end of the foreign district. Jared strolled past him when he stopped, placed the large bowl on top of one of the boulders lining the shore, and shook away the stiffness in his arms. By the time he'd eased the ache in his muscles, Armon had stripped to the waist, folded his clothes, and piled them near one of the towering walls.

"I am not going skinny dipping with you," Jared said.

"Thank the gods for that." Armon pulled off his boots, laid them atop his clothes, knelt on one knee, and started rolling up his breeches. "Well?"

"Well what?"

"Are you going to get ready, or do you plan on sparring fully clothed and getting heat stroke?"

"Ah." Jared unbuttoned his jacket, shrugged it off, and draped it over the nearest boulder. "What about these?" he asked with a nod to the bowl and its contents.

"The water's for drinking. The pastries are for eating when we're finished." Armon finished rolling up his breeches, retrieved the food and drink, and placed it in a shady area under the wall. He then removed the smaller bowl and set it on the ground, stretched out the netting, and wrapped it around the top of the larger bowl before tying the corners together underneath to hold it in place. After giving the netting a quick tap, he picked up the smaller bowl and waded into the lake. "Bring the big bowl when you're ready."

Jared stripped off his tunic and undershirt, his eyes never leaving Armon as he paddled in the lake. *What is he up to?*

'Maybe he's going to drown you.'

With a bowl?

'Maybe you should drown him.'

"Jared?"

Jared flinched, realised he'd been staring, and turned away. "Coming!" He yanked off his boots, rolled his stockings up to his knees, snatched up his discarded clothes, and tossed them down next to Armon's. After grabbing the bowl, he waded into the lake, exploring the ground with his toes before taking each step. The gravel beneath the surface was slippery with silt, but after a few steps, it thinned, giving way to thick, squelching mud.

Armon crouched down, scooped up some mud with the small bowl, and dropped it onto the netting covering the larger one. "Sift the mud through the net. Throw away the stones. And watch out for—"

"Fuck!" Jared jerked his hand from the bowl. A tiny, hard-shelled creature dangled from his mud-caked hand, its sharp-edged pincer latched to his thumb.

"—crabs." Armon tossed his bowl onto the one Jared held, grabbed Jared's wrist with one hand, and squeezed the crab's pincer with the other.

The pincer opened a fraction. Jared snatched his thumb clear. He shook his hand again—as if doing so could stop the throbbing pain—and squeezed it between his side and arm to stop the slow trickle of blood.

Armon held the struggling crab out at arm's length, watched it for a second, then tossed it aside. He looked round at Jared, the side of his mouth lifting.

Jared answered the suppressed smile with a glare. "It's not funny. That hurt."

"Aww. Poor little dandy boy. Would you like me to kiss it better?" Armon reached for Jared's hand.

Jared snatched it away, twisting and stepping back. The mud gave beneath his standing heel, sending his right leg skidding out from beneath him. His left foot missed the ground. He tumbled, arms pinwheeling, and crashed into the lake shoulder first. Armon's grasping hand flashed above him, then his head plunged beneath the waves.

His buttocks crashed against the muddy lakebed. Water rushed to fill his open mouth. He kicked and thrashed, arms paddling towards the surface, heels digging furrows in the mud. Then fingers clamped down on his wrist and pulled.

Water cascaded off him as he broke the surface. He spat out a mouthful of water, dragged in a lungful of fresh air, coughed up more water, gasped, spluttered, and drew breath.

Armon made no effort to hide his laughter this time.

"Not. Funny." Jared pressed his lips together to keep from laughing as well.

"You've got a... a weed... in your hair." Armon doubled over, his hands pressed to his stomach.

Jared patted at his head, found the straggly green weed, and plucked it free. After a brief inspection, he held one end against his forehead and let the rest dangle between his eyes. "Do you think Sanworth would like it?"

Armon pointed a finger at Jared's head, opened his mouth to speak, and broke down laughing again.

Jared placed a hand on Armon's shoulder and shoved.

Armon had time for a startled yelp before he disappeared beneath the waves. He came up a moment later, coughing and spluttering, and armed with a handful of mud. "You... you... swine!" He launched the mud at Jared's head.

Jared ducked the flying missile, lost his footing, and had to scrabble to stay upright.

Armon caught his elbow and steadied him before he fell. "Did you lose the bowls?"

"The bowls?" Jared stared at Armon, uncomprehending.

Armon pointed to his empty hands.

"The bowls!" A frantic search followed as Jared dropped into a half-crouch and patted blindly at the mud. He found the bowls several feet away, nestled amongst a cluster of rocks. "What do we want all this mud for anyway?"

"To protect our skin from the sun. Unless you want to look like an overripe tomato that's been pickled for a month?"

⊷⊶

Pale mud squelched between Jared's fingers as he pressed the last of it against the small of Armon's back. It made an odd slurping, popping sound when he pulled his hand away, as though to protest the separation. He stepped back and chuckled. "You look like a mud monster come to life."

"You're not any prettier yourself, you know." Armon slipped a hand into his breeches pocket and pulled out a set of fighting batons. "Catch."

Jared snatched the batons from the air above his head. The mud on top of his shoulders cracked, small flakes breaking off and falling to the ground. His face already felt dry and stretched where the first layer of mud had dried. He touched his cheeks, and the mud crumbled. "You sure this will work?" he asked, showing Armon the grit stuck to his finger.

"Only one way to find out." Armon dropped into a crouch, empty hands held loosely in front of him. "Show me what you can do with those things. Don't hold back."

Jared dropped into a matching crouch, careful to keep his weight on his toes. He risked a quick glance at his feet, shifted his left leg to correct his stance, and winced when a sharp bit of gravel dug into his toe.

Armon nodded to signal he was ready.

Jared feinted, shifting his weight to his left before lunging to his right, one baton extended, its tip aimed at Armon's shoulder.

Armon rocked back, evading contact, but otherwise didn't react.

Jared lunged again, skipping forward, jabbing repeatedly with his right baton, aiming for Armon's hip, his arm, his stomach.

Pebbles clacked together under Armon's shifting feet. He dodged once. Twice. Raised his forearm to parry.

Jared swept his left baton in high, aiming to bring it in over Armon's arm.

Armon spun, pushing Jared's right hand wide with his forearm and grabbing the left baton in his free hand. He twisted and pulled.

Rather than release the baton, Jared let Armon's pull draw him forward and dropped into a roll. His evasion took him past Armon's legs and ground gravel into his naked back. He gritted his teeth against the pain, tucked his right foot beneath him, and pushed. Spinning as he stood, he turned to face Armon, one baton high, one low, ready to block Armon's follow through.

Armon had backpedalled, however, and now waited several feet away. "Any sign of Verner Olsson at the embassy yet?"

Jared shook his head and strode forward, his batons at his sides. "I haven't seen him." His first attack had been too obvious; too straight forward to fool Armon.

"What about Karolina?"

Another headshake. He broke into a run, throwing his left baton underarm, aiming for Armon's head.

Armon ducked—

—and Jared dove between his legs, twisting as he fell, his right hand driving upwards.

Armon shifted his weight to his right leg and lifted his left foot off the ground, stamping down as Jared passed beneath him, driving his foot into his chest. The baton clipped his thigh at the same moment, pushing his right leg out from beneath him, knocking him off balance and leaving all his weight pressed down on Jared's ribs.

Jared bucked and lashed out. His flailing baton struck the back of Armon's knee, his fingers wrapped around Armon's ankle, and he pulled.

The twin attacks knocked Armon to his hands and knees.

Jared wriggled clear and scrambled to his feet. He pirouetted, baton swinging before him in a vicious sweep, held at the perfect height to connect with Armon's rising shoulders.

Armon twisted aside, snatched up the baton Jared had thrown, and rolled to his feet. He came out of the roll in a ready crouch, weaving the baton back-and-forth in front of his chest. "Almost," he said between laboured breaths.

Jared switched to a side-on stance, standing with his left foot in front of his right, right hand extended behind him, and fingers wrapped around the remaining baton. He watched Armon's feet, his eyes, his swaying hand, searching for an opening.

'Stop thinking so much and attack.'

Jared flicked his arm, faking another throw, but the feint failed to elicit a flinch.

'He can see you thinking, you know. You telegraph everything.'
Jared took a step forward.
Armon took a matching step back.
How would you know?
'I can sense your muscles tensing; feel every tell-tale twitch. Give me control. Let me show you.'
Jared roared to drown out the Voice and charged. A lose stone gave way beneath his foot. His ankle twisted. He brought his other foot round to correct his balance, but his thrust flew wide.

Armon slammed his baton into Jared's stomach and followed through with a punch to his lower back.

The double blow left him breathless and staggering. He glanced left then right but saw no sight of Armon. Then gravel crunched behind him. He turned—

—and Armon's leg sweep took out his feet.

For a heart-stopping second, he was airborne, then he landed with a rib-jarring thud.

Armon padded over to him and offered him a hand. "I found out why Aina's been chasing you," he said, helping Jared to his feet.

Jared stood with his hands on his knees, fighting for breath. It took all his concentration to keep from throwing up. "Why?"

"Because she wanted to examine the merchandise. Apparently, she asked Salem how much he charged for your, uh, additional services."

The urge to vomit redoubled. Jared moved his hands from his knees to his waist, straightened, and heaved in a breath. "W-what did he say?"

"That your earring has six gems in it, and she'd have to pay the going rate."

"He wouldn't—"

"Probably not. But you're out of her price range anyway."

"How…?"

"Did I find out?"

Jared nodded.

"She was bragging about it to a friend. You're quite the curiosity here. It didn't take the gossip long to spread." Armon bent down and picked up the baton Jared hadn't even realised he'd dropped. "Break time's over." He handed Jared the batons, took two steps backward, and dropped into a defensive crouch. "And don't charge in like a maniac this time. This is a serious training session, not a mindless brawl."

8/13/32 KAF (Two)

Jared studied himself in the mirror, tilted his head from one side to the other, then ran his fingers through his hair. He flipped up the collar of the dress coat—sky blue with silver edging—and flipped it down again. Next, he turned his attention to his buttons, each one a perfect silver rose. He fastened them one-by-one, checked his reflection in the mirror, and unfastened the top three again. The fancy ruffles on his shirt spilt through the gap between the coat's lapels. Shaking his head, he went to refasten the buttons and froze.

Sky blue. The same colour as the shirt he'd worn on the day Morgain had him arrested. That shirt had been trimmed with gold, not silver, but still… *Had she noticed? With everything else that happened that day, had she actually noticed?*

He refastened the buttons with trembling fingers, reached down for the hem of the coat, and tugged it to straighten out the wrinkles. Then he stared.

It wasn't just the colour of the jacket that reminded him of that morning, it was his whole routine. He had dressed to impress her then, so who was he trying to impress now?

"It makes me look fat," he said, in response to Sanworth's quiet cough. "And old." He turned to face the little tailor. "I look like I should be slumped in a worn-out armchair, with an empty wineglass in one hand and the head of my favourite hound beneath the other."

"Nonsense." Sanworth stepped forward and fiddled with Jared's clothes—rearranging a cuff here, straightening a button there. "You look positively regal. Very dashing. You will have women swooning at your feet."

"Or laughing every time I turn my back," Jared muttered, turning to the mirror. The cut of the coat did flatter him, hugging his chest and upper arms, flaring out at the waist and elbows, and cut back at the front to reveal his thighs. The darker blue of the breeches underneath stopped him looking like a strutting peacock and helped his legs look well-toned. But his eyes kept drifting back to the ruffles at wrist and neck, and the folds of silk running down the centre of his chest. "Perhaps with another shirt?"

Sanworth sighed, clutching his chest and swaying, his gestures exaggerated to reflect his hurt. "That shirt is a masterpiece."

"It's too much."

Sanworth waved Jared out of the way and proceeded to sift through the shirts and tunics hanging in the wardrobe, muttering under his breath. He picked out a plain, butter-yellow tunic and held it against Jared's shoulder. After a moment, he shook his head and returned it to the wardrobe. "Perhaps this one," he said, holding up a cream tunic with billowing forearms.

Jared slipped off the dress coat and swapped the ruffled shirt for the tunic, assisted by Sanworth at every step. Sanworth treated him as though he had no idea how to dress by himself, making it a chore to ignore the fussing as he pulled the coat back on.

The tunic was an improvement, but he still felt like a preening idiot. Its sleeves swamped his arms, and its lace cuffs draped down the backs of his hands, making the garment impractical and effeminate. "Could you make the arms narrower?"

"Don't be absurd. These sleeves are the height of courtly fashion."

'Sure. If you happen to be the court jester.'

Jared bit the insides of his cheeks to stop a burst of laughter.

Sanworth pulled him around, took several steps back, and looked him up and down. "Something's missing. A necklace, perhaps?" He returned to the wardrobe and opened the thin drawer housing the jewellery.

Jared peered over Sanworth's shoulder. Most of the jewellery was plain; simple chains in gold and silver with matching brooches in a variety of sizes, some etched with geometric patterns and some studded with small jewels. Two of the thicker chains held pendants—a black and blue enamel spider on one and a stag's head, the eyes studded with diamonds, on the other.

Only one piece failed to blend in; a woven, cotton band resting on a velvet cushion at the front of the drawer. At a little over a foot long and an inch wide, the strip of cloth would have been unremarkable but for the oval cartouche at its the centre. Embroidered with a clover leaf set in a yellow circle within a red background, it matched the hidden tattoo on Armon's neck. Jared picked it up and flipped it over, revealing the paired clasps at its ends. "What's this?"

"Something for later. This outfit is better suited to a silver chain. A heavy one."

Sanworth tried to take the cloth band, but Jared tightened his grip, his stomach knotting. "Tell me."

"Uh… well…" Sanworth twisted his collar then tugged at his sleeves. "It's a reminder. From Lady Morgain."

"A reminder?" Jared traced the edges of the cartouche with his thumb. "What did she say, exactly?"

"That, uh, she wants you to wear the symbol of the al-Rafael family to remind you you, uh, belong to her now. That you are bound to her, body and soul."

"It's a slave collar, then?" Jared squeezed with his thumb, crushing the delicate embroidery.

"No. Gods, no. Slave collars have locks, after all." Sanworth giggled, a high-pitched, nerve-ridden titter. His eyes met Jared's, and he stumbled back a step. "It's a symbol of fidelity. A reminder to you and, uh, anyone who may be tempted by you, that you are faithful to her now. She requests that you, uh, only take it off when you're alone."

"I see."

Sanworth held his hand out. "May I?"

Jared handed him the choker. The fit was tight, but not uncomfortably so. And the velvet lining was soft against his skin, though the metal clasps still bit into the back of his neck. He swallowed, testing the choker's give. It didn't press so hard he wouldn't be able to eat, but he would always know it was there. He felt like a bird, newly recovered from injury and desperate to fly. He had climbed from the nest, walked the length of the branch, leapt into the air… and plummeted earthward, his clipped wings unable to carry him across the sky.

'Don't wear it then.'

I don't intend to.

He reached behind his neck, unhooked the clasps, and laid the choker back in the drawer.

"Uh…" Sanworth looked from the choker to Jared and back.

"We're alone, aren't we?"

Sanworth nodded.

"You said a chain would be better?"

"Yes. Right." Sanworth returned to the drawer to pick through the chains.

Jared sighed and glanced out the tiny window, resigned to losing the rest of the afternoon to playing dress-up.

⚮

Night had fallen. Flames danced atop the torch in the sconce by the door, on the candles on the dresser, and in the burner below the mirror inside the wardrobe. Jared's gaze drifted towards the window. Swathes of grey blocked out the stars; the first real cloud cover he'd seen since his arrival. He sighed and looked back at the wardrobe—or, more specifically, at the last of the drawers.

He'd tried on all the clothes—fifteen full outfits in all—along with the matching accessories. Sanworth had inspected every piece, chalking a couple of coats that were too small and pinning another in need of trimming. Three pairs of breeches also required minor adjustments, along with a pair of ankle boots that rubbed at the heels.

After the ruffled shirt and baggy-sleeved tunic, he'd been dreading what Sanworth would produce next, but he'd been pleasantly surprised. Most of the clothes turned out to be elegant and clean cut, with simple, flattering lines, in a selection of shades that complimented his colouring. He hated to admit it, but Morgain had chosen well.

The same couldn't be said about Sanworth, however. He'd taken the liberty of adding one of his own designs to the collection, an experimental style he'd labelled fashionably poor. What could have been an acceptable, if somewhat undersized, pair of breeches and matching half-jacket had been ruined by slashes to the arms and legs, designed to give them the appearance of a pauper's rags.

Fashionably poor, indeed.

Jared sighed and opened the last drawer. A plain oak box rested within. He stared at it, his heart beating a too-fast rhythm against his ribs. His stomach cramped.

Sanworth reached past him and opened the lid.

Jared stared into the box and blinked, once, then twice. He'd expected a monstrosity of metal and leather, not an exquisite masterwork. He touched the gold filigreed plate, then traced the path of a stem with his finger, following it from the base of the plate to the centre. A tiny thorn sliced his skin. He snatched his hand back with a wince and sucked at the minute cut. Swapping hands, he ran his finger over a delicate silver rose, amazed at the detail the smith had captured. Intertwined, thorny stems covered the entire triangular plate, interspersed with a half-dozen perfect blooms. The beauty of it gave him pause, but it was a deception, a mask designed to hide the ugliness underneath.

He placed his thumb against the edge of the plate and flipped it up, causing two fine chains attached to its point to slide across the box's satin lining. A concave steel sheet lined the underside of the plate, joined to a metal belt by a pair of hinges. The sheath and pouch hidden underneath looked like miniature cages, the bars spaced less than a finger's width apart. Cold sweat chilled Jared's forehead.

"I must insist you try it on," Sanworth said, his voice strained. He backed away several paces to stand by the door.

"Now?"

"The sooner you try it, the more time I will have to make any, uh, adjustments."

Jared kept his eyes fixed on the belt. Sanworth was the pawn here— an intermediary sent to humiliate him on Morgain's behalf—but he still felt the urge to cross the room and strangle him. First, he had Salem threatening to lock him in a belt if he so much as looked at a woman the wrong way, and now he had to endure this? He didn't check to see if Sanworth was watching before he stripped off his clothes and threw them on the bed.

For a moment, he just stood there, chest heaving as he struggled to breathe. Then he picked up the belt with shaking hands and flipped it over to examine the back. A tiny padlock threaded through a loop in the centre, but it was open and keyless. He slid it free and set it on the dresser.

The thin chains holding the faceplate closed came next. They ran through a pair of eyelets in the back of the belt, about four inches from its centre, and met in the middle, where they would be held in place by the padlock. He pulled them down. Hoops on their ends stopped them from coming free from the eyelets.

Sanworth's reflection shifted as he glanced up and away again. He stood with his head bowed, hands clasped before him and fingers twitching.

Jared turned to face him, his lips parted in a forced smile. He flipped open the belt, the overlapping back halves swinging out on side hinges like a double gate, and stepped into it, keeping his gaze locked on Sanworth the whole time.

Sanworth glanced up just as Jared fed his penis into the sheath, met Jared's gaze, and turned bright red.

Jared looked down before his own face coloured and checked everything was in place. When he looked up again, Sanworth had turned his back. Nervous laughter bubbled up inside him. He swallowed it down. "You, uh, need to do the rest."

"I d-do?" Sanworth continued to stare at the door.

"You know you do." Jared didn't want to turn around—didn't want to see himself in the mirror—but he had no choice; the room was too small for anything else. He turned and glanced at the belt's reflection.

It's not so bad.

It formed a larger-then-normal bulge, but the faceplate had been shaped to follow the lines of his body. With clothes covering it, it would be close to invisible. And if he wore a codpiece on top, the worst he could be accused of was adding a little extra padding.

Sanworth's reflection appeared in the mirror behind Jared's shoulder.

"Make sure the chains are tight. I don't want them flapping about and whipping me." Jared winked.

Sanworth's face went from bright red to mottled puce. He averted his gaze.

Jared suppressed a vindictive smile. If he had to suffer through this ignominy, it was only fair Sanworth suffer as well.

The chains pressed against his skin as they were pulled into place, each individual link identifiable thanks to the lack of padding. Cotton drawers might ease the pressure and prevent chaffing. Then again, if he were stuck in the belt for days, or possibly weeks, the resultant mess didn't bear thinking about.

A snick sounded at his back.

Sanworth scuttled away.

Jared's blood turned to ice. "You locked it?"

"L-lady Morgain insisted."

"But..." Jared reached behind him, took hold of the padlock, and tugged. "You *locked* it?"

"Just f-following orders."

"But you have the key?" Jared tugged harder. "Tell me you have the key."

"N-no." Sanworth groped behind him, his fingers probing along the door. "No key."

No key? How can there be no key? There must be a key. There must.
'Calm down.'

He pulled on the padlock again; a useless, foolish act. *Not again. Please, not again.*

'I said, 'calm down'.'

He swallowed a rising sob and stared at himself in the mirror; at his blood-shot eyes and flaring nostrils—at the Voice's reflection hovering beneath his own, its brow furrowed and lips downturned—and released the padlock.

'The key must be somewhere.'
Right. Of course.

"If you don't have the key, who does?"

"I-it was in the package—"

"The one you gave to Armon?"

"Yes."

Jared took a deep breath and exhaled. Armon wouldn't keep him locked in the belt forever—he'd gone to too much effort to lessen the hostility between them—but that didn't mean he'd let him out anytime soon either. He'd received the package that morning, after all. He could have said something sooner if he'd wanted to.

'Why would he? He wants you under control.'
But things are different now.
'Are they? How can you be sure?'
The training—
'Furthers his own ends.'
Our agreement—
'Nothing but words.'

Jared shook his head and looked up just as Sanworth turned the handle and cracked open the door. "Any other surprises I should know about?"

Sanworth dropped his hand. "I d-don't think so." He gathered up the pile of clothes he'd set aside. "I'll make the adjustments to these and bring them back when they're done."

"Thank you."

Sanworth let himself out.

He'd been gone less than two minutes when a knock rattled the door.

"Just a minute." Jared retrieved his discarded breeches and pulled them on, grabbed the nearest tunic and slipped it over his head. He opened the door to find a royal courier waiting outside. "Yes?"

"Jared up-Arran?"

"Yes."

"I've got a letter for you from the mainland. Sorry it's late, but I had to deliver the priority mail first."

"Of course. Thank you." Jared hunted his dresser for the customary tip, found a pair of rounds, and accepted the letter in return. Once the courier had left, he pushed the door closed and sidled into the corner to read under the torchlight.

His mouth went as dry as the Redlan lake at the height of summer when he read the familiar, blocky text on the envelope.

"Jared up-Arran ~ Canri"

"Elise."

He flipped it over with shaking hands, broke the seal, and pulled out the letter.

"Jared,"

An ink spot marred the space next to his name. From her quill resting on the paper, preparing to write 'dear heart', before she changed her mind? Or merely a stray drip as she paused to gather her thoughts? He brushed his thumb across the missing endearment, a similar emptiness filling his chest, and continued.

"I hope this letter finds you well. Thank you for your warning and your concern. Your cousin has been kind enough to take me in. He confirmed some of what you told me, and I pray, for your sake, you find a way to escape.

"Before everything fell apart, I had a gift commissioned for you. I do not wish to give you false hope, but I have placed it in the envelope. Though I still care for you deeply, your infidelity broke my heart. What we had, or could have had, can never be repaired.

"However, I cannot bring myself to sell it, so I send it to you in memory of what we once shared.

"Elise."

He set the letter on the dresser and tipped the envelope up over his palm. A ring fell out; a simple silver band. He held it up to the torchlight and read the engraving inside.

"My love. My life. Forever. Elise."

He slipped the ring onto his finger and sank onto his bed.

What have I done?

He'd ruined everything. Let his fear destroy something magical—a bond he hadn't imagined possible.

She had loved him. And he... he *had* loved her.

But he'd also been a coward, too afraid of pledging himself to Elise—of settling down and having children—to see what he was throwing away.

He sat on the edge of the bed for an eternity, rotating the ring around and around on his finger, staring at nothing. Then a sob burst from his throat. He put his elbows on his knees, lowered his head into his hands, and wept.

❧❧

Time become immeasurable, devoid of light, sound, or thought. Hours or minutes or days could have passed by the time a gentle knock broke the silence.

Jared didn't even lift his head from his hands. If the gods were kind, whoever was there would assume he was asleep and leave him in peace.

The knocking came again, more forceful this time.

He sighed.

Go away. Please. Just go. A. Way.

The knocking came a third time.

He wiped his eyes then scrubbed at his face before lifting his head. Most of the candles had gone out, leaving the room cast in flickering shadows, the only light coming from the dying torch by the door.

A fourth knock. A solid thud loud enough to wake everyone in the embassy.

He slipped Elise's ring from his finger and twirled it between his thumb and forefinger. Torchlight caught the edges of the engraving, setting the words on fire.

Did I really love her?

He brought the ring to a stop and let it drop into his palm.

Did I really care?

The door handle clicked as it started to turn. He slipped the ring into his pocket, snatched Elise's letter from his dresser, and slid it under his pillow. With luck, whoever was on the other side of the door would see him lost in thought and leave.

The door opened, a shadow fell across his legs, and the door thunked closed.

He looked up.

Armon stared down at him, his forehead creased by a heavy frown.

Ashen fire welled in Jared's core. He surged to his feet, driven by the deluge of heat. "When were you going to tell me?"

"Tell you what?" Armon backed up, his frown collapsing into a puzzled knot.

Jared paused.

'Please tell me you don't believe his little act. He's lying to you. He always lies to you.'

He closed the gap to Armon in a single, powerful stride. "Don't pretend you don't know."

Armon held his hands out from his sides, palms up and fingers spread. "I'm not pretending."

"I was there when Sanworth gave you the package this morning. I know you've seen it."

"Jared, I have no idea wh—"

Jared grabbed Armon's shirtfront and slammed him into the door. "Don't. Lie. The package he was supposed to give to Salem. I saw you take it."

"Oh. That package." Armon lifted a hand toward his chest, only to drop it again when Jared growled. "I haven't had a chance to open it yet."

Jared eased back a fraction. "You haven't?"

Armon shook his head. "Look for yourself. It's in my inside pocket."

Jared tightened his grip on Armon with one hand and searched inside his jacket with the other. His fingers brushed against the leather wrapped package, and he pulled it out. Then he let Armon go, giving him another shove before he sank back onto his bed, the package clutched to his chest. A quick examination confirmed the leather wrapping was undamaged; the wax seal intact. He tossed the package back to Armon and sagged against the wall. "Sorry. I assumed…"

Armon caught the package and placed it on the dresser. Taut muscles made his movements rigid as he picked up a candle and lit it with the torch. A flick of his left wrist dropped a thin dagger into his palm. He turned to Jared, lips lifted in a mocking grin.

"I couldn't help myself," Jared whispered, staring through Armon. "He kept saying you were lying. That you just wanted to use me. I was so sure…"

Armon's grin faded. He pushed the candle back onto the holder's spike and held the blade in the flame. "Who?"

Jared blinked. *Who? Who what? What had he…? Oh, gods.* He swayed and shook his head.

Armon's knuckles turned white on the dagger hilt. "Tell me."

"The Voice. In my head."

Armon stared. He tried to speak several times, but his voice distorted and cracked. The stink of hot metal and singed hair filled the air. He yelped and dropped the knife. "What sort of voice?" he asked before jamming his finger in his mouth.

"Just a voice. Just me but... different."

"Just you?" Armon mumbled around his finger. He took it from his mouth, flexed it, and winced. "But everyone argues with themselves sometimes. It's perfectly natural." He kept his voice light, but the wrinkle across the bridge of his nose revealed his doubt.

And if I tell you it wants you dead? Jared shook his head. Armon wouldn't understand. Nobody would. "I guess."

"You've been through a lot. I'd probably be paranoid too if I were in your position." Armon jabbed a finger at the hilt of his dagger and jerked his hand back the moment he made contact. "It's when you start debating with yourself in public that you have a problem."

Jared forced himself to laugh. He stood and approached the dresser as Armon tested the hilt again.

Armon picked up the dagger and returned its blade to the flame. When it started to glow, he removed it from the heat and set to work on the package, sliding the blade between the seal and the leather, using its heat to melt the wax. He gave it a series of little twists, prying it clear. About two thirds of the seal had come free when the wax cracked, splitting down the middle. With a curse, he reheated the blade, removed the remainder of the seal, and set the wax to one side. He spread out the contents of the package—at least a dozen sealed letters—over the dresser. "Which of these am I supposed to have read?"

Jared frowned. All the letters looked the same. Each had been enclosed in a sheet of smooth, white paper, with the corners folded inwards so their edges overlapped. A stamped seal held each letter closed. Some were thicker than others, hiding extra sheets within, but none bore writing or marks on the outside. He picked them up one at time, feeling the contents. The fifth one held something small and hard. He handed it over. "This one, I think."

Armon took the letter and slit the seal, managing to remove it in one piece this time. He tipped the contents—a letter and a small brass key— into his hand. After handing Jared the key, he unfolded the letter and read it out loud.

"Ambassador,

"Thank you for looking after my pet. I hope he hasn't caused you too much trouble. As promised, I have had him fitted with a new belt. The key is enclosed. If there are any problems with the fit, please discuss it with Master far-Fay."

Armon set the letter on the dresser, face down. "It isn't signed."

"My pet?"

Armon shrugged. "That's what it says."

"What are you going to do with it?"

Armon smiled and shook his head. "What do you think I should do?"

"It sounds like he's expecting the letter. And the key. If he doesn't receive them, he'll know something's wrong. He'll blame Sanworth and accuse him of stealing, or worse."

"And...?"

"And he'll have him arrested. Questioned. Sanworth will tell him about you. About us. Everything you've worked for will be ruined."

"So...?"

Jared made a fist around the key. "You should give it back." He uncurled his fingers and dropped it into Armon's outstretched hand.

Armon pocketed the key and refolded the letter. "Thank you." He collected the rest of the letters and wrapped them in the leather. "I'll check the rest then reseal them. Get Sanworth to deliver them in the morning."

"But you broke—"

"I have a duplicate of Morgain's signet ring. I just needed to keep the wax." Armon headed for the door.

"Why did you come?"

"Hmm?"

"You didn't come here to show me the letters."

"I saw the torchlight. It's past midnight. I wanted to make sure nothing had happened." Armon let himself out.

'You see?' The Voice said the moment Armon was gone. *'He's using you. He's even got you convinced you're doing the right thing.'*

And what do you think Salem would do to me if he found out the truth?

'Send you home, I imagine.'

And you think that would be a good thing?

❧❧

Armon paused outside Jared's door and pressed his ear to the wood. Silence. Good. He'd half expected Jared to start raving the second he left. He stepped out of the doorway just as Mevin turned into the corridor.

Mevin stopped and snapped his fist to his chest. "Sir."

Armon lifted his own fist in salute. "All clear?"

"Yes, sir."

"Very good. Carry on." Armon dropped the salute and strode down the corridor. If Mevin wondered what he'd been up to, he had the sense not to give voice to his curiosity.

He turned into the side corridor and quickened his stride, determined to reach Tessa's room before Mevin's patrol route brought him within sight of the opening. He didn't risk knocking on her door, not wishing her neighbours to know of his visit, but he did make enough noise opening it to alert her to his presence.

A handful of candles burned in a chandelier above a small table in the corner, illuminating Tessa and the dozen papers spread out before her. She stared at him across the shadows, one hand resting on the tabletop, the other hidden from sight.

Armon slipped inside.

Tessa extracted her hand from below the table and reclined in her chair. "This is an unexpected visit."

Armon closed the door. "I've been talking to Jared. We may have a problem"

9/13/32 KAF (One)

A rumble of thunder accompanied Jared's arrival at the reception, its deep vibrations shaking the walls and floor, momentarily drowning out the relentless downpour. He slipped inside and closed the door.

Stanin was already seated at his desk. Ambassador Salem stood behind him, leaning over his right shoulder, talking quietly and pointing to a document on the desk. He glanced at Jared, thick brows furrowed in disapproval and eyes filled with contempt, nodded pointedly to the sand timer, and returned his attention to the document, dismissing Jared with a simple turn of his head.

Jared accepted the rebuke in silence—it could have been far worse, after all—and set about preparing for the day. He sorted the drinks first, placing those the expected visitors favoured on top of the sideboard and storing the rest in the cupboard. Glasses came next. Each one needed to be checked, polished, and matched with the appropriate drink. A tedious job, but one which gave him time to work on the Canri vocabulary Armon had given him to learn.

Förhandling—pronounced fur-hand-ling—meant negotiation.

Överenskommelse or överenskommelsen—agreement.

'You're wasting your time.'

Oenighet—oo-in-a-hert—disagreement.

'Without context, the words are meaningless.'

Förslag—fur-slog—proposal.

'The lessons are a diversion, something to distract you from the real reason he brought you here.'

And what reason would that be?

'How would I know? I'm stuck inside your mind, not his.'

Värdelös. Worthless.

'Hide from the truth if you must. It will only make the betrayal more painful when it comes.'

Kränkande. Insulting.

The door on the far side of the room opened. Alsam Azier emerged from his office with Tessa at his side.

Tessa looked stunning in a sleeveless, full-length white dress. The bodice was form-hugging, showing off her muscular but feminine curves, the skirt slender and lightly pleated, with buttoned slits down both sides. A shawl draped her shoulders, buttoned at the neck, with a pair of fine, wool ropes sweeping down from the button, passing under her arms, and connecting to the shawl at the back. She met his gaze and nodded, the blood-red jewels in her silver hairnet sparkling in the torchlight when she dipped her head.

Jared edged towards her, drawn by her warm smile. Her open face. Her perfect form.

"Ah-ha!" Azier's bellow rebounded off the walls, shattering the momentary connection. "Just the man for the job."

Jared turned away to hide his blush. *If Tessa noticed my stare... What was I thinking?*

'That she's a beautiful, athletic, healthy woman who needs the attention of a real man?'

No. She's married. I wouldn't—couldn't—do that to them.

'What makes you think you have a choice?'

Blood stirred in Jared's loins, swelling his flesh, pressing his skin against the crisscrossing bars of his chastity belt.

That... that's...

'Impossible?' The Voice laughed.

The stirring stopped as suddenly as it began, but it left him sweating, his heart hammering, his chest tight. *I won't let you do this.*

'You don't have a choice.'

"You," Azier said, his bellow loud enough to make Jared flinch, "by the sideboard."

Jared turned and pointed to himself, though he was the only one in the room Azier could have meant.

"Yes. You. What's your name again?"

Jared swallowed and wet his lips. "J-Jared, sir." He glanced at the other occupants of the room, but none of them appeared to have noticed his momentary distraction.

"Ah, yes, Jared." Azier clapped his meaty hands together. "You used to be a courier, didn't you?"

"Yes, sir."

"You know horse flesh then?"

"Yes, sir."

"Good. Ambassador Salem?"

"Mmm? Yes, Azier?" Salem didn't look up to answer.

"Can we borrow your man here for the day?"

"My man?" Salem broke off his scrutiny of the document to look around the room. "You mean Jared?"

"That's the one."

Salem's lips twisted. "Why, by the all the gods, would you want him?"

"Lady Zandra is going to assess some slave stock for me. Your man knows flesh." Azier waved his hand in Jared's direction, the enthusiastic gesture lifting his tunic, releasing an unsettling aroma of musk mixed with stale sweat. "His knowledge may prove useful."

"Will they be alone together?"

"No," Tessa said, her raised voice drowning out Azier's simultaneous reply. "We'll be travelling with an armed escort, Ambassador."

"I see." Salem studied her for a moment before nodding. "Take him for the day. I don't see what harm it will do." He turned his gaze on Jared, a knowing smile on his lips. "Not now, hmm, Jared?" His gaze flicked down to Jared's groin and up again.

Jared clasped his hands in front of himself in a needless attempt to mask the hidden cage. "No, sir." The words came out as a whisper. "But I don't know—"

"Speak up, man." Azier said. "I can't hear a word you're mumbling."

Jared turned from Salem to Azier. "I don't know anything about slaves, sir."

"Nonsense. You know how to tell if a horse is sick, don't you?"

"Yes, sir. But—"

"And you know the signs of abuse?"

"Yes, sir."

"Then you'll do fine. Flesh is flesh, after all"—Azier slapped his ample midriff—"whether it walks on two legs or four. Now off with you." He flicked his hands in Jared's direction, shooing him in the same way others would shoo a dog. "I don't have time to stand here jabbering all day. And, Lady Zandra..."

"Yes, Azier?"

"Take some of our stock with you. The smaller boy and two of the females. The youngest ones. See if they spark any interest, but don't sell them unless you're offered an exceptional price."

"For you, Azier, it will be my pleasure."

"Thank you, my lady. Until later." Azier cupped Tessa's hand in his, lifted it to his lips, and kissed the back of her fingers.

Tessa dipped her head in return, whispered something in his ear, and made for the door, waving for Jared to follow. She stopped in the corridor outside and turned to the patrolmen on duty. "Which of you is running messages?"

The guard on the left, a middle-aged man with a thick beard and moustache, dipped his head. "I am, Lady Zandra."

"Go to the patrol leader and inform him I require an escort—three men will be adequate—to accompany me into the city. Have them meet me in the courtyard in an hour."

"At once, Lady Zandra." The man saluted and left.

Tessa signalled for Jared to walk beside her and led him away from the doors.

"I really don't know anything about slaves," Jared said after they'd turned the corner. "It's not like I can age them with their teeth or check their hoofs for damage."

Tessa flashed him a smile but said nothing.

"I've never even owned a slave before."

Tessa slowed and turned to face him. "You're not one of those people who thinks slavery is wrong, are you?"

"No. I just... I don't see what use I'll be."

"And what makes you think I care for your opinion on slaves?"

"But I thought... You didn't object."

"After working so hard to get you out of there?" Tessa turned into an unfamiliar corridor. "Why would I?"

"You got me out of there? But it was Azier who—"

"It was Azier who thought you were the answer to my problem. A problem I spent almost an hour explaining to him. Indirectly, of course." She stopped outside the third of four identical doors. "He thought he was coming to my rescue, suggesting you accompany me. I doubt he would be pleased if he discovered the truth."

"Which is?"

"That we need to talk." She glanced up and down the corridor, opened the door, and extended an arm in a clear invitation for Jared to enter first.

A low-burning brazier illuminated the small room. Cushions and a thick rug offered an informal seating area to the left, whilst a low table and chairs provided a more formal arrangement on the right. A large sideboard filled part of the back wall, in between the side wall and a second door. Jared stopped partway between the two areas and looked back.

Tessa smiled as she walked past him to the sideboard, retrieved a pair of glasses, and poured them both a drink. She set the glasses on the low table, sat in one of the chairs, and motioned for him to join her.

"Talk about what?" Jared asked, not daring to step closer. They were alone, in her private rooms, likely without Armon's knowledge. The last thing he wanted was her husband walking in and finding them—

"Armon's worried about you."

"He is? Then he knows—?"

"Yes."

Jared's breath came a little easier, but he still didn't move to join her. He didn't know if he could trust himself—

'Trust me, you mean.'

No, myself. I don't know if I can trust myself—

"This would be easier if you sat down."

Jared acknowledged the truth of Tessa's words with a chuckle, pulled out the chair across from her, and sat. He caught the glass she pushed towards him and cupped it in his hands.

Tessa nudged her own glass forward an inch and slid her hand down its smooth side to rest on the table. "There's no easy way to put this. Armon thinks you're insane."

"Why would he—?"

"You told him you were hearing voices last night."

"Not voices, a voice, but I explained—"

"No. You accepted the excuse Armon made for you. He didn't want to push you when you'd already attacked him once."

"I see." Jared took a sip of the drink. It tasted fruity, like berries, cool and soothing, until the alcohol hit the back of his throat. He coughed. "It was nothing. Honestly. I was tired. Stressed—"

"You think he's the only one who's noticed? You've been distracted. Distant. You would have been trampled to death if I hadn't pulled you clear of the horse on the night we arrived."

"I was tired. It'd been a long day, and seeing Ruskin injured the way he was..."

Tessa's soft expression slipped, her brows drawing together to form a knot above her nose. "Please, Jared, talk to me. I want to help. We both do."

Jared stared into his glass, studying the deep brown liquid, watching the flicker of orange-yellow light in its depths. Part of him wanted to confess everything. To tell Tessa the truth, share the burden, find some relief. But part of him held back, afraid of how she would react, what she would do.

And how can she help even if I do tell her? She can't jump into my head and pull out the Voice or douse me with some miracle concoction to drive it away.

But just sharing the burden might help. If Tessa and Armon both knew, they would know to watch him, to distract him if he showed signs of losing control.

He shifted in his seat, the rustling of his clothes seeming overloud in the quiet room. *When did the thunder stop?* He hadn't heard it for several minutes now, although the rain continued to patter on the roof overhead. He didn't know what to do; what to say.

Tessa reached across the table and rested her hand on his wrist. "Whatever it is, we won't use it against you. I won't even tell Armon what you say if you don't want me to."

'*Kiss her.*'

Jared yanked his hand away. His glass tipped. Liquid sloshed across the table, soaking Tessa's arm.

She jumped to her feet, her yelp of surprise barely audible over the clatter of her chair. For a frozen second, they stared at each other, then she grabbed a towel from the sideboard and mopped up the spilt drink before it could drip on the floor.

Jared righted his glass, then picked it up, twirled it, and let it drop again. Picked it up. Twirled it. "I'm sorry. I didn't mean to... to..." He waved his hand, indicating the empty glass. "I didn't stain your dress, did I?"

Tessa glanced down at the tiny damp spots on her skirt, laughed, and shook her head. "I don't much care for dresses anyway. Too restrictive." She tossed the towel back onto the sideboard and her smile faded. "Why did you pull back from me?"

"Armon—"

"No. Your eyes flashed. I saw them. What did this... this *voice*... say?"

"Nothing..."

Tessa leant back in her seat and crossed her arms, never taking her eyes from his face. She waited, not judging, not demanding.

His hands began to shake. He set the glass down and pushed it away. "It told me to kiss you."

The corners of Tessa's lips twitched. "Should I be flattered?"

"Not really. It wants me to kill Salem. And Armon."

"Do you know why?"

"It wants revenge. For the abuse. The humiliation. And I think… I think it's evil."

The Voice cackled inside his head.

"How—?"

"I saw its face."

It was Tessa's turn to hesitate. She reached out to him only to draw back before her hand touched his. "Why don't you start from the beginning? Tell me everything."

Jared stood on the balls of his feet with his back to Tessa and his muscles tensed, poised to flee. He hadn't been able to sit still long, not once he'd started talking. He didn't want to see the pity in her eyes, nor the disgust, condemnation, or other feelings his confession had provoked. Whatever she was thinking right now, he doubted it was good.

"Has it managed to take control?" Tessa asked.

Jared shook his head. "Not fully. It's shown me its face, manipulated my body's responses, even helped me during the hog wrestling, but most of the time, it just… talks." He sighed and turned to face her, although he still couldn't bring himself to look at her face. "But it's the things it says. It's insidious. Constantly digging. Constantly looking for reasons to hate."

Tessa rose and walked across the room. She rested one hand on Jared's shoulder, cupped his chin with the other, and forced him to meet her gaze. Her eyes glistened with moisture, but there was no hatred there. "I'm going to help you through this. We both are. Armon's a good man. He won't abandon you. Not to this."

"How? What can you—what can *anyone*—do? I don't even know if this voice is a long-buried part of me, or if it's some… some *thing* that's found its way inside my head." He laughed and lifted his hands before dropping them in frustration. "Even that makes me sound crazy. People don't get possessed. Which means it must be part of me. Some long-hidden, evil part of me."

"You don't have an evil bone in your body."

"How can you say that? You barely know me."

"I've spent most of my life hunting evil. Believe me, you're not an evil man."

"But—"

"Have you killed before?"

"I've hunted rabbits and—"

Tessa's mouth quirked. "People. Have you ever killed people?"

"No."

"And when this voice urges you to commit murder, does it make you feel good?"

"No. But when Armon threatened to kill Elise, I dreamt of killing him for days."

"I'd be pissed off if someone threatened my family too. That doesn't make me evil. Or you."

"It doesn't say much for Armon though." Jared tried to smile, to show it was a joke, but his laughter stuck in his throat.

"No, it doesn't, but when he's with Morgain…" Tessa lowered her hands and turned away. "If I could find a way to get him away from her, I would. He was hers first though. She'll always pull him back."

"He hates it, you know. How she makes him feel. He told me."

"I know." Tessa turned back to him, blinking back tears. "But this isn't about me and Armon, this is about you."

"And what do you propose to do with me?"

"Talk to Armon about it, for a start. After that?" Tessa sucked on her bottom lip and shook her head. "I'm not sure. I've never had to deal with a crazy man before."

Jared laughed, startling himself. "Thank you."

"I'll be back in a minute."

Jared watched Tessa stroll to the second door, admiring her swaying hips and effortless walk, and smiled to himself, enjoying the view without any desire to do more. *You won't win, you know. I will never be yours.*

Tessa returned a short time later. "Armon asked me to give you this." She extended her fist.

Jared held his hand out, palm up.

Tessa pressed her hand to his and opened her fingers. When she pulled her hand away, he held a small, brass key.

His throat clamped shut, forcing him to swallow several times before he could speak. "He didn't give it to Salem?"

"He had it copied first. He asked me to tell you you're improving, but you're not sly enough yet."

Jared wrapped his fingers around the key. "Thank him for me."

Tessa nodded. "Be careful where you use it. If Salem discovers you have it..."

"I will. I promise. Thank you."

Tessa returned to the table and poured herself a drink. "You should change. Our escort will be ready soon."

"What's wrong with this?" Jared asked, gesturing at his clothes.

"Nothing. If you happen to be out for a stroll in the sunshine."

"Good point." Jared opened his coat pocket, eyed the tiny compartment, and decided it would be safer if he carried the key in his hand.

9/13/32 KAF (Two)

First, they headed to the stables to pick up the slaves. When Jared queried the arrangement, Tessa shrugged. "They're livestock. Where else would they be kept?"

He accepted the explanation without comment and went to saddle Sherna.

Sherna whinnied when she spotted him, seeking out his hands when he drew close. Her breath tickled his skin.

He laughed and dug into the pocket of his riding breeches. "Your apple, my dear. As promised." The offering was meagre—the skin of the apple spotted and wrinkled, and the quartered flesh too dry—but she snaffled it up with an eager snort. "Make the most of it, dear one. I can't afford too many more. They charged me a copper round for that. A whole round. I could buy a dozen apples for that back home."

He continued to talk as he worked, using his voice to keep her calm whilst he checked her coat.

Tessa entered the stable a few minutes later. She strolled up the aisle, stopping when she reached Sherna's stall. "Everything all right?"

"Everything's fine." He smiled and nodded, hoping the gesture came across as reassuring rather than crazed.

"Good." Tessa smiled and headed to her own mount's stall.

"I hope the storm didn't upset you." Jared said as he slid Sherna's saddle-blanket into place. "The lightning's stopped now, but I'm afraid you're going to get wet." He lifted his saddle off the stall wall and settled it across her back. "But at least you'll get a decent run out. Better than being stuck here, doing laps of the paddock."

Footsteps scuffed the dirt near the entrance. "The slaves are ready, my lady!"

Jared paused long enough to peer over the stall door. A patrolman stood in the entrance, his rain-flattened hair and stubble conspiring to give him a scruffy appearance despite his immaculate uniform.

Tessa emerged from her stall at the same moment. Her gaze followed Jared's. "And your mounts?"

"Melf and Winton are fetching them, my lady."

"Thank you…?"

"Gregory, my lady."

"Thank you, Gregory. We'll be there shortly."

Sherna butted her nose into the small of Jared's back.

He staggered forward, caught the top of the door with one hand and pushed her head to the side with the other. "All right, all right. I'll pay attention." He laughed as he turned and scratched the side of her neck.

Once he had her saddled, he led her from her stall and walked her up and down the aisle to stretch her legs whilst they waited for Tessa. She tossed her head and snorted, eager for exercise after her unusual confinements, first aboard ship and then within the paddock and stables.

Tessa joined him a few minutes later. They led their horses out side-by-side.

The patrolmen were mounted and waiting, the slaves roped together in a line behind Gregory's horse. All three wore sackcloth tunics, belted at the waist, and simple, wood-soled sandals.

Jared's eyes met the boy's as he walked past. He shuddered, recalling one of Godsman Angus's lectures.

"All slaves are soulless, boy, and it's up to the rest of us to offer them guidance. Some have the misfortune of being born soulless. Some come to us from distant lands, their souls withered and perished. Some, the worst, choose to throw their souls away, committing crimes so heinous their souls are driven from their bodies. They may walk and talk and act like the rest of us, boy, but, deep down, they're all empty."

Looking into the boy's eyes, he could well believe it. He showed no sign of awareness. He didn't look up in response to Jared's scrutiny; didn't gaze around at his surroundings. He merely stared straight ahead, seeing nothing, his eyes dead.

Not so the girls. They, at least, gave the impression they were human, hunching their shoulders against the rain, eyeing the guards with a modicum of fear and shuffling closer together, as though seeking to draw strength from one another. The one at the back leant forward to whisper something in the second girl's ear. The second girl giggled and glanced in Jared's direction, her eyes wide and wondering.

Jared strode past them, stopped Sherna next to Tessa's mare, and vaulted into the saddle.

Sherna tossed her head and side-stepped, demanding her head.

Jared gave the reins a quick tug to remind her who was in charge. "She's a little restless," he said in response to Tessa's amused smile.

"If you say so." Tessa clucked her tongue and tapped her mare's sides with her heels. The mare started walking. Sherna kept pace beside her. Gregory followed with his line of slaves, Winton and Melf flanking them.

Their path took them deep into the foreign district. The large residences and open-front shops surrounding the market square gave way to more modest buildings. They passed down a street lined with single-storey houses, each one with its own small front garden. Children played on the lawns or the street outside, watched by mothers and grandmothers whilst they worked, all of them oblivious to the slow-falling rain.

From there, they turned onto a narrower street, this one lined by three-storey flats—narrow, ugly things with steps on the sides of the buildings to give access to the rooms above. The buildings were clean and undamaged, kept that way, he assumed, by the Canri magic, but the children here played unsupervised and wore little more than rags. "So different," Jared said as he glanced back at the street they'd just left.

"It's all part of Canri's pattern," Tessa said, as if that explained everything.

The next junction revealed more flats in all directions.

"Where's all the industry? The work?" Jared asked.

Nobody answered.

Ten minutes later, they arrived at the wall marking the border of the foreign district. One of the gate guards stepped forward and greeted the travellers in Canri.

Tessa responded, her tone even and polite. She showed the guard a letter marked with Azier's seal. After several minutes of haggling, the guard extended a hand. Tessa slipped some coins from her purse and pressed them into his palm.

"He wants to see your license," Tessa said, looking at Jared.

Jared fixed the guard with a hard stare and held it for a count of ten before he retrieved the license from his inside pocket and handed it over.

The guard studied the document, nodded, and gave it back. He said something else to Tessa, signalled to his companion, and stepped aside to let them through the gate.

Two mounted Canri soldiers waited for the party on the other side. They took up position in front of Tessa and Jared.

"Wh—?" Jared started to ask.

"Guides," Tessa said. "They don't want their 'illustrious guests' getting lost."

"Don't want us seeing what we shouldn't, more like," one of the patrolmen muttered.

"Now, now, Melf, I won't be having none of that," Gregory said.

"Sorry, sir."

Jared bit the inside of his cheek to stop a laugh. "I take it foreigners aren't welcome here."

"Not without a work permit," Tessa replied, her own voice light. "And no, that licence of yours does *not* count."

"As if I would—"

Tessa's laughter brought Jared's protest up short.

The rain had turned to a steady drizzle when Armon exited the barracks. He tipped his head back to let the water wash over his face, then raised his arms skyward and stretched. Two hours sitting hunched over a table, discussing potential holes in security, redesigning and reassigning patrol routes, and checking and rechecking supplies was enough for any man. He shook his arms, wiped the drizzle from his eyes, and turned towards the embassy.

He'd made it halfway across the courtyard when the embassy doors opened and Mevin stepped out. Armon waved to the young medic then waited for him to approach. "Is Lady Zandra back already?"

"Err, no, sir."

"Then why are you here?" Armon let a slight hint of disapproval touch his voice.

Mevin shuffled his feet. "I was here with the others, waiting to escort her, when I got a summons from Ambassador Salem, sir. By the time he dismissed me, she'd already left."

"She left without a full escort?"

"No, sir. Gregory went with her instead. He's the one who delivered Salem's message."

Gregory? A tiny thorn of fear stabbed Armon deep in his gut. Gregory was one of three men assigned to his patrol shortly before they departed. All three had come with glowing reports from their previous patrols, but there'd been no time to make in-depth enquiries. He'd tried to spend time with each of them, but Gregory remained distant. The man was a veteran—he respected the chain of command—and chatting with his superiors was simply not done. *Tessa should be safe enough with him, but...* "What did Salem want?"

"He had a touch of stomach cramps, sir. Wanted me to check him over."

Armon nodded. It was a reasonable request, if an ill-timed one.

"Do you need anything else, sir?"

"Mmm? No—Yes. Was anyone waiting to see the ambassador?"

"A Canri woman, sir. Black hair. Black eyes. Very striking, sir, despite her age. She had a hardness to her. And this way of looking at me that made me want to shiver. You've met her, I think. She was sitting at your table during the feast."

"Karolina Andersdotter."

"Sir?"

"One of the Canri matriarchs. Thank you, Mevin."

"Sir." Mevin saluted and took his leave.

Jared would be disappointed when he discovered he'd missed her. *Probably for the best though. He's a lousy judge of women.* A smile flickered over Armon's lips, but his amusement quickly faded. He didn't like the sudden change; didn't like Tessa being escorted by a man he hadn't assigned, or the convenient timing of Salem's illness. It could be simple coincidence, but—

He shook his head. Speculation would gain him nothing but worry. Tessa could take care of herself. *And I*—he started towards the embassy—*I will make polite enquiries about the ambassador's health.*

The first signs of the missing industry became evident as Jared and the other members of their small party followed their guides through the tunnel beneath the thick wall. The smell reached him first, a faint but unpleasant mix of blood, offal, and urine. Then a shout echoed above the clip of the horses' hoofs. A clang. The clatter of wood. He ducked as they passed through the second gate, then his grip grew slack on his reins and pommel.

Everything looked... flat. There was a scattering of houses—*or are they shacks?*—but they were a distance away, nearer to the lake than the gate through which he'd ridden. There wasn't a dash of greenery in sight either, just a massive grid of sandstone-tiled squares separated by a series of crisscrossing blue and red roads.

Huge, open-air tanneries dominated the nearest squares. The closest held row upon row of vertical wood frames, each one housing a stretched skin, and each skin in a different stage of preparation. Men and women moved about the square, some tending to the individual skins whilst others scooped up off-cuts or scrubbed the tiles clear of blood and gobbets of flesh.

"Why do they bother?" Melf asked, guiding his horse alongside Sherna.

"Hmm?"

"Scrubbing like that. Why bother, if that magic of theirs will vanish all the muck anyway?"

Jared shrugged. "Maybe the clouds stop it working."

"Or maybe they don't see the magic as a reason to be lazy," Tessa said, amusement in her voice. "They still need to clean up after themselves outside the city, after all." She glanced over at their scowling guides, clucked her tongue, and kneed her mare to get her moving.

Jared encouraged Sherna to match pace with her whilst Melf dropped back to his position beside the slaves.

A dozen large tanning vats filled the next square, along with several mounds of dung. Two or three children occupied each vat, stomping the dung into the hides, whilst a couple of shovel-carrying older children darted between them, topping the vats up as needed.

Jared lifted a hand to his nose as they passed, but the smell grew no worse, suppressed, he presumed, by the Canri magic, and further masked by the scented oil burners lining the square.

A scuffle and a curse jolted him from his scrutiny. He pulled on Sherna's left-hand rein, turning her in a half-circle, vaguely aware of Tessa doing the same.

The slave boy lay sprawled on his back, his bound hands pulled full-stretch above his head. Bloody scrapes on his legs and elbows suggested he'd been dragged for several feet. Too-wide eyes filled a too-pale face, but then the rope went slack, and he resumed his dull, lifeless stare.

Melf dismounted and hauled the boy back to his feet. Jared turned Sherna with a vicious tug and an unneeded kick.

The tanneries gave way to giant, outdoor butcheries, each one filled with rows of chopping blocks. On the left, workers skinned the animals, separating the hides from the bodies, ready for the tanneries. Butchers dismembered the carcasses in the next square along, wasting nothing, not even the blood, which ran along gullies in the chopping boards before being funnelled into buckets underneath.

Jared glanced back at the boy again, the remembered words of the godsman echoing once more in his head.

"You only get one soul, boy. One chance to do things right."

One soul. And a boy of what? Ten or twelve? Has already lost his?

He crushed Sherna's reins in his fist.

One soul lost... And one soul gained?

Is that what you are? Another soul fighting for control?

All those lost souls had to go somewhere, after all.

"Prehen Damis judges us all, boy," Godsman Angus had said. *"Those found worthy carry their soul into their next life, those found wanting are separated, their souls trapped within the Vortex until they redeem themselves."*

So no stray souls. It was a foolish notion, anyway. Souls abandoned those who sinned. And this thing—this Voice—was a sinner, first seeking to get him killed, and then compelling him to kill instead.

So what does that make Tessa?

A sinner, certainly. A killer? Yes. Or so she claims. But soulless? Would a soulless killer have spared Armon's life? Or treated me with understanding and compassion? If the godsman's teaching's to be believed, she's a walking contradiction.

"What are you thinking about?" Tessa asked.

Jared flinched, startling Sherna into a side-stepping dance. He gave her neck a reassuring pat. "Slaves and souls."

"And what conclusions have you come to?" Tessa asked, her smile and tone suggesting she knew exactly what he'd been thinking.

"That such matters are best left to the godsmen to ponder. Speaking of which, why are there none in the delegation?"

"Godsmen?"

Jared nodded.

"The Canri wouldn't permit it. They don't want preachers of other faiths within their walls, poisoning their people's minds."

"A pity. I had some questions..."

"Questions? And here I was thinking you weren't the religious type."

"I'm not, I just thought—"

"Do you know what the godsmen do to people they consider insane?"

"No. Wha—?"

"They claim they've been touched by the gods and take them into their retreats."

"Lock them up, you mean?"

Tessa nodded. "To 'keep them safe.'"

"Do you think…?" Jared swallowed back the lump forming in his throat. "Do you think they would think me touched?"

"Perhaps."

He let the conversation drop.

The butcheries had given way to smoke houses whilst they talked. The district's only buildings—the structures he initially mistook for shacks—were hexagonal, with wooden walls and sloping, clay-tiled roofs. Thin wisps of smoke escaped through narrow vents, along with the scents of curing fish and meat.

Is it possible the godsmen are right? Have I been touched by the gods? He clamped his teeth shut on a laugh. Now that *was* lunacy. As if the gods would care about him or will him to kill.

Not the gods, then, or a second soul. Which leaves what, exactly? Some sort of parasite? But surely if such a thing existed, I'd have heard of it before now?

No. This Voice. This thing. It's part of me. It had told him as much. *'I am you. You are me.'* That's what it said. *Does that mean I am evil? That I'm the one without a soul?*

"Jared?" Tessa asked

Jared jerked his head around but managed not to startle Sherna this time. "Yes?"

"Try not to worry about it. You'll only make yourself feel worse."

Easily said, when you don't have a crazy Voice in your head. He nodded.

At the crossroads between smokehouses, he caught a glimpse of the fisheries—huge circular pools dug into the earth near the shore, each one connected to the lake by a man-made stream—but he had no chance to take in more as their guides turned them towards a small gate in the district's far wall.

"Tessa?" he asked, when the pools dropped out of sight.

"Yes?"

"Is Armon really a slave?"

Tessa grew still, all expression slipping from her face. When she spoke, her voice was chill. "What makes you think that?"

"He showed me his tattoo the first time we met. The one on his neck. And he *is* a bastard of the Blood. By law—"

"By law, all those of the Blood born out of wedlock must be enslaved. I know." Bitterness gave her words a ragged edge.

"So? Is he?"

Tessa let out a long sigh, and her tension melted with it. "Officially? No. Morgain has never demanded it. But technically? Yes. He is. Not that he'll admit it. Not even to himself."

"He said Morgain wants to change the law to protect him."

"Yes."

"How can she? All laws governing slaves come from the godsmen. They're the only ones who can determine who has a soul."

"Are you really so naïve?"

"It's not naivety, it's the truth—"

"The *truth* is that slave laws were created to stop a revolt. Men had slaves long before the godsmen arrived, preaching the words of their gods. If they'd tried to outlaw slavery, they'd never have survived."

"The laws were given to the godsmen by the gods. They—"

"Who taught you all this?"

"Ryal's godsman."

"And you've never thought to question it?"

"He discouraged questions."

"That explains a lot."

A deep-throated yell to "Stop!" brought their conversation to an abrupt halt. Jared and Tessa both turned in their saddles.

One of the slave girls had slipped her bonds and was racing down the street, her sandals slap-slapping with every step.

Melf yanked on his mount's reins, spinning it in a tight circle, and kicked its sides. His mare drew level with the girl in seconds. He leant to his left, arm outstretched, and grabbed a fistful of her tunic.

She screamed, even as she was hauled, thrashing and kicking, into the air and across the front of Melf's saddle.

He returned to the group at a more sedate pace and inclined his head. "Sorry about that, my lady. This one's a little feisty."

❧❧

Armon's stomach rumbled in response to the mouth-watering aroma of fresh-cooked bread and roast chicken. It had been too long since breakfast, and breakfast had been too small. He rested his fingers on the dining table and studied the spread before him.

A pair of boiled eggs rested atop slices of chicken and honeyed pork, arranged on a nest of gravy-soaked flatbread. Fresh fruits and a few sweet pastries filled a second plate, whilst a mug of chilled ale flavoured with berries completed the meal. He moistened his lips in anticipation and reached for the cutlery.

The dining room door opened with a swish. Armon glanced towards it without moving his head. Ambassador Salem strolled inside with Stanin trailing behind.

About time they made an appearance.

They'd been locked in a meeting with their Canri counterparts when he'd visited the reception after speaking to Mevin. Perhaps now he'd get a chance to ask Salem about Gregory's reassignment.

He cut one of the chicken slices into triangles and ate a piece as he watched the pair cross the dining room to the service tables. Salem collected a plate and selected his food with quick, decisive movements. Stanin shuffled after him, jabbing at the serving platters like a pigeon, taking tiny samples from each. Armon ducked his head and stuffed another triangle into his mouth.

Shadows fell across his table a few seconds later. Salem and Stanin set their trays down without waiting for an invitation.

Armon acknowledged them with a nod and continued to eat.

"Patrol Leader." Salem settled into the chair across from Armon, sitting straighter than a meerkat on high alert, and kept his cuffs clear of his plate with a measured flick.

"Ambassador," Armon said between mouthfuls. "You're feeling better, I hope?"

Salem tilted his head to the side. "Better?"

"You requested my medic's assistance earlier. Stomach cramps, I believe."

"Ah, yes. It was nothing serious."

Armon cut one of his eggs in half. "Nothing serious? You called my medic away from his duties, and you're telling me it was for 'nothing serious'?" He stuffed the egg in his mouth.

"What would you have me do, send for one of those Canri fakers instead?"

"Mevin was supposed to be escorting Lady Zandra into the city."

"Another of your men went in his stead, I presume?"

"Yes, but—"

"Don't you trust your men?"

"Of course I do—"

"Then I fail to see the problem." Salem didn't raise his voice, but his words carried a hard edge.

Armon speared the second half of his egg, imagining it was the ambassador's head. A series of high-pitched clicks came from Stanin's direction as he attacked each of his tiny samples in turn. Salem ate more sedately, handling his cutlery more like a bloodborn noble than an elevated commoner. Armon swallowed a mouthful of ale.

Salem finished his slice of game pie and placed his cutlery on his plate. "How secure is the embassy, Patrol Leader?"

Armon set his mug down. "Completely, Ambassador."

Salem pushed his plate to one side, forcing Stanin and Armon to do the same. "I heard you were having some staffing problems this morning."

Who, by the Vortex, told him that? Armon reclined in his chair to mask the tightness building in his shoulders. "I needed to increase the number of men guarding the stables, to keep an eye on the slaves Azier is planning to purchase. With three men there, and five needed to guard the gates and doors here, it leaves numbers a little thin for the regular and random patrols."

"I think that's a matter I can help you with." Salem took a sip of his wine. "My men can watch the front doors and the entrance to the reception. That would free up three of yours."

Armon ran his thumb down the side of his mug. Salem didn't strike him as the helpful type, which meant he either wanted Armon's men out of the way or he had reason to suspect them. Armon glanced at Stanin, but he appeared more interested in mourning the remains of his meal than adding to the conversation. Armon looked back at the ambassador. "I cannot allow that, sir. The safety of this embassy and the people in it are my respon—"

"Are you questioning the competence of my bodyguards, Patrol Leader?"

"Of course not, but I can't—"

"You can, and you will. It's not difficult."

"Regulations state—"

Salem slapped the table with his palm. A tiny twitch tugged at his lips. "Tell me, Patrol Leader, what's the penalty for insubordination?"

Armon dug his fingernails into his skin. There would be time enough to throttle the pompous fool when the deal was done. Right now, he needed to stay in character. "Anything from punishment rations and docked pay to loss of rank or a dishonourable discharge, depending on the severity of the offence."

"Punishment rations?"

"Bread and water, served twice a day." *Like you needed to ask.*

"Then I sentence you to five days of punishment rations for refusing a direct order." The twitch turned into a thin-lipped smile; one he had no doubt perfected by practising in front of a mirror.

"I was only—"

"Ten days." Salem hooked Armon's tray with a finger and pulled it away. "Stanin will take care of the necessary paperwork."

Armon clamped his mouth shut. Patrol Leader Malkem was a stickler for the rules, not an argumentative idiot.

"You have no more objections?"

"No, sir."

"Good. Stanin, have that young medic... What was his name again?"

"Mevin."

"Have Mevin oversee the patrol leader's punishment. I don't want him growing too weak to perform his duties." Salem turned to Armon. "Any further repeat of this behaviour, and I'll have you placed in solitary for the remainder of our stay here. Is that clear, Patrol Leader?"

"Crystal, sir."

"Good. You may leave."

Armon kept his eyes lowered and stood, sending his chair skidding across the stone floor. He crossed the room in five strides, wrenched open the door, and stalked outside. His stomach growled in protest.

Melf kept the slave girl draped across his saddle for the remainder of the journey. She'd stopped screaming once he rejoined the party, but she continued to squirm and struggle until he slapped the side of her head. Jared glanced back at her several times as they neared the gate out of the industrial district, shifting in his saddle each time, discomforted by the mix of hatred and despair in her eyes.

Or perhaps he only saw what he expected to see, imagining emotions in those stark eyes that simply weren't there. *She's just an animal, after all.*

Just *an animal? Like Sherna's just an animal?* He leant forward and stroked her neck. *And Sherna can't feel? Can't reciprocate my kindness? Won't react if she senses a threat?*

Tessa edged her mare closer and nudged Jared's knee. "This isn't going to be a problem, is it?"

He straightened, glanced at Tessa, and shook his head.

"You sure? I'll understand if you dislike trading in human flesh."

He glanced over his shoulder one more time before they passed through the gate, turned back to Tessa, and forced a smile. "It's fine. Honestly."

The narrowness of the tunnel beyond the gate forced them to ride single file. Their guides turned left when they exited the tunnel and led them to a small, open-fronted stable block.

Tessa slipped from the saddle and handed her mare's reins to one of the stable hands. Jared dismounted and paused to give Sherna a hearty pat before he joined her.

They waited to the side of the small, fenced-in yard whilst Gregory and Winton dismounted. Then Melf drew up at Gregory's side and handed the girl over to him.

She dangled, limp, between them, forcing Gregory to step back and lean precariously to one side to pull her down. Her legs slid off the horse's back and dropped, her head jerked back, and then she kicked, catching Gregory on the inside of the leg. Her feet hit the ground and she ran, stumbling sideways as she struggled to get her balance.

Gregory reacted first, grabbing a handful of her hair and hauling her back.

The edge of the fence rail dug into Jared's fingers. He released his pent breath and relaxed his grip.

"Is the Voice bothering you?" Tessa asked with a pointed glance at his hands.

"No. It hasn't said a word since it told me to kiss you."

"Good."

Melf finished retying the girl to the slave line and crossed the yard to join them. "She shouldn't cause any more trouble, my lady. I double-knotted the rope."

"Thank you, Melf."

Melf saluted and took his place at the back of the line. Gregory moved forward to replace him, falling in on Tessa's right.

"Remember what you're looking for," Tessa said, looking to Gregory then Jared. "Disease, untreated wounds, and signs of abuse. Azier wants slaves who are whole, healthy, and strong."

"Yes, my lady," Gregory said.

Jared inclined his head.

Their guides finished speaking with the stable master, and one of them approached Tessa. They exchanged a few words in Canri, and the guide left again.

"Time to go, gentlemen," Tessa said.

Gregory acknowledged her words with a nod and raised a hand to Melf and Winton. The two patrolmen returned the signal, and the party departed the yard.

"I want no juveniles and nobody who's too old to survive the voyage home," Tessa said as they followed the guides along a road running between a high wooden fence and the district's outer wall. "If you suspect the traders are trying to hide the slaves' ages, let me know. I won't deal with cheats."

They turned onto a second road running perpendicular to the first. The high fence continued to parallel the road on their right whilst a second, identical fence penned them in on the left.

"And be careful what you say," Tessa added. "The Canri aren't idiots. There's a good chance at least one of them will understand the Kingdom tongue."

Three men stepped through a gate in the right-hand fence. Tessa fell silent. Jared recognised two of them. Andreas, Canri's baton-fighting champion, and Oskar, the young fighter who'd trounced him at the feast. Seen side-by-side, the similarities between them were striking. They shared the same facial structure, colouring, and build, though Oskar walked with a cocky, almost arrogant swagger whilst Andreas's more relaxed strides spoke of his well-earned confidence. The third man could have been Andreas's double, had he not lacked the champion's musculature and easy gait.

The three men approached, and Andreas extended his hand. Tessa clasped his arm below the elbow.

Jared missed whatever greeting passed between them, distracted by Oskar's insolent glare. Their gazes met, and Oskar smirked, pointed to Jared's right leg, and mimed a kick.

Andreas leant to the side, whispered in Oskar's ear, and turned back to Tessa. "You have met my youngest brother, I believe," Andreas said, switching to the Kingdom tongue. "Please, accept my apologies for his disrespectful attitude. He is a boy still."

Oskar turned on his brother, his hand raised.

Andreas slapped the back of Oskar's head. "And this," he said, carrying on as though he hadn't been interrupted, "is our middle brother, Esbjorn. He runs the family affairs within the city."

Esbjorn bowed his head to Tessa. He was not a warrior like his brothers. He carried no weapons, and his full-length, wraparound tunic looked better suited to a marketplace than a fighting ring. But he looked fit, and his eyes danced about constantly, watching everything, seemingly missing nothing. He glanced at Jared and flashed what might have been a friendly smile or a predatory warning.

'What I wouldn't give to be inside his head. So alert. So thoughtful. I bet he wouldn't ignore me when I tried to help.'

You're back then?

'Back? You think I have somewhere else to go?'

You know what I mean.

'You were boring me. All this confessing and philosophising. Such a waste of time. I bet Esbjorn doesn't waste time thinking about things like that.'

How would you know?

'I've been inside men like him before. Real men. Not like you.'

You've been...? Then you're real, not some crazed part of me? Which makes you what? A lost soul? A ghost? A—

Pain flared in his side, sharp and sudden, like the bite from a bottle gnat.

"Focus," Tessa hissed.

Jared looked at the three Canri in front of him. Oskar and Andreas didn't appear to have noticed his distraction, but Esbjorn stared at him with narrowed eyes and pursed lips.

What's he thinking? What did he see?

'I imagine he saw Tessa jab you with her elbow and is now wondering what signal she gave you.'

You don't think—

'Of course not. It takes a moment to think a thought. A fraction of a second. What is there to see?'

Something must have made Tessa and Armon suspicious. I–

'You think too much.'

"Have you come to buy or sell today?" Andreas asked.

"A little of both, I hope." Tessa stepped sideways, giving the Canri a clear view of the slaves behind her.

Oskar dismissed them with a derisory glance and a sniff, but Andreas studied them with more care before leaning towards Esbjorn and whispering a few quick words. Esbjorn nodded, replied in kind, and stepped towards the waiting slaves.

He inspected the boy first, forcing his eyelids open and peering into his eyes, cupping his chin with a strong hand and twisting his head from side to side, checking the boy's ears and the back of his neck. He ran his fingers through the boy's hair, squeezed the muscles in his legs and arms, and poked at his back and sides.

Throughout the inspection, Esbjorn's expression remained calm and professional, but in the end, he shook his head and pushed the boy to one side. He turned to Andreas and said something in Canri, his tone making it clear he was unimpressed. He moved to the first of the girls and repeated the inspection with similar results.

Oskar snorted, earning himself another slap from his older brother.

Esbjorn moved on.

The second girl, the one who had tried to run, garnered more attention. She refused to stand still whilst Esbjorn checked her, jerking her head away when he peered into her eyes, trying to bite him when he reached for her chin. She kicked and bucked, struggling to avoid his touch.

By the end of the inspection, Esbjorn was grinning. He reported to Andreas again.

Andreas turned to Tessa. "This one shows good spirit. She is strong. A fighter. The other two, they are meek and lifeless. No good for us. You would do better taking them to a bordellägare—a, uh, house of whoring—where their exoticness will make up for their softness."

Esbjorn continued to study the second girl. He reached for her shoulder. She spat in his face. His lips curled up in a cruel smile, and a predatory glint filled his eyes. He ran his gaze up and down her body. His next words were spoken softly, as though he meant them for himself. "Jag vill ha henne."—*"I want her."*

A burst of laughter escaped Oskar's lips. He clapped a hand to his mouth and pretended to cough but failed to hide the amusement in his eyes.

Esbjorn turned on his younger brother, angry words streaming from his lips, flowing so swiftly they blurred into a single, indecipherable sound.

Oskar's cheeks flushed. He lowered his head, swallowing back his laughter. "Förlåt mig."—"*Forgive me.*"

Andreas stepped between his brothers, waving them to silence. "Esbjorn asks how much she is."

"Why don't we leave such mundane matters for later?" Tessa asked. "I would see the merchandise in your pens first."

Esbjorn waited for Andreas's translation then dipped his head in agreement.

Whatever else was said went over Jared's head. *That look in Esbjorn's eyes. That... desire.* He swallowed vomit, took a deep breath, and swallowed again. *Slave or not, the girl deserves better.*

"Jared?" Tessa asked as she rested a hand on his shoulder.

He looked at her, then glanced around.

Oskar, Winton, and Melf were leading the slaves through the gate in the fence. Andreas and Esbjorn stood off to one side. And Gregory... Gregory waited for them a respectable distance away.

Even so, Jared's words were a bare whisper when he said, "He's going to rape her."

"Does it matter? She's only a slave, after all." Tessa's words lacked emotion, her tone more suited to a mundane discussion over lunch. But her eyes burned, challenging him. "She's soulless. Emotionless. She won't feel a thing."

"Don't you care?"

"Of course I care! But there's nothing I can do about it. Nothing either of us can do."

"You could refuse to sell her. Or price her too high."

Tessa leant in even closer. "I'm a merchant. Every day I keep a slave it costs me—or, in this case, my trading partner—money. If I appear to be anything but eager to sell, people will start asking questions, and I cannot afford to have people asking questions. I have a part to play, and I intend to play it. Whether I like it or not is irrelevant."

"But he's going to rape her."

"And here I was thinking you didn't care."

9/13/32 KAF (Three)

Armon tossed the folder onto the table, dropped onto the hard, wooden seat, and sighed. He should have been in bed, catching up on his sleep before his evening shift, but instead he had to work out the rota. Again.

A wave of quiet rippled through the barracks as the off-duty men abandoned their conversations and turned to watch.

Pavel set his book aside and lifted his head from his pillow. "I thought we sorted that this morning."

"We did." Armon opened the folder and spread the rota sheets across the table.

"But?"

"But the ambassador decided to be helpful and relieve us of some of our duties."

Pavel sat up. "Want a hand?"

"Please." Armon pulled out a fresh sheet of paper, retrieved a pencil from the folder, and started listing the names, times, and dates of everyone scheduled to guard the embassy door and reception area.

Pavel settled into the chair next to him, glanced at the list, and proceeded to cross off the corresponding names on the rota. "How do you want them spread out?"

"Two on patrol here, one inside and one out. No set patterns. One at the stables doing the same." Armon finished and set the pencil aside, happy to let Pavel work out the details. He leant back in his chair and did his best to ignore his gurgling stomach as it digested the remains of his interrupted meal.

"Do you still want to cover the stables tonight?"

Armon nodded. "I need to make sure everything's secure when the new slaves arrive. Best I do it myself. No point giving Azier reason to complain." He crossed his arms and closed his eyes.

Tessa would be at the slave pens by now, inspecting the merchandise, surrounded by an armed escort, with her own skills to rely on besides. She was in no danger. Nobody in Canri intended her harm. So why was it that, every time he thought of her, he felt weighed down by dread? Because she was with Jared? Or because Gregory had taken Mevin's place? He didn't know, couldn't be sure. *A bit of both, probably.*

The gasses in his stomach churned.

The front door creaked.

He opened his eyes.

Mevin entered, carrying a mug of water and a chunk of bread.

Armon groaned.

"What did you do this time?" Pavel asked, a moronic grin spreading across his face.

"My job."

"Your breakfast, sir." Mevin set the meagre meal on the table. "I know it's a little late, but... well... I heard the ambassador snatched your lunch away before you had a chance to eat."

"Thank you, Mevin."

Pavel's gaze traced Mevin's path to the door then snapped back to Armon. "You upset the ambassador?"

"I pointed out he had no right to pull my men off guard duty. The rules clearly state—"

Pavel guffawed. "You questioned his orders?"

"I... yes... you could describe it that way."

"Will you never learn?"

"Probably not." Armon tore off a piece of bread and dunked it in the water. "But someone has to follow the rules, otherwise there'd be no point in having them."

Pavel shook his head, still chuckling, and finished fixing the rota.

The gate through which Melf and Winton had taken the slaves led to the first of the slave pens—a fenced in area filled with cages, the smallest of which held a single slave each whilst the largest housed several dozen. They were arranged in a grid, with the largest cage taking up the length of the back fence. Two cages sat in front of the first, then three, then four, and so forth, until the line of ten cages at the front. Neat gravel paths ran between them, spacing them so a slave in one could have no physical contact with a slave in another.

"Oskar and I brought these in yesterday," Andreas said. "They came from a village on the southern border of our family lands. They objected to our rule and rebelled. The men and women in these cages, they are the ones who survived."

Andreas continued his explanation as he led Tessa between two of the smaller cages, but Jared dropped back, his steps slowing as he looked inside the pens.

The slaves in the nearest cages appeared to be clean, clothed, and well fed. Some carried wounds, presumably suffered in the rebellion, but their injuries had been tended—cleaned and stitched or bandaged. But it was the cages that turned his stomach. Those nearest denied their occupants space to lie down. And every one stood open to the elements, their roofs nothing more than criss-crossing iron bars. The day's incessant rain had turned the ground to boggy mud. And whilst the pen's high, solid fences provided some shelter from the wind, when the sun reached its zenith, they would provide no protection from its burning rays.

Jared still suffered nightmares of his time in Ryal's pitch black dungeon, but this? This was a different kind of horror altogether. No wonder the slave boy looked so disinterested, so... dead.

And Armon wants even more slavery? He's mad.

And yet...

And yet those men and women watching him from their cages didn't look miserable or sad, frightened or cowed. Some looked curious, some defiant. One or two even looked down their noses at him, as if he were a flatworm and they the lords and ladies. They were not Canri, these viridian-skinned, heavy-browed men, women, and children, but they carried themselves with the same superior air.

Jared dragged his gaze away from the pens. Tessa and Andreas had almost reached the end of the first row of cages. He hurried to catch up.

"Were you looking for anything in particular?" Andreas was asking when Jared reached them.

Tessa shook her head. "Strong slaves. Healthy ones, who are intelligent enough to learn the Kingdom tongue—or enough of it to understand commands. One or two men with weapons' training. I also have several clients who might be interested in more… exotic… slaves if the price is right."

"Why don't I show you around then? Esbjorn and Oskar can stay with your men. If you want a second opinion, you can always call them over."

"That is most kind of you. Thank you, Andreas." The smile Tessa gave Andreas would have made Armon jealous. It certainly quickened Jared's pulse.

He turned away before she noticed.

'Why don't you seduce her? I'm sure she'd bed you if you asked her to.'

Piss off.

The Voice laughed.

Footsteps sounded at Jared's back as Andreas led Tessa deeper into the pen. He didn't turn to follow. The slave in the final solitary cage held all his attention.

The man sat cross-legged in the centre of the cage, oblivious to the muddy puddle forming around him and the rain falling on the back of his unprotected head. His long, black hair was plastered to his scalp, the rainwater running down the strands to gather into droplets that fell onto his thickset shoulders. Leather armour covered his legs and torso but couldn't disguise his bulging muscles. He had metal studs in the soles of his boots and thick iron rings on most of his fingers.

Jared took a step towards the cage, then another, trying to get a closer look at the slave's face, but the man kept his head bowed, his features hidden in shadows.

More footsteps crunched towards him. Oskar appeared at his side, his thin grin more predatory than inviting. "Want see, yes?"

"I…" Jared bent forward but still couldn't see the man's face. *Why does it matter? He's a stranger. After today, I'll probably never see him again.* He straightened. "Yes."

Oskar's eyebrows flickered, nudging upwards before contracting into a frown. He glanced towards the slave. When he turned back, his grin widened to show the tips of his teeth. "Come." He caught Jared by the elbow and pulled him forward. "Look. Buy." He dragged Jared to the cage door.

The man within never stirred.

"In?" Oskar asked. He pulled a large set of keys from his pocket and began searching through them.

"I…" Jared hesitated, eyeing Oskar from the corner of his eye. Oskar had despised him since the moment they'd met. *This sudden helpfulness—*

"In?" Oskar repeated as he slid a key into the lock.

Jared started to shake his head, but his gaze dropped to the slave again, drawn as inexorably as a butterfly to a flower. Something tugged at his brain, the touch as faint as the brush of a feather.

This is madness.

He lifted his gaze to meet Oskar's. "Yes. In."

Oskar grinned as he turned the key, pulled the door open, and waved Jared inside. If the man in the cage heard the door opening, he gave no sign of it. Jared paused with his foot on the edge of the threshold.

'What's wrong, dandy boy? Are you afraid?'

The tug came again, less subtle this time.

He stepped inside.

The door crashed into its frame. The lock snicked.

The slave launched himself from the ground, thrusting up and forward with his powerful legs. He slammed into Jared, lifting him from his feet and carrying him backwards.

The sound registered first—the sickening crunch of metal striking flesh—then agony lanced across his back like the lashes from a dozen burning brands. He found himself pinned to the cage wall, his feet dangling a foot above the ground and one of the slave's heavy forearms pressed against his throat. He tried to draw a deep breath but could only manage short, pain-filled gasps. The slave's brilliant blue eyes dominated his vision. Then the slave grinned, revealing two rows of filed teeth. He growled something incomprehensible and leant forward, opening his mouth wide.

The bars of the cage dug into Jared's back. The press of the slave's forearm cut off his breath. He clutched the slave's wrist, pulled, twisted, and squeezed. Kicked at his legs and knees. Hammered a fist into the inside of his elbow. The slave proved as immovable as a house.

His strength fading, he switched tack and dug his nails into the slave's forearm, pressed down until he broke the skin, and pulled.

The slave didn't even flinch.

Jared's lungs burned.

His vision blurred.

He heard distant shouts. Nearby laughter.

'You're an idiot, you know that? Anyone would think you wanted to get yourself killed.'

Then help me!

His awareness shifted. He could still see, but everything looked fuzzy, as though he were peering through thick glass; could still hear, but the sounds were distorted, as though he were listening underwater; could still feel, but—

Prehen Damis, help me.

—he couldn't move; couldn't twitch so much as a finger. But he sensed his leg tensing, his oxygen-starved muscles screaming in protest. His foot made a small, jerky kick.

Wha—?

'You asked me to help you. And unlike your useless gods, I listen when you call.'

His leg lifted. His knee slammed into the slave's groin. All without a single thought from *him*.

The slave grunted and lost his hold.

Everything snapped into focus—

—and he fell. His feet hit the ground, skidded in the slick mud, and shot out from under him. His backside followed. The force of the impact rippled up his spine.

You... you...

'I saved your life, you ungrateful coward.'

He tucked his legs in—legs which responded to his will—and grabbed at the bars above his head, desperate to get to his feet before the slave came at him again.

But the slave had already been disabled. Esbjorn and several other slavers had him pinned against the opposite side of the cage, his arms and legs held in place by large hooks attached to poles thrust through the bars of the cage. He stared at Jared and grinned. Blood coated his teeth and dribbled down his chin.

Blood?

Jared sank back to the ground, a throbbing fire coming alight in his left shoulder. He glanced at it and swallowed. The slave had bit him! Blood pooled in the ugly teeth marks and soaked the ragged edges of the hole in his jacket.

The cage door opened. Andreas entered, wrapped his arms around Jared's torso, and pulled him out. Oskar shut and locked the door behind them.

At a command from Esbjorn, the slavers unhooked their poles, releasing the slave.

"Can you stand?" Andreas asked.

Jared nodded. Andreas released his hold. Jared's legs trembled, but he managed not to fall.

"Please accept my apologies for this… incident. Tarval is a trained Hyal warrior. He was bred to kill. Oskar should never have let you in." Andreas glared at Oskar. "I will have him beaten if—"

"That will not be necessary, thank you, Andreas," Tessa said.

'And where was she *during all of this? Not helping you, that's for certain.'*

She stepped up beside Jared and gently probed his throat. "Can you breathe?"

Jared nodded, not trusting himself to speak.

She shifted her attention to his shoulder, her fingers hovering just above the bite. "This needs to be cleaned."

"Esbjorn can take care of it," Andreas said. "We have a medical hut nearby. He does not know a word of your Kingdom speech though."

"Then he and Jared will get along swimmingly. Jared doesn't speak a word of Canri."

Jared ran his fingers across his bandaged shoulder, pausing at the dip, poking it. The slave—Tarval—hadn't just bitten him, his sharpened teeth had torn through leather and skin and ripped out flesh, leaving him with an ugly, throbbing hole in his shoulder.

'That'll teach you to feel sorry for slaves.'

I didn't—

'Poor, soulless creatures. Trapped in their tiny cages. Helpless. Alone.'

I never—

'Ripped from their homes. Mistreated. Abused.'

I—

"Jared!" Tessa nudged his arm.

"What?"

"Stop poking it. You'll make it worse."

"Sorry." *Sorry?* Jared scoffed at his inane response and lowered his hand.

"How's your throat?"

"Sore."

"It sounds it. Try not to talk."

He nodded, more than happy to take her advice.

They were still in the slave pens. Andreas had dismissed Oskar and left Esbjorn with the patrolmen. They had toured two pens so far and were halfway around the third. Andreas took pride in his part as their guide, stopping before each cage to introduce the people inside, explaining why they were there, giving details of their history and naming their tribe. He would pick out two or three from each cage, pointing out their strong points, glossing over any issues.

Tessa picked out more, querying their backgrounds and their skills. Then she would turn to Jared and ask what he thought.

He tried to study them as Esbjorn had, looking for signs of illness or wasting, despondency or disease, but it was hard to do through the bars of a cage. Nor did he know what he was looking for. Or why.

"He looks strong and healthy," he said of one man. And of the woman in the next cage, "She looks sickly. Her eyes are dull, and her skin is too shiny."

And then there were the children. Some clung to their parents' legs or backs. Others tried to hide behind their mothers' skirts. When Andreas ordered one young woman forward, her daughter, only two or three years old, started to wail. Jared had to walk away then, lest Andreas read his discomfort on his face.

'Feeling sorry for them again? Have you learnt nothing?'

Jared ignored the taunt—and several others—and concentrated on playing his role.

"I saw how you broke Tarval's hold," Tessa said as they waited for Andreas to retrieve a recalcitrant slave. "You did well."

"I didn't—"

"I saw you knee him in the balls."

"No. *I* didn't. It was the Voice."

"It took control?"

"I asked it to help and—" Jared spotted Andreas approaching and broke off.

Tessa stared at him with the intensity of a nursing cat minding her blind young. Then she turned away, her face all polite smiles again, and waited for Andreas to re-join them.

❧❦

Sleep refused to come. The pillow felt lumpy, the room stuffy, his body restless, his mind a whirr. Armon rolled onto his side, thumped the pillow, rolled onto his back, stared at the ceiling for a count of ten, and closed his eyes. The rain fell against the shutter, tap, tap, tap. The men in the barracks chatted and laughed, their hushed voices loud enough to fill the room. He groaned, gritted his teeth, and rolled onto his other side. His leg twitched. His scalp itched. He fell back onto his back, stretched his arms above his head, and hissed. He drew in a deep breath. A second. A third. Willed his mind to rest.

Something crashed outside. A great pealing clang filled the air. Men cursed and shouted. A woman's voice, shrill and piercing, rose above the rest. Armon swore, kicked free of his tangled blankets, and stood.

The trip to his desk took three shuffled steps. He sank onto the chair, placed his elbows on the edge of the desk, rested his head in his hands, and sighed.

It should have been simple. Stanin and Jared were to monitor the negotiations, Tessa would keep an eye on Azier, he would use his position to track all the comings and goings, and between them, they would spot any potential sticking points before anything went wrong.

Only, within a day of arriving, he'd discovered Stanin had lied to him—continued to lie to him—had even gone so far as to deny any wrongdoing when confronted.

And Jared's ability to pick up the Canri language was close to non-existent. The dandy boy needed three or four months of intense, one-to-one tuition, and Armon couldn't give it to him. As it stood, he was next to useless.

And they were becoming friends.

Friends!

All of that he could deal with, work around, or fix.

Salem, on the other hand?

He hadn't trusted Salem since the moment he met him. He was too smug, too arrogant, too full of himself. Too successful for it to be pure skill and luck.

But there had been nothing except his own suspicion to go on. Nothing, that is, until this morning.

It might have been coincidence that Salem called for Mevin just as the medic was preparing to escort Lady Zandra into the city. Might have been coincidence that Gregory, a man Armon barely knew, had escorted her instead.

He doubted it. Doubted it so much he wanted to race after them, drag Gregory away, and ensure Tessa was safe. But he could not, dare not, follow her.

He dropped his head into his hands, dug his fingers into his scalp, and groaned.

✦✦

Jared followed Andreas and Tessa back to the road, his gaze fixed on the path so he didn't have to look at the caged slaves.

"We do have another pen where we keep the older slaves and young orphans," Andreas said, "but I do not think you will find anything of interest there."

"To business then." Tessa said.

"It will be a pleasure." Andreas linked arms with Tessa and led her towards a small hut wedged between two of the tall fences.

"The slave who took a bite out of Jared," Tessa said, "what was his name?"

"Tarval."

"Tarval. How much would he cost?"

Andreas paused outside the hut's doorway. "Surely a lady like you would not be interested in purchasing a warrior?"

"No. But I have clients in the Kingdom who might. If I could tell them how much a man like him would cost, or purchase him at a price I know would earn me a fair profit..."

"Of course. We can discuss it inside." Andreas opened the door and waved Tessa through. He put a hand out to block Jared's path, however, and offered Tessa an apologetic bow. "I am sorry, Lady Zandra, but servants are not allowed."

Tessa nodded. "Go back and wait with the horses, Jared."

"But—"

"Just go."

Jared bowed to Tessa and Andreas in turn and headed back the way they'd come. He didn't rush. The negotiations could go on for a while, and he didn't have a lot to do whilst he waited. Perhaps if Mevin had been with them, he'd have had a chat and a laugh, but he didn't know Melf, Winton, or Gregory well enough to engage them in idle conversation. He'd wait at the stables. Give Sherna a proper rub down.

He turned onto the main road and headed towards the stables. There were more slave pens behind him, owned by other families or merchants, but their tour with Andreas had taken so long he doubted there'd be time to visit them. That, at least, provided a spark of sunshine in an otherwise miserable day. He'd seen enough caged people to last him a lifetime.

'They're no more caged than you.'

Jared ground his teeth and willed the Voice to silence. He might as well have willed the rain to fall upwards, or the sun to cease its travels across the sky.

'The bars may not be so solid, the boundaries less defined, but you are caged nonetheless.'

What's your point?

'Isn't it about time you did something about it?'

I am.

The Voice made a sound that might have been a snort.

Subtlety is lost on you, isn't it?

'What subtlety? You're not doing anything.'

Armon and I have an agreement. He—

'Is lying. I've told you that already.'

And I've told you I don't care what you think. This is my mind, my body, and my life. I will decide what to do with it. Not. You.

'I should have let Tarval kill you.'

You would have died too.

An eerie silence filled Jared's mind, turning his blood to ice and sending a shiver down his spine. He blinked, and a face—*his* face—floated in front of him, its eyes burning as if aflame, its mouth open in silent laughter.

He blinked again and the vision vanished. His toe caught the edge of a paving stone.

He stumbled and grabbed at the fence to steady himself. His legs trembled, heavy and unresponsive, almost as though—

No! *I'm still weak from Tarval's attack, that's all. Weak and tired.* He started towards the stables. His stride improved with every step, his legs regaining their strength.

Sherna whinnied when he entered the stable yard.

He whistled back. "Heya, girl." He scratched between her ears when he reached her and laughed when she snuffed at his pockets. "Give me a minute. Let me see if I can find you a treat."

He turned. Metal flashed, sunlight glinting off a brass buckle. His reflection stared at him from the highly polished surface. His face, his eyes, his smile.

'What did you expect? Flames and manic laughter?'

Jared shivered.

Sherna snorted and tossed her head.

Jared tore his gaze away from his reflection and stiffened.

Gregory watched him from the yard entrance, one hand resting on the jamb, the other on his belt near his sword hilt. He met Jared's gaze and smirked, revealing stained teeth and several pockmarks on his cheeks and chin.

Jared stroked Sherna's neck, the familiar feel of her hair and muscles easing the knot forming in his stomach. "Can I help you?"

"I came to get my chewbac." Gregory pushed off the jamb and stepped into the yard. "Left it in the pocket on my saddle." He continued to stare, rubbing his hilt with his thumb. "Guess we all have our little habits." He chuckled and shrugged, breaking eye contact.

Little habits? Jared pivoted to keep Gregory in view as he strolled towards the dun mare on the far side of the yard. *Had he seen something? Heard something? How long had he been standing there?*

Gregory plucked a small packet from under the flap of the mare's saddle, lifted it in salute, and strolled back the way he'd come. Jared stared after him until the high fences of the pens blocked him from view.

9/13/32 KAF (Four)

The stable smelt of horse, damp wood, and day-old hay. And almonds. Armon scooped a handful from the nearest pouch then let them slide through his fingers, back onto the pile. He hated almonds. And hay. Hay made him sneeze.

He rested a hand on top of the nearest stall door and gave it a tug, an instinctive habit born of years of patrolling. The door didn't budge. He moved on to the next one.

The horse in the stall, a small chestnut mare, stopped eating long enough to give him a look that, had it come from a human, he would have considered derisive.

Soft footsteps warned him of another's approach. They stopped, and a quiet, familiar voice asked, "Sir?"

Armon turned his step into a pivot and faced the newcomer. "Yes, Mevin?"

"The pens are ready for inspection, sir."

"Thank you, Mevin." Armon gave the rest of the stalls a hasty check before falling into step beside the young medic. "How are you finding Canri?"

"It's different, sir. What I've seen of it. But then, it's the same too. All that fancy decorating at the embassy, and the huge feast, it's just them's what's got showing off to impress those as what's not. And they talk funny and have their religion no-one's allowed to know about, but they still got to eat and shit and piss like the rest of us."

Armon swallowed a chuckle and nodded. "True enough, Mevin. True enough." He stepped outside just as the sun slipped below the horizon, its failing light turning the undersides of the remaining clouds a deep vermilion. He glanced across the paddock towards the gate, but it remained closed. Tessa was late.

"It's like I told Jared," Mevin said. "People are people, wherever they are."

Armon turned left, following the dirt path around to the side entrance. "Have you spoken to him recently?"

"Who, sir?"

"Jared."

"No, sir."

The stench of human waste, sweat, and used straw assaulted Armon's nostrils when he stepped through the side door. He paused to give his eyes time to adjust to the dim light provided by the burners and narrow windows. The first two stalls—or, more accurately, cells—were occupied by the slaves Azier had brought with him. They were a filthy, pathetic lot. "All the locks and hinges have been checked?"

"Yes, sir." Mevin led Armon to the nearest unoccupied stall and pulled on the door. The bars rattled like marbles in a tin but held firm.

Armon flicked the double catches open, stepped inside, and closed the door behind him. "Lock me in."

"Yes, sir."

He turned in a slow circle, running his hands up and down the walls forming the rear and sides of the stall, pushing on random bricks to check they held firm. Then he got down on his knees and pulled back the fresh straw to ensure nothing was hidden in or beneath it. Satisfied, he turned back to the locked door, first testing it with raw strength before slipping his hand between the bars and trying to flip open the complex catches from the inside. He failed.

Perhaps something thinner.

He returned to the pile of straw and picked it apart, testing each strand until he found one strong enough. He slipped it through the bars. After much wiggling and finger-contorting, he managed to hit the catch. The strand bent in half. He dropped it. "It should hold. There are secondary locks?"

"The lever on the wall near the door. It operates bolts in the floor."

"For all the stalls?"

"Yes, sir."

"It should be secure. You can let me out now."

Mevin took a step back and crossed his arms, his face expressionless. He shook his head.

"Not funny, Mevin." Armon thrust an arm through the bars, lunging for Mevin's jacket. Mevin scuttled out of reach. Armon closed his eyes and took a breath. "Let me out of here. Now."

"I can't, sir. Ambassador's orders. He decided rations were too lenient."

Armon's chest muscles tightened, shortening his breath. "That man—"

Mevin's face crumpled. He doubled over laughing. "I'm sorry, sir, but... but... your face..."

"My face. Yes. Very amusing. Now let me out. Please."

Mevin wiped tears from his eyes with one hand whilst flicking the catches open with the other. "I can't wait to tell the others—"

"Breathe one word of this to the men, and I'll put you on double drills for a month."

Mevin's laughter died on his lips. "You're serious?"

"I'll oversee the punishment myself. Do you know what it would do to discipline if I started letting people get away with playing practical jokes?"

"But—"

"Especially on senior officers."

"I'm sorry, sir. I was j-just having some fun."

Armon turned his back to hide his own grin. "Have the rest of the stalls been searched and prepared?"

"Yes, sir."

"Then—"

"They're here, sir," a new voice interjected a second before its owner, Pavel, entered the slave block. He nodded to Mevin then snapped his heels together and thumped fist to chest in salute.

Armon acknowledged the salute with a dip of his head and patted the air to tell his sub-patrol leader to relax. "How many?"

"Two of the originals plus five new ones."

"Put ours back where they came from. The new ones can go at the far end, one to a stall, for now. Help Mevin prepare in here. I'll greet Lady Zandra."

"You soft on her, sir?" Mevin asked.

Armon spun. "Excuse me?"

"You got this look in your eyes when you said her name..."

Did I? The skin over Armon's forehead grew taut, his muscles knotting. Mevin's observation had been made without malice, but if word spread of a connection between himself and Tessa it could put them both at risk. "I know better than to go chasing my betters, lad. As should you."

"O-of course, sir. I shouldn't have asked."

"You're right. You shouldn't." Armon chose to leave it at that.

His knees almost buckled when he stepped into the paddock. Tessa stood near the central stable's entrance, talking with the soldiers who'd escorted her. For a moment, he could only stand and stare, fighting the urge to grin at her like a lovesick lunatic. He'd been so certain something bad would happen; that she'd be hurt. Yet there she was, a commanding figure in her white riding dress, issuing orders to men who'd dedicated a lifetime to soldiering, acting as though it was something she did every day of her life. Those men would have reacted very differently if they'd realised the truth; if they knew a flick of her wrist or a pat on a shoulder could end their lives. But they saw what she wanted them to see: a rich, self-assured merchant.

She turned to speak to someone behind her. Her gaze met his. The skin around her eyes wrinkled, and she flashed him her beautiful smile, the one she reserved especially for him.

That moment of eye contact lasted less than a second, but it was enough to dispel the last of his tension. He stepped forward into the space Melf had vacated. "Welcome back, Lady Zandra."

"Patrol Leader." She acknowledged him with a quick nod, finished giving instructions to the men, and turned to face him. "I didn't expect you to welcome me yourself."

"I heard you were bringing in fresh livestock. I wanted to make sure the stalls were prepared."

"Very proper of you, Patrol Leader. I'll be sure to mention your thoroughness to your superiors."

Armon dipped his head. "You honour me, my lady." He checked no-one was looking and winked.

"Rascal." A dimple appeared in her left cheek, a sure sign she was biting it to keep from laughing.

He coughed to hide his own smile and offered her his arm.

She rested her hand in his, as was proper, but then she tickled his palm.

Another cough masked a strangled laugh. Melf rounded the corner of the stable. Armon edged closer to Tessa. "Did Gregory give you any problems?"

"Gregory? No. Why—?"

"I'll explain later."

Melf stopped a respectable distance away and saluted. "The slaves are all in their stalls, Lady Zandra."

"Thank you, Melf. Care to lead the way, Patrol Leader?"

"It will be my pleasure." Armon guided Tessa around the stables to the side door, careful to stay a half-step ahead of her without appearing to drag her along. He lowered his arm when they reached the door and stepped aside, allowing her to enter the slave block in front of him. He followed a pace behind, blinking to help his eyes adjust.

Tessa stepped to one side, giving him a clear view of the end cell.

Armon grinned. "He is perfect."

"I thought so."

Armon took several steps forward, never taking his eyes off the giant dominating the end cell. Something primal rose up inside him; a need to meet the challenge in the giant's deep blue eyes and prove himself. He rested one hand on the hilt of his sword and wrapped the other around the handle of his dagger.

The slave had to be closer to seven feet than six, every inch of him solid muscle. He held himself perfectly poised; perfectly still. A true fighter.

Tessa dropped a hand onto his shoulder. "Stay back. He's a cannibal. He's already tasted Kingdom flesh today."

Armon looked back. "He has?"

"One of the slavers thought it would be funny to let Jared into his cell. Tarval—the slave—almost killed him. Took a bite out of his shoulder as well."

"Is Jared—?"

"He's fine. His neck's a little bruised, but he'll recover."

Armon stepped back. "Did you get a chance to talk to him?"

"This morning. We'll talk about it later."

"Is it serious?"

"It could be."

Armon looked back at the slave. "Does he speak Canri?"

"Enough to obey basic commands. That's why I bought the interpreter." Tessa pointed to a wiry, grey-haired, old man in the next stall.

"Will he accept the proposal?"

"From what I could learn about him, it's possible." Tessa reached into her belt pouch and pulled out a sheet of rough paper. She handed it to Armon.

"What—?"

"His dietary requirements."

"But he's a slave."

"A very important, very expensive slave."

Armon's eyes dropped to the list. "A whole chicken? He gets a whole chicken?" His stomach rumbled in protest.

∽⳼∾

Armon watched the moonlight caress Tessa's face, shadows dancing across her mouth and lips as a cloud drifted past the safehouse window. "He wants to kiss you?"

The corners of Tessa's eyes pinched. "Have you listened to a word I said?"

"Yes. Of course. But… he wants to kiss you?"

"No. The voice in his head told him to kiss me. It's not the same thing."

"Isn't it?" Armon leant back. The old wooden chair creaked beneath him. "How can you be sure? How do you know this isn't an elaborate hoax he concocted to make you feel sorry for him and get you into his bed?"

Tessa's soft laugh carried a mix of mockery and frustration. "You think he's capable of that?"

"Well… no. But still…"

"Besides, I'm more concerned about it wanting him to kill you."

It was Armon's turn to laugh. "That will never happen."

"Not if Jared's in control, no, but…" Tessa stepped away from the gap in the shutter. A shaft of moonlight cut through the room like a glowing knife, dust motes dancing along its length. "This thing—this voice, or entity, or whatever it is—I don't think it can be defeated easily."

"Trust me in this, Tess. I've been training him for weeks. I know what he's capable of. And what he's not."

"And I know what I saw. Tarval had him pinned by the neck, suspended above the ground, and half-dead. He didn't have the strength to hold up his own head, and yet he managed to knee Tarval in the groin hard enough to break his grip."

"A lucky hit."

"A precise hit. An expert hit."

"Facing death makes people desperate. They find new reserves—"

"No. He told me himself, the voice took over."

Armon ran a finger through the dust on the table, tracing random patterns through the muck. He hadn't expected to find dust here, but perhaps the Canri magic didn't work where the sun rarely shone, or perhaps it sensed the house had long been abandoned and had no reason to keep it clean. "All right. Let's assume, for now, this 'voice' is more than a ploy. Let's assume it's real. The beginnings of insanity or something. What can we do?"

"Keep it secret, for a start."

Armon scratched at his arm, not even aware he was doing so until Tessa caught his hands in hers and pulled them away. He glanced down at the red welts and squeezed her hands in thanks.

She smiled, a touch of sadness in her eyes. "Did you forget to drink the tea?"

"Mevin took it off me."

"Why would he—?"

"Salem put me on punishment rations and—don't look at me like that—and he put Mevin in charge of the rationing."

Tessa slipped into the chair opposite, still holding his hands, and rested her elbows on the table. "And?"

"And he caught me brewing the tea in my room when he brought dinner. He confiscated it, reminded me any drink except water was forbidden, then asked me what it was for."

"And?" Tessa prompted a second time.

"And he lectured me on the stupidity of buying medicines from Canri street merchants. Told me someone had probably slipped something into my food or drink, and the itching was likely a side-effect, or a sign of mild addiction."

"And?"

"And I grumbled and muttered and let him take the tea."

"Could he be right?"

Armon shook his head. "It's happened both times I've visited the city, and only ever affects me when I'm within the walls. As soon as I leave, it stops. That's not an addiction."

Tessa loosened her grip and rubbed the backs of his hands with her thumbs. "I'll buy you more tomorrow. I could ask if they have anything to help Jared whilst I'm there."

Armon sucked on his lip for a moment then shook his head. "We don't know how the Canri people feel about the insane. If word gets out that one of our delegation is mad, it might damage the negotiations."

"Then I'll tell them it's for one of the slaves. No-one will care."

"I suppose I could teach him some focus and meditation techniques. They might help."

"It's a start. And there's always the public library—"

"You think you can read Canri well enough?"

"No, but you—"

"Would look very out of place and create a lot of suspicion if I went there. And what would I say to the clerks? 'Do you have any books on people hearing voices and going insane?'"

Tessa laughed. She lifted Armon's hand in hers, ran her thumb across his fingers, and kissed them. "What's wrong, love?"

"Did I do the wrong thing, bringing him here?"

"Why would—?"

"Because his madness began when Morgain arrested him." Armon noticed Tessa's lips part slightly and grinned. "You see? I was listening."

"I never doubted it."

Armon just stared for a moment, grinning like a lovesick pup. Then he remembered what they were discussing, and his smile fell. "Did I cause all this?"

"I don't see how."

"If I hadn't told Morgain—"

"If you hadn't told Morgain, she'd have found out anyway, and when she did, she'd have taken her revenge. If pain, fear, and stress triggered this insanity, the only one to blame is Morgain."

Armon sighed. "This would be much easier if I still hated him."

"You never hated him."

"I—"

"You hated the idea of him." Tessa leant forward, her grip tightening. "You hated that she'd found someone else. You let your jealousy rule your head."

"Tessa—"

"Don't!" She slapped her hands onto the table, pinning his beneath them. "Don't even try denying it. You may not be her lover, but I know you want her."

Armon flinched at every word, the venom in Tessa's voice striking at his heart. He stared at her, open-mouthed, before turning away, his face burning. "I would never—"

"You would. If she gave you the chance, you would."

Armon's hands trembled under her fingers. He snatched them away, tucked them under his armpits. Tears pricked the backs of his eyes. A lump filled his throat. Silence surrounded him, the moment stretching out forever as he searched for a reply. "Then why...?"

"Why am I still with you? Because I love you, you fool." The hint of a smile tugged at Tessa's lips. "And because, one day, you will see the truth." Her smile broadened, her chin dipping in a firm nod.

Armon swallowed the lump and blinked back the tears before they could fall. He was *not* in the habit of crying. It was the influence of this city—the incessant Canri magic clawing at his insides—making him weak. "I love you too."

"Enough of this. I will not have you sitting here feeling sorry for yourself because of her." Tessa half-rose from her seat, reached across the table, and caught his wrists.

He resisted her pull at first, but then relented, managing a soft smile, and let her take his hands once more.

She settled back onto her chair. "You did not cause Jared's insanity. You may have told Morgain of his affair, but he's the one who cheated on her, and she's the one who tortured him. None of that was your fault."

"I wanted him to suffer."

"And now you regret it. And that's why I'm still with you. Why I haven't given you up."

"I need to get him away from her."

"And you?"

Armon hesitated, feeling the tension in her hands. He felt like he was poised on the edge of a cliff with a great weight bearing down on him, about to push him off. He stared into oblivion and tried to step back. "Tessa, I..." Too soon. She had asked him too soon. "Jared isn't our only problem."

Tessa's face sagged, her hands going limp in his. For a moment, he thought she would push the matter, but then she sighed and shook her head. "Gregory?"

"Gregory," he confirmed.

Dust continued to float through the beam of moonlight, the particles dancing and spinning as they slipped in and out of the spectral stream. Armon sighed. The rush of expelled breath set the dust motes swirling.

Tessa hadn't shared his concern over Gregory. She'd agreed the timing was suspicious but felt the redeployment of Armon's patrolmen and the placement of Salem's bodyguards in their place held much greater significance. Those acts, combined with Stanin's recurring trips to the market, pointed at some form of clandestine activity. An activity Salem didn't want Armon, or his men, to know about.

But how, Armon had argued, would moving his men away from the reception and embassy entrance help? His patrolmen still guarded the main gates. Anyone arriving or leaving would still need to pass them.

"Unless..." Tessa had sat straighter in her chair as she spoke, her eyes glowing like diamonds in the reflected moonlight. *"Could there be another entrance?"*

Such a simple question, and suddenly everything fit. But if there was a second entrance into the embassy it meant he, or more accurately, Patrol Leader Malkem, had failed. He'd ordered the buildings and grounds searched when they first arrived. He and his men had found nothing. Which meant that, if there was a second entrance, the ambassador would have an excuse to have Malkem dismissed whenever he chose.

It also begged the question: where? Not within sight of the main gates, or his men would still see whoever Salem was hiding come and go. *In the back wall, perhaps? Or underground?* Armon couldn't search for it himself, not openly. Nor could he risk having his men do so. If Salem did distrust Malkem, then doing anything unusual would only confirm his doubts.

Tessa had offered to search for him, but he vetoed the idea. So far, there was no reason to think Salem knew of her involvement—Gregory's reassignment to her escort aside—but if they were seen together too often...

Tessa would find a reason to speak to him tomorrow, to give him the tea. But after that there would be no more secret meetings, no sneaking about to see each other after dark. Not until he could confirm if he was or wasn't being watched.

The thought of not seeing her—of her being so close and yet out of his reach—created a gut-shredding ache deep inside. But perhaps it was for the best after what had been said.

Why couldn't I just say yes?

Would it be so bad to start over somewhere new, just Tessa and me? He could be himself, the man he'd always wanted to be. No more sneaking. No more hiding. No more pretending. Just Tessa and him. Together. Safe.

Except it wouldn't be that easy. Morgain would never give him up. And he couldn't leave either. Not yet.

It wouldn't just be Morgain he'd be abandoning, it'd be his dreams and ambitions. Everything he'd worked for his entire life.

The laws he wanted to change.

The lives he wanted to improve.

His freedom.

If he left Morgain now, he'd never be free. She wouldn't just demand his capture, she'd name him for what he was. Her slave. Once the law changed—

The law? He snorted and rubbed a faded scar on his forefinger, old pain flaring sharp.

"Come here, you filthy brat." A massive hand locked onto his, ragged nails slicing skin. "I'll teach you to expose yourself, rutting like a mindless animal."

Armon jerked to his feet, fleeing the long-dead grasp. His chair clattered to the floor.

"Shh!" Morgain's hair whipped around her shoulders, sunlight dancing across it in ribbons of fiery gold. "I have something special for you in my room. But it's a secret. No-one else must know."

Armon growled and righted the chair, the shadow of a fist closing over his again.

"I didn't do anything. I swear. Morgain invited me. She said—" His collar was yanked tight, cutting off his air. Then he was being dragged backwards, away from the bed, away from Morgain with her top clutched to her bared chest, her tongue playing along the teasing curve of her lips.

He tightened his grip on the chair back, raised it above his head, and swept it down with a roar. It crashed against the table and shattered, sending splinters of chair leg flying. Dust rose in thick, choking clouds.

Morgain gyrated on the bed, hips swaying, hands caressing.

He swung the chair again.

She touched her lips.

A third time.

Her neck.

A fourth.

Her hips.

Each touch ignited fresh fire in his untested loins.

Each twist and turn filled his stomach with sickening bile.

She hooked the hem of her top and slid it off, leant forward and crooked her finger. Her naked breasts jiggled, enticing him forward. He reached for her, lips pursed in anticipation.

She giggled, pulled back, and screamed.

Armon glared at the broken spoke clutched in his hand and threw it aside.

Morgain had caught him that day. Wormed her hook and drawn him in as expertly as a master fisherman.

She'd known it, too. The teasing never stopped. The hints and suggestions. She dangled herself just out of reach, a carrot to guarantee his obedience. What he felt for her was pure desire, an animal lust that sickened him even as it drove him on. He'd never expected to love someone. Never expected anyone to love him back.

And then he'd met Tessa.

Tessa, who'd been sent to kill him and ended up marrying him instead.

He loved her. Loved her so much he felt hollow whenever life forced them to part.

And yet...

And yet he knew one day he would lose her if he couldn't bring himself to walk away.

The second chair fared no better than the first. Nor the third. The tabletop cracked and buckled under the onslaught until, with a loud groan, it collapsed. He stood over it, a chair-back clutched in his hands, his chest heaving and his blood thundering in his ears. He roared again, putting all his anger into the wordless scream, and threw the chair-back across the room.

Only one chair survived his tantrum, standing incongruously amongst the piles of shattered wood.

How could he condemn Jared for being unfaithful when he wanted to do the same?

He stalked across the room, his eyes fixed on the panelled door. His hands contracted into fists. He swung without thought, without purpose, punched the door—

—and screamed.

Solid wood. The door had been built with solid wood. He cradled his fist to his chest, rubbing his forearm in a pointless attempt to ease the ache. The sudden pain doused the fire in his blood as effectively as a torrent of iced water.

He stared at the carnage in disbelief.

What sort of a monster am I?

He turned his arm over and probed the back of his hand. Blood seeped from several shallow cuts, but no bones poked out. He wiggled his fingers. A wave of agony shot down his arm.

He gritted his teeth and concentrated on breathing until the pain eased. Gathering his courage, he tried twisting his wrist.

It moved, thank the gods, and the pain didn't seem quite so bad. *Nothing broken then.* He hoped. He'd get Mevin to check it when he returned to the barracks, though how he'd explain the injury he didn't know.

He'd warned Pavel he'd be late, claiming he'd be scouting the route between the stables and the embassy for any potential problems, but that excuse wouldn't stand up to scrutiny if he didn't return soon.

He glanced about the room one last time before leaving, shaking his head at the mess of wooden shards and splinters, the collapsed table in the middle of the floor. He'd reduced it to kindling, destroying it as surely as he would his relationship with Tessa if he didn't change something soon.

He checked himself then, picking several splinters out of his uniform and knocking more free from his hair.

His anger had vanished, spent like fireworks at a Mournday fair.

But it would come back.

It always did.

9/13/32 KAF (Five)

Armon flexed his hand, fending off the stiffness from the blossoming bruise. He glanced in both directions. Melf wasn't due to pass through for another ten minutes, but there was no curfew in place, meaning any of the embassy's residents could walk by at any moment. He rapped on the door in front of him three times and slipped inside.

"Armon?" Tessa asked, her voice slurred as if from sleep.

"Yes." He closed the door and padded to the couch. She lay curled at one end, the coals from a dying brazier lighting her and the book draped over the cushion near her hand. "Reading something good?"

She blinked and hid a yawn behind her hand. "You shouldn't be here."

"I know. But I couldn't leave things the way I did. You're the one I love, and I needed you to know." He crouched and rested his hand on her leg. "Yes, part of me lusts for Morgain, but you…" He swallowed and gazed into her eyes. "You are the one who makes me whole. I love you, Tessa. And I would give the world and everything in it to make you happy." He shuffled closer and reached for her hand. "I know it's asking a lot, but give me time, please. I'll find a way to untangle myself from this mess, to break free of her and not have to hide anymore. You're my wife. And one day, one day soon, the entire world will know it."

Tessa smiled, despite the dregs of a frown tugging down the corners of her brow. She clasped his hand and pulled him forward, leaning towards him at the same time. "I love you, too."

He parted his lips for a kiss.

Not a quick, hot kiss born of passion, but a slower, more intimate joining birthed in the twining of their hearts.

⧽⧼

Faint orange light leaked through the narrow cracks in the shutter, enough to limn the edges of the furniture and allow Jared to locate his flint. He fumbled several times before he managed to generate a spark. It caught the tip of the candle wick, glowed for a moment, and puffed out.

"Come on!" He struck the flint again—hard enough for the steel to skip and graze his fingertip—and cursed. Sparks flew, and the fire took. The flame danced atop the candle, causing shadows to stretch and shrink across the room.

He dropped steel and flint into the half-open drawer, picked up the candle, and used it to light the second one atop the dresser. After stabbing the first candle back on its holder, he leant against the dresser with fists planted, arms straight, and head bowed.

Tremors coursed through him, his muscles cramping. The day had been too long; too full of unexpected drama.

He lifted his head and stared at his reflection. Grey-blue shadows underlined his eyes, and jagged, bloody veins marred their whites. His skin looked ashen, despite his tan, and purple bruises covered his throat.

At least the choker Morgain insisted I wear will serve some purpose.

He chuckled, then winced as the rush of air irritated his windpipe. The hole in his shoulder continued to throb in counterpoint to his pulse.

"Gods and fishes, how did I come to this?"

Has it really been less than two months since my life turned on its head? Less than two months since I first heard the Voice?

And he'd dismissed it out of hand; blamed its whispers on exhaustion and hunger.

He snorted and pushed away from the dresser.

If he'd had any doubts about the threat it posed, today's 'possession' had wiped them out. It had controlled him for a second, but that second had terrified him to the core. To have no control over his own body—to have it act without his say so…

If the Voice can do that, what else is it capable of?

'Why don't you ask me and find out?'

Because I'm sick of your endless lies.

Lies. Taunts. Threats. But if it wanted him dead, why had it saved him today?

'Because we are better—stronger—together.'

You'll forgive me if I choose not to believe you.

Jared sighed, shrugged off his jacket, and tossed it onto his clothes chest.

Pointless worrying about it now.

He could barely think clearly enough to use a flint, never mind make sense of a being that shouldn't exist. Things would look better after he'd slept. And Tessa had promised to help, though what she could do he didn't know. How did one go about fighting a disembodied voice? And what good would it do him if he couldn't even go home afterwards?

He pulled off his shirt and threw it on top of his jacket.

He hadn't found a shred of evidence to take to Ryal; hadn't learnt a single detail of Morgain's plans. Oh, he'd made a deal with Armon that might bear fruit, but he hadn't discovered anything useful about Salem or Stanin to give him either. If he didn't learn something soon, he'd end up returning to the Kingdom as Morgain's pet. Death at the Voice's hand might prove a better fate.

'Unification would be even better.'

Unification? Jared bowed his head and rubbed at his eyes. *I'll see you destroyed before I let that happen.*

The Voice's laughter echoed inside his head.

CHARACTERS, GODS, AND THINGS

Characters (Kingdom):

Jared up-Arran: Courier and minor member of the Blood (Kingdom nobility)

Lady Morgain al-Rafael: Ruler of the al-Rafael Region.

Armon bal-Rafael (AKA Malkem): Morgain's spymaster.

Elise: Scullery maid. Jared's lover.

Ryal al-Arran: Jared's cousin.

James: Ryal's adviser.

Kieron: Ryal's son.

Regal and Sherna: Jared's stallion and Jared's mare.

Art: Old man who works in the stables.

Tessa (AKA Lady Zandra): Assassin posing as a merchant.

Lady Zandra: See Tessa.

Malkem, Patrol Leader: Alias used by Armon whilst in Canri.

Ambassador Salem: Joint leader of the Kingdom delegation.

Stanin: Salem's head scribe.

Alsam Azier: Joint leader of the Kingdom delegation.

Ruskin: Kingdom merchant who competed in the games.

Mevin: Patrol medic.

The Voice: The (rather unimaginative) name Jared has given the voice he hears in his mind.

Pavel, sub-patrol leader: Second in command of the Kingdom patrol.

Sanworth far-Fay: Lady Morgain's tailor.

Gregory: One of the Patrolmen escorting the delegation.

Winton: One of the Patrolmen escorting the delegation.

Melf: One of the Patrolmen escorting the delegation.

Characters (Canri):

Davin: Canri guide who welcomed the delegation to Canri.
Arvid: Canri man at the feast.
Magistra Justus: Magistra for the foreign district.
Vortai Yngve: Vortai for the foreign district.
Furste Hjalmar: A Canri prince.
Verner Olsson: Canri trader involved in the trade negotiations.
Oskar Kristofson (Blue Eyes): Young Canri fighter who defeated Jared in the games. Andreas and Esbjorn's younger brother.
Andreas Kristofson: Canri baton fighting champion. Esbjorn and Oscar's older brother.
Pol Artursson: Competitor in the welcome games.
Karolina Andersdotter: Mysterious Canri woman with black eyes.
Marta Aasen: A Canri merchant.
Aina: Marta's companion.
Esbjorn Kristofson: Slave trader. Andreas's middle brother.
Tarval: Warrior slave who bit Jared.

The Kingdom Calendar:

There are 28 days in every Kingdom month, and 13 months in a year. Years are named after the King who is reigning at the time. The count starts at the beginning of the first full year of their reign and ends the year they die/abdicate.

Kingdom Coinage:

Octain: Eight-sided gold coin. Can be split into eight 'bits', each worth two pentains.
Pentain: Five-sided silver coin: Can be split into five 'bits', each worth five rounds.
Round: Round copper coin. Can be split in half.

Canri Coinage:

Quart: Large round gold coin. Two quarts are roughly equal to three Kingdom Octains.
Quartain: Large copper coin. Equal to six Kingdom rounds.

Kingdom Gods:

Prehen Damis: God of Souls and ruler of the Vortex—the place where souls are held between lives.

Mortis Damis: God of Death. The full moon is said to be his unblinking eye.

Kingdom Saying:

Vortex take you: Equivalent to 'go to Hell'.

Acknowledgements

I'd like to take a moment to thank everyone who's provided their help and support during the writing of this book.

Thank you to my parents for their encouragement and early feedback.

Thank you to my editor, Rama Devi, for pushing me to add more similes to my work. (Something I'm still learning to do consistently.)

Thank you to my critique partners Turtle... who?, Cassandra Myles, Jay Squires, Tessa Kay, JJ Rowe, and Shelly Campbell for your invaluable insight, leading me to strengthen both characters and the story line.

Thank you to my beta readers June Duncan, Jessica Nel, Angela Massey, Roy Owen, Adrienne Pitre, Karen Thomson, and everyone else who popped in to comment on a chapter or two.

And finally, thank you to everyone who has bought and read this book. I hope you enjoyed the story!

For more information on my books (including maps), my blog *How to Bake Yourself a Book*, and a free short story *The Glass Butterfly* via my newsletter, please visit: https://asthomson.com

www.ingramcontent.com/pod-product-compliance
Lightning Source LLC
Chambersburg PA
CBHW051009180726
48291CB00006B/2037